Alexander Strachan

The Life of the Rev. Samuel Leigh

Missionary to the Settlers and Savages of Australia and New Zealand

Alexander Strachan

The Life of the Rev. Samuel Leigh
Missionary to the Settlers and Savages of Australia and New Zealand

ISBN/EAN: 9783337151720

Printed in Europe, USA, Canada, Australia, Japan

Cover: Foto ©Raphael Reischuk / pixelio.de

More available books at **www.hansebooks.com**

LIFE OF THE REV. SAMUEL LEIGH,

Missionary to the

Settlers and Savages of Australia and New Zealand.

ILLUSTRATED EDITION.

THE LIFE

OF THE

REV. SAMUEL LEIGH,

MISSIONARY TO THE SETTLERS AND SAVAGES OF AUSTRALIA
AND NEW ZEALAND:

WITH

A HISTORY OF THE ORIGIN AND PROGRESS OF THE
MISSIONS IN THOSE COLONIES.

BY THE LATE
REV. ALEXANDER STRACHAN.

ILLUSTRATED EDITION.

LONDON:
THE WESLEYAN MISSION HOUSE,
BISHOPSGATE STREET WITHIN.
1870.

DEDICATION.

TO THE

SECRETARIES AND COMMITTEE OF THE WESLEYAN
MISSIONARY SOCIETY,

AND TO THE

SUBSCRIBERS AT HOME AND ABROAD.

GENTLEMEN AND CHRISTIAN FRIENDS,

IT did not fall within the province of the author
of this volume, either to expound the constitution of
your Society, or to analyse the principles on which its
affairs have been conducted. His object has been,
1. To give a comprehensive view of the moral degradation and social wretchedness of the settlers and
natives of New South Wales and New Zealand; to
point out the means that have been established, and
maintained from year to year by your generous contributions, for their civil and religious elevation, and to
mark the effects of those means upon their principles
and habits: 2. To supply such information as should
enable you to form a just estimate of the privations,
labours, and appalling dangers to which many of your
foreign agents have been subjected, while endeavouring to carry out your benevolent purposes, and to
secure the higher objects of their mission: 3. To show

you that, having succceded in putting down cannibalism, infanticide, and polygamy, and in organizing
churches, setting up educational institutions, and
advancing the interests of civilization, commerce, and
Christianity, wherever you have planted your missionaries, it is now your imperative duty to send your
system into the interior of those colonies, and, by a
simultaneous and vigorously-sustained effort, establish amongst the savages that roam in these "dark
places of the earth" the means of grace, and opportunities of salvation. I have presumed to inscribe
this volume to you, being persuaded that, as members of the Wesleyan Missionary Society, you feel a
deep interest in the subjects on which I have written.

I am, Gentlemen and Christian friends,

With sentiments of sincere regard,

Respectfully yours,

ALEXANDER STRACHAN.

PREFACE.

By a mysterious arrangement of Divine Providence, the writer of this volume was brought into personal intercourse with the Rev. Samuel Leigh during the last year of his life. He stood by his side at a public meeting, when a sudden attack of congestion of the brain interrupted his speech on the Australian mission, and plainly indicated that his days were numbered. A friend of his, alike distinguished by eloquence in the pulpit and ability as a writer, said to him one day, "Mr. Leigh, your life has been such an eventful one, that I should like to record the main facts of it, and give them to the church." This spontaneous offer, from one of whom he entertained the most exalted opinion, greatly affected him. After alluding to it on the following day, in terms of respectful affection, he looked at the author, and said, significantly, "I have confidence in you." The writer excused himself, on the ground that no person, in his judgment, was qualified for such an undertaking, who had not made himself thoroughly acquainted, either by personal observation or a laborious process of reading and reflection, with the geography of the countries in which he had laboured, and with the genius, habits, and pursuits of the natives of those countries. As every day diminished the hope of Mr. Leigh's recovery, and enhanced the responsibility of the writer, he felt compelled, by the force of circumstances, to yield to what had obviously become *his* duty. Every desirable facility was kindly afforded: free access to Mr. Leigh himself at all times, the use of his own journals and those of his early coadjutors, as also an extensive foreign and domestic correspondence extending over a period of thirty years. The Wesleyan Mission-House offered to submit to his inspection the valuable and confidential communications of its foreign agents. The privilege of examining those documents might, very properly, have been accompanied with an intimation that prudence and discrimination would be expected in making selections for publication; but no such intimation was given, and the occasion only supplied additional evidence of the integrity, honour, and fraternal kindness which characterize the brethren at the head of that establishment. It is equally due to the secretaries of the Church Missionary Society, thus publicly to acknowledge the frankness and courtesy with which they offered to place within the reach of the author any of their documents that might be selected as calculated to afford assistance in the prosecution of his work. The materials for this volume being chiefly derived from those original and authentic sources, the work does not, in any degree, interfere with the interesting narratives of the Rev. Messrs. Waterhouse, Lawry, and Bumby.

In forming an estimate of the character and acts of public bodies and private individuals, the writer has been influenced solely by the concurrence of circumstances, or the evidence of facts; and, having no interests to serve but such as involve the public good, or the progress of religion in the world, he has endeavoured to write with candour and impartiality. Few examples have been recorded in the annals of the church, since the apostolic age, more strikingly illustrative of the providence and grace of God than the Life of the Rev. Samuel Leigh.

In this edition the translations from the native tongue have been examined and corrected by a Maori scholar, long connected with the Church mission in New Zealand.

ILLUSTRATIONS.

CONTENTS.

CHAPTER I.

CHAPTER II.

CHAPTER III.

CHAPTER IV.

CHAPTER V.

CHAPTER VI.

CHAPTER VII.

CHAPTER VIII.

CHAPTER IX.

CHAPTER X.

CHAPTER XI.

CHAPTER XII.

CHAPTER XIII.

CHAPTER XIV.

CHAPTER XV.

CHAPTER XVI.

CHAPTER XVII.

CHAPTER I.

HIS EARLY LIFE—IS APPOINTED TO NEW SOUTH WALES—INCIDENTS AT
SEA—ARRIVES IN PORT JACKSON.

CREATION was intended to afford new developements of the Divine perfections. "For the invisible things of Him from the creation of the world are clearly seen, being understood by the things that are made, even His eternal power and Godhead." It was, no doubt, the primary object of the Divine government to bring out those infinite and sublime realities with increasing perspicuity; to lay open to the inspection of angels and men the peculiarities of the Divine economy; and thus to demonstrate, with accumulative evidence, that "God is, and that He is a rewarder of them that diligently seek Him." In conformity with those principles, the stupendous events recorded in the annals of the past, whether sacred or profane, must be interpreted; and it is only under their guidance that we can trace, with any degree of accuracy, the outline of the future in the prophetic scriptures. Whilst every dispensation of God is intended to lead men to acknowledge His existence and supremacy, it is also calculated to draw them into a sweet and filial relationship to Himself.

But men generally view the aspects of Providence as they do the works of nature: the man who is struck with the magnificence and splendour of the sun seldom pauses to examine the illuminating power of the glow-worm, though in its organization the one is as illustrative of the wisdom and omnipotence of the Creator as the other. The traveller who stands in admiration as he lifts his eye and surveys the grandeur of Mount Lebanon, treads upon the violet, which is much more exquisite in its structure and colouring than the most stately cedars that adorn the scenery around him. The revelations of the telescope are wonderful; but they are not more remarkable than those of the microscope. In dealing with the fields of space and the planets, the Great Architect had ample scope for the arrangement and adjustment of His materials; but look at that minute form of life, scarcely perceptible to the eye when placed upon a polished surface. How surprising that animated matter should be brought within such a circumference! that the principle of life, the delicate members of the body, the various senses, and the laws of instinct, should be combined within such narrow limits!

The same heedlessness is shown in contemplating the dealings of God with men. Extraordinary occurrences awaken general attention, and fill the mind with emotions of joy or feelings of apprehension; while ordinary events are allowed to pass from our recollection, without leaving any salutary impressions behind them. We are apt to lose ourselves in generalities. We may well admire that illustrious scheme of mercy, which issued in "leading captivity captive, and in giving gifts unto men;" and adore that wisdom which added "diversity" to those gifts. For, "He gave some, apostles; and some, prophets; and some, evangelists; and some, pastors and teachers; for the perfecting of the saints, for the work of the ministry, for the edifying of the body of Christ: till we all come in the unity of the faith, and of the knowledge of the Son of God, unto a perfect man, unto the measure of the stature of the fulness of Christ."

But we must not confound with this general arrangement those particular dispensations which devolved upon individuals all those offices, and supplied them with corresponding qualifications. Paul, who, as an apostle, "was born out of due time," was sent "far hence unto the Gentiles," "to open their eyes, and turn them from darkness to light, and from the power of Satan unto God: that they might receive forgiveness of sins, and inheritance among them which were sanctified by faith" in Christ Jesus. And what did this commission imply, but a renunciation of his country, and of all the endearments of social life and of permanent friendships? The Heathen world lay before him like an illimitable desert,

> "Where wilds, immeasurably spread,
> Seem lengthening as ye go;"

or like a vast hospital, where all is loathsomeness and disease. This desert he was to cultivate until it should become redolent of moral beauty; and to travel from ward to ward in this hospital, distributing amongst the sick and dying the "leaves of the tree of life, which are for the healing of the nations." If he took up this commission at all, he was to take it with all its responsibilities: "He must bear my name," said Christ to Ananias, "before the Gentiles, and kings, and the children of Israel: for I will show him how great things he must suffer for my name's sake." With a decision and fortitude unparalleled in the history of mankind, he detached himself from all secular pursuits, and consecrated his future life to the prosecution of this great enterprise. His worst fears were more than realized in his experience: "For the Holy Ghost witnesseth," says he, "in every city, saying that bonds and afflictions abide me. But none of these things move me, neither count I my life dear unto myself, so that I might finish my course with joy, and the ministry, which I have received of the Lord Jesus, to testify the gospel of the grace of God."

With a call as distinct and valid as was that of Paul, though differing in external circumstances, did the subject of the following narrative undertake a mission to barbarous and ferocious men, from whose violence he stood "in jeopardy every hour." He was called to pass through all the variety of trials enumerated by the apostle, in the following comprehensive summary:—"In journeyings often, in perils of waters, in perils of robbers, in perils by mine own countrymen, in perils by the Heathen, in perils in the city, in perils in the wilderness, in perils in the sea, in perils among false brethren; in weariness and painfulness, in watchings often, in hunger and thirst, in fastings often, in cold and nakedness." But in him was verified the prediction of David: "He that goeth forth and weepeth, bearing precious seed, shall doubtless come again with rejoicing, bringing his sheaves with him." Before, however, conducting the reader to the scenes of his sufferings and triumphs, we shall furnish a brief account of that process by which he was prepared to discharge, with so much honour to himself and benefit to others, the momentous duties of his office.

Mr. Samuel Leigh was a native of Milton, a beautiful village one mile distant from Hanley, in Staffordshire. He was born on the 1st of September, 1785, and spent the earlier years of his life in learning and recreation. As he advanced towards the fifteenth year of his age, he became increasingly thoughtful and reflective. The solemnities of a future judgment and its consequences more deeply impressed his mind, and exercised a salutary and restraining influence over his habits and pursuits. Those impressions ripened into religious principles, which often led him to seek the solitude of the fields for devotional purposes.

There was little, at that period, in the spiritual condition of the Church of England to attract him to her altars. The Wesleyans occasionally visited the village, and conducted their service in any obscure cottage within their reach. By availing himself of all the outward helps which the established Church and the Dissenters in the neighbourhood supplied, by the daily perusal of the scriptures, and by earnest prayer, he obtained a sense of pardon through faith in Christ Jesus. He now felt it to be his duty to assume a public profession of religion; and, after mature consideration, united himself to the Independent church of Hanley, which was comparatively weak, and the congregation small.

His first concern was, to know in what way he could best promote the interests of this little community. He saw around him numbers, of all ages and of both sexes, living in a state of moral delirium, and hastening to perdition. It occurred to him, that, by taking a whole pew in the chapel, he might be able to persuade some of these ungodly people to attend public worship; and he had the happiness of seeing this first and ingenious experiment crowned with the most gratifying results. Were professing Christians generally to imitate the conduct of this young man, it would soon become necessary for our spiritual Israel to enlarge her tents, by lengthening her cords and strengthening her stakes. This simple but effectual method of serving the cause of Christ, may be adopted, not only by those of moderate abilities and limited means, but by all who cultivate habits of diligence, economy, and zeal. The value of time, the worth of the soul, and the importance of knowledge, were then presented to Mr. Leigh's mind in a new light, and called into vigorous exercise all his intellectual faculties.

As he "increased in wisdom and in favour with God and man," it soon became apparent to the church that he was a "chosen vessel," destined to be a standard-bearer in the "sacramental host of God's elect." His talents were first exercised in the private and social means of grace; afterwards he became a lay-helper, and went out into the adjacent villages, expounding the scriptures, and exhorting the people to "flee from the wrath to come." Though not indifferent to doctrinal truth, he was yet more intent upon converting men, than shaping his creed to a conformity to either Calvinism or Arminianism; and more earnest in his endeavours to promote the glory of Christ, in the increase and union of His church, than to advance the interests of sectarianism. Hence, for five years, he divided his labours between the Independents and the Methodists, and so conducted himself as to command the confidence and esteem of both denominations.

During the whole of this period he felt a deep conviction that he was called of God to "preach among the Gentiles the unsearchable riches of Christ;" but a veil was thrown over the field of his future labours, and the precise time when he was to enter upon his work. At that period, the Congregationalists had a seminary, of some celebrity, at Gosport, for the classical and theological improvement of candidates for their ministry.

This institution, which was humble in its origin, but grand and philanthropic in its objects, trained several distinguished men, for various departments of usefulness in the church, both at home and abroad; men, whose names will adorn the history of the respective countries in which they laboured, suffered, and died.

The founder of this theological school was David Bogue, D.D., a native of Coldingham, near Eyemouth, Berwickshire. He received the rudiments of learning in the Grammar School of Dunce, the birth-place of the celebrated Duns Scotus. He afterwards prosecuted his studies in Greek, Latin, Hebrew, Mathematics, Philosophy, and Divinity, for nine years, at the University of Edinburgh. After taking a Master's degree, and passing through the accustomed examination as to his theological knowledge, literary attainments, and acquaintance with church-history, he was licensed as a preacher of the gospel in the Church of Scotland. Receiving an invitation to take charge of a Scotch church at Amsterdam, he went over to Holland. The Dutch Government was prepared to settle an ample income upon him for life; but he found the people so completely immersed in the pursuit of gain, and so averse from the things of God, that he declined the offer, and returned to London. Being on a visit to a friend at Tichfield, he was earnestly solicited to occupy the pulpit in the Independent chapel of Gosport. Their minister, preferring the study of the civil law to that of the gospel, had relinquished his charge, and was qualifying himself for the bar. He rose rapidly in his new profession, was knighted, and sent to India as Sir James Watson, to succeed Sir William Jones. On hearing Dr. Bogue, the church gave him a unanimous call to be their pastor. This call he accepted.

In the year 1789, George Welch, Esq., a pious and opulent banker in London, felt impressed with the necessity of doing something for the dark places of his own country, as well as for the Heathen abroad. He proposed to select a few young men, of deep piety, good natural abilities, and a moderate education, and place them under some able tutor, to be instructed in classics and theology for, at least, three years. At the expiration of that period, they were to go out as preachers of the gospel. The banker selected Dr. Bogue as the tutor, and sent him three students. Such was the origin of an institution which rapidly expanded and rose, under the supervision of the doctor, to considerable eminence.

By the advice of his friends, Mr. Leigh resolved to avail himself of the assistance which this institution offered, in the prosecution of his studies. Having agreed to the terms, which were three years' residence, at forty pounds *per annum*, he entered the academy.

One of his fellow-students was a young man from Aberdeenshire. He was a native of Henethmont, near Huntly, and had been brought up as a shepherd's boy. A returned missionary, having visited Huntly, held a public meeting; at which he gave such an account of the condition of the Heathen, and of the progress and effects of Christianity abroad, as greatly impressed the shepherd's boy, who was present on that occasion. The impressions then made upon this youth could not be obliterated. When the severity of the weather compelled the sheep to seek shelter from the storm, he was accustomed to creep in amongst them, and, while enjoying their protection and warmth, he prayed for himself and the Heathen. He soon acquired a taste for reading, and improved himself in various branches of learning and general knowledge. He excited the attention of the Independent minister of the village, the Rev. G. Cowie; who, after directing his studies for a short time, recommended him to Dr. Phillips and several other persons in the city of Aberdeen. Those gentlemen were astonished when the lad presented himself in a Highland cap, and other articles of dress, little corresponding with aspirations for literary fame. "Man judgeth by the outward appearance;" and, in this case, the evidence was decisive. He was soon ordered to withdraw; and, after some severe animadversions on the gentleman who had sent him, it was at once agreed to send him home. Before the youth was called in, Dr. Phillips expressed his regret that, before deciding his fate, they had not asked him to engage in prayer. On entering the room, they requested him to pray: he instantly fell upon his knees, and addressed God with such humility and fervour, expressing, at the same time, such thoughts and sentiments, as surprised the gentlemen present. When they arose from their knees, they looked at each other and at the lad, and felt ashamed. They now agreed to send him to the missionary seminary at Gosport. He soon distinguished himself there. In 1812, he became the literary coadjutor of Dr. Morrison in China; and, as Dr. Milne, assisted that gentleman in the translation of the Old-Testament scriptures into the language of that country. Dr. Milne was a man of rare attainments, and of signal devotedness to the cause of Christ. After a short but brilliant career of service, he was called to receive his crown of glory in 1822.

Another of the students was the Rev. Mr. Le Brun, whose sufferings and successes, in the Isle of France, are recorded in the history of the London Missionary Society. Mr. Thom, afterwards Dr. Thom, who went out to the Cape of Good Hope, and became pastor of the Dutch church there, was also associated with Mr. Leigh in the various studies and duties of the institution.

The history of these four students is strikingly illustrative of the Divine sovereignty: "that not many wise men after the flesh, not many mighty, not many noble, are called: but God hath chosen the foolish things of the world to confound the wise; and God hath chosen the weak things of the world to confound the things which are mighty; and base things of the world, and things which are despised, hath God chosen, yea, and things which are not, to bring to nought things that are: that no flesh should glory in His presence."

Mr. Leigh brought into all his academic investigations and pursuits a mind thoroughly imbued with the "love of the truth," and resolved to combine the acquisition of learning with progressive piety. Nature had shaped him in a mould that gave him a peculiar adaptation for missionary work. Endowed with a robust constitution, a cheerful disposition, affable manners, and a noble and disinterested generosity, his whole character was at once transparent and attractive. His mental peculiarities were obvious to all who were acquainted with him. From the day of his conversion to the close of his public life, he seemed wholly incapable of any obliquity of purpose. His mind was quick in its perceptions, prompt in its decisions, and resolute in prosecuting whatever he took in hand. Once satisfied that the proposed object was good, in accordance with the great scheme of his life, and calculated to promote the glory of God in the improvement of man, he was deaf to all insinuations as to hardships and dangers; his only concern was to find out the readiest method of securing it, at all risks to himself. Relying on the validity of the Divine promise, "Lo, I am with you alway, even to the end of the world," his "faith laughed at impossibilities, and cried, 'It shall be done.'" This constitutional temperament rendered him an interested spectator of all that occurred around him in his new situation at Gosport. He entertained a high opinion of Dr. Bogue; and, whether he referred to him as a Christian gentleman or a tutor, he always spoke of him in strong terms of commendation.

A glance at the regulations of the establishment, the number and order of the classes, and a few days' residence, convinced Mr. Leigh that the utmost industry would be necessary, on his part, to enable him to keep pace with their educational system. No duty devolving upon the students subjected them to greater vexation than the preparation of methodical discourses, founded upon some text of scripture, which they were required to deliver in the presence of the principal and tutors of the college. As this was a weekly exercise, it fell upon each student with an inconvenient frequency; while the remarks and criticisms to which the discourse was subjected, extending to doctrine, arrangement, style, and manner, were not always complimentary. It requires a rare combination of parts to enable any professor to conduct such discussions to the mutual benefit of any considerable number of young men. In this establishment the results were not very satisfactory to any party. The fastidiousness and severity of the preceptor frequently led to the practice of art and deception on the part of the pupil. One of them, being very much irritated one day by the strictures which were made upon his homily, said, "Gentlemen, I forgot to inform you, at the close of my sermon, that what I had delivered embodied the substance of a very able exposition of the text by the Rev. Dr. B., of London."

After a laborious study of every branch of biblical literature, Dr. Bogue had most conscientiously embraced that system of Christian theology so ably set forth and defended in the writings of Calvin. Every divergence from the strict principles of that system was regarded by him as indicating a downward tendency to error and Arminianism. Mr. Leigh had adopted the moderate views of Baxter, and the weekly discussions referred to failed to bring him to a nearer approximation to the collegiate standard of orthodoxy. After being in the establishment for some time, he informed the doctor that investigation and prayer had produced a conviction in his mind, that Arminianism was more agreeable to the word of God than the theology of Calvin, whose dogmas appeared to him to be absurd and contradictory. Being unable any longer to approve of the doctrinal instruction given in the college, he felt that consistency required him quietly to withdraw. In this resolution the principal acquiesced, and they parted with feelings of mutual regret.

Having communicated his views and intentions to his brother-in-law, who was a member of the Wesleyan church, he mentioned the case to the Rev. Joseph Sutcliffe, M.A., on whose recommendation Mr. Leigh was received into the Society at Portsmouth; where he remained as the superintendent's assistant till the ensuing Conference. After due examination, he was accepted by the Conference, and appointed to the Shaftesbury circuit. Here he laboured, with increasing zeal and usefulness, for two years; often preaching four, and not unfrequently five, times on the Lord's day. He commenced several schools, which he found, on his return to the circuit after an absence of thirty years, in great efficiency; as also five local preachers on the Plan, who had been brought to the knowledge of Christ by his instrumentality. At the district-meeting his superintendent, the

Rev. Benjamin Wood, desired the chairman to administer some cautionary advice to his young man, as the labours he imposed upon himself were such, that human nature could not long sustain them. The Rev. Jonathan Edmondson, M.A., who presided, remarked, that experience would teach him moderation; and that if he had not a little fervour now, he was not likely to acquire it as he advanced in life.

During this period, Mr. Leigh was keeping up a regular correspondence with his mother and sister, and in every letter reminding them of his call to the missionary work. He told them that his mind dwelt upon it in the day-time, and that in the night-season he often dreamed that he was crossing the seas with a message of peace to the Heathen; that he was detained by the authority of his mother; and that he could not leave the country comfortably until she was prepared to concur in what he believed to be the will of God. His mother was unconverted, and could see no sufficient reason for his leaving her, in old age and widowhood, to enter upon so hazardous an undertaking. In some of her letters she remonstrated, expostulated, and entreated; at other times she wrote in tears, and expressed her deep regret, that, in consequence of his obstinacy, the calamity she had long anticipated was obviously becoming inevitable. The filial submission of the son to a questionable stretch of parental authority, often affected her. Soon after he left Shaftesbury, he received a letter from her, in which she said, "Son Samuel, if the Lord has called thee to be a missionary, he will no doubt enable me to give thee up. May the Lord himself go with thee!" "On reading this letter," said he, "I felt as 'merry and lightsome' as Christian, when 'his burden was loosened from his shoulders, and fell off his back.' I sat down and wrote, by the next post, to the Rev. Joseph Benson, offering to go to any part of the world."

He had recently had an interview with Dr. Coke, at Portsmouth, who was preparing to sail for Ceylon; which had given a fresh impulse to his missionary zeal. Just at this juncture the committee received an earnest application from Montreal and Quebec, requesting that a young minister might be sent there, without loss of time. The Conference of 1814, which assembled in Bristol, appointed Mr. Leigh to North America, and sent him up to London to prepare for the voyage. Having completed his outfit, the secretaries gave him permission to visit his mother before leaving the country. "Give us your address," said Dr. Clarke; "and a promise that you will return to London by the first conveyance, after receiving our letter requesting you to do so."

Mr. Leigh took the coach for Staffordshire that night at

eleven o'clock.   On arriving at home, he found that his mother's grief at parting with her son was greatly augmented by the sudden and severe illness of his sister, who was then in a dying state.   The seven o'clock post of that evening brought him a letter from the secretaries, stating that the ship was to sail immediately; that his passage was taken and paid for; and that he must come at once to London.   After perusing the letter, he rose up hastily, and paced the room.   The eye of a mother is always quick and penetrating.   Observing his perturbed feelings, she said, "Samuel, what is the matter? tell me, directly."   He replied, "I am sent for, and must go." "Always obey those who are over you," said his mother, with deep emotion, "and you will generally be right.   The will of the Lord be done!"   He stepped into the next room, to take a parting look at his dear sister.   She had not been able to recognise him; the power of utterance was gone; and she lay, as if in a sweet sleep, in utter unconsciousness of what was transpiring around her.   He knelt down by her bed-side, and, after commending her departing spirit into the hands of God, and his mother to the protection of Providence, he embraced them, and parted, to see them no more till the "resurrection of the just."   Here is a scene that would not have disgraced the apostolic age: the contemplation of it is calculated to melt the most insensible heart.   What a sublime subject for the pencil of the artist!   How admonitory to a slumbering church; and to such of her members as dwell with self-complacency on the sacrifices they have made for the evangelization of the Heathen!

While Mr. Leigh walked from his mother's house to the coach, a distance of about a mile, he was absorbed in thought, and overwhelmed with grief.   The words of David, wrung from his lips by the severity of his trials, came to his recollection, and afforded relief: "Why art thou cast down, O my soul? and why art thou disquieted within me?   Hope thou in God: for I shall yet praise Him, who is the health of my countenance, and my God."   Nothing, however, passed through his mind, implying a reflection on Divine Providence; he felt no misgivings as to his present duty, and entertained no gloomy or desponding apprehensions respecting the future.   He took his seat on the coach that night, having been just six hours in his mother's company.

On reaching London, which he did in time for the sailing of the vessel, he was informed that a letter had been received from Montreal that morning, requesting that no missionary might be sent there for the present, as the country was in a very disturbed state.   The half of the passage-money was returned, and the ship sailed without him. This occurrence, which was a source of disappointment. and vexation to all parties, turned out to be a dispensation of "judgment and of mercy;" for, within three weeks, intelligence was received of the total loss of the vessel, and of all on board, passengers and seamen, with the exception of four individuals. Thus God continues, from time to time, to assert His supremacy: "He doeth according to His will in the army of heaven, and among the inhabitants of the earth: and none can stay His hand, or say unto Him, What doest Thou?"

Just at this time, a voice from another quarter of the globe reached the committee, saying, "Come over, and help us." As the communication is full of interest, not only as it marks the commencement of a new era in the history of the country whence it came, but also as it led to results far more extensive and glorious than could have been anticipated by the most sanguine Christian philanthropist, we subjoin the substance of it:—

"There are probably twenty thousand souls in this colony of New South Wales, natives of the British Isles, with their descendants. From the description of people sent hither, much good cannot be expected. The higher ranks of those who were formerly convicts, are, in general, either entirely occupied in amassing wealth, or rioting in sensuality. The lower orders are, indeed, the filth and offscouring of the earth, in point of wickedness. Long accustomed to idleness and iniquity of every kind, here they indulge their vicious inclinations without a blush. Drunkenness, adultery, sabbath-breaking, and blasphemy, are no longer considered even as indecencies. All those ties of moral order, and feelings of propriety, which bind society together, are not only relaxed, but almost extinct. This is the general character of the convicts, high and low; and, excepting the civil and military departments of the Government, there is no other difference than that which wealth naturally creates, in the means which it affords for greater indulgence in vice. The policy of the present Government is just, mild, humane, and encouraging. The climate is uncommonly fine and healthy, and peculiarly favourable to an English constitution. The country is beautiful and exceedingly fertile, and intersected with roads. The necessaries and luxuries of life are abundant, and easily to be obtained; and the mode of living and social habits of the people are nearly the same as in England.

"Sydney, the principal town and seat of Government, is populous and extensive. Nearly one-half of the colonists live there, and there a preacher would find much to do. Paramatta, a populous village, is situated sixteen miles up the country, nearly in the centre of the colony. Within from five to ten miles of Paramatta, on every side, are the following settlements; namely, Liverpool, Prospect, Concord, Baulkham-Hills, Castle-Hill, and Kissing-Point. Twenty miles inland from Paramatta lies the village of Windsor, on the banks of the Hawkesbury River. Sydney town would be the first and principal place; then Paramatta, in the centre of the settlements around it; and, lastly, Windsor, and the Hawkesbury country. At first there was but one family of Wesleyans, now we have nineteen persons meeting in class.

"We call upon you in our own behalf: leave us not forsaken in this benighted land. We call upon you in behalf of our children: let them not be left to perish for lack of knowledge. We call upon you in behalf of those who have neither opportunity nor inclination to speak for themselves: leave them not in their blood. We call upon you in the name of the outcasts of society, landing daily upon our shores: administer to them that word of life which may make their exile a blessing. Send *us* that gospel which you have received from the Lord to preach to every creature. Send amongst us one of yourselves, and many shall rise up and bless you.

"In order to make some provision for the cause of God amongst us, we have vested a certain sum of money in horned cattle; which sum will be allowed to accumulate by the natural increase of the cattle. We look forward with a certain confidence, by the blessing of God, to be able in a few years, from this fund, entirely to support the work amongst us. This fund we have by deed conveyed to proper trustees, to be applied exclusively to this object. We would suggest, 1. That the missionary be a single man; 2. That he be legally qualified; 3. That he be rendered independent of us and every one else in the colony; 4. That he have a good supply of wearing apparel, house-furniture, and books: in short, send us a preacher tolerably supplied with those articles, and, by God's blessing, he shall be no further expense to you."

Messrs. Bowden and Hoskins, by whom this document was signed, were formerly Wesleyan schoolmasters in London. They were recommended to the colonial chaplain by Joseph Butterworth, Esq., M.P., and appointed to take charge of the charity-schools of Sydney. They agreed to meet in class on March 6th, 1812, and held the first class-meeting on the evening of that day. There were present the schoolmasters and their wives, three of the senior girls from the school, two soldiers, and Mrs. I., and J. F.; making, in all, twelve individuals.

A class of six members was formed at Windsor by Mr. E. He was a native of Ireland, and had been educated for the bar. In a moment of severe temptation, he committed forgery, was convicted, and sentenced to death. While preparing for the day of execution, his heart was changed, and he obtained peace with God. Several extenuating circumstances having come to the knowledge of the Government, his sentence was commuted to transportation for life. He carried into banishment the sacred scriptures, and the fear of God. He was much and deservedly respected, being intelligent, consistent, zealous, and humble. On the week-days he taught a school; and on the Lord's day went into the neighbouring villages, where he read the Liturgy and explained the word of God.

The committee regarded the appeal from Australia as the call of God, and proceeded at once to make arrangements for the departure of Mr. Leigh to that country. As the colonists had promised to pay the current expenses of the mission, the committee were of opinion that he might depend upon their making a decent provision for his maintenance. To this proposal he objected. "I go," said he, "as your missionary; depending upon you, and holding myself responsible to you for my conduct; and not as the hired agent of the colonists, of whom I know nothing." This decision prevented much subsequent misunderstanding; for the "investment of capital in horned cattle, and the conveyance of the fund accruing from that investment to trustees for the benefit of the mission," of which they had written, were found to refer rather to their good intentions, than to any practical plan they had actually adopted for the purpose of extending Christianity in the country.

On the 30th of September, 1814, Mr. Leigh appeared before Sir William Domville, Baronet, Lord Mayor of London, and made the declarations, and took the oaths, prescribed by law; "in faith and testimony whereof," said his lordship, "I have caused the seal of the office of mayoralty, of the said city of London, to be put and affixed to this licence." On October 3rd, Mr. Leigh was "set apart for the work of the ministry, by the imposition of hands, as a person well qualified to feed the flock of Christ, and to administer the holy sacraments." The parchment certifying this fact is signed by ADAM CLARKE, LL.D., F.S.A., then President; SAMUEL BRADBURN; THOMAS VASEY; and JOHN GAULTER.

It was now discovered that all attempts to establish a mission in New South Wales, without the sanction and co-operation of the Home Government, would prove abortive; and Dr. Clarke was requested to submit the case to His Majesty's Ministers. "On the 3rd of November," says the doctor, "I wrote to the

Right Honourable Lord Viscount Sidmouth, stating that I had been applied to for a missionary to go out to New South Wales, and that I had been applied to, also, for a schoolmaster;—that the schoolmaster and mistress of our charity-school in Great Queen-street had gone out thither; and they, with several other settlers, prayed that we should send them over one of our preachers; that I had found a suitable person, Mr. Samuel Leigh, who was capable of acting in this *double capacity*, and for whose prudence and loyalty I did not hesitate to pledge myself; and I wished to know whether His Majesty's Government would do any thing towards accrediting the said Samuel Leigh. To this letter I received the answer and memorandum, copies of which I here subjoin.—ADAM CLARKE."

"Whitehall, November 19th, 1814.

"DEAR SIR,—I have to thank you for having favoured me with another part of the important work in which you are engaged, and for the letter with which it was accompanied. My acknowledgments have been delayed by my desire to give you, at the same time, an answer respecting Samuel Leigh; which, as I am pressed for time, you will, I hope, excuse me for enclosing in the form of a memorandum.

"I remain, with sincere esteem, dear Sir,

"Your faithful and obedient servant,

"SIDMOUTH."

"Memorandum:—The Governor of New South Wales has applied to Government for some schoolmasters to be sent out to that colony. Mr. Samuel Leigh, a person recommended by Dr. Adam Clarke, appears fit to be employed in that situation. The allowance is £50 *per annum*, and a passage provided at the expense of Government. If it should be considered more advisable for Mr. Leigh to go out as a missionary, the Society for Propagating the Gospel in Foreign Parts will grant him an outfit, and must (by regulation) apply to the Colonial Department for a passage, with letters of introduction to the Governor of New South Wales. No salary is allowed by Government; but if, after a residence of two years, he shall be considered by the Society as disabled by age and infirmity, £100 *per annum* will be granted to him for life by Government; or, if he dies in the service, a pension of £50 *per annum* will be allowed to his widow.—SIDMOUTH."

His lordship's kindness had assumed a form and taken a direction which the doctor had not anticipated, and which he felt to be extremely embarrassing. His reply to his lordship is dated Harpur-street, November 22nd, 1814. "I feel highly obliged," he observes, "by the very kind attention your lordship has paid to my request, relative to Mr. Samuel Leigh. But, not expecting such a favour as your lordship proposes, and finding a vessel bound for New South Wales, I had, on the strong recommendation of a friend, taken, and (but two or three days before I was honoured by your lordship's obliging offer) paid for, his passage. As I did not know of any other vessel going out for that place, and the captain proposing to sail as on this day, and some others pressing him to let them have the berth, I was obliged to close with him by paying the money. I wish Mr. Leigh to act in a *twofold character,*— namely, as an instructor of youth in useful learning, and a teacher of the adults in the knowledge of God, and their duty to their fellows ; and for earnest, prudent, well-directed endeavours of this kind, your lordship knows, from the constitution of the colony, there must be the greatest necessity. But I am now at a loss how I can avail myself of your lordship's generous offers. I feel extreme delicacy in thus troubling your lordship, but should be very happy to receive your lordship's further directions, under the present circumstances of the case."

As the noble secretary was not prepared to sanction the *double capacity* in which it was proposed to send Mr. Leigh to the colony, he closed the correspondence with a dignity and courtesy becoming a great statesman :—

" Whitehall, November 30th, 1814.

" DEAR SIR,—As I find, by yours of the 22nd instant, that you have provided Mr. Samuel Leigh with a passage to New South Wales, nothing further appears wanting to accomplish your wishes, than that of his being recommended to the Governor of the colony, to *act in the capacity of schoolmaster.* I shall immediately recommend Mr. Leigh to Lord Bathurst, through whom all correspondence passes with the Governor of New South Wales, who, I have no doubt, will direct the Governor to appoint him to *such situation* in the colony.

" I am, dear Sir,
" Your obedient servant,
" SIDMOUTH."

Each page of the correspondence is endorsed " A. CLARKE."

The necessary arrangements being completed, Mr. Leigh went on board the ship " Hebe," at Portsmouth, and joined the East and West India fleets which lay in St. Helen's Bay, waiting for sailing orders. The commodore gave the signal to weigh anchors on the morning of February 28th, 1815 ; and they were gently borne away from their native shores by an easy breeze. Mr. Leigh felt as others felt when casting his eyes, for probably the last time, upon the land of his fathers. The

West-India fleet separated from them at sea, and sailed under convoy to its destination.

A violent gale sprang up on the 6th of March, which scattered the fleet, and drove the "Hebe," with several other ships, out of their course. At daylight, on the following morning, the captain observed two suspicious-looking sails bearing down upon them under a press of canvass. "Mr. Leigh," said he, "if these are privateers, we stand no chance. If they are French, those of us who may survive the skirmish will be lodged in a French prison." Mr. Leigh replied, "Sir, I am going to New South Wales as a missionary; and if I go through a French prison, it is not of much consequence to me." He felt assured that God was sending him with a special message to Australia, and relied upon Providence for protection while on his way to deliver it. The ship's papers were put into a bag, with a cannon-ball, and placed in the hands of a lady-passenger, who, at a given signal, was to throw them overboard. The captain ordered the ship to be prepared for action, the decks to be cleared, and all on board to be supplied with arms and ammunition. The bustle that ensued produced a great sensation, and led the most sceptical to look serious. The children became much excited on seeing their parents in tears, and hearing them pray to God for mercy; and, concluding that some awful calamity was coming upon them, ran about inquiring into the cause of their distress. While the enemy was taking up his position, the general order was given, "Men, be calm, be steady, obey your officers, defend yourselves!" At that moment it was discovered that one of the ships was English, and the other American, sailing under false colours. The captain of the English ship was permitted to come on board the "Hebe;" and, after a short interview, the strangers withdrew, and not a shot was fired on either side. During a few awful moments of suspense, when they expected a broadside from the enemy, and stood ready to return the fire, a gentleman-passenger became so agitated, that it was with difficulty he was restrained from committing suicide: he repeatedly attempted to throw himself into the sea, preferring, as he said, being drowned, to the casualties of a sea-fight. "All is well! all is well!" soon spread through the ship, and changed the current of feeling from fear and sorrow to one simultaneous flow of satisfaction and thanksgiving.

On the evening of the same day a storm of unusual severity came on, which continued, without much intermission, for nine days. All their live stock perished, and almost every thing on deck was swept away. They were going to throw the guns overboard, when the captain changed his mind, and ordered them to steer for the Bay of Biscay. They reached the Bay in safety, and rode out the storm.

This succession of trials sobered all on board, and paved the way for the introduction of a regular series of religious services. One day, during the tempest, the captain entered Mr. Leigh's cabin, and inquired whether he would oblige him by " asking a blessing before and returning thanks after their meals, and by reading prayers and preaching a sermon on the Lord's day."

Mr. Leigh, who had been waiting for an opportunity to propose a similar arrangement, cheerfully undertook those duties. But for some time their beneficial influence was completely neutralized by the inconsistent conduct of the captain himself. He was an able and vigilant officer, but an habitual swearer, and seemed to study how he might give variety of form and emphasis to his oaths. His general conduct was characterized by firmness, decision, and punctuality; while dignity and courtesy were agreeably blended in his intercourse with all on board. He had the ship's bell rung exactly at nine o'clock in the morning, and expected and required the first-class passengers to be seated when he came below to preside at the breakfast-table. When any irregularity occurred in this respect, he would express his disapprobation in oaths, and conclude by asking Mr. Leigh to say grace. This practice was amusing to the doctor and a few others, who were sceptical; frightened some of the ladies, who were delicate and nervous; but gave general offence to the more serious part of the company. Mr. Leigh felt it to be his duty to call his attention to so unseemly an exhibition. While he was thinking of the least offensive method of doing this, the captain broke out into such a paroxysm of swearing as he sat at dinner, that Mr. Leigh involuntarily leaned his head forward until it touched the table. The captain, observing this, said, with considerable emotion, " I perceive, Mr. Leigh, you do not like it." " Like what?" said Mr. Leigh. He replied, "So much swearing." " Indeed," said Mr. Leigh, " I do not; it does no good to any one, and must ultimately prove very injurious to your own interests." Addressing him, the captain said, with great solemnity of manner, " Sir, I will in future avoid a practice which evidently gives you much pain."

A few days afterwards he expressed a wish that Mr. Leigh would make it convenient to pay some attention to the children on board. " They are fifteen in number," he remarked ; " they are running all over the ship; and a little discipline and instruction will, in my opinion, be of essential service to them." Mr. Leigh lifted a sheet of paper, on which he had written the outline of a method of instruction he had prepared; and informed him that, on its receiving his sanction, and that of the parents of the children, it should be instantly adopted. The children were to assemble at ten o'clock in the morning; the Psalms and Lessons for the day were to be read and explained; and those exercises were to be begun and concluded with singing and prayer. On the Lord's day they were to attend prayers and preaching in the forenoon, and be subjected to a general catechetical examination in the afternoon. Several of the passengers asked permission to be present during the exposition of the scriptures, while the singing drew the sailors and others in groups around the skylights, where they also could hear.

On the following Sunday, March 11th, the regular services were again interrupted. "In the morning," he remarks in his journal, "a ship was reported to be in sight. Being watched, she was observed to have her eye upon us, and to be making all sail to come up with us. As she approached, the captain concluded, after examining her with his glass, that she was an American cruiser. He ordered the decks to be cleared, the guns to be loaded, and all that could use arms to be furnished with fire-arms or cutlasses. Before coming within range of our guns, she told us by signal, that she was an English privateer. Her chief officer was allowed to come on board the 'Hebe;' and, after a little parleying, he took a glass of grog, wished us a safe voyage, and bade us good morning. We had to pass through the same ordeal in the evening, as a ship, bearing Spanish colours, seemed to be making all haste to overtake us. During the uneasiness, bustle, and confusion that ensued, it was announced, 'She has changed her course: all is well!'

"After an anxious day we retired to rest. The two following days were delightfully employed in religious duties; but, at twelve o'clock on the night of the 13th, all hands were ordered to turn out. When they mustered on the deck, the captain informed them that a large ship was close upon them; that, by the aid of the moon, he had discovered her to be a ship of war; and that resistance on their part would be useless, as one of her broadsides would send them to the bottom. They must, therefore, either submit to be taken, or, knowing their ship to be a first-rate sailer, endeavour to escape by putting on more canvass. After a moment's consultation with the officers, all hands were employed to get out of the reach of so disagreeable a neighbour. The enemy perceived their object, and sent a cannon-ball with a signal to surrender. The captain ordered the ship to lay-to. After remaining two hours in distressing suspense, an officer and twelve men boarded the

'Hebe.' 'Our commander,' said they, 'wishes to know why you have left the convoy, and if you are in want of any thing. We are cruising for the protection of British commerce.' The captain informed them that they had been separated from the convoy by stress of weather, thanked them for their kind offer of assistance, and ordered the ship to be put under sail. The next day the weather was tremendous." How true to fact is David's description of a similar scene!—"They that go down to the sea in ships, that ·do business in great waters; these see the works of the Lord, and His wonders in the deep. For He commandeth, and raiseth the stormy wind, which lifteth up the waves thereof. They mount up to the heaven, they go down again to the depths : their soul is melted because of. trouble. They reel to and fro, and stagger like a drunken man, and are at their wit's end. Then they cry unto the Lord in their trouble, and He bringeth them out of their distresses. He maketh the storm a calm, so that the waves thereof are still. Then are they glad because they be quiet; so He bringeth them unto their desired haven."

"March 21st.—The weather has moderated. All are now cheerful : my young people evidently improve, and the adults of every class are more attentive to their religious duties. On the 23rd we were again disconcerted by the appearance of four brigs, under circumstances that created some alarm. As our ship was well manned, and provided with arms and ammunition, the captain issued the order to prepare for action. As the brigs neared us, they hoisted friendly flags, and bore away in another direction. Good Friday was observed with due solemnity. O may we be saved by the precious blood of Christ !"

"'We have had extraordinary weather of late,' said one of the sailors. 'I expected nothing else,' said another, 'after taking Jonah on board.' 'For my part,' said a third, 'I believe the missionary to be a good man; but as he is going to convert the convicts of New South Wales, the devil seems determined to stop him if he can.' 'I have been convinced for some time,' said a fourth, 'that we shall all go to the bottom before we reach Port Jackson.' 'Well,' said a fifth, 'when we are going down, I shall keep as close to the missionary as I can; for then I shall stand some chance of getting into heaven with him.' The more sober-minded and reflective frequently remark, 'It is no wonder that we have such tempests and troubles : we are so indifferent about religion.'

"April 15th.—We have just heard of the disasters that have happened to the convoy and fleet which left England with us. Many of the ships have reached Madeira with only half their men, their masts down, and their bulwarks swept away. Blessed be God! we and our ship are still spared. I am pleased beyond measure with our children: they come running into my cabin during the day, to repeat hymns and passages of scripture which they have committed to memory.

"17th.—At the close of a delightful sabbath, seven of our men were sent out to raise the anchor, in doing which they capsized the boat. Only one of them could swim, and he made for the ship. When he came alongside, he was so exhausted, that, for some time, he could not hold the rope that was thrown overboard to save him. The others seized the oars, or clung to the boat, and thus sustained themselves, until they were picked up by a boat from the ship.

"20th.—We have a fine breeze: all are in good spirits; we dwell together in peace. On the 27th, one of our men disobeyed the second mate: he was placed in irons, and afterwards put on board a man-of-war.

"May 2nd.—The passengers begin to feel the inconvenience of the heat, and to complain of the tediousness of the voyage. For the first time cards were introduced. I walked the deck until my usual time for retiring to rest. Knowing that a public reproof would be resented, I said, as I passed the card-party to my cabin, 'Good night, ladies and gentlemen. I pray God to save us this night from destruction.' This observation spoiled their game; for they soon separated, and went to bed.

"15th.—I was not able to perform Divine service last Lord's day, having fallen from the deck on to the cabin floor. My arm was nearly broken, and I was much bruised. It was truly refreshing to see the mariners and passengers sitting in different parts of the ship, reading the books and tracts which I had from time to time distributed amongst them. Our boatswain and gunner have certainly experienced the converting grace of God.

"22nd.—Last Sunday we held public worship: and a most precious season we felt it to be. The ship's bell rings at ten, that they may prepare for the service: it rings again at half-past ten, when all assemble with their Bibles and Prayer-Books. We present the appearance of a little church.

"June 1st.—Being informed that one of the officers had borrowed the gunner's Bible, I presented him with a copy, for which he seemed truly grateful. I also offered one to the captain, which he thankfully accepted, and assured me that he would not only preserve it as a memorial of our friendship, but also carefully and frequently read it. O may it be the instrument of his salvation!

"13th.—I have been on board nineteen weeks; and, thank God! I have been comfortable and happy.

"15th.—O what a day has this been! The anticipated storm came on; and, in a short time, the sea ran mountains high. The gunner was ill, and received orders to keep his bed; but, on hearing that the men were unable to take-in the main-sheet, he jumped up and ascended the shrouds to assist his comrades. The saddle of the mainyard gave way, and he, being weak, lost his hold, and fell into the sea. His strong jacket being open, he floated on the waves. We saw him fall, and the great gulls descending upon him; but, though he remained above water more than ten minutes, the state of the elements rendered it impossible for us to save him. He had become truly pious, and I have no doubt of his salvation.

"17th.—Yesterday was a day of more than ordinary serious-ness: I endeavoured to improve the death of the gunner. The captain was much moved: Lord, teach him to number his days!

"30th.—The children were examined, and gave much satis-faction. Such as could read the scriptures were presented with a Bible, and one shilling in silver."

Mr. Leigh devoted one hour, morning and evening, to the instruction of a young emigrant in Latin and geography; so that the whole of his time was profitably occupied. The Lord "confirmed the word of His servant, and performed the counsel of His messenger;" so that, no doubt, impressions were made which neither the progress of time nor the future vicissitudes of life could entirely obliterate.

They had been exposed to a heavy gale for several days in succession, when the wind suddenly and entirely ceased to blow. The sea had been stirred to its depths, and the waves continued to scud past them like a multitude of lofty mountains in pursuit of each other. The doctor, who was particularly struck with this state of the ocean, stepped up to Mr. Leigh, and observed, "If Jesus Christ were on board, you would call this a miracle." "Not at all," said Mr. Leigh; "it is not like one of His mira-cles." "The analogy is, in my opinion," said the doctor, "complete; for in the New Testament we read, that 'He rebuked the wind, and there was a calm.'" Mr. Leigh replied, "I have frequently observed, that gentlemen of your sentiments seldom do justice to the scriptures. The passage which you have partially quoted says, 'He arose, and rebuked the wind and the *raging of the water;* and *they ceased,* and there was a calm.'" Without a single remark the doctor retired, but returned in a short time with the New Testament in his hand. Pointing to the passage with his finger, he said, "You have quoted the text correctly. I had not previously noticed the effect of His word upon *both elements.* I am now prepared to admit that what is here said to have occurred is much more *like* a miracle than any thing we have witnessed to-day." From this period he treated Mr. Leigh and Christianity with marked respect; and on more occasions than one defended both, when attacked by others.

A lady from Liverpool having given birth to a daughter, a most interesting service was held on the occasion of its baptism. The name of the ship, "Hebe," was imposed upon the infant; and she was solemnly dedicated to God in the presence of the officers, the seamen, and passengers. Mr. Leigh delivered an appropriate address on the relative duties, and urged all present to an immediate and personal consecration of themselves to Christ. The religious exercises, which had been continued with but occasional interruptions throughout the voyage, had so united all parties on board, by the social and kindly intercourse they occasioned, that, when they came to separate from each other on the shores of Australia, the scene was truly affecting.

They sailed into Port Jackson on the 10th of August, 1815, after a voyage of about five months. When the captain had transferred the command of the ship to the pilot, he said, "Mr. Leigh, you have, no doubt, observed the fidelity with which I have kept my promise to abstain from swearing. I have not uttered an oath for the last four months." This gave Mr. Leigh an opportunity of reminding him, that the faithful observance of his promise was a proof of the moral power which God had bestowed upon man, and that He would hold him responsible for the due exercise of that power. He concluded by saying, "I am sure that your own mind must reflect with satisfaction upon the victory you have achieved over a sinful and an inveterate habit." "I have been at sea," said the captain, "for the last thirty years; but no previous voyage has yielded the gratification to my own mind that this has done." When the vessel was safely moored, Mr. Leigh and others went on shore.

CHAPTER II.

IS INTRODUCED TO THE GOVERNOR—SOCIAL CONDITION OF THE PEOPLE —FORMS A CIRCUIT OF ONE HUNDRED AND FIFTY MILES—EXPOSED TO IMMINENT DANGER.

ON landing in Sydney Harbour, Mr. Leigh inquired for Mr. E.; and, on approaching the residence of that gentleman, found him standing in the door. Expecting a hearty reception, he walked up to him, and, taking him frankly by the hand, said, "I am a Wesleyan missionary, just arrived from England by the ship 'Hebe.'" "Indeed!" said Mr. E., "I am sorry to inform you, that it is now doubtful whether the governor will allow you to remain in the country in that capacity. You had better, however, walk in, and remain in my house until that question can be settled." The manner and observation of Mr. E. gave a severe shock to a mind naturally sanguine and ardent. Mr. E. introduced him to his family, and invited him to partake of refreshments : but he became so variously exercised, as he sat at table, that, feeling it impossible to be either cheerful or communicative, he expressed a wish to retire to his bed-room. He spent the evening in serious reflection, and the greater part of the night in self-examination and prayer. The last sight which he witnessed at home—his aged mother in tears, and his sister on her death-bed,—the loss of the ship by which he was to have gone to America,—the labours and trials of the voyage, —and now the prospect of his ministry being interdicted— rushed upon his recollection, and, like the confluence of many streams, almost overwhelmed him. He was called to breakfast in the morning, and took the place assigned to him at table; but his appetite was gone. After family prayer, arrangements were made for landing his luggage, and getting it placed in a situation of security. In looking over the packages, Mr. E. observed, "It does not appear that you have brought any household furniture : in our application to the committee, we particularly requested them to send 'furniture for a *house.*'" "The committee understood you," said Mr. Leigh, "to apply for furniture for a *horse*, and I have brought an excellent second-hand military saddle, bridle, and all other requisites." From the indistinctness of the writing, the secretaries had been led to substitute the word "horse" for "*house.*"

It was regarded as a primary duty on the part of Mr. Leigh, to pay his respects to His Excellency the governor, present his credentials, and, if possible, obtain his official sanction. Accordingly, next day, at eleven o'clock, he called at the government-house, and sent-in his name and designation. After waiting some time, he was ushered into the presence of His Excellency by his aide-de-camp, and received with much formality. Addressing himself to Mr. Leigh, he inquired, "Who sent you here in the capacity of a Wesleyan missionary ?" "The committee of the Society," said Mr. Leigh, "at the request of several British emigrants, and, as I understand, with the concurrence of His Majesty's Government." The governor replied, "I regret you have come here as a missionary, and feel sorry that I cannot give you any encouragement in that capacity." "The documents which I have now the honour of presenting to Your Excellency," said Mr. Leigh, "will show you that I am legally and duly authorized to preach the gospel in any part of His Majesty's dominions." The governor turned round upon his heel, and remarked, "You have come to a strange country. Those documents are of no value here. It is necessary we should be jealous and cautious; for, a few years since, we had a religious rebellion, aggravated by the bitter hostility of both Papists and Protestants. If you will take office under government, I will find you a situation in which you may become rich, and one in which you will be much more comfortable than in going about preaching in such a colony as this." After thanking His Excellency for his generous offer, Mr. Leigh informed him, that, having come to New South Wales as a Wesleyan missionary, he could not act in any other capacity while he remained in the country. He then briefly stated the objects of his mission, and the means he intended to employ for the attainment of those objects. The governor, who had listened with marked attention to his statement, observed, "If those be your objects, they are certainly of the first importance; and, if you will endeavour to compass them by the means you have now specified, I cannot but wish you all the success you can reasonably expect or desire. Call at the surveyor-general's office; present my compliments, and say, that I wish him to afford you every facility in his power in travelling from one township to another." At the close of the interview, His Excellency advanced towards Mr. Leigh, and shook hands with him in the most cordial manner.

Having thus secured the countenance and protection of the colonial government, Mr. Leigh began to mature his plans for a systematic attack upon the ignorance and immorality with which he was surrounded. We would remind the reader, that the state of society in that colony differed in many respects from that of every other appendage to the British crown. People look at a well-regulated commonwealth as they do at a magnificent building. They are struck with the nice adjustment of materials in the edifice, and the variety and richness of its decorations; but they overlook the labours of the men who quarried those materials, who chiselled them into beauteous forms, and blended them in symmetrical proportions. We shall not be able to "see the grace of God," as displayed in the extended fields of Australia, nor the obligations of the church to the men who first grafted the evangelical scion on the "wild olive-tree" of that continent, without glancing at the actual state of things when they commenced their labours.

The selection of New South Wales as a penal settlement originated in the separation of the North-American provinces from England. In that selection the Government proposed, "1. To rid the mother-country, from time to time, of the yearly increasing number of prisoners who were accumulating in the jails.

AUSTRALIAN BLACK AND FAMILY.

2. To afford a proper place for the punishment of criminals, as well as for their progressive and ultimate reformation.   And, 3. To form a free colony out of the materials which the reformed prisoners would supply, in addition to families of free emigrants who might be induced to settle in the country."   With these laudable objects in view, the Government fitted out a small fleet, with two years' provisions on board, for upwards of one thousand individuals; seven hundred and fifty-seven being convicts.   This fleet sailed into Port Jackson, under the command of Captain Phillips, governor of the new colony, on the 26th of June, 1788.   The massive timber that had remained undisturbed for ages, and the brushwood interlaced and covering the ground like net-work, fell in all directions under the saw, the axe, and the hedge-bill.   Tents were pitched; the live-stock was landed; the safe custody of the convicts provided for; the stores deposited in temporary buildings; and the colony, amounting to a thousand and thirty individuals, established.

The natives came down upon the colonists in considerable numbers, and hostilities soon commenced; in the course of which, many cruelties were committed on both sides.   The effects of the musket were incomprehensible to the savages: they saw their men fall as by magic, at a much greater distance from the enemy than could be reached by the most dexterous use of either the spear or the bomerang, while the instrument of destruction was invisible.   Being terror-struck, and feeling themselves unable to cope with civilized man, they fell back into the depths of their native forests.   It is not our intention to trace the vicissitudes through which the colony has passed since that period; but, looking at its unprecedented progress in population, intelligence, commerce, and religion, we may say that "a nation has been born in a day."   The poetic prediction, uttered when the first Europeans struck their tents in Sydney Cove, and regarded at the time as being just possible during the revolution of ages, is being rapidly fulfilled.   The poet represents HOPE, standing upon a rock, and encouraging Art and Labour, under the influence of Peace, to pursue the employments necessary to give security and happiness to an infant settlement.

> Where Sydney Cove her lucid bosom swells,
> Courts her young navies, and the storm repels,
> High on a rock, amid the troubled air,
> HOPE stood sublime, and waved her golden hair,
> Calm'd with her rosy smile the tossing deep,
> And with sweet accents charm'd the winds to sleep.
> To each wild plain she stretch'd her snowy hand,
> High-waving wood, and sea-encircled strand.
> "Hear me," she cried, "ye rising realms! record
> Time's opening scenes, and truth's unerring word:—

> *There* shall broad streets their stately walls extend,
> The circus widen and the crescent bend;
> *There*, ray'd from cities o'er the cultured land,
> Shall bright canals and solid roads expand.
> *There*, the proud arch, Colossus-like, bestride
> Yon glittering streams, and bound the chafing tide;
> Embellish'd villas crown the landscape-scene,
> Farms wave with gold, and orchards blush between.
> *There*, shall tall spires and dome-capt towers ascend,
> And piers and quays their massy structures blend:
> While with each breeze approaching vessels glide,
> And northern treasures dance on every tide!"
> Then ceased the nymph: tumultuous echoes roar,
> And JOY's loud voice was heard from shore to shore.
> Her graceful steps descending press'd the plain,
> And PEACE, and ART, and LABOUR join'd her train.

The improvement of a country is ordinarily, like the cultivation of the soil, slow and laborious. Regarding the apostles as spiritual husbandmen, the "field" assigned to them was "the world." They were to enclose it, drain it of its idolatries, "break up the fallow ground," sow it with the seed of the kingdom, and God was to "give the increase." During the first twenty-nine years, the government of New South Wales was employed in forming institutions adapted to the peculiarities of their social condition, in adjusting the civil rights of the different classes in the country, and in promoting their physical comfort. Although multitudes had been annually landed upon their shores, thousands of whom were the very offscouring of European society, yet no adequate means had been employed for their moral or intellectual elevation. The severe inflictions of justice were not sufficient to suppress the frequency of dishonesty and bloodshed; and there were few instructors in the land to remind them of the worth of their souls, or of their responsibility to God.

Few scenes could have been more discouraging than that which presented itself to the newly-arrived missionary. Beyond the frontiers of the colony, there lay a nation of savages, covering a territory extending, in a direct line, two thousand miles, and numbering nearly two hundred thousand souls. In the colony itself was a vast community of convicts, who—"being filled with all unrighteousness, fornication, wickedness, covetousness, maliciousness; full of envy, murder, debate, deceit, malignity; whisperers, backbiters, haters of God, despiteful, proud, boasters, inventors of evil things, disobedient to parents, without understanding, covenant-breakers, without natural affection, implacable, unmerciful"—were suffering the "due reward of their deeds," and living "without God in the world." The free settlers and squatters were thinly spread over a large section of the country, and removed but a few degrees from the preceding classes in ignorance and vice.

In the mean time, what had the legislature done to stem the tide of ungodliness that was undermining the foundations of the social edifice, and threatening to sweep every vestige of truth, honour, and honesty from the country? It had provided military establishments, jails, and gibbets! It is true that the colonial government, as administered by Major-General Macquarie, was conciliatory in a high degree; but the criminal laws were still sanguinary. Such indeed were, at that period, the laws of the mother-country and of the other states of Europe. The Government maintained, that men who had forfeited their civil rights, and been convicted of every conceivable atrocity, ought to be subjected to a severe system of disciplinary control. It will be admitted, we presume, that such a system required to be worked with an equal regard to justice and mercy, to prevent its degenerating into one of oppression, inhumanity, and cruelty. Since then, the laws have been happily ameliorated; and the principal object now sought to be attained, by secondary punishment, is the moral, intellectual, and spiritual reformation of the criminal.

Governor Macquarie evinced a deep and humane interest in every expedient that seemed calculated to reclaim the convict, or promote his personal well-being. "His maxim," says Montgomery Martin, "was to make every convict consider his European life as a past existence, and his Australian one a new era, where he would find honesty to be the best policy, and good conduct its own unfailing reward. He raised to the Commission of the Peace a few who had been convicts; patronized the thoroughly-reformed; gave others colonial situations; and distributed among them large quantities of land. But noble, generous, and philanthropic as were the motives which dictated such conduct, it has been regretted that he was not more discriminating in the exercise of his patronage." He suggested and executed several new and comprehensive plans for the general improvement of the country, and the extension of the colonial trade and commerce. He erected many public buildings, constructed hundreds of miles of public roads, and established several model-farms. Without depreciating the talents of the able statesmen by whom he has been succeeded, we have no doubt, looking at the difficulties which he had to overcome, the few facilities which the colony supplied for aiding him in his arduous undertakings, and the bold and equitable principles of government which he permanently established, that the historians of other times will accord to him the honour of having laid the foundation of what must become, in the course of years, a great, populous, and wealthy state. Macquarie maintained a nicely-balanced administration; as remote from extreme severity as from culpable remissness. He combined with official dignity the blandness of a gentleman and the generosity of a national benefactor. After serving his country, in various important offices, with distinguished ability and honour, he retired to Scotland, where, after a painful affliction, he died in peace.

The changes which he introduced into the capital itself were as judicious and extensive, as they were necessary and beneficial. Each proprietor had been allowed to build on his land when and how his caprice dictated; so that, no attention having been paid to the laying-out of the streets, the town of Sydney was exceedingly rude and irregular. It did not contain one thousand houses; and, with the exception of a few private residences, these were generally small and of mean appearance. After much opposition and many efforts, His Excellency at last succeeded in establishing a perfect regularity in most of the streets; and even reduced to a degree of uniformity that confused mass of buildings known by the name of the "Rocks," which for many years was "more like the abode of savages than the residence of a civilized people." From the earliest times of the colony there had congregated, in this part of the town, the worst characters in the country;—the felon, whose ill-directed punishment had only rendered him more obdurate, cunning, and slothful;—the prostitute who, if such a thing be possible, had sunk yet lower; the *fence*, watching for a livelihood, by plundering the plunderer;—and many who, without great positive vices, were drawn, through ignorance or the want of energetic resolution, into the vortex of ruin. The following is a true picture of the actual state of the inhabitants of this section of the town:—

"We went into a house, which had been deprived of its licence on account of the practices and characters admitted by its landlord. We found it full to suffocation, in defiance of all law, of the lowest women, sailors, and ruffians, who supported themselves by waylaying and robbing, and often murderously wounding, any intoxicated sea-officer, newly-arrived emigrant, or up-country settler, who might chance to wander into their infernal precincts; and as part of the occupation of the women was to act as lures, of course this was no rare occurrence. The door was kept barred, and there was an outlet behind up the 'Rocks.' When our meal was over, I, who had no inclination to join in the frightful doses of raw spirits which those around me were swallowing, fell into conversation with a young woman who was sitting beside me. She was sallow and thin, and coughed almost incessantly. She told me, that she was given over by the doctors. When I asked her how she could think of coming into such a place, under such circumstances, she said she knew it to be wrong, but she could not sleep at night, and wanted company: 'when her sister came here,' (so they speak in the sisterhood of misfortune,) 'she came too.' My attention became wholly abstracted from the fierce riot around; I heard nothing but the broken voice that was answering my questions; I saw nothing but my own mental visions of the woes it told, till some one threw open the window-shutters and said it was sunrise. The return of daylight seemed the signal for a general dissolution of the assembly. I found that a few outcasts, like the invalid herself, had agreed to give a portion of their guilty earnings to support her while she lived.

"Several days passed without my having seen her: at last I found her in a little weather-boarded shed, in a small bed on the bare ground. The poor sufferer was too hoarse to speak, or rather could make no sound. She had caught the influenza, which was then about, and is the only fatal epidemic of the colony. Added to her previous complaint, it had made perfect havoc of her little remaining strength. Her eye was lustrous and wild, her face clammy all over with the heat, and her breathing one protracted struggle. If my Lord ——, who took her from her father and mother ten years ago, at the age of sixteen, could have looked from amidst his luxury into this shed, he must have hated his escutcheon. As I could not understand what she was trying to say, I went out and got a pencil and paper, for she had had a first-rate education. An old Italian, who had been a prisoner, but who was now boating on the river, told me she understood his language as well as he did himself, 'and talked it like a lady.' She must also have had a good knowledge of music; for she knew the names of almost all the pieces played by the military band. She wrote on the paper that she should like to have a doctor. Off I went to Dr. Bland, the first medical practitioner in the colony. I met him at his own door. Like himself, when I described the case, that good man turned and went with me directly. As soon as he saw Jane, he pronounced the case to be hopeless. I went out, took a large first-floor room for her in a nice, cool, shady place, and had her removed to it, another unfortunate volunteering to go with her as a nurse. Having completed those matters, I felt as if I had never been in such perfect enjoyment of all the highest faculties of my being. Forget-fulness of self is surely the gate into the Divine places of the universe; and thus this night, for at least a little while, I was allowed to walk with God! I visited her frequently before she died, and read to her nearly the whole of the New Testament, of which she became more and more fond. I did not see her die; but they say it was the change of a minute—a wandering of thought into bewilderment—bewilderment becoming unconsciousness—unconsciousness settling into death. She was interred in the 'sand-hills.'

"If the world were searched from end to end, no where could there be found such another volume of unutterable woe as is bound up in this little spot. Here lie Jews, Protestants, Presbyterians, and Catholics: all wanderers far from home and kindred. What elements are here! Misfortunes wonderful, indescribable delusions, and direct criminality! The betrayed, driven from society, has become the betrayer, from the necessities of hunger, nakedness, and cold. To reclaim these outcasts is woman's mission."

The runaway convicts were generally concealed in the "Rocks." They were in strict hiding during the day-time, and only showed out at night, creeping through the darkness, up and down those intricate streets, to the place of assignation for concocting some desperate deed, or thence to the place of perpetration. Almost every house of the lower orders in this district partook, at this period, more or less of the same lawless character. It was astonishing what numbers kept illegal spirit-shops; what numbers, again, of those were receivers of stolen property; and what numbers either harboured bush-rangers on their premises, or received them and purchased their plunder at night. "So that this whole field of society may be said to have been undermined, where the superficial and visible life, bad as it was, concealed another unspeakably worse." Many of the constables themselves were no better than the rest. As might be expected, the police courts presented, from week to week, melancholy proof of the demoralized condition of the people. On a Monday forenoon, scores of men, women, and children might be seen, who had been dragged off the streets on the preceding night for drunkenness, fighting, and similar offences, standing before the magistrate to receive their sentences. "Six hours to the stocks"—"Ten days to the cells"—"Twenty days to the treadmill"—or, "Fifty lashes," were generally the awards of the bench. Among the motley group of culprits thus convicted of drunkenness, riot, and theft, might be seen elderly and young women dressed in silks.

In the vicinity of Sydney, and on all the principal roads leading to the interior of the colony, the most serious depredations were frequently committed by the bush-rangers. They were generally well-mounted and armed, and travelled in bodies of from two or three to half-a-dozen. Their main object being plunder, they seldom committed murder, unless resisted in their attempts at the commission of robbery. The numerous receivers of their stolen property, in Sydney, and especially amongst the inhabitants of the "Rocks," provided them from time to time with supplies of ammunition, food, and clothing; and informed them when valuable stores were about to leave Sydney, and by what roads; also, what gentlemen were supposed to keep money in their houses, and how they might be most easily robbed.

Does the reader inquire what had been done by the established Church to meet the spiritual necessities of her expatriated children, now perishing for lack of knowledge in a strange land? In the exuberance of her zeal she had sent out four colonial chaplains, at the expense of the state. These were indeed excellent men; but their attention was chiefly confined to the military and the convicts; and, besides, what were these among so many? To attempt the establishment of a Christian mission amongst such a population as has just been described, was surely one of the loftiest exercises of Christian benevolence! It was like entering the charnel-house, and "preaching Christ, as the resurrection and the life," to the dead; or making an experiment with the "balm of Gilead," after every other remedy had failed. Never was the efficacy of the gospel more severely tested; never were its triumphs more signal or complete! Men —who had despised parental authority at home, had outlived all regard for truth and honesty, had passed through the discipline of the prison and the treadmill, and who had finished their convict-life in the chain-gang—trembled, like Felix, under the gospel, became exemplary members of the state and of the church, rose to distinction and affluence, and bequeathed their fortune to the humane and benevolent institutions of the country. As might be expected, the sterility of this wilderness could only be subdued "by the sweat of the brow;" yet some of the first labourers have lived to see it bring forth "thirty, sixty, and even an hundred fold."

"When I commenced my mission in Australia," said Mr. Leigh, "there were only four clergymen of the Church of England, and but few communicants; now, there are ninety-three thousand, one hundred and thirty-seven persons in connexion with that church. Then, there was no Presbyterian minister in the colony; now, the members of the Church of Scotland number eighteen thousand, one hundred and fifty-six. Then, there were only fourteen accredited Wesleyans; now, there are above ten thousand, and nearly as many children receiving instruction in their day and Sunday schools. May we not say, in the language of admiration and gratitude, 'What hath God wrought!'" Surely it is our duty carefully to mark the progressive steps by which these wonderful results have been reached, and to "glorify God" in the men whom Divine Providence selected and employed in the work.

Being alone, with limited means and no patronage, Mr. Leigh felt it necessary to form his establishment in Sydney upon very economical principles. The few Wesleyans, who had sent to England for a missionary, had rented a house in the "Rocks," in which they assembled from sabbath to sabbath for exhortation and prayer. The partition-walls of this building were removed, and the interior fitted up as a place of religious worship. Here Divine service was celebrated on the Lord's day, at six o'clock in the morning, and again at the same hour in the evening. The congregations soon presented a singular variety. Persons attended who belonged to nearly all the great divisions of the human race, and of almost every shade of complexion; with European emigrants, soldiers, and convicts.

As for the juvenile portion of the inhabitants, they were growing up in ignorance and profligacy. Being in daily intercourse with drunkards, thieves, and prostitutes, they became familiar with crime, and imposed no restraint upon their passions or appetites while they could elude the vigilance of justice. Having received no educational training, nor been subjected to any domestic control, they were, in thorough depravity, on a level with the savage. They were emphatically "a seed of evil-doers, children that were corrupters."

The missionary soon became known to the inhabitants of the "Rocks," and well acquainted with their true character. Finding the adults generally deaf to reason, and impervious to conviction, he resolved to make a determined effort to rescue, at least, some of their children from impending ruin. With this object in view, he re-organized the Sunday-school, which just existed, and placed it upon a new and improved basis. Having obtained the assistance of a few pious soldiers and reformed convicts, he soon collected a considerable number of scholars. The blessing of God was upon the institution in a remarkable degree. While the children were obtaining a knowledge of the first principles of revealed religion, Mr. Leigh was brought into a constant and profitable intercourse with their families.

One of the most valuable auxiliaries in this and in every other good work, was Sergeant James Scott. Mr. Scott was converted and joined the Wesleyan church in the West Indies. The detachment to which he belonged was ordered to New South Wales, where he distinguished himself by the able and conscientious discharge of his duty as a non-commissioned officer. Having seen much service, and being now considerably advanced in life, he was anxious to retire from the army. On an application being made for a discharge to the officer in command, the case was referred to the governor. On looking at the Regulations of the Army, the governor informed him, that he could not retire upon a pension without returning to England. His Excellency had a high opinion of Mr. Scott, and, being wishful to retain him in the colony, offered him a clerkship in the commissariat department. He had not been long in the office, before one of the magistrates, between whom and the governor there existed some misunderstanding, applied to him for permission to inspect some of his books. Mr. Scott would neither give up the books, nor allow him to examine them in the office. When His Excellency was informed of the circumstance, he was so impressed with the integrity of Scott, that he at once promoted him, and gave him an official appointment. Those gracious interpositions of Providence were regarded by Mr. Scott as being intended to draw him into closer communion with God and His church, and seemed only to quicken his zeal and expand his benevolence. He opened his own dwelling-house for religious worship on the week-nights; and there Mr. Leigh had the pleasure of preaching, to his family and neighbours, from week to week, "the unsearchable riches of Christ." Mr. Scott himself began to exhort, and subsequently became a local preacher.

In the mean time, the congregations at the chapel had greatly increased, and were become more regular and settled. Just at this juncture an estate, consisting of a piece of land and several houses, situated in Princes-street, were offered for sale. The whole was purchased by Mr. Scott. He enclosed a portion of the land for his own use, and laid it out as a garden. Part of his purchase he sold to the little Wesleyan society for £300, who so altered the premises as to provide a comfortable residence for the missionary, and a mission-house for the transaction of business.

The Lord having raised up two or three lay-helpers, Mr. Leigh purchased a horse, and began to make excursions into the country. A gentleman in Sydney expressed a wish that he would visit a friend of his at the settlement of Castlereagh. "I will give you," said he, "a letter of introduction to him: he will be glad to see you; for, like yourself, he is a Staffordshire man." Mr. Leigh mounted his horse, and reached Castlereagh late in the evening. On riding up to the fence enclosing the premises, he observed the gentleman standing in the door. "Sir," said Mr. Leigh, "I have a letter from your friend, Mr. M., of Sydney. He wishes you to allow me, as a Wesleyan missionary, to preach to your people." The haughty settler replied, peremptorily, "I shall do nothing of the kind." "Perhaps," said Mr. Leigh, "you will be so kind as to allow my horse to remain in your yard all night, and permit me to sleep in your barn? I shall pay you whatever you may demand for our accommodation." The gentleman repeated, in a tone and with a vehemence that settled the question, "I will do nothing of the kind." "Do you think," inquired Mr. Leigh, "that any one in the settlement will take me in for the night?" "I think John Lees will," said the farmer: "he lives about two miles off, in that direction,"—pointing with his finger.

Mr. Leigh turned his horse, and rode, as fast as the entangling nature of the underwood would admit, in search of the homestead of John Lees. On arriving at his wood-hut, he knocked with the end of his whip at the door, and called out, "Will you receive a Wesleyan missionary?" The door opened, and out came a little, stiff, ruddy lad, who laid hold of the bridle with one hand, and the stirrup with the other, and said, "Get off, sir! my father will be glad to see you." Mr. Leigh dismounted, and entered the hut. His astonishment may well be conceived, when he observed a number of persons sitting round a three-legged table in the most orderly manner. Directing the attention of the stranger to some books that lay on the table, old Lees said, "We were just going to have family worship. Perhaps you will have no objection to take that duty off my hands." "Not at all," said Mr. Leigh; and, taking up the Bible, opened it on Isaiah xxxv.: "The wilderness and the solitary place shall be glad for them; and the desert shall rejoice and blossom as the rose." Here he was obliged to pause, and allow the tears to flow, until he could again command the power of utterance. He then proceeded with the second verse: "It shall blossom abundantly, and rejoice even with joy and singing: the glory of Lebanon shall be given unto it, the excellency of Carmel and Sharon, they shall see the glory of the Lord, and the excellency of our God;" but he could proceed no further. Five minutes before, he had felt himself to be a stranger in a strange land, enclosed in the woods of Australia at a late hour, and without a home: now he was in Bethel; while the verses which he had read opened to his view the moral renovation of the world. He was quite overcome; and his manly spirit, that could unbutton his waistcoat to receive the spear of the man-eater, was unable to breast the tide of its own feelings. The gurgling of restrained emotion interrupted the harmonious flow of their evening song, while their prayers, offered in broken sentences, were the simple expression of humble and adoring gratitude. When they rose from their knees, the farmer crossed the floor, and, seizing Mr. Leigh's hand, squeezed it until he felt as if the blood were dropping from the points of his fingers. "We have been praying for three years," said Lees, "that God would send us a missionary : now that you are come, we are right glad to see you. We had not even heard of your arrival in the colony." After supper they retired to rest, exclaiming, "We have seen strange things to-day."

Next day Lees gave the missionary an account of the circumstances under which he became serious. He was formerly a soldier, belonging to the New South Wales corps. After the corps was disbanded, the government granted him a small allotment of land, with some other aid, to commence the "settler's life." He married, and soon had a rising family. After hard work, several acres of tall trees were felled by his own axe, and the timber burnt off. His live stock increased, and he began to thrive. But his former propensity for strong drink, checked for a while by industry, again developed itself, and grew on him, till he bore all the marks of a reckless, confirmed drunkard. It happened in his case, as in a thousand others, that one useful article after another went, till part of his land and all his live stock were gone, *except one pig*, now fat, and ready for the knife. The unhappy man was contemplating the sale of this *last pig*, to pay off a debt which he had contracted for spirituous liquors, when a circumstance occurred which changed the whole course of his future life, and, we believe, his final destiny. While in bed one night, and in a sound sleep, his mind wandered to the usual place of conviviality : he was in the act of grasping the spirit-bottle to fill another glass, when, to his terror, he observed a snake rising out of the bottle with expanded jaws, and striking its fangs in all directions. Its deadly eye, flashing fire, was fixed upon him, and occasioned a convulsive horror, which awoke him. He thanked God that it was but a dream ; yet the impression then made upon his mind could never be obliterated. He regarded the whole scene as indicating the inseparable connexion between intemperance, suffering, and death. The more he reflected upon it, the more deeply was he convinced of his guilt and danger. His distress of mind so increased, that he resolved to go over to Windsor, a distance of twelve miles, to consult the assistant colonial chaplain, the Rev. W. Cartwright. That gentleman spoke earnestly and kindly to him, recommending the reading of the scriptures, much prayer, and a believing appropriation of the promised mercy of God in Christ Jesus. "Having obtained help of God," he continued in the diligent use of these means up to the time of Mr. Leigh's arrival.

Having finished his affecting narrative, he called his people together, and desired the missionary to address them. Having done so, Mr. Leigh prepared for a long journey through the woods. He wished to obtain a guide, but could not succeed in hiring one. "If Providence," said Lees, "has brought you across the sea to this country to convert men, you may depend upon it, you will not be left to perish in the woods of New South Wales. You will have a difficult journey, I tell you; for the bush is very close, and the distance cannot be much less than forty miles. I will show you the direction in which the place lies to which you are going. Put your trust in God, and make the best of your way to it." The missionary soon found that there was no exaggeration in Lees's statement, either as to the length or difficulty of the journey. He carried a good axe, and was frequently obliged to alight, and cut a passage for himself and horse through the closely-compacted underwood.

While the animal was forcing his head and shoulders through a dense coppice that obstructed his progress, he suddenly started, and, falling back almost upon his haunches, stood trembling as if he would drop upon the ground. Mr. Leigh struck him; but he would not move. He then descended from the saddle, and took hold of the bridle to lead him. Turning his eye to the right, he observed the foliage moving, and heard a rustling noise; instantly a snake, nine or ten feet long, made his appearance, and deliberately crossed in front of Mr. Leigh and his horse, within a few feet of the spot where they stood. In passing, he threw off an effluvium, that induced sickness and vomiting. His bite would have proved fatal to either man or horse in a few hours; but he evinced no disposition to interrupt the travellers. Sometimes the cattle or sheep disturb them, or lie down upon them, when they become irritated, and bite severely, and generally fatally. Soon after the bite, the carcase of the animal swells to an enormous size, and bursts.

Mr. Leigh resumed his journey; and, shaping his course by the descending sun, and marking the trees along the whole line of his progress, for the guidance of others, reached the settlement to which he was going, at a late hour, and much fatigued. Next day he examined the neighbourhood, and returned to Sydney.

His next visit of observation was to Paramatta. This town was situated at the distance of fifteen miles by land, and eighteen by water, from Sydney. The town consisted principally of one street about a mile in length. The population, which was chiefly composed of small traders, publicans, artisans, and labourers, did not exceed, at that period, twelve hundred persons. The situation of the town was exceedingly delightful. It lay in a spacious hollow, covered with the richest verdure, and surrounded by hills of a moderate elevation. Nothing could exceed the beauty of the scenery which presented itself on all sides as the voyager proceeded from the capital to this provincial town by water;—the sea generally smooth as a lake, or but gently rippled by a slight breeze; innumerable little promontories, covered with wood to the water's edge, stretching into the sea, and forming a corresponding number of beautiful little bays and inlets in endless succession and variety. As the inmates of the jails of Great Britain were poured upon the shores of Australia with a rapidity and in such numbers as had not been anticipated, the colonial government made arrangements for removing a portion of the troops and prisoners to Paramatta.

This was the second place in the colony into which Christianity was introduced. Divine service was first celebrated here in 1791; just three years from the first landing of the English. Mr. Shepherd, of Kissing Point, was present on that occasion, and gave Mr. Leigh, in writing, the account we here subjoin:—
" The first assembly of people for the worship of God I ever witnessed in this country, was at Paramatta. We assembled in a carpenter's shop near the house of Governor Phillips. The military chaplain, the Rev. Richard Johnson, officiated. He subsequently divided his labours between the barracks and prisons of Sydney and Paramatta. I soon became acquainted with several persons who, I had reason to believe, enjoyed the favour of God. We agreed to meet privately for religious conversation and prayer. The place selected for our meetings was the banks of the little river which flows into the quarry. Here, under the open canopy of heaven, we read the word of God, prayed for Divine grace and the guidance of Divine Providence, and sang a hymn before we parted. Those meetings were continued for seven years. In 1798, the missionaries of the London Missionary Society, who had been driven from Otaheita, landed in New South Wales, and took up their residence at Paramatta. One of them, the Rev. James Cover, preached on the sabbath afternoon, from, 'Behold, I stand at the door, and knock : if any man hear my voice, and open the door, I will come in to him, and will sup with him, and he with me.' At the close of the service, two men from Kissing Point, who had been deeply impressed by the sermon, informed the preacher that many in their settlement were living like Heathens; that, if he would come over and preach to them, they would give him a hearty reception, and get a good congregation. Next sabbath, Mr. Cover and a few Christian friends walked to Kissing Point, and held a meeting for the exposition of scripture, and the worship of God. Much interest was excited. Perceiving a number of fine children running about, 'like the wild ass's colt,' Mr. Cover advised the people to build a school, and get them educated. They entered heartily into the undertaking ; and, as I was appointed to raise subscriptions, I witnessed the frankness with which all contributed. 'I like your object,' said Captain Patterson, 'and

will give you two pounds.' 'I as much approve of it,' said his lady, 'as my husband, and will give you other two pounds.' His Excellency the governor appointed Mr. Hughes schoolmaster. The house was soon finished, and the colonial chaplain opened it by celebrating Divine worship. We had no bishop; but the presence of the Lord consecrated the place. The missionaries preached on the Lord's day; and, after the arrival of the Rev. Samuel Marsden, he came out, and conducted a service on the week-night. Most of the young people in the district were educated at this school; and several of them are now honourably employed in preaching Christ in the islands of the sea."

The female convicts, amounting to several hundreds, were generally quartered at Paramatta. They were confined within the walls of an extensive building called "the factory," where they were kept under a strict, if not a severe, discipline, and engaged in various feminine occupations.

The governor, who had always manifested a deep commiseration for the mental and physical ignorance and degradation of the aborigines, and who had employed various humane and benevolent projects to overcome their repugnance to the society and habits of civilized men, and bring them to a free and beneficial intercourse with the colonists, resolved to establish an institution here for the education of their children. After it had been in operation for a short time, His Excellency issued a proclamation, inviting the natives to meet him in Paramatta on the 28th of January. On the day appointed, about two hundred natives, headed by their chiefs, entered the market-place at ten o'clock in the forenoon. Having seated themselves on the ground in a circle, the governor, accompanied by all the members of the native institution, entered, and walked round, inquiring after the several tribes, their chiefs, and residences. The chiefs were then assembled by themselves, when His Excellency confirmed them in their rank, and conferred upon them badges of distinction. Lady Macquarie, having arrived with the children of the institution, now entered the circle. Several of the children were examined; and it was delightful to witness the interest evinced by the chiefs on the occasion. One of them turned round to the governor, and, pointing to one of the children, exclaimed, with extraordinary emotion, "Governor, that's my pickaninny!" Several of the female natives were observed to shed tears. After an ample dinner of roast beef, and its usual accompaniments, they separated, wondering, as they retired to the bush, at this unprecedented display of European grandeur, intelligence, and hospitality. Such was the first dawning of civilization on this nation of savages.

There was only one church in the town, in which the Rev.

Samuel Marsden, senior chaplain, officiated. This distinguished man was a native of Leeds. He was in early life a member of the Wesleyan society in that town; and several branches of his family still remain in connexion with that body. By a peculiar train of providential events, he was led to connect himself with the Church of England, and had assigned to him the chaplaincy of New South Wales. Characterized by a sound judgment, fervent piety, and enlightened zeal, he acquired great influence with the public, and long commanded the confidence and respect of the civil and military authorities in the colony.

We are aware of the severe strictures of Dr. Lang upon what he regarded as being the secular character of Mr. Marsden, and the incongruity of his combining the office of · minister and magistrate. But though we admit, as a general principle, that to associate the ministerial office with the secular offices of state is, under ordinary circumstances, a degradation of the clerical character; yet it must not be overlooked that Marsden was put into the commission of the peace at a time when the government required the most vigorous co-operation of all the loyalty and intelligence in the country. We have no hesitation in saying, that the characteristic prejudices of this writer led him to form and to publish an erroneous estimate of Mr. Marsden's principles and conduct.

The religion of the senior chaplain was not an occasional emotion awakened by some new developement of the justice or mercy of God, but a vital and spiritual warmth, shedding its influence over his whole soul, and drawing out its sympathies and charities towards all men. Hence he put himself in communication with persons of all nations, when brought within his reach, whether civilized or savage. He presented to the eye a manly attitude, while his manner was peculiarly familiar and attractive. The very cannibal seemed to lose his ferocity in the presence of so much respectful and confiding attention. This apostolic man, finding that his own church was not prepared to respond to his numerous applications for missionaries, encouraged, by every means in his power, the agents of the London Missionary Society on the one hand, and opened the way to New Zealand to the Wesleyans on the other. To the former he sent, in 1815, the "historical books of the New Testament, Catechisms, and Hymn-Books, in the native tongue of several of the islands; and caused many copies of the Old Testament to be printed in New South Wales, in the language of Otaheita." In July, 1817, he had the happiness of hearing, that the inhabitants "of eight islands had renounced idolatry; that the immolation of human victims had ceased; that infanticide was suppressed; that Christianity had become general throughout these islands; that chapels had arisen instead of *morais;* that the sabbath-day was strictly observed; that about four thousand had learned to read, and many of them to write; and that part of the Gospels which had been translated into the native tongue, was then being printed." The work to which he gave so great an impulse has been in steady progress ever since; and there is reason to believe that very shortly all the islands of the Pacific will be gathered into the fold of Christ.

The senior chaplain received Mr. Leigh at Paramatta with great cordiality, and wished him "God speed!" The missionary commenced preaching in a private house, but some time afterwards obtained the government school-room, and formed a small class of invalided soldiers. One of his first converts was John W——: he was a native of Brighton, and a convict. The farmer to whom he was assigned, employed him as his stockman. This occupation rendered it necessary that he should travel and spend much of his time in the woods. He was consequently in frequent contact with the natives, who were constantly traversing the bush in search of their enemies or of food. A small party of them came suddenly upon him one day, and, as they appeared wild and mischievous, he prepared to defend himself. He was well armed, and expert in the use of the musket; but they succeeded in spearing him. He, however, escaped with his life; and the wound, the spear not having been a poisoned one, soon healed; but he was wholly unfitted for his duties, and obliged to leave his situation. He removed to Paramatta, in the hope of meeting with some light employment there. His almost miraculous escape from destruction, and partial recovery to health, made a strong impression upon his mind, and led him to hear the missionary. He was deeply convinced of sin; and, after many distressing conflicts, entered the fold of Christ. As he had a small family entirely dependent upon his own industry, he was advised to get a little horse and cart. It was suggested that by putting a board across the cart, he might carry a few passengers and light parcels to Sydney. With the assistance of a few friends, he commenced, and soon became known in the town. The integrity and punctuality with which he executed the orders confided to him, his obliging manner, and unwearied diligence, gained him the confidence and patronage of the public. His business increased so much, that he was obliged to get a larger horse and a covered conveyance. He became a great favourite; another horse was added to his establishment, and a stage-coach substituted for the covered cart. He would not be bound to carry any passenger who either swore or became quarrelsome on the coach. When any thing of the kind occurred, he would pull up and inform the party, no matter who he might be, that he was acting contrary to his regulations, and that he must desist, or quit the coach. He gained more than he lost by his firmness and consistency. The gentlemen settlers entered into a subscription, sent to London for four superb sets of harness, and set him up with a coach and four horses. John's was the first public conveyance in Australia. He had an affecting recollection of his early life, and of the distress and disgrace in which he had involved his parents. After the death of his father, he kept up a filial correspondence with his mother; and, as the Lord prospered him, he settled £20 *per annum* upon her for life. His children were also made partakers of the grace of God; and his son, the Rev. J. W., is now preaching that gospel, which, as a moral lever, raised his family to comfort and respectability.

After preaching at Paramatta on the Sunday, Mr. Leigh went to Seven Hills, a distance of only three miles, and preached at a settler's house on Monday evening. A journey of twenty miles brought him to Windsor on Tuesday night.

This town is built upon a hill, close by the river Hawkesbury, which now forms the boundary of the county, and which, after flowing one hundred and forty miles, pours its waters into Broken Bay. The buildings were weather-boarded without, and lathed and plastered within. There was a government-house, military and convict barracks, a court-house, and a jail. The population did not exceed three hundred; composed chiefly of farmers and their servants, with a few small traders, mechanics, and general labourers. They were mostly English, Welsh, Scotch, and Irish. They were rude and intemperate; while many of them had completely outlived all respect for even the "form of godliness." A sermon on the Lord's day was the only religious agency which the state supplied to check the turbulence and profligacy of the people. The lands in the neighbourhood of the town were exceedingly fertile; but this advantage was more than counterbalanced by their extreme liability to inundations from the Hawkesbury. This river had been known to rise to the height of ninety-three feet above its ordinary level. Inundations of seventy or eighty feet were of frequent occurrence; and the consequences to the settlers were often fatal to themselves and families, and always ruinous to their property. The town itself, which stands only a hundred feet above the level of the Hawkesbury, has hitherto escaped these tremendous overflowings; but as its elevation above the highest known floods is only a few feet, it cannot be considered free from danger. The clouds, attracted by the Blue Mountains, burst upon their lofty ridges, when the waters, rushing down with irresistible force, spread themselves in all directions for twenty miles, preventing all intercourse between the town and country for several days together. The chaos of confusion and distress that presents itself on these occasions, cannot easily be conceived by any one who has not been a witness of its horrors. A vast expanse of water, of which the eye cannot in many directions discover the limits, every where interspersed with growing timber, and crowded with poultry, pigs, horses, and cattle; stacks and houses, having frequently men, women, and children clinging to them for protection, and shrieking out in an agony of despair for assistance;—are the principal objects by which these scenes of death and devastation are characterized. These inundations have happened since the establishment of the colony, upon an average, about once in four years.

After a heavy fall of rain, Mr. Leigh was obliged, like other travellers, to apply the whip and spur and put his horse to his utmost speed, that he might keep in advance of the rising waters, and reach the town before they had taken possession of its entrances. The Rev. W. Cartwright says, in a note to Mr. Leigh, "The sun rose with uncommon splendour; and though an interval of gloom succeeded, yet, during the performance of Divine service, the heavens were beautifully serene. But no sooner were the doors and gates of the sanctuary shut, than the clouds collected, and the voice of God was heard in the thunder. The senior chaplain and myself stepped into a boat which was waiting for us in *one of the streets of Windsor*, and steered in a direct course over fields, and houses, and trees, and landed safe within twenty yards of our own door."

After some negotiation, the missionary succeeded in renting a *skillion*, or out-house, which he opened for Divine worship. The service was well attended; and all conducted themselves with quietness and propriety, excepting one individual. He was a notoriously profane convict, who had been subjected to the most humiliating degradation, and passed through the severest sufferings. Every expedient which the penal laws would sanction was tried, in order to bend this daring and incorrigible offender to the observance of his duty; but the sinning principle in him had become a "law," so that he seemed to be evil in an incarnate form, rather than human nature, corrupt indeed, but yet capable of the ameliorating influences of instruction and grace. This man entered the preaching-room, and, by various gesticulations and noises, interrupted the service, and created confusion. The other convicts expostulated with him, reminding him that the missionary was under the protection of the governor; and that, were he to complain to His Excellency, they would all be restricted and punished. He was so far influenced by these considerations that he retired, and left the congregation to worship God in peace.

On Monday morning this man had occasion to go into the bush. The hot marshy jungles of New South Wales are infested with musquitoes. A sort of stinging ant leaps upon the person, like a grasshopper, and inflicts an irritable wound: while the marsh leech, a virulent and active tormentor, insinuates himself near the skin, in spite of all means of defence, and often fills the shoes with blood. The thickets abound with venomous snakes. "There are, at least, thirty varieties: of which all but one are dangerous in the highest degree." Though few accidents happen to either the aborigines or colonists from their bite, they yet require to be guarded against. In travelling on foot, Mr. Leigh invariably wore leather leggings as a protection. But the unhappy man already mentioned entered the bush, without any regard to his own safety, and was bitten by a snake in the foot. In his previous desperate career of wickedness his other foot had suffered amputation, and he was obliged to use an artificial one. After receiving the bite of the snake, he seemed to have resolved on returning home immediately; but the intensity of the poison soon developed itself, and his wooden leg so retarded his progress that he was unable to clear the bush. When the muster-roll was called over, it was ascertained that he was missing; a party was sent out to search for him, and apprehend him. They discovered his body, lying in the outskirts of the wood: he was quite dead. Mr. Leigh and several officers went to the place, and held an inquest on the body. It was swollen to twice its natural size, and the features were so distorted, and his likeness so completely obliterated, that, but for his wooden leg and the convict-dress, he could not have been identified. The commander offered a reward to any of the convicts who would dig a grave, and bury the corpse. Mr. Leigh and a military officer accompanied this little band of volunteers. As the weather was sultry, the body could not be approached. They scooped out a grave at a distance, and then, with long poles, rolled the corpse into its last resting-place. After the grave was filled up, Mr. Leigh delivered an address, and returned from this melancholy spectacle. "He that being often reproved hardeneth his neck, shall suddenly be destroyed, and that without remedy."

Mr. Leigh employed the whole of Wednesday and Thursday in visiting the settlers, in Windsor and its vicinity, from house to house.

On Friday morning he rode to Portland Head. There was no religious teacher in that settlement. On Saturday forenoon he went round the neighbourhood, and published that he would preach that evening in the corn-shed of T. B., at seven o'clock. The attendance was so encouraging, that, at the close of the service, he told them that he would preach again, in the same place, on the following morning, which was Sunday, at the same hour. A few Presbyterians had erected a small house in the wood, in which they assembled on the Lord's day for reading the scriptures and prayer. They earnestly requested the missionary to give them a sermon in this lonely sanctuary at eleven o'clock. The news of his arrival had spread with surprising rapidity, considering how thinly this part of the country was populated at that time. When he reached the meeting-house, he found several persons who had come thirty miles to hear the word of God. They had crossed two rivers, and travelled along roads scarcely passable. "It was truly animating," he observed, "to see those distant settlers approaching this retired spot, in their one-horse carts, and arranging their vehicles round the house of prayer." The service brought the land of their fathers and early times to their recollection; and many a tear fell that day.

From thence Mr. Leigh travelled five miles to Wilberforce, and preached at a farmer's house, at two o'clock in the afternoon. When he came within sight of the house, the good woman began to prepare his dinner; and when he arrived, he found the *damper* and tea upon the table. Surrounded by his earnest congregation, he partook of her hospitality; then all of them united joyfully in the worship of God.

On concluding the service he mounted his horse, and rode five miles further to Windsor, where he preached again in the evening at seven o'clock. Having travelled twenty miles, and conducted four public services, he retired to rest, at a late hour, wearied, but happy.

On the following day he rode to Richmond, a distance of only three miles, where he preached in a private house. It was then a rising town, and contained a considerable population. "The scenery around the town," said Mr. Leigh, "is varied and beautiful in a high degree. I was astonished when I crossed the main street, and, for the first time, looked down on the celebrated Australian river, the Hawkesbury, as it flowed, smooth and deep, at the other side of the eminence on which the settlement stands."

"When I reached the high-lands," said Knight, "and looked across the alluvial tract, which, in the language of the residents, is called *the low-lands*, and saw the fine expanse of rich cultivated land, with the Hawkesbury on the other side, and the dark blue misty mountain-outline beyond, I felt at once that I was in the country of the husbandman. Whichever way I looked, I could see fields of the tall green Indian corn, with its lofty tassel-tops, bending and waving under the fresh breeze that was sweeping over it.   Here, again, a square of orchard, loaded with splendid peaches, broke the uniformity of the surface.   There a piece of ground newly ploughed, or with the teams at work upon it,—and here a square of wheat-stubble, on which a boy tended a herd of pigs as they picked up the scattered grain,—still further varied the prospect: and, every few fields apart, some more or less simple edifice marked the homestead.   In the neighbourhood I found all kinds of vegetables and fruit-trees flourishing.   I saw a boy driving to the pigs a cart laden with peaches, which he had gathered from under the trees in the orchard.   In another place I found a large tract planted with a species of tobacco.   The men who were working among the plants were convicts, lent by the government to the settler on whose land they were at work. Their huts, which were at the edge of the tobacco-ground, were merely a few upright sheets of bark, with interstices of many inches, and only part of a roof." There was nothing, however, in the moral or religious condition of the people in harmony with the beautiful arrangements of nature or the fruitfulness of the soil.   Yet, notwithstanding the ignorance and licentiousness which every where abounded, the commencement of the labours of the missionary was regarded as forming a new era in the history of their township.

On Tuesday morning he set out for Castlereagh.   His road lay parallel with the Blue Mountains.   He held several religious services at the huts of the settlers on his way, and concluded the day with a sermon at the house of John Lees in the evening.

On the day following he left Mr. Lees at an early hour, for Macquarie Grove, the residence of Mr. Hassal, where he arrived in time to hold an evening service.   This was a dangerous and fatiguing journey.   He had to find his way through one unbroken forest, without road or path of any kind, for thirty miles. He had to force his horse between the trees and through the entangled brushwood, frequently using his axe, and directing his course by the sun; whose rays were so condensed in the wood, that the brass mountings of the saddle burned the hand on being touched.

He rode to Liverpool on Thursday, a distance of twenty miles.   The town was then in its infancy; having been founded by Governor Macquarie, about the time that Mr. Leigh received his appointment to New South Wales.   On his arrival, he found the usual accompaniments of a town in that colony,—barracks for soldiers and convicts, several settlers, a few traders, artisans, publicans, and labourers.   There was no place of worship.   A small weather-boarded school-room had been built, a short time before, by subscription.   Here Mr. Leigh preached his first sermon, and promised to visit them again as soon as possible. The soil around the town is of a very indifferent quality; but as Liverpool occupies a central situation, between Sydney and some fertile districts in the counties of Camden, Argyle, and Westmoreland, it is likely to be a place of considerable importance. In consequence of its proximity to the Blue Mountains, which rise seven thousand feet above the level of the sea, and attract the clouds, it is occasionally visited with tremendous thunder-storms.

"I once spent a night," says a Presbyterian clergyman, "far away from any human habitation, among the mountains beyond Liverpool, during one of the most awful thunder-storms ever experienced in the country. The repeated flashes of lightning rendered darkness visible. The coruscations and lurid glare made it appear as if the atmosphere was on fire. The air was tainted with a sulphuric smell. The loud and rapid peals of thunder, reverberating from mountain to mountain, seemed like the artillery of heaven let loose to accomplish nature's dissolution. This war among the elements was succeeded by torrents of rain, to which I was completely exposed: for, soon after the thunder-storm had begun, I took the precaution of removing my bed from under the trees, for fear of attracting the lightning. Many a tree was that night struck, and instantly shivered to atoms: I slept none. My horses, which stood near me, refused to eat. When daylight appeared, extensive and fearful was the havoc effected by the combined power of the lightning and whirlwind. Trees which happened to attract the electric fluid were completely stripped of their bark, and split down the centre from top to bottom: while their branches, some of them a ton weight, were rent from the main trunk, and scattered in all directions, often to the distance of one hundred yards."

Mr. Leigh was overtaken by a similar tempest while travelling, one day in harvest, on the side of the Nepean River. The rain fell in torrents. Himself and horse seemed to be wrapped in sheets of lightning, and the wind blew a hurricane. He at last came within sight of a hut, and diverged from his path to seek shelter. As he approached it, he saw a tall ruffianly-looking man and a female emerging from the bush. The man called out to him, with strong Irish accent, "Get into the cabin, sir, and take your horse with you." These persons were the settler and his wife. The storm had driven them from the harvest-field; and, in returning home, the female had brought with her a sheaf of barley, which she carried on her head. On coming up to Mr. Leigh, the man took hold of the bridle, and pulled the horse into the hut. When they all got in, the cabin was full. While the man was getting up the fire, his wife was rubbing the barley out of the straw in her apron.　She then sifted it on the table, put it into a frying-pan, and dried it well over the fire.　Taking a little hand-mill, she ground it, made it into dough, and baked it in the frying-pan.　The fire being now at liberty, she put-on an old saucepan with some water, put some tea into the water, with three eggs, and boiled them all together.　Taking the eggs out, and pouring the water from the tea-leaves, she placed the whole upon the table, observing, "You see, sir, we live in a very homely way here: but you are very welcome."　In the mean time the horse was served with a small portion of the barley. Mr. Leigh took one egg without hesitation, the second with a degree of reluctance, and nothing but the importunity of his hostess could have induced him to take the third.　The man went out, and gathered a bundle of grass for the horse; and while it was eating, the missionary spoke kindly and earnestly to them about the necessity of preparing to meet God.　They would not let him go, until he had given them a promise that he would visit them again, when he should come into that part of the country.　He was frequently obliged to place himself wholly in the hands of this class of settlers, in lonely situations, where robbery and murder might have been perpetrated with impunity; and met with nothing but uniform kindness and hospitality.　"About nine months since," he observes, "we were much disturbed by the natives, who speared a number of stockmen and others in the interior of the country.　The governor sent out several detachments of soldiers, who drove them from the settlements, and shot many of them in the woods.　I have often been exposed to their rage; but hitherto the Lord has preserved me.　While travelling in the bush one day, far from any European dwelling, I observed a tribe of natives coming upon me. While I paused and hesitated, it seemed to be suggested to me, 'Go forward in the name of the Lord.'　I did so; and as I passed through them on horseback, they bowed in silence. I can say, that on many occasions the Lord has delivered me out of the hands of bloody and cruel men.　I have gone through troops of savages in safety.　Blessed be the name of the Lord! August, 1817.　LEIGH."　On the following day, Friday, Mr. Leigh returned to Sydney.

He had now traversed the most important and populous districts in the colony, and made arrangements for supplying them with regular services at convenient intervals.　The circuit which he thus formed, included the principal towns in the provinces, with several out-settlements, and extended one hundred and fifty miles.　He proposed spending fourteen days in the city, and ten days in going round this circuit of one hundred and fifty miles, alternately.　He could not multiply himself; but he could multiply his labours by riding up and down through the several townships, breaking, as he went along, the bread of life to perishing thousands. By adopting this plan, he was enabled to carry the gospel where it had never been preached before; and to awaken, throughout the country, that desire for religious instruction which has led to the establishment of churches of all denominations.

The example which he thus presented has been closely imitated; and now the established Churches of England and Scotland, and the various Nonconforming churches, have their preaching-stations and lay agents. Nor can the claims of the country be met, even now, but by working the same system with energy. "In a populous district on the Hume River," says Mackenzie, "the people are two hundred miles from the nearest church or clergyman. There is neither missionary, catechist, nor schoolmaster, in all the district. It cannot boast even of a burial-ground: and hence the dead are generally buried in sight of the huts. These graves may be seen here and there in the forest, fenced-in by a few rails. The very form of Christianity is lost among them. In one place the people kept, they knew not how long, the Friday instead of the sabbath day. One man stated, that, having been accustomed, when young, to shave on the Saturday night, he knew when the sabbath came by the length of his beard. Their children, eight or nine years of age, are still unbaptized. All that is wanted to change the habits of the people, are a few proper men to *itinerate* among them. They ought to have prudence, unconquerable zeal, and fervent piety. They should be good riders, able to sleep under a tree, and capable of enduring fatigue. They should learn to swim; and think it no hardship to dine, in the hut of a native, on a half-roasted opossum."

Mr. Leigh's plan required a large amount of lay agency; and, just as Providence supplied it, did he press it into his service. To settle the preliminaries of a scheme that contemplated nothing less than the diffusion of vital Christianity over so large a section of Australia, necessarily occupied much time, and involved great mental anxiety, physical effort, and pecuniary responsibility. So soon as the sphere of his labours had assumed a definite shape, he made the following communication to the committee:—

"I have just returned from my eighth tour through the different colonial settlements. My circuit extends one hundred and fifty miles, which distance I travel in ten days. I have fourteen preaching-stations, and have formed six classes,—three in Sydney, one at Paramatta, one at Windsor, and one at Castlereagh. We have established four Sunday-schools, which are in a satisfactory state. When I go into the country on the Sunday, I preach at ten o'clock in the morning; dine, ride seven miles, and preach at two; ride six miles, and preach at five; from thence I ride six miles more, and preach at seven in the evening. My constitution, I fear, will not long stand so much exertion in the heat of the day. But what can I do? The sight of the people flocking to the house of God, some with chairs, and others with stools on their shoulders, to sit upon, urges me to persevere; and, while I am praying and weeping for their salvation, I forget my fatigue. A poor man walked fourteen miles the other day to converse with me about his soul. We want chapels at several places, and more missionaries. The state of society here is awful. With regard to myself, I desire to live every moment to God, and to die in the missionary field."

To a correspondent in India he writes,—" Our place of worship in Sydney will hold about two hundred people, and it is generally crowded. I can only supply the country places once in three weeks. The clergy give me every encouragement. I have fifty-eight communicants. The intelligence from Otaheita is truly animating. The king has been converted, and has assumed a profession of Christianity. Numbers of the natives have renounced idolatry; and the Sunday-schools are in prosperity. What can we fear, if God be with us? Let us go on, 'looking to Jesus,' who has said, 'Lo, I am with you alway, even unto the end of the world.'"

CHAPTER III.

FORMATION OF HUMANE AND RELIGIOUS INSTITUTIONS—LABOURS—
PRIVATIONS—PERILS—SUFFERINGS.

How beautiful in their adaptations are the figures employed in scripture, to describe the enlargement of the " kingdom of God" in the world! Isaiah compares it to the sudden and unexpected fertility of a " wilderness." " The desert," says he, " shall rejoice and blossom as the rose:" formerly it was " a solitary place," now it is covered with the " glory of Lebanon," and the " excellency," the luxuriance and fragrance, " of Carmel and Sharon." Daniel changes the figure; but marks, with equal distinctness, its aggressive character. He represents it as a stone, " cut out without hands;" and predicts, that, after " smiting" the empires symbolized by the image of Nebuchadnezzar, it should " become a great mountain, and fill the whole earth." Our Lord, speaking of it as " a grain of mustard-seed," " which indeed is the least of all seeds," describes it as rising into magnitude, and extending its branches to a vast circumference.   Let any one examine the import of those figures, and look at the advantages which Christianity confers upon mankind, and he will at once perceive the justness of the analogy.   We shall bring an illustration or two from some of those institutions which owed their origin to the Wesleyan mission in Australia.

The established Church had expounded the truth for thirty years; but she had made no effectual application of it to the public mind.   She had, no doubt, converted men; but she had no skill in uniting her converts in works of practical usefulness. She had plenty of materials within her reach; but she had no experienced artisans to form them into an engine of sufficient power to raise the mental or moral condition of the people.

But no sooner did the missionary meet with a pious soldier and a free convict adapted to his purpose, than he sent them out to visit the poor, and pray with the dying.   They soon collected evidence to prove, that several outcasts had actually died for want of the common necessaries of life.   There did not then exist any public provision for the relief of the destitute. The two visitors agreed to give each sixpence a week to the most necessitous case they should meet with.   As they prosecuted their labours, the cases so multiplied, that they were led to lay the deplorable condition of the poor before the little Society.   Their simple detail of facts awakened general sympathy, and led to the formation of a small committee.   Mr. Leigh mentioned the subject to the Rev. W. Cartwright, who at once offered to become a member of the committee, and render them all the assistance in his power.   They met once a week, divided the town into districts, appointed a visitor to each district, and made a general appeal to the people for assistance.   Subscriptions flowed in on all hands; so that they were able to supply articles of food and clothing to great numbers of individuals. The visitors, who read and explained the scriptures in the dwellings of the poor, and prayed with them, brought such reports to the committee, from week to week, as greatly affected and encouraged them.   They felt it to be " more blessed to give than to receive;" and were so delightfully employed in " doing and receiving good," that, before their suspicions were excited, they were £40 in debt.   This discovery brought them to a stand-still.   At a meeting of the committee, it was agreed that they should go in a body to a wealthy merchant, of the name of JONES, show him their books, and ask him to advance goods on credit for the next three months.   Their institution, which was becoming generally known, was rising in public estimation.   On stating the object of their visit to Mr. Jones, and showing him how much they had been enabled to accomplish with a comparatively small sum of money, he said, "Gentlemen, I will comply with your request, and execute your order to-day." They returned to the vestry, and, while they were deliberating on the state of their affairs, the cart arrived with the goods. On opening the invoice, they discovered that the account, amounting to £20, was receipted. There was another enclosure, which, on examination, proved to be a check upon Mr. Jones's banker for £40, the amount of their debt. When the announcement was made to the meeting, they rose up simultaneously, and then falling down upon their knees, the clergyman and the missionary gave God thanks with joyful lips.

This unexpected and handsome donation of money and goods inspired them with fresh zeal; and, before they parted, they resolved to apply to His Excellency for a government building, that they might bring the sick poor into one place. The governor complied with their request, and, by the assistance of a few generous friends, they were enabled to prepare accommodations for fifty individuals. They called it "THE SYDNEY ASYLUM FOR THE POOR." It was soon filled with persons of various nations; among whom were several aggravated cases of indigence and disease. Here they had medical attendance, with every domestic comfort, and religious services twice on the Lord's day, and three times on the evenings of the week-days. This new establishment increased their expenditure beyond all their calculations; so that, at Christmas, when their books were balanced, they found themselves again in debt. Their subscriptions had increased, and they had multiplied evidences of the utility of their labours; but their income did not cover their expenses. They now determined to bring their circumstances under the observation of the governor. At an interview which they obtained, His Excellency said, "I am well acquainted with your proceedings. The management is admirable, and you are doing much good. But I question whether you will be able to maintain your establishment. I wish you to go on for the present; and I will issue an order for the immediate payment of the debt you have incurred."

A zealous churchman wrote home to Lord Bathurst, the colonial secretary, describing the growing importance of the "Sydney Asylum for the Poor," and expressing a wish that the management might be transferred, by authority, from the Methodists to the clergy and members of the Church of England. When Lord Bathurst's dispatch arrived, in reply, His Excellency the governor called the committee together; and, after expressing his great surprise that any private individual should have presumed to address the government without his knowledge, read the document. It declared that "the management of 'THE SYDNEY ASYLUM FOR THE POOR' must remain in the hands of those with whom the institution originated; that the accounts must be audited, as heretofore, once a year; and that the governor was authorized to pay, from the colonial revenue, its annual deficiency of income." His Excellency, laying the dispatch on the table, observed, "Gentlemen, I entirely concur in Lord Bathurst's sentiments." "Since then," said Mr. Leigh, "this has become a magnificent establishment. Thousands have been fed and cured, and instructed in their religious duties; and many have gone from it to glory. Who could have anticipated such results from the two sixpences of the soldier and the convict?"

The frequent intercourse of the sick visitors with the poor at their own dwellings laid open the domestic condition of the people generally, and brought to light a fact which accounted, in some degree, for the alarming prevalence of ignorance and vice. It had been remarked, that, throughout the districts into which the town was divided, very few copies of the scriptures had been met with. This discovery led Mr. Leigh, and the major of the military band, to visit every house in the city. This laborious canvass proved, that, on the average, there was but one Bible to every ten families; and these had been supplied, chiefly, by the Naval and Military Bible Society. Dining one day, soon after, with one of the magistrates, Mr. Leigh stated, that he had ascertained, from personal inspection, that there were but few copies of the word of God amongst the people; that he held in his hand a Report of the Colombo Bible Society, and that a similar institution was much wanted, and would prove a great blessing, in New South Wales. The magistrate, with whom he left the Report, put it into the hands of Lady Macquarie. On reading it, her ladyship was much struck with a beautiful letter, written by the lady of Governor Brownrig, of Ceylon. On finishing its perusal, she said, "Governor, cannot we have a Bible Society here?" "I am not aware," said His Excellency, "that there is any thing in the way of our attempting the formation of such an institution." He sent for several gentlemen, military officers, and the clergymen; and desired their opinion as to the propriety of establishing a Bible Society for the colony. The gentlemen assembled approved of the object; but gave it as their opinion, that it would be imprudent to call a meeting for such a purpose, in the present state of public feeling; besides, there were no Bibles in the colony, either for sale or gratuitous distribution. After respectfully delivering their opinions, they withdrew. The next

Gazette, however, contained an advertisement calling a meeting to be held, in the court-house, three weeks from that date, for the formation of a Bible Society,—the governor to preside on the occasion.

During the intervening three weeks, several heavy packages addressed to His Excellency were received from England. They were found to contain Bibles and Testaments, which had been shipped by the British and Foreign Bible Society. The following letter, which was addressed by Mr. Leigh to the secretaries of the above Society, soon after his arrival in New South Wales, accounts for this seasonable and abundant supply of the word of God :—

"GENTLEMEN,—I take this opportunity of thanking you for the parcel of Bibles and Testaments which I received, through the medium of Lady Grey, at Portsmouth. The Portuguese Testaments I distributed at Madeira, except three. A gentleman, brother to a priest, assured me, that many persons in Madeira would be glad to receive and read the New Testament. I had reason to believe that this statement was correct, from the numerous applications I had for the word of God. The English copies I have given away in this colony; and 'have had the satisfaction of seeing, in passing and re-passing through the bush, shepherds and stockmen reading the sacred book with deep attention. Were a Bible Society originated here, I am sure that Governor Macquarie and the clergy would cheerfully give their assistance. Should your Society favour me with another supply, you may depend upon a faithful distribution of your bounty."

When the day arrived for holding the meeting, nearly all the respectable people in Sydney attended. They were addressed with great effect by the governor, the judge-advocate, and the senior chaplain. No meeting had been previously held in the colony equal to this, in numbers, respectability, and unanimity; while its effects were general, permanent, and practical. Mr. Leigh and one of the governor's aide-de-camps were appointed collectors. Branch Societies were afterwards formed, in several provincial towns, which, after having supplied their respective neighbourhoods with the sacred volume, have remitted to the parent Society above £10,000.

The rapid movements and extraordinary labours of the missionary awakened the suspicion and jealousy of several of the subordinate agents, both of the church and state. While on a tour through the provinces, the governor invited the magistrates, military officers, and chaplain of Windsor to dine with him. During dinner, the resident magistrate inquired whether

His Excellency were aware that a missionary was going up and down in the several townships, collecting large bodies of people together, and persuading them to become Methodists. Unless some restraint were laid upon him, they would soon, in his opinion, become a colony of Methodists. He concluded by recommending, that *missionary Leigh be sent to work in the chain-gang, in the coal-mines of Newcastle.* "You had better," said an officer present, "let missionary Leigh remain where he is, and keep a vigilant eye upon him." The governor replied, "Gentlemen, I am neither unacquainted with the person to whom you refer, nor with his proceedings. As I did not, in the first instance, approve of his mission, I have, I assure you, kept a vigilant eye upon him. I have now sufficient evidence, that he is doing good every where." Then, turning to the magistrate who preferred the complaint, His Excellency added, "Sir, when Mr. Leigh comes here again, I desire that you will call the servants of the government into the store-room, that he may preach to them. Remember, I wish this to be regularly done in future."

Soon after this affair, of which Mr. Leigh knew nothing at the time, the colonial secretary sent for him, and told him, that the Rev. J. Y., of Liverpool, had complained to the governor, that when he came into that town he had the bell rung to summon the people to his service. In the opinion of the reverend gentleman, such a practice was putting Dissent too much upon a footing of equality with the Church of England. The governor had gone into the country, but had requested him, the secretary, to inquire into the facts of the case. "I am surprised," said Mr. Leigh, "to hear this statement. It is true that the bell has been rung; but at whose instance, I am not able to say. I will make inquiry, and let you know." He did so; and informed the secretary, that the magistrate, Thomas Moore, Esq., had caused the bell to be rung, that his own family, the military, settlers, and convicts might know the time for commencing the service. When the case was reported to the governor, he said, "Tell missionary Leigh to go on quietly and patiently, as he has done, and I will protect him."

The Rev. J. Y. then applied to the Rev. Samuel Marsden, and requested that, as senior chaplain, he would interfere and prevent the ringing of the bell in future. Mr. Marsden sent for the missionary immediately; and, in the presence of the complainant, stated the grounds of complaint. "My reverend friend," said Mr. Leigh, "has acted a very unkind part in this business. My own ministry created that desire for religious instruction to which he is indebted for his present appointment. On your recommendation he obtained orders in England; but, till then, he was, like myself, a poor missionary, in Tahiti. I dined at his house but lately, and he did not even allude to this grievance. He thanked me for the attention I had paid to the spiritual interests of his wife, who was converted by attending my ministry, while he was absent from the colony. He might have said, that 'he had somewhat against me.' But, sir, he has carried this frivolous and groundless complaint to the governor; and had I not been well known to His Excellency, I might at this moment have been under orders to quit the country. The bell has been rung at the request of your friend, Thomas Moore, Esq.; but my opinion was neither asked nor expressed on the subject." Addressing himself to the Rev. J. Y., the senior chaplain observed, "Sir, I am surprised at your conduct: you have done very wrong: you have grieved me much." Mr. Y. replied, "When I received ordination, the bishop charged me to have nothing to do with Dissenters." "That may be," said Mr. Marsden; "but he could not mean, that you were to persecute them! Mr. Leigh has nothing to do with your bishop, and I cannot allow him to be treated as if he were an enemy to our Church. You must not, in future, interfere with him. When he commenced his service in Liverpool, there was no desire amongst the people there to hear the word of God, nor was there a teacher of any kind within twenty miles of the town. You have 'entered into his labours.' "

Soon after these unpleasant occurrences, Mr. Leigh met the governor, as he was returning from the country. His Excellency ordered his carriage to stop, and inquired of him how he was getting on; why he had not applied for land, that, like the clergy and others, he might improve his condition by breeding cattle and sheep; and assured him, that he would feel a pleasure in assisting him in any way that he might suggest. After expressing his obligations to His Excellency for his condescension and generous offers, he respectfully intimated that he was sent there for purely spiritual objects; but that, though he could not accept of any gifts for his own use, he felt at liberty to avail himself of any offer that might be made of land, on which to build chapels or school-houses for the benefit of the Society. "Whenever you want a site," said the governor, "for either of those purposes, after making your selection, call at the surveyor-general's office, and, if it be unappropriated, present my compliments, and desire him to mark it off for your Society." The general muster of the colonists, which took place once in three years, was at hand. On those occasions, each colonist presented a schedule containing an inventory of his property in land, houses, cattle, and grain. On looking over the missionary's schedule, the governor inquired, "Mr.

Leigh, have you nothing to return but your old horse? You seem to have neither cattle nor grain yet. Why, you will always be poor at this rate." Above five hundred gentlemen were present, including magistrates, clergymen, military officers, and wealthy settlers, who had come to pay their respects to His Excellency; and in their presence Mr. Leigh briefly explained the regulations of the Missionary Committee, and the design of the mission.

A letter from a pious soldier, then doing duty at Newcastle, about forty-eight hours' sail from Sydney, first called his attention to that settlement. He stated in his letter, that he held a prayer-meeting every night, when not on duty; that these meetings were well attended; that several convicts were inquiring what they must do to be saved; and urged him to come over, and give them a sermon. Mr. Leigh availed himself of the first opportunity for visiting and strengthening the hands of this humble pioneer. On arriving in Newcastle, he found but few settlers; amounting, with their families, to not more than thirty individuals. There was a small detachment of troops, and four hundred and seventy convicts. These were supposed to be irreclaimable offenders. They had been imprisoned in Great Britain. Many of them had been tried for highway robbery, house-breaking, forgery, and murder. Several had been condemned to death, respited, and afterwards transported. On their arrival in New South Wales, they had resumed their old habits, committed various crimes, were tried in the criminal court of Sydney, and re-transported to this place, where they were worked in chains from sunrise to sunset. They were chiefly employed in burning lime, and procuring coal and timber, for the government. Here labour and discipline combined to bring the profligate to a premature grave. "The wages of sin is death." The governor, who had just been in the settlement, on a tour of inspection, returned home deeply affected by the scenes which he had witnessed there. As those scenes no longer exist, we gladly throw a veil over them. His Excellency was grieved to find, that those wretched prisoners had no spiritual instructor to press upon them, in the last moments of life, either "repentance towards God, or faith in the Lord Jesus Christ." "I must," he observed to the Rev. W. Cooper, "build a church for the establishment at Newcastle. I really cannot any longer endure the existing state of things there. I will give instructions for commencing the work immediately; and you must go over at once and lay the foundation-stone, with as much solemnity as possible." The reverend chaplain went over; and the religious services were peculiarly awakening, solemn, and impressive. The convicts themselves seemed to think, that a happier day was dawning upon them. The church was neat; and, being finished with a spire, formed a striking and interesting object in the landscape.

There was some ecclesiastical difficulty in the way of obtaining a resident clergyman; and Mr. Leigh was requested to supply the church as frequently as possible. The distance, however, was so great, and the regular work of his own mission so fully occupied his time, that he could give them only an occasional sermon. The convicts were conducted to church by the military; they behaved well, and several of them soon showed great improvement in their disposition and habits. The surrounding country is remarkable for its beauty and fertility: it is now the residence of a bishop of the established Church. Just in proportion as knowledge and conviction pervaded the minds of the people, did they evince a desire to have places of worship, and the ordinances of religion regularly administered, in their respective townships. Several individuals, who had either lived in obscurity, or been grossly immoral, seemed to be suddenly called forth, as if by a special interposition of providence and grace, to occupy new and comparatively high positions in society. The change in those persons was so unexpected and remarkable, that it was universally admitted they had become "new creatures in Christ Jesus." .

One of the most prominent of this class was Mr. John Lees, of Castlereagh. From his first connexion with the missionary, he had exerted himself to the utmost to promote the general interests of the mission, and especially to bring his own neighbours into fellowship with the church of Christ. The blessing of the Lord was upon him; and he determined to render his prosperity subservient to the glory of God and the benefit of man. With these objects in view, he resolved to build a place of worship at his own expense, and give the exclusive right of occupation to the missionary. When finished, the appropriation of this little building to the purposes of religious worship was signalized by much of the Divine presence. It was noticed by Mr. Leigh in the following terms: "On the 7th of October, 1817, I opened a chapel at Castlereagh, built and given to the mission by Mr. John Lees. While I stood and looked at the people coming in carts, from various quarters and remote distances, I was reminded of the scriptural figure of 'doves flying to their windows,' and of the American camp-meetings. The place was soon filled with attentive hearers. I addressed them from, 'The Lord hath done great things for us, whereof we are glad.' After the public service in the evening, the people were unwilling to leave the place; so we held a prayer-meeting: and truly Jacob's God was with us." At the close of these services,

Mr. Lees said, "I have not yet done my duty: having made some provision for the worship of God, I must now contribute something towards supplying the building with the ministry of God's word. I cannot, at present, give money; but I will give one acre of my best land: I will plough it, sow it, reap it, thresh and sell the produce, and you shall have whatever it brings, without any deduction." The missionary took one end of the Gunter's chain, and the farmer the other; and they measured off the devoted acre. After applying the produce of this acre, for several years, to the mission, he observed, "It was a fortunate thing for me that I gave you that acre of land; for, since that time, my neighbours have all observed that my wheat has grown thicker and stronger than theirs."

At this period Mr. Leigh was peculiarly buoyant, and confident of ultimate success. In writing to his mother, he said, "I am truly happy in my work; and, although I cannot boast of any great things done, as yet, in this mission, I believe that those who come after me will have the pleasure of making known, to the friends of missions, great and glorious results. God has promised it. The Saviour has sealed the promise with His blood. The Holy Spirit has given the earnest; and the end is sure: 'My word shall not return unto me void,' saith the Lord. Yes; when you and I shall be in heaven, thousands upon earth will praise God and the Lamb for this mission. We want more missionaries. The harvest truly is great: multitudes are perishing, and I am here alone. You are saving something for me: here is a call: give it now: after your death I shall be provided for. O God, thou who hast the hearts of all men in thy hands, send us faithful 'labourers into this vineyard!'"

To another correspondent he writes, "You say, 'Return to England.' Were I to attempt it, I should expect to be engulfed by the waves before I could get clear of the shores of New South Wales. Let no man despise the day of small things. God has promised that 'all the ends of the earth shall see His salvation.' In the prosecution of my mission, I am as happy with a crust of bread and a draught from the brook, as when I used to dine on your roast beef. But I am sometimes without even a crust. Travelling in the woods one day lately, I became quite confused, and lost all idea of the direction in which the settlement lay to which I was going. After riding until I was exhausted, I threw the reins upon the neck of my horse, and allowed him to shape his own course. He brought me, at last, to a stockman's hut. I alighted, and begged that he would give me something to eat. He said that his master had just left, and that he was not allowed to give any thing away in his absence. He had thrown some Indian corn to the fowls, who were picking it up in the back yard. I cheerfully joined the fowls, to which he offered no objection; and felt refreshed and strengthened by this providential repast. Here I obtained fresh instructions, set out again, and reached Liverpool at a late hour. The Indian corn which I had eaten with the fowls made me ill for a fortnight. What can one missionary do in such a country as this? Yet I have seen many penitential tears. I sometimes travel twenty miles, preach to twenty persons, retire to rest with twenty thousand blessings, and go off again in the morning, singing for joy. Pray that I may be filled with faith in Christ, and with a burning zeal for the spread of His gospel."

From the number of capital convictions in the criminal court of Sydney, and the frequency of executions, he was obliged to devote, in conjunction with the chaplains, a considerable portion of his time to visiting the cells of the condemned, and attending them in their last moments. It was no uncommon occurrence for six or eight to be executed in a morning. In December there lay, under sentence of death, four of the most notorious villains that had ever disgraced Australian society. They had committed almost every conceivable offence against the person and property of man. They were Irish Roman Catholics. They refused the assistance of the chaplain, and told the missionary that he was not of the true church, and that his scriptures were lies. They wished to confess; but there was no priest in the country. They sincerely hoped, they said, that, by praying to the Virgin Mary, the holy apostles, and the blessed saints, the Lord would be induced to show them mercy, and that their priests at home would get them out of purgatory. The earnest expostulations of the minister they treated with supreme contempt; "like the deaf adder that stoppeth her ear, which will not hearken to the voice of charmers, charming never so wisely." "I accompanied them," said Mr. Leigh, "to the place of execution, distant about half a mile. When they came within sight of the gibbet, one of them, who had appeared more reserved and thoughtful than the others, turned round and said, with much feeling, 'Sir, I depend entirely upon Jesus Christ for salvation. Will you pray for me?' I did pray for him; and never did I see a man more deeply affected, or more earnest in prayer. I had hope in his death. The other three were exasperated by his conduct, and evidently died under the delusion of a corrupt faith."

The scenes occurring at the trial of the convicts were sometimes peculiarly affecting. At the preceding assizes, a father and son were arraigned on a charge of sheep-stealing. They were convicted on the clearest evidence, and both were condemned to be executed at the same time. When the sentence was pronounced, the elder prisoner stood forward, and addressed the court in the most pathetic terms. He admitted his own guilt, but begged to remind the judge of the youth of his son, who had been drawn into the commission of the offence by his father's persuasion and example, and whose previous good conduct rendered him not unworthy the royal clemency. If his son were spared, he, the father, would die cheerfully. Here the lad interrupted his father: he observed that, if his father were executed, it would break his mother's heart, and the family would be left destitute; that he had heard his father say, that, if he got off this time, he would not steal another sheep; and that, as to himself, he was too young to be of any service to the family, and would not be missed. He did hope that the judge would spare the life of his father. The hearts of all present were melted. The judge ordered the prisoners to be removed, and the court to be adjourned; while he abruptly withdrew to his private room. In a few days the sentence of the prisoners was commuted to transportation for life to the penal settlement of Newcastle.

An insidious and malignant letter was inserted in the "Sydney Gazette," calculated, if not intended, to excite the most determined opposition to the mission. While the friends of the mission were considering how they might best vindicate their proceedings, the governor issued his General Orders. In those Orders His Excellency said, "I deem it necessary, in justice to my own feelings, and also to the highly respectable and benevolent persons and societies engaged in missionary labours, which have ever received my sanction and support, thus publicly to express my disapprobation of a letter recently published in the 'Sydney Gazette,' and calculated to prejudice the public against those excellent men and their useful institution." Any organized hostility to the mission, after this official announcement, would have had the appearance of a direct opposition to the colonial government. The authoritative interposition of the governor averted the consequences of a religious controversy.

At this time, Mr. Leigh had the happiness to receive seven missionaries and a lay gentleman, sent out by the London Missionary Society to strengthen and extend their missions in the islands of the Pacific. "While they remained in the colony," said Mr. Leigh, "all of them have acted in perfect unison with myself, and been zealously employed in preaching in various parts of my circuit. They conducted themselves, while under my observation, like men of God. The Rev. W. E., one of their number, took for his text, the first time he occupied my pulpit in Sydney, 'I hear that there be divisions among you; and I partly believe it.' I told him, at the close of the service, that the text was rather inappropriate, for we had not much to divide; and that, at present, there was no schism in our church. He was then a young man: he has since distinguished himself in several spheres of missionary labour, and in various departments of literature. With the spirit and bearing of the Rev. John Williams I was particularly struck. He was obviously a man of a devotional spirit, prudent in all his proceedings, patient in trials, and persevering in difficulties."

The name of the lay gentleman who accompanied them was Gyles. He had, for many years, been employed as the manager of a plantation in Jamaica, and was consequently well acquainted with the cultivation of the cane and the manufacture of sugar. The directors of the Society, being assured that their missions had produced a new organization of society in many of the South-Sea Islands, were anxious to promote habits of industry, and lead in the train of Christianity all the commercial advantages of civilization. Their missionaries had successfully cultivated coffee, cotton, and sugar-cane; and, although their experiments had been conducted upon a small scale, they were sufficient to prove that, under judicious management, those products might be manufactured as articles of trade and commerce. The superintendence of this secular department of the mission was confided to Mr. Gyles. He was engaged for four years; during which time it was supposed he would be able to raise the cane, instruct the natives in the art of manufacturing the sugar, and leave them capable of conducting the business themselves.

The Rev. Samuel Marsden greatly approved of this experiment. Writing to a friend, he observed: "I am happy to inform you that the labours of the missionaries have been greatly blessed at the Society Islands. The missionaries have begun to translate the scriptures, and have now a printing-press at work. The Society have also sent out materials for manufacturing sugar; and the missionaries will set the natives to grow cotton. I hope, in a little time, we shall have a cargo of sugar at Port Jackson from Otaheita, which will lessen the heavy expenses of the mission. The colony will furnish a market for all the sugar that can be made for a long time at the Society Islands. I cannot but entertain the pleasing hope that all the inhabitants of the numerous islands will, in due time, receive the blessings of the gospel. The British settlement in New Holland is a very wonderful circumstance in these eventful times. The islands in the Great Pacific Ocean could not have been settled, unless there had been a settlement formed previously in this country. The missionaries could never have maintained their ground, had they not been encouraged and

supported from Port Jackson.   How mysterious and wonderful
are the ways of God!   The exiles of the British nation are sent
before to prepare the way of the Lord."

While Mr. Gyles remained in Sydney, he was wholly occupied in completing his arrangements for entering, at once, upon
his duties on his arrival in Tahiti.   Learning that the son of a
highly respectable West-India merchant, of the name of Matthews, lived at no great distance from Sydney, and that he was
well acquainted with the manufacture and working of the
sugar-mill, he resolved to pay him a visit.   As Mr. Leigh had
met Mr. Matthews a few times in Sydney, Mr. Gyles begged
that he would accompany him to that gentleman's house.
Getting the best information they could respecting the settlement in which Mr. Matthews resided, they set out on their
journey.   Having crossed the Lane Cove, an arm of the sea,
they soon entered the woods.   Here the coppice was so dense,
that their progress was not only slow, but laborious.   Night
came on, with heavy rain.   They were both satisfied that they
had either been misinformed as to the distance, or had lost
their way.   Having taken no provision with them, they became
both hungry and faint.   As the night advanced, the dark clouds
that surrounded them began to break, and the moon gradually
rose upon them with Australian splendour.   About midnight
they came to two large trees that had been blown down, and
obstructed their progress.   Leaning against the trees, they consulted together as to what was best to be done.   In such
circumstances they knew that it would be dangerous to go to
sleep; for, if there were no snakes in that particular locality,
they must sleep at a great risk in their wet clothes.   It was
ultimately agreed, that one of them should rest upon one of
the trees, while the other stood by and watched.   Mr. Gyles,
having stretched himself upon the tree for a short time, got up
cold and stiff; and while Mr. Leigh was taking his place, he
heard a sound like the barking of a dog.   He exclaimed, "Lift
me up, Mr. Gyles."   "Why," said Gyles, "what is the matter?"   "I have heard," he replied, "the bark of a dog.   Let
us shout as loud as we can; for, if he be a domestic dog, he
will bark again; but if he be a native dog, he will not."   They
both shouted, and the barking of the dog was distinctly heard.
They continued to shout, and thus kept the dog in a state of
irritation, following, at the same time, in the direction of the
sound, until they arrived at a fence.   "Now let us get over,"
said Mr. Leigh; "for I am sure there is a homestead in the
neighbourhood."   Laying hold of the fence, and raising themselves up to get over, they observed five men on the other side,
with their muskets levelled.   The men called out, "If you

advance another step, we will fire into you." A momentary pause ensued; after which, Mr. Leigh, who was a stranger to fear, threw himself over the fence, and was instantly collared by the men. One of them turned his head round to the moon, and, looking into his face, cried out, " What! is this missionary Leigh?" Mr. Leigh, knowing his voice, replied, " It is, Mr. Matthews." "Thank God," said Mr. Matthews, "we have not shot you! Come in, come in, and I will give you our reasons for acting as we have done. We fully intended to have shot you."

What from the want of food, the severity of the night, and the fatigue of the journey, they were scarcely able to walk. Mr. Matthews conducted them to the house, which they had been seeking all day; and, while the servants were preparing refreshments, the travellers were wrapped up in warm blankets, and put to bed. By the morning they were much refreshed, and able to join the family at the breakfast-table. Mr. Matthews then stated, that yesterday, being St. Patrick's day, his people resolved to have a *spree* in the evening; that their hilarity was interrupted by the barking of the watch-dogs; that on sending out the servants to ascertain the cause of the incessant noise of the dogs, they returned to say, that they heard several voices in the woods, and that they were approaching our residence. "We instantly concluded," said Mr. Matthews, "that a body of bush-rangers was coming upon us; and, not knowing their number, five of us loaded our muskets, and came out, determined to shoot them in defence of ourselves and property. Your making a stand, though it was but for a moment, saved you."

After mutual congratulations and united thanksgivings to God, Mr. Gyles explained the object of their visit. Mr. Matthews entered, at once, into the views and plans of Mr. Gyles; and offered to have the necessary machinery made on his own premises, and under his own superintendence. He sent Messrs. Leigh and Gyles home to Sydney; completed, in due time, his contract; and shipped the sugar-mill and its appendages for Tahiti, where Mr. Gyles himself arrived in August, 1818. He carried with him a letter and several presents from Mr. Leigh to the king. The king was pleased with this mark of respect, and acknowledged it in the following terms :—

"DEAR FRIEND,—I wish you every blessing, and also your family, through Jesus Christ. I have received your letter, which was written on the 12th of May, and also the things you sent me. I feel much pleased that you wrote to me, and also for the things you sent. I have commenced a journey round Tahiti to animate the people to attend the word of God, and to send abroad the missionary to all lands: that is our work at present. In May there will be laws established here, at Tahiti, to make straight the crooked parts: when straight, it will be well. I am well, and hope you and your family are well.

"I wish you every blessing, through Jesus Christ.

"POMARE."

Mr. Gyles removed to Eimeo, where he erected his machinery. He enclosed a considerable tract of ground in the fertile and extensive valley at the head of the beautiful Bay of Opunoku, usually called Taloo Harbour. Sugar-cane was procured from the gardens of the adjacent districts, and sugar made in the presence of the natives, who were delighted on discovering that an article, so highly esteemed, could be made on their own shores, from the spontaneous produce of their own soil. This well-intentioned scheme, which was meant to be an auxiliary to Christianity, was rendered abortive by the misrepresentations of the captain of a South-Sea trader. He informed the king, that, should the attempt to manufacture sugar succeed, indivi-duals from distant countries, possessing influence and large resources, would establish themselves in the islands, and, with an armed force, which he would in vain attempt to oppose, cither destroy the inhabitants, or reduce them to slavery; that Mr. Gyles had come from the West Indies, where foreigners had entered in a friendly spirit, but afterwards brought troops, exterminated the inhabitants, and remained masters of the islands. The king was so far influenced by those statements, that it was thought best, in deference to his wishes, to advise Mr. Gyles to return to New South Wales, by the first conveyance: which he accordingly did.

The political state of the East Indies rendered it necessary to remove all the troops, that could be spared, from the colony to that country. The men draughted for that service included nearly all the pious soldiers who were members of the mission-ary church. These men were ornaments to Christian society, and had occupied, for some time, various departments of use-fulness. They were commanded by Colonel Moore, who, to mark his approbation of their conduct, gave them the privilege of passing the sentinels after regimental hours. By this relaxa-tion of barrack-discipline, they were enabled, when not on duty, to attend all the week-night services. When they embarked, the colonel ordered the officers to afford them every facility for holding their religious meetings while at sea. He had always encouraged Mr. Leigh in the prosecution of his mission, and evinced a lively interest in its success. The destination of those troops was Madras, where they arrived in safety. They soon ascertained that the Rev. James Lynch had arrived, and formed a church of twelve members, who were all persons of colour. The military class-leader, Sergeant Ross, said in a letter to Mr. Leigh, " I was struck with the fervour of their devotion, and the solemnity of their worship. The few times we met with them were indeed 'times of refreshing from the presence of the Lord.' We had also several profitable interviews with Messrs. Loveless and Knill, of the London Missionary Society; and, although we are now removed one hundred miles from them, we keep up a profitable correspondence. So soon as we got settled, I called our little band together to my house, when we agreed to meet in class on Tuesday evenings, as we had been accustomed to do at Sydney. We petitioned the colonel for liberty and protection in the exercise of religious worship. He replied, ' You shall have both.' We have bought and fitted up a house, at our own expense, and opened it for exhortation and prayer. Mr. Lynch, being on a tour through the country, visited us, and met our class. The Lord was with us of a truth ! This being the first Wesleyan preaching-house ever built upon the territories of the East-India Company, he desired me to give him a drawing of it, and an account in writing of our commencement. We are blessed with a pious chaplain ; but, in my opinion, the missionary system alone can meet the claims of India. There is evidently a great work of preparation going on amongst the people around us."

While those pious soldiers gave a fresh impulse to the infant church at Madras, and exhibited, by their example, a steady light, in the midst of surrounding darkness, their removal from Sydney was painfully felt by that Society at their devotional meetings, and in working their Sunday-schools and Tract Society. But the promise, " As thy days, so shall thy strength be," is as applicable to the church collectively, as to her individual members. The diminution of their numbers brought the Sydney Society into closer compact, and led to increased exertion and more earnest prayer. The Lord, who maintains His sovereignty, and yet responds to the intercessions of His people, vouchsafed a special blessing to His own ordinances. As the " son of man " had the pleasure of seeing that, by prophesying, the Spirit of the Lord was brought down upon the " bones," which were " very many, and very dry ;" so Mr. Leigh had the gratification of seeing the word of the Lord " running " amongst the people, and being " glorified," in the conversion of a number sufficient to fill up the vacancies occasioned by the change that had taken place in the colonial forces.

But, while he seemed to others to "rejoice as a strong man to run a race," he had become the subject of deep emotion, and of considerable physical suffering. He had been two years in the colony without having received a single letter from England. These had been years of wasting labours and constant anxiety. "It is not natural for me to complain," he would say, "but my public duties and mental perplexities are sometimes more than I can well sustain. I go to the post-office, on the arrival of the mail, full of expectation, and return disappointed and grieved. I am generally relieved by prayer and tears." During the war, the correspondence between Great Britain and her distant colonies was very irregular. The missionaries of another Society were seven years without hearing from their official directors. But the cases must be extraordinary that can warrant even the appearance of remissness in public bodies, whether they be ecclesiastical or commercial, in maintaining a free and frequent correspondence with their foreign agents. The semblance of indifference on their part to the personal safety and comfort of their servants abroad, will be found generally to strengthen the temptation to unfaithfulness, while it weakens the sense of responsibility.

The long rides which Mr. Leigh was obliged to take in the heat of the day; his having frequently to lie down at night upon the ground, with his great-coat for his only covering, and his saddle-bags for his pillow; made a visible impression upon his constitution, and reduced him to a state of extreme weakness. The Rev. Samuel Marsden, having heard of the state of his health, sent for him; and, after expressing the most fraternal solicitude, urged him to take a voyage by sea. "You are aware," he observed, "that in 1814 I established some lay settlers in New Zealand. Since then, I have always had several of the natives living with me: I think this will tend greatly to enlarge their views, to increase their thirst for knowledge, and make them acquainted with the comforts of civil life. They will also learn the use of our sabbaths, the meaning of public worship as well as family; and, on their return to their own land, will impart to their friends what they have seen and heard. The New-Zealanders are considered the most warlike savages known, and are all cannibals; yet they have been kind to my lay settlers, and are even partial to them. They have begun to cultivate their land, and to raise various productions. The climate is fine, the land fertile, the country in all parts well watered, and every thing favourable, in a local and natural point of view, for its becoming a great country. It has fine rivers, abounds with valuable timber, while its streams and shores are full of excellent fish. I am sending over a ship with stores for my lay settlers. I will give you a free passage, and make such arrangements as shall secure every comfort at sea, and your personal safety while you remain in New Zealand. When you have considered what I now propose, let me see you again."

Up to this period less was known in Europe of New Zealand, than of any other island in the Pacific Ocean. The occasional intercourse which had taken place between the natives of these islands and civilized men, had tended only to generate mutual hostility. Having observed that Europeans thought it no crime to murder and plunder those islanders upon the most trivial occasions, and often from mere wantonness, the sympathies of the Rev. Samuel Marsden were moved towards them. He cultivated an acquaintance with such chiefs as occasionally visited Port Jackson, studied the national character, acquired the confidence of those chiefs, and resolved to reclaim the population of the country to Christ and civilization. The announcement of his plan for the accomplishment of these objects was treated with ridicule; and the destruction of the first men that should land upon the shores of the country was predicted. He was reminded that Tasman, who first visited them, had a boat's crew murdered on landing; that Mariner had twenty-eight of his men murdered on the beach; that ten of Captain Furneaux's crew were surrounded, murdered, and eaten; and that from eighty to one hundred persons, on board the ship "Boyd," met a similar fate. He was assured that the appearance of his sails on the seas of New Zealand would lead to a confederacy amongst the tribes along the coast to seize his ship, and cut off both crew and settlers.

Mr. Marsden's intercourse with the chiefs led him to the conclusion, that the above massacres were to be regarded only as acts of retaliation for numerous unprovoked deeds of cruelty and injustice practised upon the natives by white men. Duaterra, a chief of some authority, had resided in Mr. Marsden's family for nearly three years, and had formed a strong and sincere attachment to that gentleman. He assured the chaplain that, if teachers were sent to his country, he would guarantee their safety, and treat them with hospitality. Mr. Marsden, having studied his character well, knew how far he could depend upon his promises of protection in his native land. The ship "Active" was purchased; and, being well manned and armed, was sent over to New Zealand, to try the disposition of the natives, and test the integrity of Duaterra. After visiting the territories of Duaterra, and satisfying themselves as to the practicability of Mr. Marsden's scheme, they returned to New South Wales, bringing Duaterra and two other chiefs on board.

Their report was so favourable, that all necessary preparations were now made for returning to New Zealand to establish the settlement.   Mr. Marsden resolved to go himself, and share in the glory or hazard of the enterprise. He selected Messrs. Hall, King, and Kendall, and their families, as the persons to be located amongst the savages. The one was a schoolmaster, the other a carpenter, and the third a shoemaker. They were to follow their respective trades, teach them to the natives, induce them to adopt European habits, and prepare them to receive Christian instruction. ¬ The governor invested the schoolmaster with the office of resident magistrate, and issued a proclamation, informing all captains of ships visiting New Zealand, that they would be held responsible to British law for any acts of cruelty or injustice which they might perpetrate upon the persons or property of the natives. After they were ready to sail, the governor hesitated as to the propriety of giving them permission to leave the colony on so dangerous an undertaking. It was with extreme reluctance that he parted with the senior chaplain ; and no persuasion could induce him to extend their leave of absence beyond four months.

The "Active" sailed from Port Jackson November 19th, 1814. Thirty-five persons were on board, with numerous animals, and various stores. They had been at sea but a few days, when the chiefs on board became gloomy, sullen, and reserved. Duaterra, in replying to some questions proposed to him by Mr. Marsden, said, "From the very depths of my soul do I regret having given you the slightest encouragement to leave New South Wales. A gentleman in Sydney informed me, that the consequence of granting protection to your settlers will be that others will be introduced, who will take our lands and kill our people." As might be expected, such a statement created a great sensation on board the "Active." Mr. Marsden assured Duaterra that their motives were disinterested, and that, unless they could depend with entire confidence upon himself and the other two chiefs sailing with them for protection, he would order the ship to return immediately to the colony. After consulting the other chiefs, and taking a little time for reflection, Duaterra informed Mr. Marsden, that it was very probable that the other chiefs, 'Hongi and Korrakorra, would be prompted to acts of violence on getting to their own country; but that, if he would establish his settlement at the Bay of Islands, he and his tribe would be able to afford ample protection. On this assurance being given, the captain was ordered to sail for the Bay of Islands. They entered the Bay on the 22nd of December. After several friendly interviews with the natives, they landed.

Divine service was celebrated, for the first time in these lands, on the following Sunday, being Christmas-day. Duaterra had made a reading-desk of an old canoe, and prepared seats

CARVED HOUSE, NEW ZEALAND.

for the Europeans with some planks, which had been brought to the ground. The whole population of the neighbourhood assembled on the occasion. Korrakorra drew up his warriors, and marched them, rank and file, into the enclosure; while all that could be spared from the ship were landed, to join in the service. The chiefs were dressed in regimentals, which had been presented to them by Governor Macquarie, with their swords by their sides; while the savages stuck their spears in the ground. Mr. Marsden conducted the service in a very impressive manner. Duaterra acted as interpreter. No doubt the prayers of that day moved heaven, and occasioned "joy in the presence of the angels of God." At the close of the service about three hundred natives surrounded Mr. Marsden, and commenced their war-dance, shouting and yelling in demonstration of their joy.

It was now deemed safe and necessary to proceed at once to procure timber, and erect suitable buildings for the families of the settlers. On witnessing these proceedings, Duaterra became much excited, and exclaimed, with an air of triumph, "New Zealand will be a great country in two years. I will export grain to Port Jackson, in exchange for spades, axes, hoes, tea, and sugar." The grand object of his life, for the last ten years,—an object which was the constant subject of his conversation, namely, the civilization of his countrymen,— was, in his opinion, about to be speedily realized. Under this impression, he made arrangements for an extensive cultivation, and formed a plan for building a new town with regular streets, after the European mode, in a beautiful situation, which commanded a view of the mouth of the harbour and adjacent country. Mr. Marsden accompanied him to the place, and examined the ground fixed upon for the town. He pointed out the situation where the church was to stand, and said that the streets were to be laid out before Mr. Marsden left the country. At the very time when these plans were to have been executed, Duaterra was stretched upon his death-bed. "I could not but view him," said the chaplain, "as he lay languishing beneath his affliction, with wonder and astonishment, and could scarcely bring myself to believe that the Divine Goodness would remove from the earth a man whose life appeared of such infinite importance to his country, which was just emerging from gross darkness and barbarism. I fondly hoped that he had only commenced his career. He was a savage of clear comprehension, quick perception, of a sound judgment, and void of fear. At the same time, he was mild, affable, and pleasing in his manners. He was in the prime and vigour of manhood, being about thirty years of age, and extremely active."

Mr. Marsden's term of absence having expired, the "Active" was unmoored, and sailed for the colony. Duaterra, the statesman and warrior, on whom, more than upon any other individual, the emancipation of his country from savageism seemed to depend, died four days after Mr. Marsden left New Zealand. The senior chaplain felt a deep interest in the fate of the lay settlers whom he had left behind, and availed himself of every opportunity that offered for supplying their wants, and encouraging them in their labours. He was of opinion that a short residence in New Zealand would improve the health of Mr. Leigh, and, at the same time, greatly serve the interests of the infant settlement.

While Mr. Leigh was deliberating about the voyage, the Rev. Walter Lawry arrived from England. He had had an agreeable passage of four months and eight days. He sailed in a convict-ship, and preached regularly to the prisoners, the military, and the mariners on the gun-deck. Many heard the word with gladness, and several "received it in the love thereof." He had the most satisfactory evidence of the repentance and conversion of these men. One of the passengers and the captain's clerk trained a choir of singers, which added much to the interest of their public services. Those two gentlemen were exceedingly zealous and useful in promoting the instruction and reformation of the convicts.

On the day after Mr. Lawry's arrival, May 2nd, 1818, Mr. Leigh returned from the country. He had been separated from his ministerial brethren for three years; and when he saw Mr. Lawry, he kissed him, and exclaimed, "Bless the Lord, O my soul! and forget not all His benefits." Mr. Leigh and J. Eager, Esq., introduced Mr. Lawry to the governor, who received him with marked cordiality, and wished him much success in the work in which he was engaged. On retiring, Mr. Leigh observed, "Who that duly considers the benefits of civil government, can refrain from saying, 'God save the king!'" Mr. Lawry spent the Sunday in Sydney, and preached twice with much acceptance and power. He subsequently waited on the resident chaplain, "from whom," said he, "I received that hearty welcome which might be expected from a holy minister of Christ. I lost no time in paying my respects to the reverend the senior chaplain, who lives at Paramatta, and was not surprised that his 'praise should be in all the churches.' The fields here are white to the harvest; and what may we not expect from a people thus prepared of the Lord? Mr. Leigh is every thing I could wish in a colleague. In commencing this mission he has not only been alone, like a sparrow upon the house-top, but has endured calumny and opposition from those from whom he expected assistance. I need not dwell upon his wanderings in these forests without food, having no shelter by day, and frequently no bed by night. His patient soul endured all in quietness; and the effects of his labours will be seen after many days. By his exemplary conduct he has established himself in the good opinion of almost every one here, from His Excellency the governor to the fisherman at the stall. We are agreed to live upon two meals a day, if we may have another missionary and a printing-press."

As soon as Mr. Lawry had been introduced to the principal friends, and was made acquainted with the working of the circuit, Mr. Leigh felt himself at liberty to accept the generous offer of Mr. Marsden, and embarked for New Zealand. The distance was only fourteen hundred miles; but the weather was tempestuous, and the ship a bad sailer, so that they were twice the usual time upon the ocean. The lay settlers received him, as he expected they would, like Christian men.

CHAPTER IV.

VISITS NEW ZEALAND—STATE OF THE COUNTRY—RETURNS TO ENGLAND —ARRANGES FOR ESTABLISHING THE NEW-ZEALAND MISSION.

THE Rev. Samuel Marsden had requested Mr. Leigh to inquire into the proceedings of his lay settlers at the Bay of Islands, and, if possible, to extend their usefulness. The preliminary process by which they were attempting to bring out the results of missionary labours, was quite new to Mr. Leigh. An experiment was in progress which he feared was founded upon the most fallacious principles, and calculated to issue in nothing but disappointment. "The discoveries of ancient and modern navigation," says Gibbon, "and the domestic history or traditions of the most enlightened nations, represent the *human savage* naked, both in body and mind, and destitute of laws, of arts, of ideas, and almost of language. From this abject condition, *perhaps the primitive and universal state of man*, he has *gradually risen* to command the animals, to fertilize the earth, to traverse the ocean, and to measure the heavens." This may be regarded as a fair representation, not only of the sentiments of the author, but also of Hume, Lord Kames, Helvetius, and many of the philosophers of the modern schools of Germany and France. But do the records of history afford a single instance in which a nation has *gradually elevated itself, by its own inherent energies*, from a state of extreme barbarism to a state of great intellectual refinement? The uniform testimony of history proves, that if man had been a savage at first, he would have remained a savage for ever. We may unhesitatingly affirm, that no nation has risen from savageism to civilization until some civilizing impulse has been communicated, and a leverage applied from without, of sufficient power to raise it from its former level. But, if recourse is to be had to the civilizing process, in what order should it be applied? Is it to be the pioneer of Christianity, or to supplement it?

At the period to which we refer, the uniform answer of the reviewers, of the magazine and newspaper writers, and of a considerable portion of the clergy, of all denominations, was, "If the Heathens are to be won back to the rank and standing of civilized men, you must make them good mechanics, and then make them good Christians, if you can." "Men must be rational and civilized," observed Dr. Lardner, "*before they can* be Christians: knowledge has a happy tendency to enlarge the mind, and to encourage generous sentiments." "Barbarous nations," said the bishop of Carlisle, "are unable to bear the truth, and vicious and immoral ones are incapable of bringing forth the fruits thereof. *Christianity cannot* immediately transform the minds of men, and totally change the general temper and complexion of *any people*." These views being entertained and avowed by some of the highest authorities in the church and state, Mr. Marsden himself was induced, when in England, to embrace them, and selected New Zealand as the field in which their validity was to be tested.

Mr. Leigh believed the calling of Missionary Societies to be a spiritual calling, and that the office of the missionary should be restricted to spiritual objects. No deviation from this general principle could, in his opinion, be justified but by extraordinary circumstances. Nor can we see the utility of setting up, amongst savages, a system that renders it necessary to combine instructions in the art of making a nail, building a hut, or manufacturing a plough, with incidental observations on the perfections of God, the principles of His moral government, or the plan of man's redemption. The primary object of missionary institutions is, to reveal God's method of salvation to the world. He "commandeth all men every where to repent;" this repentance is to issue in faith in Christ; this faith is to reform the habits of man; this reformation is to spread until it has removed all the obnoxious maxims of civil government, and bound the members of the commonwealth together in fraternal love. In the economy of grace, as in that of nature, design and arrangement are apparent. As the various parts of creation passed from under the plastic hand of the Creator, they rose to that position in the fields of space which His wisdom had assigned to them. Thus, "the greater light was to rule the day, and

the lesser light to rule the night;" the summer was to succeed
the spring, and the autumn to precede the winter.   To interfere
with this established order, would be to derange the whole system of nature and providence.   So, in the economy of grace,
God has a method emphatically His own; yet, in dealing with
men at home and Heathens abroad, not only have the schools
of philosophy, but the church herself, frequently interfered with
this order.   God begins with the understanding and heart;
they, with the hands and feet.   He would purify the fountain;
they would filter the streams.   He would convert the soul;
they would civilize the life.   He demands the first attention and
homage of man; they would qualify man for his religious duties,
by teaching him the multiplication-table, and the art of holding
the plough.   To attempt to bring men to religion by the appli-
ances of civilization, is to act the part of an unskilful physician,
who undertakes to cure a chronic affection of the heart by the
first application of an external remedy; or that of the mechanic,
who thinks he can make his time-piece go right by adjusting
the pointers.   Mistaken men! the mischief lies deeper.   Sin is
a spiritual malady, and can be reached only by a spiritual
agency.

The lay settlers in New Zealand held meetings for conversation and prayer; but they were not allowed to preach.   They
followed their secular callings, and had but little opportunity, as
they had little inducement, to attempt the religious instruction
of the natives.   Missionary Leigh found that Christianity had
not extended its benefits beyond the circumference of a few
miles.   The temporal expectations of the carpenter were exceeded; whilst those of the other two brethren were disappointed and blighted.   They owed the preservation of their
lives, from day to day, under God, to the patronage of Mr.
Marsden.   He was regarded as being their chief; and the kindness and liberality which he had shown to the native chieftains
and their sons, placed them, as they admitted, under great obligations to him.   Those missionary mechanics were much depressed; and little misunderstandings between their families had
led to a suspension of their religious meetings.   A village only
a few miles distant had not been visited for three years; whilst
their intercourse with the natives was more secular than spiritual
in its nature.

Missionary Leigh came at a crisis, and stepped in as a mediator.   Their differences were soon healed by mutual explanation
and prayer.   He established daily meetings for the exposition
of scripture and united intercession.   Although attenuated by
affliction, he yet felt that his present position involved a special
call for exertion.   He laboured to convince them, that they

were expected to abstract as large a proportion of their time from worldly pursuits as might be compatible with a due regard to the temporal welfare of their families, and to devote it sedulously to the instruction of the natives. He was anxious to become acquainted with the condition and habits of the people around him; but, having no knowledge of their language, except what he had acquired from occasional interviews with such of them as had visited Sydney and Paramatta, he was obliged to converse with them through a friend.

On the second Sunday after his arrival, he went out in the afternoon to a village not far from the settlement. As he entered it, he was shocked to see twelve heads of men, neatly arranged on the right-hand side of the path. They were beautifully tattooed, and presented a calm and placid aspect. This exhibition brought some of the most savage and atrocious developements of human nature under his own immediate observation. He felt, at the moment, that he had entered the "region and shadow of death," and was treading a soil but recently moistened with the blood of man. What an instructive study is here laid open to those philosophers who plead for the dignity of human nature, the sufficiency of human reason, and the excellency of natural religion! Mr. Leigh sent for the chief, and said to him, "I did not expect to witness so revolting a spectacle in your village. Why have you placed those heads in such a situation?" He replied, with an air of contempt, "Because I expected you to buy them!" "*Buy them!*" said Mr. Leigh, with considerable vehemence, "I buy spars, pigs, and flax, but not the heads of men." On returning through the same village in the evening, he perceived that the heads had been removed. On meeting the chief, he inquired why he had removed the heads. "Because," he observed, "you did not like to see them, and wished that you might not see any more. But the captain of the next ship will, in all probability, purchase them."

Coming to a hut, much superior in appearance to those around it, Mr. Leigh crouched down; and, on looking in, discovered a living child lying naked, between two large stones. He crept in on his hands and knees, the entrance being very low, and, wrapping the infant in his pocket-handkerchief, brought it out. Several persons, having observed him, raised the cry, "The white man has gone into the queen's hut!" The people were soon in motion; and the queen herself arriving, demanded to know what business he had there. Holding up the child, he said, "I went in to save the life of this infant. Why was it left alone, naked, and upon the floor of the hut?" The queen replied, "I have been planting potatoes, and could not attend to it. But I do not regret it; for your handkerchief, having touched my pickaninny, is forfeited—it is now my property." He judged it prudent to let her have it. He then went into their plantations, and expostulated with such as he found working on the Lord's day. They declared that their gods were good for nothing: they did not give them a sabbath. "They kept them *mahi, mahi,* until they were *máte, máte,* then it was *mahi, mahi,* until they were *máte mōe.*" "They said, *Work, work,* until they were *sick, sick,* and then they said, *Work, work,* until they were *sick dead.*"

His attention to the child, and his affable manner with the natives, secured their confidence and esteem. He visited six of the nearest villages in succession, assembled the people, and inquired whether they were willing to receive instruction. They generally replied in the affirmative, and assured him that if the white teachers would come regularly, they would stay at home themselves, and bring their children to be taught. He formed those villages into a circuit, and made a plan, to which the lay missionaries attached their names. They conducted a religious service in each village, every Lord's day.

Having witnessed, with much satisfaction, the improved zeal and usefulness of his lay brethren, and brought them to adopt a regular system of labour, Mr. Leigh felt persuaded that he might leave the work in their own hands, and return to New South Wales. This course had become necessary, as, owing either to his incessant application to duty, or to his disease having assumed a more aggravated form, there was scarcely any perceptible improvement in the state of his health. The homeward voyage, however, from New Zealand to Port Jackson, had a very beneficial effect upon both his health and spirits.

On landing at Sydney, his first concern was to know how the affairs of the mission had been conducted during his absence; and it yielded him no small degree of satisfaction to learn, that the cause of religion had been making a steady progress, and that the circuit, generally, presented an encouraging appearance. The report of his colleague was peculiarly animating. He observed, "As to the success of the gospel in the colony, I have no doubt; and I exult in it for many reasons. This is certainly one of the most important spheres of labour under the direction of the committee. From us, in a few years, I expect to see missionaries sallying forth to those islands which spot the sea on every side of us: the Friendly Isles, the Feejees, New Hebrides, New Caledonia, New Zealand, New Georgia: and then to the north again, very contiguous to us, are the Islands of New Guinea, New Ireland, Celebes, Timor, Borneo, Gilolo, and a great cluster of thickly-inhabited missionary fields: but we want more missionaries. I thank God, my health has been good. My mind has been happy; and I do not regret having journeyed so far to be a helper in this great work."

The congregations had so increased, that additional accommodation had become indispensable; but the societies were small, and building very expensive. Not only were all kinds of materials very high in price, but a common mechanic could not be engaged for less than ten shillings a day. Several individuals, however, not immediately connected with the mission, encouraged the erection of larger and more suitable places of worship. One day, while Mr. Leigh was dining with the resident magistrate of Liverpool, Thomas Moore, Esq., that gentleman said to him, " I have been thinking what I should give you towards the erection of larger and more commodious chapels. I have concluded to give you £20 for one at Sydney, £10 for one at Paramatta, and £10 for one at Windsor." Others followed this noble example; so that, in a very short time, a handsome sum was subscribed.

The Rev. Samuel Marsden, being informed of their intention to build a chapel in the town of Windsor, where he had considerable property, offered the donation of a sufficient quantity of land on which to erect both a mission-house and chapel. In the note in which he made this offer, he said, " To give you the right hand of fellowship, is no more than my indispensable duty. You may rely with confidence upon my continued support and co-operation in all your laudable attempts to benefit the inhabitants of this populous colony. I am fully persuaded, that your ministerial labours will tend to promote the welfare of these settlements, as well as the eternal interests of immortal souls. The importation of convicts from Europe is very great every year. Hundreds have just landed on our shores, from various parts of the British empire; hundreds are now in the harbour, ready to disembark; and hundreds more are on the bosom of the great deep, and hourly expected. We must not expect that governors, magistrates, and politicians can find a remedy for the moral diseases with which those convicts are infected: Heaven itself has provided the only remedy, which is the blessed Balm of Gilead. We must expect great discouragements; but let us go on sounding the rams' horns; the walls of Jericho will and must fall in time. We are feeble; but the Lord is mighty, and will bring Israel to Mount Zion. I pray that the Divine blessing may attend all your labours for the salvation of men in this colony."   "Behold, how good and how pleasant it is for brethren to dwell together in unity!" The above attestation in favour of this mission, from the pen of so competent and disinterested a witness as Mr. Marsden, who thoroughly understood the principles on which it had been conducted, and had seen its practical results, is highly complimentary to the ability and zeal with which its affairs had been conducted by missionary Leigh. Let this testimony be placed in contrast with the opinions of those gentlemen who, having spent six or nine months in the country, examining its geological peculiarities, or collecting botanical subjects, have written respecting this noble enterprise in the most disparaging and flippant manner.

Mr. Leigh was not a man to be diverted from his purpose by ordinary occurrences. Assisted by his colleague, he proceeded to lay the foundation of the Windsor chapel, September 13th, 1818. Mr. Lawry conducted the devotional parts of the service, and Mr. Leigh preached from Ezra iii. 11: "And all the people shouted with a great shout, when they praised the Lord, because the foundation of the house of the Lord was laid." The opening of this neat and commodious building, which took place early in 1819, excited much public interest, and brought several families under the influence of the gospel, who had, for many years, abandoned even the outward forms of religion.

The congregation in Sydney had for some time been subjected to the greatest inconvenience, from the unsuitableness and size of the building which they occupied in that city. It did not contain more than two hundred hearers, while the situation was exceedingly objectionable. The society, though improving in numbers and respectability, was not, as yet, able to undertake a building at all in keeping with the rapidly advancing population and architectural elegance of the metropolis. Just at this season of encouragement and trial, Mr. Scott, who had sold them the estate on which the mission-house stood, said to Mr. Leigh, "I intend, God willing, to build a chapel upon my garden ground, and give it to the mission. I feel this to be a duty which I owe to Divine Providence." He soon afterwards laid the foundation-stone with great joy; and, after spending five hundred guineas upon the erection, secured the exclusive right of occupation to the Wesleyan missionaries. It was appropriated to the worship of God in March, 1819; on which occasion Mr. Leigh preached in the old chapel in the morning, and Mr. Lawry in the new one in the evening. Referring to these services, Mr. Leigh writes: "The congregations were large and attentive. I cannot express what I felt during the evening service as I looked round upon the audience, and reflected on the wonderful change that had taken place since I first preached in Sydney 'Rocks.' I was 'lost in wonder, love, and praise!'" This building, which was of dressed stone, presented a neat appearance, and was capable of containing four hundred hearers. And there it still stands, to tell to the citizens of yet another generation, how solicitous their deceased friend was that the worship of God should be perpetuated amongst them. May we not ask, What are all the magnificent structures, which the wealth and gratitude of the British people have reared, to commemorate the triumphs of the national flag over their prostrate enemies, the eloquence of their statesmen, or the munificence of their benefactors, when compared with this beautiful house of prayer? When the achievements of those illustrious warriors and statesmen shall have been blotted from human recollection, and the monuments that record them shall have been reduced to their original form, it will be said of this unpretending edifice, this asylum for the lost, "that this man was born there." This free-will offering to Christ was but a type of Mr. Scott's principles. Those principles were so disinterested and expansive, that they only wanted the means to have erected places of worship and school-houses for the entire population of Australia.

The town of Sydney had been divided into small sections, a tract society established, and every house supplied periodically with religious tracts. This humble instrumentality had been the means of awakening general inquiry, and of leading many to observe the sabbath, and attend the means of grace, who had not been within the walls of a place of worship since they left the land of their nativity.

The new chapel did not long meet the demand for seat accommodation. The recollection of the past inspired the people with fresh hopes, and present success increased the ardour of their zeal. While every thing connected with religion assumed a new and cheering aspect, His Excellency the governor, and Thomas Wylde, Esq., offered a piece of land, from their respective estates, in Macquarie-street, sufficiently large for chapel and educational purposes. The Wesleyans resolved to keep pace with the leadings of Providence and the liberality of their friends; and agreed to erect, upon the above site, a building of stone, fifty feet by thirty. They selected the 1st day of January, 1819, for commencing the work. "I was induced," said Mr. Leigh, in a letter to his brother, Ralph Leigh, Esq., "to lay the foundation-stone on New-Year's morning, because it is a season of special intercession with all the Protestant churches of Great Britain and Ireland; and perhaps the abundant blessings we received on that occasion were sent in answer to their prayers."

That branch of the mission which was established at Paramatta had been so conducted as to secure the respect of the public, the confidence of the resident clergy, and the co-operation of the colonial government. His Excellency, having heard of the increasing numbers who were anxious to hear the missionaries if they had a larger place of worship, generously offered them a suitable piece of ground on which to erect a chapel adapted to the altered habits and increasing population of the town.

But while the fruits of the mission were thus multiplying in all the settlements, the missionary himself was fast sinking under the pressure of duty and disease. His friends at home and abroad had expostulated with him in the most earnest terms: "You are killing yourself," said the Rev. Joseph Benson, "by doing what neither God nor the committee expect or require." But when he looked at the criminal lists, and the number of executions, the condition of the convicts, the spiritual destitution of the colonists, and the crime and destruction prevailing amongst the natives in the interior, he was carried forward by an irresistible impulse.

The church at Newcastle, with a congregation of eight hundred hearers, being without a clergyman, the governor applied to Mr. Leigh for assistance. The spirit was willing, though the flesh was weak; and he consented to go. He sailed in one of the government ships, and resumed his labours amongst the thieves and murderers of that settlement; but increasing indisposition rendered his speedy return to Sydney indispensable. He was now incapacitated for all public duty; and, for some time, his friends despaired of his life. He possessed a calm and settled assurance of God's favour, and awaited the issue of his affliction in cheerful resignation.

But how mysterious are the dispensations of Divine Providence! They are always, however, in perfect accordance with His own declaration: "My thoughts are not your thoughts, neither are your ways my ways, saith the Lord. For as the heavens are higher than the earth, so are my ways higher than your ways, and my thoughts than your thoughts." Nor does this present any new phases in the general aspect of Providence. After it had been clearly demonstrated, that human philosophy was insufficient to curb the passions or regulate the habits of mankind, that Christianity was a revelation from God, and that "the foolishness of preaching" was the chosen instrument of salvation to the world; do we find Paul, then in the zenith of his glory, imprisoned in Rome, and John in the island of Patmos? But the one was writing his inimitable Epistles, and thus laying a train destined to spring a mine that was to shake the throne of the Cæsars, and, in its vast reverberations, demolish every idol-temple throughout the Roman empire; while the other was preparing his apocalyptic history of the church, through all intervening ages, to the end of time. So the affliction of missionary Leigh, apparently so unseasonable, invigorated all the graces of the Spirit in his experience, and prepared him for a more arduous campaign in the service of Christ. He resembled the husbandman, who, having sustained the toils and privations of the spring, watches with satisfaction the rising blade in his corn-fields, and looks forward to autumn with hope; but is suddenly struck down, without being permitted to reap the increase.

The physicians of Sydney were of opinion, that nothing but a long voyage could justify the slightest hope of Mr. Leigh's ultimate recovery. The stewards apprized the committee in London of this opinion in an official note, dated February 24th, 1820. In it they observe: "Mr. Leigh has fairly worn himself out in this mission. For three years he travelled through this uncultivated and extensive colony alone and without help, during the burning heat of summer, and the cold and wet of winter. We all perceived what would be the result of such incessant labour, and only wonder that he sustained it so long. It is the unanimous opinion of all the medical men here, that the only chance of recovery is a voyage to England. After much persuasion, he has consented to return home. He is exceedingly respected in this country. Should his health be restored, the committee cannot send any man who will be so acceptable to the people as Mr. Leigh. In the name of the friends of the mission, we request that, so soon as it may be considered safe, Mr. Leigh may be sent out to us again, in preference to any other person."

"My fellow-labourer," said the Rev. R. Cartwright, "I heard on Saturday of your intended voyage to England. I have for some time observed your declining state of health; but assuredly the Lord is fitting you for some eminent service. I rather envy than pity you, knowing that your inward man is renewed day by day. None of us have escaped, like yourself, the tongue of the slanderer. Neither in my capacity of magistrate nor chaplain have I heard any thing to your prejudice. All classes have united in the opinion, and considered Mr. Leigh a faithful servant of Jesus Christ. Your labours have been greatly blessed. Take with you the comfort of knowing, that you have the approbation of God and man. If God should restore you, stand up for us in England, and plead our cause, that we may have more help from your Society, or some other. Why may we not hope to have you again amongst us? You have a stock of knowledge which none can possess who have not passed through the same ordeal. Be assured we shall not cease to pray for you. Write to me, and give me the benefit of your experience. Should you be in the neighbourhood of Bradford, near Leeds, tell my friends there that I often think of them with tears of gratitude. And now, brother, 'I commend

you to God, and to the word of His grace, which is able to
build you up, and to give you an inheritance among all them
that are sanctified.' You must consider me, at all times, to be,
with much esteem, your affectionate brother in Christ." The
reverend gentleman commenced his Christian career amongst
the Wesleyans of Bradford. He subsequently connected himself with the established Church in that town; and, on the
recommendation of the Rev. Mr. Crosse, obtained ordination,
and an appointment to a chaplaincy in New South Wales. To
Mr. Leigh he was " a friend and a brother; " and, in all seasons
of difficulty and perplexity, was ready to administer encouragement and afford help.

The friends having completed Mr. Leigh's outfit, he took
an affectionate leave of them, and went on board. His pre-
carious state of health excited the sympathy of all in the ship,
and led them to adopt every method which medical experience
could suggest for alleviating his affliction. They sailed by
Cape Horn, and called at Pernambuco, where they were detained
a fortnight. This is a maritime province of Brazil. Mr.
Leigh availed himself of the opportunity which this unexpected
detention afforded for acquainting himself with some of the
peculiarities of the place and people. For this purpose, he
spent the greater part of every day on shore. He could not
penetrate into the interior of the country but at the risk of his
life, so that his observations were necessarily confined within a
comparatively small circumference. Nature seemed to be every
where clothed with the attributes of grandeur and beauty. The
infinite diversity, richness, and luxuriance of the vegetation,
extending as far as the eye could reach, exceeded all the scenery
which he had ever witnessed. The various tints of the foliage,
in which all the colours of the rainbow were sweetly blended,
gave a wonderful variety to the prospect; "while the myriads
of reptiles, birds, and insects studding the ground in most
brilliant colours, or sparkling like gems on the surrounding
branches and leaves," reminded him of primeval Paradise. In
the exuberance of evergreen foliage, which forms the peculiar
characteristic of the Brazilian empire, this region has the pre-
eminence over every other part of the globe. Its geographical
position, fertile soil, genial climate, noble ports, and navigable
rivers, render it, perhaps, the most valuable portion of the
western continent.

The condition of the people presented a melancholy contrast
with the bounty and loveliness of nature. The aborigines were
a sullen and ferocious race of savages, strangers to arts or
manufactures, and habituated to cannibalism. Here a population exceeding five millions of souls was sitting in "gross dark-

ness and in the shadow of death." At the period to which we refer, there were one million, nine hundred and thirty thousand slaves, chiefly employed on the sugar-estates in the interior; and six ships in the harbour newly arrived, with fresh cargoes, from the coast of Africa. Mr. Leigh frequently attended the slave-market, where hundreds of men, women, and children were offered for sale. They were quite naked. Their heads were neatly dressed, and their bodies rubbed over with oil, to give them the appearance of plumpness, and make the skin soft and glossy. Where age had silvered the hair, it was cut as short as possible, and every means employed to conceal deformity, and set off the objects of this criminal commerce. "Shall I not visit for these things? saith the Lord: and shall not my soul be avenged on such a nation as this?" To the heart of a missionary, accustomed to regard every man as a brother, and every woman as a "sister or mother," these exhibitions were exquisitely touching. The distress evinced on the separation of families proved that, although these children of nature were denied the prerogatives of manhood, they yet possessed all the peculiar and inherent properties of humanity. The slave squatted in front of his master's residence, as a substitute for a sign-board, marked the locality where the slave-merchant conducted his retail business.

Here Popery reigned without a competitor, and carried on her sorceries, none daring to question the validity of her claim to supremacy. Her architectural magnificence, her gorgeous altars, the number of her ecclesiastics, and the costliness and variety of their sacerdotal costumes, marked alike her unbounded wealth and political influence. Her numerous holidays, in which amusement and devotion were agreeably blended, and the exuberance of her paternal love in granting, upon easy terms, an exemption from the fires of purgatory, acted upon the imagination of an ignorant and credulous people, so as to render them intolerant to all who differed from them, even to bloodshedding. Their public worship was as devoid of solemnity as of spirituality.

Returning from the church one day with a lady-passenger and her two daughters, Mr. Leigh observed two Spanish ladies, richly attired, following close behind them. They made several observations on the dress and elegance of the young ladies with Mr. Leigh. "They are heretics," said one of them as they passed. "Yes," said the other, "they are heretics. But what a pity that those beautiful creatures should be fuel for hell-fire!" Mr. Leigh hastened to the water-side, and, the boat being ready, they were glad to escape from their tormentors. Having witnessed the ostentatious pageantry of Popery, under the sacred name of religion, they united in the simple worship of the true God in Christ with grateful hearts. The history of this lady, who was well known to Mr. Leigh in the colony, was remarkable. She was tried in Yorkshire for an aggravated case of horse-stealing, and sentenced to transportation. As a convict, she conducted herself with the strictest propriety, and, after a season of trial, obtained a ticket of leave. She married, commenced business in Sydney, and gradually rose to respectability and affluence. She was anxious that her daughters should have a first-rate education, and was on her way to England for the purpose of placing them at a boarding-school.

The health of Mr. Leigh had gradually improved from the time of his leaving the colony. The doctor, the captain, or the commissary had been accustomed to read the Prayers and Lessons; but his severe cough was so far relieved, that he was now able to go through the whole service himself. Having enjoyed "line upon line, precept upon precept," during the voyage, all on board had become religiously impressed by the truth; and several were unquestionably converted to God.

The ship having called at Portsmouth, Mr. Leigh landed, and forwarded to the committee an account of the state in which he had left the mission. That account, which we abbreviate and subjoin, will be perused with deep interest :—

"It has pleased God," he observes, "of his infinite goodness, to bring me back in safety to my native land. 'While I live, I will praise the Lord.' For nearly four years I was enabled to prosecute my mission without disappointing one congregation. I had many difficulties to encounter, long rides, and frequently no bed but the ground. But, though I suffered in health, I rejoiced in spirit. I visited New Zealand, in the hope of being much benefited by the change; but the improvement was scarcely perceptible to myself or others. The number of persons brought into society in New South Wales is comparatively small; but I believe they are sincere in their profession. Our congregations in Sydney are good; and the Sunday-schools afford a pleasing prospect of usefulness. The congregations in Paramatta and the interior are highly encouraging. Six months hence, several respectable towns will be provided with neat and convenient places of worship. The expense of the chapels at Sydney and Windsor will be defrayed, or nearly so, by public subscriptions. Mr. John Lees, of Castlereagh, has built a second chapel there at his own expense; and a friend at Nepean River has one in progress, which he means to give to the mission.

"But we must have more missionaries: three are indispensably necessary. Station one at Sydney, that he may visit the neighbouring settlements, at present entirely destitute of the means of grace; the second at Paramatta, whose circuit will extend seventy miles, and include eight settlements, the inhabitants of which have not hitherto heard the gospel; the third at Windsor. The missionary here will have a sphere of action thirty miles in extent. From this station the gospel will, I trust, be carried across the Blue Mountains. Without such a provision, the colonists in that territory will soon be on a level with the natives. Wilberforce is a very promising settlement: from hence to the second branch of the Hawkesbury River, a distance of sixty miles, there are many emigrants who have not seen a Christian minister since they came into the country. These are all anxious to have religious instructors. I will communicate more fully when I reach London: in the mean time, you will see that 'I have neither run in vain, nor laboured in vain.' "

It has become customary, of late, for those who look with jealousy on Christian missions, to take the Annual Reports of the different societies, and calculate the amount of success from numerical *data*. But this is as fallacious as it is unjust. The individual who adopts this rule of judging shows either profound ignorance or deep malignity. It would be as rational to take up the returns of the Australian settler, and endeavour to show that, because his produce does not give, on the average, more than one bushel of wheat to the acre, he has done nothing. But is it not something to have manufactured all the requisite implements of husbandry, to have cleared the forest of its timber and brushwood, and to have proved, by actual experiment and numerous specimens, the depth and richness of the soil? Those persons may not be aware of it, but their principles are identical with those of Simon Magus, who determined the value of " the gift of God," and the worth of the soul, by a money-standard.

Mr. Leigh, single and alone, laid the foundation of a spiritual empire, which has been widening ever since, and will be enduring as time itself. The connexion of New South Wales with the numerous islands in the South Seas, with which its commercial intercourse is constantly enlarging, gives it a higher interest as a mission-station. And how cheering, even in its dawn, is the prospect of complete success in this important division of the globe! There is every probability that Australia will become the Great Britain of the Southern Ocean, and spread Christianity, science, and commerce throughout its numerous and populous islands.

After a short stay in Portsmouth, Mr. Leigh travelled by coach to London, where he was kindly received, by the Rev. Joseph Taylor, at the Mission-House, Hatton-Garden. The unwearied attention of Mr. and Mrs. Taylor, and the superior medical treatment under which he was placed, produced a sudden and remarkable change in the state of his health. As soon as he conveniently could, he met the secretaries, the Rev. Messrs. Bunting, Taylor, and Watson. After going fully into the temporal and spiritual affairs of the South-Sea mission, he urged the necessity of extending the work in Australia, and attempting the establishment of new missions in New Zealand and the Friendly Islands: "I am prepared," said he, "to take the one, and Brother Lawry the other, of those untried fields of labour." "Sir," said Mr. Taylor, "what are you talking about? With a debt of £10,000, we are not in a condition either to enlarge the old, or undertake the establishment of new, missions." The other secretaries having concurred in the opinion of Mr. Taylor, the interview closed, and Mr. Leigh retired; but he could not sleep all that night. Next morning, when seated at breakfast, he brought the subject again before Mr. Taylor, expressing his regret that the doors which had been opened by Divine Providence for extended usefulness, should have been so peremptorily closed by the secretaries. Mr. Taylor again adduced the £10,000 in justification of the prudent, though painful, conclusion to which the secretaries had come.

Mr. Leigh, who felt as if he could not live unless he were permitted to go to New Zealand, continued in earnest prayer that God would clear away all obstructions, and carry him back again to that country. This subject filled his mind and engrossed his attention day and night. One morning as he lay in bed, reflecting alternately on the enterprise on which his heart was set, and the impossibility of dealing with the £10,000, it occurred to him, in a moment, that it was not money that he wanted; but that if he could obtain articles to be used in barter, they would subserve all the purposes of money. Elated by this new conception, he got up, struck out his new theory, prayed over it, and awaited the call to breakfast with impatience. So soon as he entered the parlour, he laid his plan before Mr. Taylor, observing, "If you will give me leave to go down to the manufacturing districts, and make a public statement of the actual circumstances of the cannibals of New Zealand, and solicit such articles as the people may be willing to contribute, I will engage to establish a mission amongst those savages, in defiance of your £10,000." Mr. Taylor replied, "Mr. Watson will be here at eleven o'clock, when you had better submit your scheme to him. It seems to me to be deserving of some consideration." Mr. Watson arrived, and listened with respectful attention to Mr. Leigh's proposal. "We cannot," said Mr. Watson, "give you the authority you require; but the conference is at hand, and the case had better be brought before that body. In the mean time, I am rather impressed in favour of your suggestion."

As Mr. Leigh was advancing towards a state of convalescence, it was thought that a few weeks in the country would greatly facilitate his restoration to health. His deep consumptive cough had subsided, and his strength and spirits were rapidly returning. He, however, had no idea of making the pursuit of health the primary object of his journey into the country. It seemed to him that, if he could ascertain the views of his brethren, and test public feeling, if it were but in a few instances, before going to conference, he would be better able to judge of the propriety of pressing upon that body the adoption of his scheme for evangelizing New Zealand. For this purpose he left London, accompanied by Mr. Taylor, and called at Louth on his way to Hull and York. At the former place they held a missionary meeting. "At this meeting," says the "Stamford Mercury," of Tuesday, July 18th, 1820, "several very instructive, eloquent, and impressive speeches were delivered by the Rev. Messrs. J. Taylor, Gregory, Cubitt, Hannah, Agar, and others; but though all these speeches were truly excellent, that of Mr. Leigh most attracted our notice. This gentleman gave some very interesting information relative to New Zealand and its people, amongst whom he resided for a short time before he sailed for England. Let it suffice to notice that, notwithstanding the almost incredible ferocity of these cannibals, they are remarkably ingenious and enterprising, very respectful to Europeans, and discovered a surprising willingness and capacity to receive instruction; and that Mr. Leigh intends shortly to sail, with six other ministers, for New Zealand, and other islands in the Pacific Ocean. We do sincerely pray that this gentleman and his assistants may be able, through the blessing of God, to convert and civilize this interesting, though degraded, race of men." Though the friends at Louth were expending nearly £1,000 upon their trust-premises, they yet nobly responded to Mr. Leigh's call for assistance in his hazardous undertaking. During this visit he lodged at the house of Mr. Horton, and secured a valuable auxiliary to the cause of missions in the son of that gentleman, the Rev. William Horton.

He met with a similar reception at Hull and York; and went to the conference at Liverpool satisfied as to the complete success of his plan, unless his brethren should put an interdict upon it. The open conference, it was believed, would afford him a suitable opportunity for submitting his scheme to the candid consideration of the Christian public. The chapel was crowded to excess, and the Lord enabled him to plead the cause of the New-Zealand savage with perspicuity and power.

After much discussion, the conference sanctioned the establishment of the mission, and authorized him to visit such provincial towns as might invite him, for the purpose of realizing the means of accomplishing that object. Several brethren, being persuaded that the religious principles and zeal of the lay members of their societies would be refreshed and invigorated by his communications, invited him at once to their respective circuits.

No man enjoyed Christian fellowship more than Mr. Leigh; and yet, when the New-Zealand case passed the conference, he became restless and unhappy. He seemed to have a special call to this particular department of his "Master's business," and was eager to enter upon its onerous duties. Having taken leave of the conference, he retired for a few days to recruit his strength, before commencing a general visitation of the circuits.

On the 18th of September, 1820, he received the following letter, addressed to the "preachers in the circuits which Mr. Leigh may visit," and signed, "Jabez Bunting." "The conference in Liverpool, having heard Mr. Samuel Leigh's statements respecting the favourable openings for the establishment of missions among the black natives of New South Wales, in Tongataboo, and the Friendly Islands, and in the populous and extensive islands of New Zealand, agreed to appoint several missionaries, including himself, to those countries; and, as many of the preachers and respectable friends who attended conference were desirous that he should visit some of the principal places in England, to receive such articles of manufacture as would be more valuable than money in the support of those missions, the conference resolved as follows : 'That Mr. Samuel Leigh having been appointed as a missionary to New Zealand, the conference authorizes the missionary committee to direct him to visit, before his departure, any places in this kingdom where it is probable that he may obtain the present of various articles of manufacture, in aid of the South-Sea missions;' and the preachers cheerfully engaged to render him all the assistance in their power. Feeling very desirous that his health may not suffer, I would suggest the propriety and necessity of his not being called upon to preach, or do any public work, but what may be absolutely necessary for the purposes of furthering his object. Under God, the establishment of those important missions depends materially upon the continuance of his life and strength; and I would sincerely hope, that he may be spared to accomplish so great a work. A king and chief from New Zealand, under whom our mission is to be established there, have lately been, for a few days, at the mission-house; and are much pleased that Mr. Leigh is going to reside in their country, and to preach to themselves, their children, and countrymen in their native language. Mr. Leigh will communicate more fully, in person, the wishes of himself and the missionary committee on the subject of his visit."

Mr. Leigh made a tour of the provinces, travelling by day, and speaking to, generally, crowded audiences almost every night. After delivering a public address in Sheffield, he received several tons of goods, including almost every article of local manufacture; such as ploughs, spinning-wheels, spades, saws, axes, and fish-hooks, together with all descriptions of ironmongery. Several of these donations were large. Mr. Holy presented one hundred dozens of forks and knives. The firm of Newton and Chambers, of Thorncliffe, contributed goods valued at £100, consisting of grates, pots, kettles, and sundries. In presenting the list of articles to Mr. Leigh, the head of that firm enclosed a £5 note for his own use. He immediately returned it, observing, "I never receive donations for myself: send it to the secretaries!" One lady sent him one hundred wedding-rings. He held an aggregate meeting in Oldham-street chapel, Manchester; after which he received prints, calicoes, wearing apparel, and curiosities, some of which were above one hundred years old, valued altogether at £500. Having stated his case to the people of Birmingham, he was soon surrounded with innumerable articles in copper, iron, and brass, saws of all kinds, axes, pins, buttons, and fish-hooks. Liverpool furnished a large assortment of wearing apparel for men, women, and children. Captain Irving, of Bristol, provided a large tent, which was found very serviceable in New Zealand; while other friends there contributed, in various ways, in furtherance of an object that excited an interest as deep as it was general.

The London Missionary Society was then holding its anniversary meeting in that city. Mr. Leigh attended the meeting, and delivered an affecting address on the state of the inhabitants of the South-Sea Islands, and the privations and sufferings which their missionaries had been called to endure amongst those barbarians. During the war, their letters and supplies from home had been cut off for seven years; in consequence of which they had been reduced to the greatest extremities.

The contributions of the people to the New-Zealand mission were packed in old casks, which had previously contained wine, beer, and porter; and were sent to Hatton-Garden in such quantities, that Mr. Taylor had some difficulty in finding warehouse-room for them in the neighbourhood.

Does the reader inquire, "What became of this vast accumulation of property? Can any satisfactory account be given of its appropriation? Was it faithfully and economically applied to the introduction and establishment of Christianity in New Zealand?"   The writer of this narrative is happy in being able to assure the surviving contributors and their families, that, after the lapse of thirty years, there exists satisfactory evidence that, in administering their bounty to the Heathen, "there was no profligate expenditure."   The goods were received as a sacred deposit: they were shipped to New South Wales, and re-shipped, as they were required, to New Zealand.   They furnished the means for purchasing the missionary estate there, for erecting appropriate premises for the purposes of the mission, and for building preaching and school houses in the adjacent villages; and were laid out with such prudence and judgment, that they almost entirely supported the mission for five years.   "Those men," said Mr. Leigh upon his death-bed, "who accuse us and our establishment of extravagance, utter slander in ignorance or enmity."

Having completed his labours in the country, he returned to London, deeply impressed with a sense of the goodness of God, and of the benevolence of His people.   In the mean time, 'Hongi and Waikato had arrived from New Zealand.   They were accompanied by Mr. Kendall, of the Church mission.   Mr. Leigh had known those chiefs in their own country.

In the early history of European intercourse with those islands, no name stands more prominent than that of 'Hongi. He ruled over a territory comprehending seventeen districts, and stretching across the land from the eastern to the western shore.   The extent of his possessions alone would have rendered him one of the most powerful chiefs in the country; but he was still more celebrated and dreaded as one of its most distinguished warriors.   His precipitate and sanguinary justice rendered him at once the terror and the glory of New Zealand. He was the Napoleon of his age; he marshalled and trained the provincial forces subject to his authority, and generally led them to victory.   But, although he was ferocious and blood-thirsty in battle, he was, at other times, all equanimity and gentleness, and not more distinguished by mild manners and kindly affections than by a natural ingenuity in several useful and ornamental arts.   He particularly excelled in carving rude figures upon wood.   Waikato, his companion, was a relative, and a young chief of an amiable disposition.

"They had come to London to see the king, the multitude of his people, what they were all doing, and the goodness of their land.   They wished to remain in England one month, and then to return home.   They desired to take back with them one hundred men; miners, to search for iron, blacksmiths, carpenters, and missionaries, to teach them arts and religion in their own tongue. They were anxious to have twenty British soldiers, and three officers to keep the soldiers in order. They would protect them, and grant them plenty of land. These are the words of 'Hongi and Waikato."

They were sent, in the first instance, in company with Mr. Kendall, to Cambridge, to be near Professor Lee; and it was principally from the materials furnished by them that Dr. Lee compiled the first grammar of the Maori language. Missionary Leigh also spent a short time with the learned professor in furtherance of the same object; and, whatever may be the literary defects of that work, it has been of undoubted utility both to missionaries and schoolmasters.

After a brief residence at Cambridge, they returned to London, where they excited much public attention by their beautifully tattooed faces. His Majesty, King George IV., admitted them to an audience, showed them the armoury in the palace, and made them several costly presents. Waikato was struck with almost every object upon which his eye fell. 'Hongi was struck with nothing but the discipline of the troops, the military stores, the coat of mail which the king presented to him, and the great elephant.

They lost no time in honouring Mr. Leigh with a visit. After a mutual interchange of compliments and inquiries, 'Hongi said, "As I have not been quite at home since I came to this land, I will stay with you while I remain in England." Mr. Leigh, knowing that, in a few months, the lifting up of the spear of 'Hongi would be equivalent to a declaration of life or death to himself and family, felt it prudent to accept of this proffered mark of respect, with as good a grace as possible. As the chief would not lie on a bed, Mr. Leigh was obliged to lay his mattrass on the floor, and sleep beside him.

He was remarkably sensitive. Whenever he was recognised as a great chief, and treated with that deference and respect which he considered due to his official dignity, he assumed the attitude and spoke with the authority of a prince. But where he was regarded only as an object of curiosity, he became sullen and indignant. A striking illustration of this peculiarity occurred at the house of a highly respectable gentleman, who had invited a large circle of friends to meet the chiefs at an evening party. 'Hongi had conducted himself with an air of conscious superiority, and that scrupulous regard to etiquette by which he was generally distinguished, until he observed some of the ladies evidently tracing the lines upon his tattooed countenance, while a smile played upon their own, implying, as he thought, a feeling of pity towards himself. He instantly rose up in a state of excitement, threw himself across three chairs, and, covering his face with his hands, remained in that posture until the company retired.

The Church Missionary Society paid much attention to him, and made him several valuable presents. In many critical moments he had thrown himself between their lay settlers and death; and never, let the cost be what it might to himself, would he allow any thing belonging to them to be destroyed.

The Wesleyan Missionary committee, being about to place life and property at the mercy of this savage, was anxious to conciliate his good-will in a way that should testify their respect for him, and, at the same time, encourage his well-known taste for the mechanical arts. At the suggestion of Mr. Leigh, they presented each chief with a box of carpenters' tools. After they had examined, with evident satisfaction, the contents of the boxes, Joseph Butterworth, Esq., M.P., observed, that the committee would have very great pleasure in adding any other article that would be particularly acceptable to them. "Then," said 'Hongi, "add, if you please, a dress for my wife." When this, with several other articles of female attire, was provided, he seemed pleased and satisfied.

The climate, or their altered mode of living, soon affected their health; and, as the winter approached, 'Hongi was seized with an affection of the chest, which placed his life in jeopardy. The most earnest expostulations could not, for a long time, reconcile him to a blister; but when he at last submitted, the effects were so beneficial, that he declared he would not leave the country, unless he were supplied with a pot of the preparation to take home with him. As soon as they could be removed, the government granted them a passage, in the ship "Spoke," to New South Wales.

The secretaries of the Church missions sent a respectful note to Mr. Leigh, desiring him to oblige them with another interview, on the subject of their New-Zealand mission. He did so; and, after expressing his views and opinions freely on the state and prospects of that mission, was leaving the office, when one of the gentlemen called him back. "Mr. Leigh," said he, "not satisfied with getting all the money you can for your new mission, you have been down into the country, I hear, collecting considerable quantities of goods: do you intend to open a great trading establishment abroad?" Mr. Leigh smiled, and observed that it was the want of money that had compelled him to have recourse to such an expedient, and he was much mistaken if his success did not provoke them to follow his example. ".It is not improbable," remarked one of the secretaries; "but if we should, we shall exercise a little more sobriety, I hope, than you seem to have done. I must tell you frankly, that I have myself been shocked at the reports of some of your speeches in the news-papers. The tales of travellers, and the injudicious representa-tions of missionaries, have done much mischief to the cause of religion. I have been obliged to reprove the tendency to exaggera-tion which I have perceived in some of our own agents." "What did you see in my speeches," inquired Mr. Leigh, "at variance with the sobriety of truth?" "Why," replied the secretary, "I read that every where you have asserted that the New-Zealanders are cannibals! No sensible person in this country will believe it, and I feel it to be my duty publicly to contradict it." "You had better not," said Mr. Leigh; "for I not only know that they eat one another, but I have seen them do it: and the evi-dence of facts is more convincing to the people of this country than the most plausible reasonings. There can be no exaggera-tion in describing the character of a man that roasts and eats his fellow." In a week or two afterwards Mr. Leigh received twenty-five volumes of books, with the following note enclosed:—

"MY DEAR SIR,—The committee of the Church Missionary Society beg that you will accept their thanks for your kind coun-sels and attention to our settlers at the Bay of Islands. They have much pleasure in presenting you with a copy of the Society's proceedings. I am,

"Very faithfully yours,
"JOSIAH PRATT."

CHAPTER V.

MARRIES AND SAILS FOR NEW SOUTH WALES—THE ABORIGINES—LANDS
IN NEW ZEALAND—WAR—CANNIBALISM.

ALMOST every arrival of the foreign mail brought to Mr. Leigh encouraging intelligence from his former spheres of labour.

The Rev. Samuel Marsden wrote from New Zealand: "It is very gratifying to our feelings, and affords us a pleasing pro-spect, to be able to perform the worship of the true God in the open air, without any sensations of fear or danger, when sur-rounded by cannibals with their spears stuck in the ground, and their *pattoo-pattoos* and daggers concealed under their mats. We could not doubt but the time was at hand for gathering into the fold of Christ this noble race of men, whose temporal and spiritual wants are inconceivably great, and call loudly on the Christian world for relief. Their misery is extreme. The prince of darkness has full dominion over their bodies and souls. Such is the tyranny that he exercises over them, that the chiefs sacrifice their slaves as a satisfaction for the death of their friends; while numbers voluntarily and superstitiously devote themselves to death. Nothing but the gospel of Christ can set them free; and we cannot hope for the gospel having its full effect without the aid of the Christian world. Suitable means must be provided for the evangelization of New Zealand; and, if this be done, there can be little doubt but that the important object will be attained."

About the same date, in 1820, Mr. Carvosso touched at Van-Diemen's Land, on his way to New South Wales, and disclosed a new field of missionary labour in that penal colony. "The people here," said he, "are literally as sheep without a shepherd. Considering the former character of these colonists, and their destitution of the means of grace, what can be expected but the greatest profligacy? The lieutenant-governor was quite agreeable to my preaching in the street, and ordered the chief constable to attend, and prevent interruption. I preached frequently to numerous, attentive, and increasing congregations. Animated by the example of the apostle of the Gentiles, I felt a strong desire to have the honour of laying the foundation of a church on this island, whose light should be seen from afar. Here is a fine opening for a 'man full of faith and of the Holy Ghost.'"

At the same time, the work was going on satisfactorily in Australia, under the active administration of Mr. Leigh's successor. In a letter addressed to Thomas Holy, Esq., of Sheffield, he observes: "I have witnessed many conversions lately, and several very promising young men are among the number of our converts. Every little thing here contains the germ of something great; and I am fully persuaded that as this is the rallying-point of all commercial and other affairs in the southern hemisphere, so it is and will be the refuge and nursery of Christian missionaries. I have been doing a little among the black natives, from whose eyes I have seen the tear fall, while I have been explaining to them the nature and intent of Christ's sufferings. I begin to have hope of them."

Immediately the scene changes, and reveals the social state of the colony: "Three men, who were executed last Friday, seemed to be truly penitent. I had paid sedulous attention to them; and so did several others. Before they ascended the platform, we sang a hymn, which produced a considerable effect upon the spectators. There were six thousand convicts present, many of whom were in tears. We knelt down upon the grass, and, after spending a short time in prayer, they ascended the scaffold. They addressed the assembled multitude with much earnestness, and with evident effect. We then sang another hymn, at the close of which the drop fell. Twelve men have been executed this session. I attended the last of them yesterday. They all evinced deep contrition of heart."

In this, and in various other ways, by the instrumentality of the missionaries, have hundreds been saved in New South Wales, whose names have never appeared on the list of communicants, nor in the Minutes of the Conference. Mr. Lawry was seasonably relieved from the pressure of public duties by the arrival of Mr. and Mrs. Carvosso; who were speedily followed by Mr. and Mrs. Mansfield.

Mr. Leigh was now maturing his plans for leaving England. Experience and observation had long convinced him, that no single man should be appointed to labour amongst a barbarous people. In the hope of promoting his own comfort, and extending his usefulness amongst the natives of New Zealand, he went down into Staffordshire, and married a lady of the name of Clewes. He had been intimately acquainted with her in early life. She was a person of good sense, deep piety, ardent zeal, and indomitable courage. In no circumstances, either by sea or land, amongst the civilized or savage, did she seem to be the subject of fear. When surrounded by tribes of armed cannibals, who waited only for a signal from their leader to transfix her with their spears, she always appeared calm, firm, and self-possessed. To Mr. Leigh she was an invaluable companion, a "Dorcas" to the widow and fatherless, and to the mission an indefatigable and successful co-adjutor.

After a sojourn in his native land of little more than eight months, during which period he had visited the principal towns in England, and attended numerous public meetings, in an indifferent state of health, we find this intrepid man sailing from Gravesend, in the ship "Brixton," April 28th, 1821, to resume his duties in the South Seas. He carried with him a suitable assortment of goods, and was accompanied by Mrs. Leigh, Mr. and Mrs. Horton, and Mr. Walker. The public services were well sustained during the voyage; the daily intercourse of the missionary party with the passengers and crew was agreeable and profitable; and various plans were suggested and discussed relative to their future proceedings.

On the 8th of August they reached Van-Diemen's Land, and cast anchor in Sullivan's Cove, Hobart Town. Very little was known of the interior of the country at that time. This beautiful island, which is one hundred and seventy miles in length, and one hundred and fifty in breadth, is remarkably fertile and healthy. The population, including prisoners and free people, amounted to eight thousand. "The aborigines," says Mr. Leigh, "have a better appearance than the natives of New South Wales. They are black, with woolly hair; their limbs are small; their bodies are exceedingly thin, arising, no doubt, from the poverty of their diet. They live by hunting, and have no knowledge of the arts. They decorate their fleecy locks with the teeth of the kangaroo, pieces of wood, or the feathers of birds. They draw a circle round each eye, and waved lines down each arm, thigh, and leg, which give them a most savage appearance. In summer they wear no clothing; in winter males and females dress themselves in the skins of the kangaroo. They believe in the existence of two spirits; the one good, the other bad. When they are on a journey, they sing in honour of the good spirit, for the purpose of securing his protection. Their voices are sweet, and their melody simple and expressive.

" The moral state of the Europeans can scarcely be described. Considering their crimes before they were banished to this colony, we may easily account for the surrounding profanity. Adultery, drunkenness, and blasphemy are sins which prevail amongst both rich and poor, male and female, bond and free. With these are inseparably connected idleness, dishonesty, quarrelling, and misery. Almost every tongue has learned to swear, and, amongst the lower classes, every hand to steal. The houses are surrounded by fierce dogs, to guard against nocturnal depredations. There is but one aged clergyman, whose labours are almost wholly confined to the town; so that the out-settlements have no religious service whatever."

During Mr. Leigh's absence in England, a small detachment of soldiers had been removed from New South Wales to Hobart Town. Sergeant Waddy and two privates, who had been members of the Sydney Society, agreed to commence a prayer-meeting. They mentioned their intention to a resident of the name of Nokes; who said he would be happy to unite with them, and, if possible, procure a house in which to hold their meetings. He obtained the use of a carpenter's shop, which soon became too small. They then rented a building, sufficient to contain two hundred hearers; and opened it for religious worship, twice on the Sunday, and on every night in the week, excepting Saturday night. Three persons were awakened, and agreed to meet in class with the three soldiers, under Mr. Nokes as their leader. The soldiers conducted the services alternately, until they were removed to Macquarie Harbour, when the whole of the duty devolved on Mr. Nokes. It was their practice to read and expound a chapter, to sing three or four hymns, and for several persons to engage in prayer. Exercising these sacred functions, they were exposed to much scorn and persecution; but the blessing of God was upon them, and they slowly increased in number and influence.

Such was the state of things when Mr. Leigh landed at Hobart Town. He waited on the lieutenant-governor, the resident magistrates, and several of the principal inhabitants of the town; and found them all favourable to the establishment of a mission in the colony. The missionaries preached on the Lord's day, and on several evenings in the week, to congregations varying from two to three hundred persons. The current expenses were too much for the limited means of the soldiers and their friends, so that a considerable debt had been incurred. Mr. Leigh stated the case to the congregation, and announced a collection for its liquidation. The people responded to this appeal with such liberality, that, with £5. 5s. added by the passengers and mariners on board the "Brixton," a sum was obtained sufficient to pay the whole of their liabilities.

His Honour, the lieutenant-governor, having offered land on which to erect any premises that might be required for the purposes of the mission, and all classes being anxious to have a resident missionary, it became a solemn question as to whether this singular conjunction of circumstances did not constitute a call from God to leave one of their number on the island. After a day spent chiefly in discussion and prayer, it was agreed that, for the present, Mr. Horton should remain. Mr. Leigh preached again in the evening, and, at the close of the service, he informed the people of the conclusion to which they had come, and introduced Mr. Horton as their future minister. They could scarcely repress their deep and lively feelings of joy; and came forward, with marked respect and gratitude, to recognise him in that capacity. This intelligent and devoted missionary entered, at once and with all his heart and soul, upon his public duties; and many have been the trials and triumphs of Christianity in the colony since that day. It is as true of good as it is of evil, "Behold, how great a matter a little fire kindleth!" The work thus commenced by the three soldiers, and carried forward by this youthful missionary and his successors, has so expanded, that, at the time we write, there are not fewer than four thousand nine hundred persons under the instruction of the Wesleyan ministers in the island.

Nor must we omit, in this short digression, to notice the obligations of the mission to Samuel Horton, Esq., cousin to the Rev. William Horton. He arrived from China in 1823, and purchased eight hundred acres of land, situated near Ross, on the banks of the Macquarie. He entered upon the cultivation of his estate; and the labours of the spring were succeeded by an abundant harvest. A severe illness ensued, which compelled him to pause, and contemplate death as the probable result of his affliction. He sought God in prayer, and was enabled to renounce the world and embrace religion. He immediately joined the Wesleyan church, and, "having obtained help of God, continues unto this day" to "adorn the doctrine of

God our Saviour in all things." On the 6th of January, 1852, this gentleman laid the foundation of a collegiate institution, the special object of which is to provide a respectable classical and commercial education for the sons of the Wesleyan ministers stationed in the South Seas. To commemorate the munificence of the founder, who, in addition to the gift of twenty acres of land, presented a donation of one thousand guineas, the building is called "Horton College."

But in an equal proportion to the progress of the truth have the elements of evil been multiplied and strengthened in Van-Diemen's Land. From the day that missionary Horton organized his little church in Hobart Town, to the year 1835, upwards of twenty-seven thousand convicts, the very scum of European society, had been floated in upon their shores. In that year the convict-population amounted to sixteen thousand, nine hundred and fifty-eight. Mr. Horton obtained access to the jails and hospitals, which he regularly visited. He established a sabbath-school, and taught a night-school in the penitentiary.

Every thing being satisfactorily settled at Hobart Town, the "Brixton" raised her anchors, stretched her canvass, and bore away for New South Wales. The separation of the missionary party, who, up to that time, had been eminently one family, was peculiarly distressing. While they were mingling their prayers and tears with those of their young friends whom they were leaving behind, the manifestation of so much Christian affection evidently moved all on board. The "Brixton" sailed into Port Jackson on Sunday, September 16th. The missionaries attended the chapel in the evening, to "pay their vows unto the Lord in the presence of all His people."

Joseph Butterworth, Esq., M.P., having applied to the senior chaplain for his candid opinion relative to the proposed mission to New Zealand, that gentleman observed, in reply, "No European is so well acquainted with New Zealand, and with the character of the inhabitants, as myself. I was lately near fifteen months amongst them, and travelled over a great part of the northern island. I crossed the country, from east to west, four times. I think one missionary alone would be very solitary and uncomfortable. If he were a single man, he would be exposed to great temptations; and, if he were married, it would be a trying situation for a single married woman to live amongst the natives. After all, the Europeans are more to be dreaded than the savages: they violate the wives and daughters of the chiefs, and abandon themselves to every villany. Mr. Leigh has returned to us improved in health. He is about to enter upon an arduous sphere of labour in New Zealand. I have known him long; and no man, in my opinion, is better suited to begin such a mission. He has been tried, and found faithful. It will give me much happiness to forward his views, as far as I can. It is my intention to visit New Zealand again, if the Lord permits; and then I hope to see Mr. Leigh settled. I stood by him when the highest authority in this land would have banished him from the country; and will do it again, if necessary."

There were two points that claimed the immediate attention of Mr. Leigh: 1. What is the present state of the work of God in New South Wales? 2. By what means may it be best sustained and extended?

To the FIRST of these inquiries the journals of the brethren supplied satisfactory answers. "At Richmond, Windsor, and Wilberforce," said Mr. Carvosso, "the congregations are improved, and the people are increasingly attentive and devout. I have paid much attention to the hospitals, and been much blessed while exhorting the patients to look to Christ for salvation. I read memoirs, and appropriate extracts from religious books, to enlarge their knowledge. I also read and explain the scriptures, give them personal advice, and pray with them. The extreme sufferings of many produced in my mind sentiments of the deepest commiseration. After preaching at Castlereagh one morning, a man lingered behind the congregation to speak with me. He had felt much under the preaching for some time, but never so much, nor so acutely, as this morning. 'I cannot,' said he, while wiping the falling tear with the sleeve of his jacket, 'refrain from weeping at the sight of my sins.' Before we parted, he promised to attend both the class and Sunday-school. On my way to Pit Town the other evening, I was not a little gratified at seeing some of the natives reaping wheat in the field, with great dexterity. My congregation very much resembled those I had seen in Cornwall; a respectable number being present, some from a distance, several women with infants, leading other branches of their family, all decently dressed, and hearing with eager attention."

During the five following months, things presented a still more encouraging aspect. "I am sure," said another missionary, "the cause to which we are attached is growing in the esteem and affection of all ranks of society. Our ministry, in most places, is well attended. I am persuaded we are taking the right method for the spread of the truth and power of religion; and that hereafter God will build up his church in the midst of this people; and though we not unfrequently now appear to be like the husbandman sowing his seed amidst thick forests and in the cavities of rocks, it will then be manifest that we have not laboured in vain. Missionary meetings have been held at Castlereagh, Richmond, Windsor, Paramatta, and Liverpool, at which places the contributions have been liberal."

Another of the brethren corroborates these statements:— " The work of God," he remarks, " still continues to prosper amongst us. The congregations are increasingly large and respectable: the numbers in society are gradually augmenting ; the prayer-meetings are well attended, and are frequently, in an eminent sense, 'times of refreshing from the presence of the Lord;' and our Sunday-schools receive accessions of both teachers and scholars. In Sydney alone we have four Sunday-schools in efficient operation. In the school at the barracks there are upwards of one hundred children of convicts, many of whom could not read at all before the school was founded. Those institutions form the foundation-stone of our liveliest hopes. Many of those interesting youths are not only acquiring a knowledge of the Divine will, but are being trained with a view to their future and general usefulness in society. Often do I fancy, while looking upon them in the house of God, that I see the embryo of a useful class-leader, then of a zealous local preacher, and then again of a faithful missionary, who will carry the tidings of salvation to some of the adjacent islands. Nor are our hopes confined to the scholars. Many of the teachers were formerly among the taught ; but now these young persons bid fair to be valuable in more important and extensive departments of labour."

The beautiful new chapel in Paramatta, built by the noble contributions of missionary Lawry and the family of his father-in-law, was opened for religious worship on the 21st of April. All the missionaries in the colony assisted at the opening services : the congregations filled the new building, and the Lord was in the midst of the people. " For the Lord hath chosen Zion ; He hath desired it for His habitation. This is my rest for ever : here will I dwell; for I have desired it. I will abundantly bless her provision : I will satisfy her poor with bread. I will also clothe her priests with salvation : and her saints shall shout aloud for joy."

The other institutions of the Wesleyan church, for the instruction of prisoners and relief of the poor, were in progressive improvement ; and " the last love-feast held in Sydney," said the minister who conducted it, " was the best, I believe, ever held in New South Wales. I could scarcely help fancying myself in England, so lively were the people, so clear their experience, and so powerfully was the presence of God felt."

SECONDLY. Mr. Leigh, having recommended an enlargement of the work in the South Seas, and been appointed general superintendent to see the plans of the committee practically applied, felt anxious that the brethren should proceed, with as little delay as possible, to their respective destinations; himself and Mrs. Leigh to New Zealand, Mr. and Mrs. Lawry to Tongataboo, Mr. and Mrs. Carvosso to Van-Diemen's Land, Mr. and Mrs. Horton to New South Wales, and Mr. Walker to form a mission amongst the natives of the colony.

Before they separated, it was judged desirable to hold the first anniversary of the Australian Missionary Society. The meeting was held in Macquarie-street chapel, Sydney, on the 1st of October, 1821, and excited an extraordinary interest. The Rev. Samuel Leigh presided, and was supported by several lay gentlemen of distinction, and magistrates from various parts of the colony. Many of the speeches were characterized by great eloquence and power. The institution had not been established more than six months; and yet, at the close of the meeting, it was found to have yielded £236.

Amongst the list of subscribers, we perceive the name of John Lees, of Castlereagh. A missionary, who was present on the occasion, has given the following graphic description of the circumstances under which John's name was introduced on the list :—" He had come down in his jolting cart, thirty-five miles, to attend the meeting. He had heard much of missionary meetings in England. They suited his taste, and he came on tip-toe of expectation. Various persons had addressed the meeting : it was drawing to a conclusion : the secretary had taken down a pretty long list of subscriptions, with the names of the contributors annexed. John, who was sitting on my right hand, now stood up, his tall, lean figure and mean costume making him very conspicuous, and said, with great seriousness, ' Mr. Secretary, put me down six guineas !' As those were not the days of great givings, the meeting was astonished. The secretary, knowing his narrow circumstances and large family, could not bring his mind to place so large a sum in connexion with John's name. This storm of benevolence from the Blue Mountains arrested the proceedings, till John, guessing the cause of the embarrassment, got up and relieved his friends. His heart was full at the thought of God's love to himself and family. Amidst flowing tears, and with broken accents, he assured the meeting of his deep sense of obligation to God his Saviour. He must be permitted, he said, to present the sum he had named, to promote a cause to which he was a great debtor. He concluded with a touching reference to two of his children, whom God had recently taken to glory. One of these, who had married a lay missionary of the Church, in New Zealand, returned to the colony, and died in the Lord. Every individual present was much affected: his name was entered on the subscription list, and his speech pronounced the best of the evening. As he literally sought first the kingdom of God and its righteousness, he found means in due time to pay his noble contribution."

On the 16th, Mr. Leigh had a lengthened interview with the senior chaplain, on the subject of the New-Zealand mission. The chaplain considered it a providential circumstance that Mr. Leigh had been in the country, and was personally known to several chiefs of authority and influence. He recommended the establishment of his mission at Mercury Bay, where there was a considerable population, and where he would be under the immediate protection of his friend 'Hongi. "I will give you letters," he observed, " of introduction to several chiefs, friends of mine; and, at the same time, urge upon the agents of the Church mission to afford you every facility in your work. The undertaking, as you are aware, is hazardous; but the Lord is with you. I should like to have a meeting of the committee of the Bible Society before you leave the colony. " Very well," said Mr. Leigh, and the time was fixed. The day appointed being inconvenient to the members of the committee, only Mr. Marsden, Captain Piper, and Mr. Leigh attended. " We shall not be able," said Captain Piper, "to proceed to business with our present number." Mr. Marsden replied, "Then let us try if we cannot do a little missionary business. I am told that you have two beautiful jackasses, Captain Piper. Now I wish to introduce the jackass into New Zealand. If you will sell them, I will make a present of them to my friend Leigh." "The jackasses to which you refer," said Captain Piper, " are indeed very fine ones. I have got them from England for two of my children; they will give them up with great reluctance; but, in the cause of missions, every thing must be sacrificed. They cost me £20, and you shall have them for the same money." ' "Then put them on board immediately," said the chaplain, "and I will consign them to my settlers at the Bay of Islands."

Mr. Leigh availed himself of the first opportunity to introduce Mr. Walker to the governor, as a "missionary to the natives of New Holland." His Excellency rejoiced to recognise him in that capacity. He had always felt a deep solicitude, he observed, for the civil and moral improvement of the aborigines; and his government, as missionary Leigh well knew, had made several rather expensive experiments, with a view to promote so desirable an object. He reminded Mr. Walker of the danger, difficulty, and self-denial necessarily attending his noble undertaking; but, at the same time, assured him that all the servants of the government would receive instructions to protect, assist, and encourage him.

A deep and general sympathy had been awakened in favour of this mission, by several appeals that had appeared in the "Sydney Gazette." The last of these was by an excellent person under the signature of *Philanthropus*. "I am now," he remarked, "closing my eleventh year's residence in the colony: and notwithstanding the various and reiterated appeals which have been made to the piety and humanity of my enlightened European brethren, in behalf of the aborigines of this land, nothing as yet, besides the government native institution, appears to be done to ameliorate their miserable and perishing condition. We therefore, with feelings of good-will to all, earnestly entreat those who are endued with benevolence and charity, to behold their peaceable and suffering fellow-creatures, without habitation, without clothing, without food, without comfort, without hope, without God! With such a sight, who can remain unmoved? Shall we manifest no sympathy or compassion for them? Are they not men and brethren? Have we not all one Father—God? one father—Adam? And shall we despise or disregard the soul or the body of our brother? 'If thou forbear to deliver,' from distress or death, 'doth not He that pondereth the heart consider it? And He that keepeth thy soul, doth not He know it? and shall not He render to every man according to his works?' O Christian! did thy Saviour show so much kindness and condescension towards thee, as to make Himself of no reputation, that He might raise thee from poverty and wretchedness, and exalt thee to happiness and glory everlasting? and canst thou be indifferent to the state of thy perishing brother? If any possess this world's goods, or any spiritual privileges, 'and see his brother have need, and shutteth up his bowels of compassion from him, how dwelleth the love of God in him?' We have heard of a projected design to promote the improvement of all the aborigines in these settlements, by endeavouring to lead them to a knowledge of Christianity and its benign influence and happy effects on mankind. But where now are its friends and supporters? Who among us will assist in the pious work of attempting to instruct and Christianize the sable tribes of New Holland?

> 'How do I pity those who dwell
> Where ignorance or darkness reigns!
> They know no heaven, they fear no hell,—
> Those endless joys, those endless pains!'"

To those barbarians, whom it was proposed, for the first time, to raise, by evangelical training, to the dignity and freedom of men, had been assigned the lowest place in the scale of intellect. This opinion has been supported by some of the highest scientific authorities. Their physical aspect differs in several respects

NATIVE HUT, AUSTRALIA.

from all the civilized races of Asia and Europe. The writer has now before him several beautifully finished portraits of natives of both sexes. They were executed by a convict, (formerly an artist of some celebrity in London,) at the expense of Mr. Leigh. In both height and weight, the New-Hollanders seem to differ but little from the English: but it would appear that one effect of continual hardships and privations, endured through a series of generations, is to eradicate from the human countenance almost all traces of beauty and proportion. The head and mouth are large, the face broad, the eyes dark and sparkling, the cheek-bones are high, and the skin of a chocolate colour. They rub their bodies over with fish-oil, to protect them from the effects of the climate, and the stings of innume-rable insects. This oil produces, in hot weather, an odour so strong that the cattle smell it at a considerable distance; and, being thus warned of the near approach of the blacks, whose spears they have been taught by experience to dread, hasten away to a place of safety. They decorate their persons with dogs' tails, having feathers fastened to them with gum, with human teeth, or the teeth of the kangaroo, and the jaw-bones of fishes.

A few branches of the *casuarina,* so disposed as to shelter them in the direction of the wind, constitute their only dwelling: against cold and rain they do not attempt to guard themselves. In the woods they make huts of the bark of a single tree, bent in the middle and placed on its two ends on the ground, afford-ing shelter to only one person. Upon the sea-coast, the huts are larger, and formed of several pieces of bark put together in the shape of a bee-hive, the entrance being in the side. These are of sufficient dimensions to hold six or eight persons. They live chiefly on fish, opossums, grubs, reptiles, and roots. Black and brown snakes abound in most parts of the country. They vary in length from three to fourteen feet. "The black snake," says Mackenzie, "I have not only seen eaten, but dined on it myself. When broiled, it is as white as an eel, and as tender as a chicken. The natives, however, will not eat of it unless it is killed by themselves. The reason is obvious: a white man seldom suc-ceeds in killing a snake with the first blow: the consequence is, that the animal, being only wounded, becomes desperate, and often, in the agony of dying, thrusts its fangs into its own body, and thus diffuses the poison through every part of it." The same author adds, "The bite of these animals is almost certain death." The spear and boomerang are used in procuring animal food. The curved and recoiling boomerang will skim over the ground twenty or thirty yards, then rise a hundred feet, and, after killing a bird perched on a branch at that height, return to the precise spot whence it was thrown. No European

has, as yet, discovered on what principle of projectiles this singular instrument is constructed.

Notwithstanding the presence of Europeans on the coast of
Australia for fifty years, here is still a vast community living in
voluntary savageism. What an anomalous race of beings!
Shrewd and intelligent, yet not possessing even the first rudiments of civilization; utterly ignorant of all the principles of
art or science, yet able to obtain a ready livelihood where a
civilized man would perish; knowing nothing of any metal, possessed of no mechanical tool, and yet able to fabricate weapons
of a most formidable description; having neither house nor
home, domesticating neither bird nor beast, cultivating neither
grain nor fruit; naked, yet unwilling to bear the restraints of
clothing; looked down upon as the lowest in the scale of humanity, yet proudly bearing themselves, and contemning the
drudgery of the men who despise them; confiding, cheerful,
kindly of disposition, yet treacherous, inflexible in revenge, and
glorying in massacre; enjoying the most unrestrained liberty,
yet in daily danger of death: living, in short, in a state of society resolved into its first elements; having no worship and but
little superstition, revering no God, dreading no devil, knowing
no law human or Divine, without rule of conduct in this life,
without hope of reward or fear of punishment in the next!

They have no writings, no signs to record past events, no
works of art, no monument of any description. They do not
acknowledge any Supreme Being, yet their belief in the existence of spirits is universal. As might be expected, their notions
of a future state are vague and unsatisfactory. It is a well-
ascertained fact, that they have been in the habit of eating the
bodies of those taken in war. They are short-lived, and have
the appearance of old men and women at the age of forty years.
This premature decay is, no doubt, partly owing to their constant exposure to alternations of heat and cold, and to their pre-
carious mode of procuring subsistence: this week they feed like
beasts of prey, and the next they may be compelled to live for
several days without food. In the absence of medical skill, of
clothing, of house-shelter, and of stored provisions, the case of
the sick amongst them, especially in the winter season, is truly
deplorable.

Polygamy is practised to a great extent, and is the occasion
of much social discord and suffering. Infanticide is, and has
long been, prevalent amongst them. Captain Sturt, while on a
journey down the Murray, witnessed a black fellow kill his
infant, by dashing its head against a stone, after which he threw
it on the fire, and then greedily devoured it! Even the celebrated Bennellong, whose society was so much courted in Eng-

land, and who was supposed to have abandoned all the habits
of savage life, buried his daughter alive! After returning to
his own country, and spending six months with His Excellency
the governor, he threw off the military costume presented to
him by the king, and ran into the woods naked. Having followed his wife's body to the grave, he astonished the Europeans
present by taking his little daughter, and placing her along with
the corpse of her dead mother in the same grave. He gave the
signal, and the grave was instantly filled up by the natives in
attendance. When remonstrated with for this unnatural act, he
coolly replied,—that, the mother being dead, no woman could
be found willing to nurse the child; and that, therefore, it must
soon die a worse death!

Here is a race distinguished by great peculiarities, well worthy
the study of the philosopher, the attention of the philanthropist,
and requiring the aid of the missionary! "This nation of
savages," says the statesman, "has been taken under the paternal government of Great Britain, and claimed as her subjects."
Yes; but we have taken possession of their country; their very
existence has been overlooked, their natural rights have been
denied, their lands have been sold by the state, and their children disinherited! Should not some reparation be made to
these simple barbarians, and some pains taken to improve them
in the arts of life? Should not some expense be incurred for
the gradual amelioration of their wretchedness? And by whom
should the burden of this work of justice and mercy be borne?
by the settlers, by whose means the land has been secured as an
extension of the dominions of their native country? or by the
British nation, which has acquired so vast a territory by such a
bloodless conquest, and upon such easy terms?

Much has been plausibly and eloquently said and written
respecting the kindness and forbearance of the European population; but we are prepared to show that there has been, at
least, equal forbearance on the part of the aborigines. Many of
the colonists along the frontiers have treated them like wild
beasts; whilst their intercourse with them has been characterized
by the grossest duplicity and fraud. The natives have seen
their wives and daughters perishing in the woods, the victims
of the most loathsome colonial diseases. Is it any wonder, if it
has been found difficult, from time to time, to soothe the angry
spirits of men, smarting under a deep sense of such unmerited
injuries? Had they been a martial and united people, they
would long since have mustered an army of sufficient numbers
to have driven their foreign invaders from their shores.

In her colonizing projects, Great Britain, with all her preten-
sions to literary and religious distinction, would have acted with

greater consistency, had she adopted the policy of the ancient Egyptians. In adjusting the population to the capabilities of their country, they sent out colonies, under experienced leaders, to people and to cultivate other fertile regions of the earth. In this way they extended their foreign commerce, and advanced the national wealth and glory. But, wherever those colonies went, they carried with them the gods, the laws, the arts, and the worship of the mother-country. In this way they spread the knowledge of science and religion over the nations of Greece, and ultimately over the world. If, when Great Britain broke up the Mogul empire in the east, dethroned the native princes, and appropriated their revenue to her own aggrandizement, she had been faithful to her commission as a Christian state, she would long since have taught the millions that people the plains of India to sing, "with a loud voice, Worthy is the Lamb that was slain to receive power, and riches, and wisdom, and strength, and honour, and glory, and blessing;" and the sable tribes that cover the mountains and forests of Australia to respond to them in the sublime language of the Psalmist, saying, "The Lord reigneth; let the earth rejoice; let the multitude of isles be glad thereof."

We would not be understood to insinuate that *nothing* has been done to concentrate and reclaim the savages of New Holland. Several schemes have been adopted, with various degrees of success. Scores have been roused from their native indolence, and brought to adopt European customs and habits of industry. They supply the colonists with wood and water, are trustworthy guides and messengers, and can both read and write. Some are also found at the communion-table, who "worship God in the spirit, and rejoice in Christ Jesus." But nothing has been done worthy of a great Christian state, or commensurate with the valid claims of the numerous and diversified tribes that lie scattered over the wide fields of the great southern continent.

Such were the character and condition of the people among whom Mr. Walker was about to establish his mission. Paramatta was to be the head-quarters; and thence the missionary was to proceed to the interior, and put himself in communication with the natives. This was a work of greater danger, difficulty, and labour than is ordinarily supposed. The different groups of natives wander about over a vast range of country, having no settled abodes; each group frequently separating itself into smaller divisions, for the sake of obtaining food, occasionally encroaching upon the territories of the neighbouring tribes, or commingling with them when on friendly terms. Their dialects differ essentially from each other; and they are themselves by no means of a communicative disposition.

When all due preparations had been made, Mr. Leigh took the newly-arrived ·missionary, and introduced him to the aborigines.   The first tribe they met with were related to the chief Bennellong, who had died a short time before.   "I happened," said Mr. Leigh, "to have a portrait of this celebrated chieftain, which had been taken in England, in my pocket at the time.   I took it out, and showed it to them.   When they looked upon his features, they were astonished, and wept aloud. 'It is Bennellong!' they cried.   'He it is!   Bennellong!   O, he was our brother and our friend!'   The scene was so affecting, that Mrs. Leigh and the missionary, who were present, mingled their tears of sympathy with the ·Heathen.   As soon as they had recovered from their grief, we entered into conversation with them; for this tribe can speak English.   As some of the missionary's expressions were unintelligible to the young people, they laughed.   The chief observed it, and instantly reproved them.   'You no laugh,' he observed, 'when the teacher speaks to you.   He be our parson.   You mind what he speaks.   He come to do black man good.   We must be good, no get drunk, no swear.   You young children, mind book. Old people no like book: very good young people learn the good book.'"   This interview made a favourable impression upon the mind of the young teacher, and led him to believe that barbarians possessing such warmth of feeling and gentleness of manners would soon be won over to the faith of Christ.

In a few days afterwards he witnessed a new developement of the native character.   "I fell in," said he, "with a tribe of natives as I was returning from Paramatta to Sydney.   Many of them were intoxicated; and, on such occasions, they are like incarnate devils.   Both the drunk and the sober knew me. I felt anxious to lead them into the woods, knowing that if the convicts met them, there would, in all probability, be fighting and bloodshed.   They followed me; but such a noise I never heard, and such barbarity I never before witnessed.   They struck the women on their heads with their *waddies* with such violence, that I expected nothing less than the death of some of them.   When one man lifted his *waddy* to strike another, I stepped in between them.   I then turned, and saw another bleeding profusely.   Before I had wiped away the blood from the head of one, another was in danger.   I said that I would not live with such a people.   This produced a clamour which made the woods ring; and all vociferated, 'Parson, do stay! Parson, don't leave us!'"   Mr. Walker applied himself diligently to the study of the native dialects, preaching, in the mean time, to the European settlers, and to such New-Hollanders as understood a little English.

It was supposed that an agricultural establishment might be connected with the mission in New South Wales, with every hope of advantage to the natives; and Mr. Leigh submitted to the governor a proposition to that effect. His Excellency replied: "Your pious and humane proposal to direct your labours towards the improvement of the natives is highly praiseworthy, and demands my best acknowledgments on the part of this government, as well as on the part of those poor ignorant people themselves, whom I consider as also placed under my immediate protection. But the Rev. R. Cartwright, the present chaplain of Liverpool, having tendered his services to superintend a native school or seminary, on a large scale, and also connecting with it an agricultural establishment in *the interior*, I deemed it advisable to refer his proposal to the consideration and approval of His Majesty's ministers, whose decision has not, as yet, arrived in the colony. As soon as you have digested your plan, bring it to me, and we will talk it over; and in any thing that I can do, by way of building a chapel, giving grants of land, awarding government servants to clear it, and tools for the natives to work with, I shall be most happy to meet your wishes." But, alas! with the small means of the missionaries, and a very limited colonial revenue, what could either they or His Excellency accomplish?

Just at this period intelligence was received from New Zealand, which left no doubt that war had broken out in that country, and that hundreds had already fallen in battle. Mr. and Mrs. Leigh were urged to remain in New South Wales until the fury of the contending tribes had, in some degree, subsided. In this, the unanimous opinion of their friends, they felt obliged to acquiesce.

On October 11th, 1821, Mr. Leigh's official duty called him to Windsor, where he baptized the infant son of the Rev. B. Carvosso. During the administration of that ordinance, he was unusually earnest and protracted in prayer. At the close of the service he said, "That child will be the subject of early piety, and inherit the true missionary spirit." This devout wish—for it can only be regarded in that light—was fully realized by the child and his parents. After an exemplary career of educational progress and filial piety, he died in great peace in the twentieth year of his age.

On December 11th Mr. Leigh waited on their Excellencies, Governor Macquarie and Governor Brisbane, to take leave, being on the eve of sailing for New Zealand. Sir Thomas informed him, that the last communication received by the government was exceedingly unfavourable. Several districts had been nearly depopulated, and there was no immediate prospect of a cessation of hostilities. He presented Mr. Leigh with great quantities of seeds of various kinds, and earnestly hoped that Divine Providence would protect him. The friends again urged the propriety of his waiting, at least, until the arrival of his assistants from England. After listening attentively to all that was advanced, Mrs. Leigh said, with deep feeling, "Samuel, I have heard nothing that has shaken my confidence in God. Our friends at home expect us to do our duty. Notwithstanding the kindness of Christian brethren here, I shall not be happy another day in the colony. We are prepared for death or life in the discharge of our duty."

On the following evening Mr. Leigh preached a farewell sermon in Macquarie-street chapel, from Phil. i. 27: "Only let your conversation be as it becometh the gospel of Christ: that whether I come and see you, or else be absent, I may hear of your affairs, that ye stand fast in one spirit, with one mind striving together for the faith of the gospel." The congregation was large, and all the missionaries in the colony attended on the occasion. One of the brethren, who was present, said, "His parting address was truly spiritual and impressive, and the whole audience was deeply affected. Three days afterwards despatches were received from the Bay of Islands, stating that, after skirmishing with each other along the coast for nearly one hundred miles, the exasperated warriors had carried the fight into the interior; and, as they granted no quarter, the slaughter had been great. Mr. and Mrs. Leigh were unmoved by the tidings, and seemed to be saved, by the grace of God, from all fear. They are determined to go amongst these cannibals, and offer them the salvation of the gospel. At four o'clock, on the morning of the 31st of December, 1821, a party of us accompanied brother and sister Leigh to their ship, where we took leave of them. May the God of missions be their defender from the violence of savage men!" In the evening, the brethren closed the year with a watch-night of great solemnity and power.

After an agreeable run, it was announced from the masthead, that New Zealand was rising to view. "When I stepped upon the deck," said Mr. Leigh, "and looked towards the shore, and then at my wife, and reflected upon the probable consequences of our landing, I felt as if divested of all spiritual strength. We were running in upon a nation of ferocious and blood-thirsty Heathens, where there was no power to protect, and while the country was convulsed by war. Never shall I forget the agony of mind I endured, until reflection brought me to feel that I was surrounded by the Divine perfections, and that a hair could not fall from our heads without the concurrence of God."

They sailed into the Bay of Islands on the 22nd of February, 1822. Those natives who had previously known Mr. Leigh hastened to bid him welcome, which they did by rubbing noses and shedding a profusion of tears. While a succession of individuals thus saluted him, until the skin was entirely rubbed from the point of his nose, they shouted, "Glad, very glad, to see the white teacher!" They examined Mrs. Leigh's dress with a troublesome minuteness, and inquired why she had left her pickaninnies on board the ship. Being informed that she had no children, they tossed their heads indignantly, and said, "Then she be no good: the white teacher be poor man."

From his old friends of the Church mission Mr. Leigh met with a cordial reception. Those brethren might have regarded him as having come into the country for the avowed purpose of setting up a rival ecclesiastical agency; but, instead of yielding to sectarian and petty jealousies, they hailed him as a fellow-labourer, and gave to him and his wife the best accommodation which their settlement afforded. Fish and potatoes were soon provided, and, after dinner, Mr. and Mrs. Leigh mingled freely with the natives; Mr. Leigh making the best possible use of the Maori words and phrases which he had learned during his former visit.

He then inquired whether the asses, sent from New South Wales, had not arrived. One of the settlers replied, "They have arrived; but they have been seized by the natives, and carried off." "Indeed!" said Mr. Leigh: "by what natives?" "By those with whom you have just been conversing," he observed. "Then let them be called," said Mr. Leigh. On their arrival, he inquired why they had carried off the asses, and what they had done with them. He informed them, that they had been purchased and sent by their friend Mr. Marsden, who had charged him to take special care of them. They stated that the "great pigs" having gone upon their *wenua tapu*, where their dead lay, they had tied their legs, put them on board a canoe, and landed them upon a desolate island. "But," said Mr. Leigh, "they did not know that the land was *tapu*, being strangers in the country." "If they did not," they observed, "the white men did; and they should have taken care of them." The loss of the asses being thus imputed to the inattention of the white men, roused the indignation of one of the settlers who was present. Imitating the rage of the natives, he defended himself and his brethren from the vile insinuation, stamping and scolding until a large wig which he wore was shaken off his head. One of the chiefs called the attention of Mr. Leigh to his countryman, remarking, "You see, teacher, he is an angry man: let him take his wig and go home: we shall have nothing to do with him."

Late in the evening the " large pigs," as they called the asses, were brought back in good condition. The people having assembled, Mr. Leigh said, "If these animals had sense, I would address them in the severest language of reprehension." He ordered their heads to be turned towards himself, when, looking them sternly in the face, he elevated his voice, and upbraided them for their base ingratitude, pointed out their indecency in having gone upon land that had been *tapu*, and expressed a hope that they would not transgress again. He assured them, that, while they respected the customs of the country, the New-Zealanders would treat them with kindness; but that if they violated those customs, they would deserve a second banishment to the desolate island from which they had just come. After this severe reproof, the natives agreed to give the asses another trial.

Two valuable horses which Mr. Marsden had previously sent over, for agricultural purposes, had been killed for the same offence. Nichols records a similar incident :—"A cock and hen were presented to a native and his wife by the captain of a trader, who told them, that, if taken care of, they would breed, and be of great service to them. The cock would be satisfied with no place for his roost but the roof of a small building, which was *tapu*, and, of course, made sacred. Here he regularly perched himself, in utter contempt of the awful prohibition. He was frequently driven from the mystical edifice, but he as often returned. At last it was determined, as the just punishment of his sacrilege, to banish him from that part of the country; which was accordingly done."

Mr. Leigh observed, that, although the number of settlers had increased since his former visit, and the arrival, a few months before, of the Rev. J. Butler, the first ordained clergyman, had given a church-form to their proceedings and worship, yet the cause of Christianity had not experienced any considerable enlargement. Feeling much solicitude on the subject, and inquiring into the cause of so lamentable a state of things, the brethren observed, that their own serious attention had, for some time, been directed to the same subject; but, after mature consideration, they had reason to believe that the depressed state of religion amongst them was to be traced to other causes than that of remissness in the discharge of their official duties. "Till within a few months," they observed, "we enjoyed comparative tranquillity, and there were not wanting many cheering indications of coming success in our labours. All the chiefs were disposed to live in peace. Many of them are sensible men, and well disposed; and would devote themselves to various useful pursuits, if they had any reasonable hope of reaping the fruits of their industry. They had made as much progress in civilization as could have been reasonably expected in the time. They gave us every encouragement to establish schools, and to go into the interior, to converse with the natives and preach the gospel. The savage customs and manners of the people in our district were much softened, and we possessed both their confidence and esteem. We employed ten natives in farming, fencing, gardening, and looking after our hogs, cows, and goats. We had eight native sawyers cutting wood. They all victualled with us, went on exceedingly well, and were improving very fast. We have ten acres of land fit for sowing this seed-time, and intend to raise on it wheat, barley, oats, and peas. Our garden, which is three-quarters of an acre, is well stocked with various sorts of vegetables and fruit-trees. The return of your friend 'Hongi has entirely changed the face of things. He and his allies have plunged the country in war, and seem determined to sweep it with the besom of destruction, unless prevented by our God."

While the following circumstances disclose the origin of this calamitous war, they throw considerable light upon the Maori character. In returning from England, 'Hongi and Waikato called at New South Wales, and spent a short time under the hospitable roof of Mr. Marsden. Here they met with Hinaki and another chief, who had taken their passage to London, that they might "see the land of the white men." 'Hongi, in describing his visit to the "country of great muskets and great ships," dwelt with significant emphasis on the grandeur of King George, and the splendour of the military spectacles he had witnessed. He had marked the reluctance of the king and his people to supply him with muskets and gunpowder. Of the intelligence, industry, and religion of the English people, he had taken but little notice. Mr. Marsden, perceiving that his bosom was fired with ambition, and that the insight he had obtained into the wealth and arms of Great Britain, had only increased the intensity of his desire for distinction and blood, endeavoured to persuade Hinaki and his companion, for the present, to give up their voyage to London, and return to their own country with 'Hongi and Waikato. With this request they complied, on hearing that the climate had nearly killed 'Hongi, and that it was extremely difficult to get muskets and gunpowder. 'Hongi gave them an account of his interviews with the committees of the Church and Wesleyan Missionary Societies, and told them that Mr. Leigh might be expected in a few weeks to commence a mission in New Zealand. After some discussion, they agreed to recommend the establishment of the mission at Mercury Bay, under the immediate protection of Hinaki and the other chief.

While Hinaki was expressing his satisfaction with this arrangement, 'Hongi said, abruptly, "Before that can be done, I have
a small affair to settle with my friend Hinaki.   During my
absence, I understand that one of my people has been killed
with a *maree*, by the River-Thames tribes, and I must have
satisfaction."   Then, turning to Hinaki, he said, with a distorted countenance and contemptuous sneer, "Go home with all
speed, and put your *pa* in the best posture of defence : for as
soon as I can get my people together, I shall fight you."   After
this unpleasant occurrence, they ate at the same table, slept
under the same roof, united in the worship of God, and sailed to
New Zealand in the same ship.   That 'Hongi might be prepared to execute his threat against Hinaki and his tribes, he
purchased large quantities of muskets, pistols, swords, and gunpowder, in Sydney, giving in exchange for those commodities
many of the valuable presents which he had received from the
king, from the missionary committees, and private gentlemen,
while in England.

During the voyage homewards, every means were employed by
Hinaki, consistent with his own dignity, to move 'Hongi from
his purpose, and secure peace; but that haughty chieftain was
implacable.   On reaching the Bay of Islands, Hinaki and his
friend hastened home to rouse the population of their respective
districts to resist the aggressions of the invader; while 'Hongi,
at the head of three thousand men, lost no time in entering
their territories.   The opposing armies met like two whirlwinds,
moving in opposite directions, and the event of the conflict was
for some time doubtful.   Hinaki and his brave followers, though
fighting upon unequal terms, made a vigorous defence.   At
length 'Hongi, who had the greatest number of muskets, and
had arranged his men in the form called in Roman tactics the
cuneus, or "wedge," placing himself at the apex, and directing
those behind him to wheel round on the enemy from right to
left, or to fall back into their original position, as opportunity
offered, shot Hinaki.   On perceiving his enemy fall mortally
wounded, 'Hongi immediately sprang forward, scooped out the
eye of the dying chief with his English knife, and instantly
swallowed it; and then, holding his hand to his throat, into
which he had plunged the knife, and from which the blood was
flowing copiously, drank as much of the warm fluid as they
could hold.   About one thousand of Hinaki's warriors fell in
the battle, three hundred of whom were roasted and eaten on
the field by the troops of 'Hongi.   Hinaki was a man of exquisite symmetry, and of extraordinary muscular power.   He
received four balls before he fell.   He had two brothers engaged
in the same battle; one of them almost as fine a man as him-

self, the other about twenty years of age: both were killed and eaten, excepting their heads, which were preserved as tokens of victory. The destruction of the natives was complete; and the place has never been inhabited since.

On his return to the Bay of Islands, 'Hongi brought twenty captives, bound hand and foot, in his canoe, whom he intended to retain as slaves. But his daughter, hearing of his arrival, and learning, at the same time, that her husband had been killed in the fight, came down to the beach, and accused her father of having been accessory to his death. To pacify her, and to make her some amends for the loss of her husband, he immediately caused the captives to be placed with their heads over the gunwale of the canoe, and, with a sword which he had received from the hand of royalty while in England, smote off the heads of sixteen of them in cold blood. Twenty more were also killed, roasted, and distributed amongst his men. And yet these costly oblations were not sufficient to appease the exasperated spirit of the widowed lady. She told her father, that he had no reason to be proud of his victory; that she considered it mean, cowardly, and cruel in him to have fought Hinaki's people with muskets, when they had only native weapons with which to defend themselves. Being determined to follow her husband to the *réinga*, she loaded a musket, and retired into the woods. She was soon missed by her friends, who, guessing the real cause of her absence, went in various directions in pursuit of her. After a tedious search, they discovered her lying in blood, but still alive: their god, they said, directed them to the spot. The ball, instead of passing through the head, as she intended, had passed through the arm near the shoulder. She soon afterwards strangled herself. Alas! there is nothing in Heathenism to relieve the mind in such extremities. Christianity brings in its doctrine of the atonement, and offers the pardon of sin, an assurance of God's favour, and eternal life through faith in Christ Jesus.

When Mr. Leigh spoke to 'Hongi about the atrocities perpetrated during his campaign against the tribes of the River Thames, he smiled, and remarked, " We must observe the customs of our country: the blood of Hinaki was sweet!"

Just at this time, the Rev. John Williams, of the London Missionary Society, cast anchor in the Bay. Writing to his father, he observed, "The large canoes are now returning from the war in every direction. The day before yesterday, several passed us; one or two of which had a man's head at the head and stern, and several prisoners they had taken in the war. One of our seamen went on shore, and saw ten heads of warriors, all preserved, brought from the field of battle. We have

FEMALE SLAVE, NEW ZEALAND.

received much kindness from the friends of the Church mission. I never was in a place so well adapted for the itinerant labours of active missionaries. The land is full of inhabitants, settled in villages about one mile distant from each other. Mr. and Mrs. Leigh, of the Wesleyan Society, are here. When they shall have acquired the language, they will be a blessing to the people. More good itinerant missionaries, with the blessing of God, will turn the lion-like New-Zealander into an industrious and peaceful citizen."

'Hongi, believing that the extreme difficulty which he experienced in procuring muskets and gunpowder was occasioned by the interference of the missionaries, shunned them, and became irritated and reserved. The natives, perceiving the change in his temper and bearing towards the brethren, also began to treat them with indifference and contempt. The labourers refused to work unless paid with muskets and powder. They entered the premises when they pleased, carried off whatever they could lay their hands on, broke down the fences, and seemed prepared for the perpetration of the greatest crimes. By the grace of God, his servants were enabled to bear those severe trials and provoking insults in the true spirit of Christian resignation. Mr. Leigh, at last, complained to 'Hongi of the conduct of the people, and desired his protection from such vexatious annoyances. During this interview he said, "Mr. Leigh, I have a grateful recollection of your kindness to me when I was in your country: I will not suffer a hand to touch you: 'Hongi has said it. You are making preparations, I suppose, for commencing your mission amongst the tribes at the River Thames and Mercury Bay. That mission will not now be necessary, as I intend to sweep that people from the earth. I would advise you to go to Ho-do-do, where my sister resides, and where you will obtain protection. But, to be plain with you, since you stand in the way of our obtaining muskets and powder, we New-Zealanders hate both your worship and your God. In our very hearts we hate them. They are not like ours. We only worship in sacred places, where no food has been either cooked or eaten. You worship any where! Our very children hate your worship: they have to turn round so many times;" (alluding to their being required to kneel at prayer;) "it is quite burdensome to them." Checking himself a little, and throwing an assumed smile over his features, he added, "When we have seen more of the Europeans, we may, perhaps, change our opinion!"

'Hongi was not in a temper to be reasoned with; and, the resolution once taken respecting the Mercury-Bay tribes, the execution followed with a surprising promptitude. He was soon at the head of one thousand fighting men, with whom he set out to renew hostilities, leaving orders to embody two thousand more, and send them after him. Before leaving, he and a detachment of his warriors applied to Mr. Leigh for the loan of his boat. After consulting with the Rev. Mr. Kendall and a few others, Mr. Leigh consented to let them have the boat. "We cannot work it," said they, "without the large oars." Mr. Leigh replied, "Then you shall have the large oars." Not satisfied with this, one of them demanded, in a very peremptory tone, the use of the little oars; to which Mr. Leigh at once objected. Putting on the ferocity of the savage, this individual renewed the demand: at the same time elevating and balancing his spear, he gave the missionary to understand that he must either give up the little oars or defend himself. Throwing open his breast, and advancing with a firm step towards the point of the spear, Mr. Leigh vociferated, "I will receive your spear; but I will not surrender the little oars!" At this moment 'Hongi, who had been in close conversation with another party, turned quickly round, and inquired into the cause of the altercation with the teacher. On being informed of the facts, he said to his infuriated warrior, "What do you mean? you are unreasonable. The teacher has given you his boat and his great oars. What would you have? You have grieved me! Flee into the woods, and never again look upon the face of 'Hongi."

It was not the value that Mr. Leigh attached to "the little oars," that led him thus to place his life in jeopardy; but, 1. To show them how sacred he considered the rights of property to be, and to teach them to respect those rights: 2. To check a rapacity which, if unchecked, would have multiplied its demands until it had reduced him to a level with themselves. Those who suppose that Mr. Leigh and his friends of the Church mission had only to explain and enforce the principles of religion and morality, and practically to conform to those principles in their intercourse with the people, are but imperfectly acquainted with the elements pervading social life in the country at the time. They had not only to lay down practical maxims, but also to stand by those maxims at the risk of every thing dear to humanity.

In their secular dealings with the natives, they laid themselves open to suspicion by the restriction which they imposed upon their articles of trade and barter. From their list they excluded those commodities which, of all others, were regarded as the most necessary and valuable. Those savages could not comprehend their motives, though they had sagacity enough to surmise that the missionaries withheld powder and muskets to prevent their rising to an equality with white men. By adopting this restrictive policy, they made themselves obnoxious to the people, and ran the risk of falling martyrs to their philanthropy. Their condition was not only embarrassing, but, on many occasions, perilous and perplexing in an extraordinary degree. They might say with the apostle, "We are troubled on every side, yet not distressed: we are perplexed, but not in despair: persecuted, but not forsaken: cast down, but not destroyed." It was in vain that the brethren expostulated with the people around them. Maddened by war, they said, "Our future condition will be as good as that of our fathers: the *réinga*" (or New-Zealander's elysium) "is a place where the spirits of the departed have every enjoyment of which their minds are capable of forming a conception!" By such reasoning as this did they shut out the exalted principles of Christianity.

'Hongi continued to prosecute the war with intense malignity for upwards of five years; during which time the whole northern part of New Zealand was over-run, from the North Cape to the populous districts of Waikato, Rotorua, and Waiapu. Great numbers were slain, and multitudes fled for refuge to the hills and to the woods. During his numerous conquests, 'Hongi gathered up the scattered fragments of many tribes, and sent them as slaves to the Bay of Islands. This was regarded at the time as a public calamity. It turned out, however, to be one of those dispensations in which the goodness and severity of Divine Providence appear conspicuous. They had been brought from various quarters to the only spot in the country where Christian truth was shining as a light in a dark place. They shared in that light: they attended the missionary schools and other means of grace: they learned to read and write; and some of them had firmly fixed in their minds the essential truths of the gospel. After a time, the rugged character of the chiefs and people in the Bay of Islands began to soften down, under the continued influence of Christianity: these slaves were liberated, and permitted to return to their respective districts and friends. Some went to the East Cape, others to Kawia, on the western shore. A few advanced down the course of the Wanganui River to its mouth. Several went to Cook's Straits, where their tribes had located themselves. Wherever they went, they spread the leaven of Christian truth, and created a desire for spiritual instruction, in regions where missionaries had never been. Messengers came to the Bay of Islands, from a distance of five hundred miles, to solicit teachers.

CHAPTER VI.

As 'Hongi had effectually closed the door against the Wesleyan mission to the River Thames and Mercury Bay, by declaring it to be his intention to prosecute the war in those districts until he had "swept the inhabitants from the earth;" and as Ho-do-do, which he had recommended, was too distant and perilous a voyage for Mr. Leigh to undertake alone; he was under the necessity of reconnoitring the coast in various directions nearer home, to ascertain the temper of the natives, and the most eligible site for a permanent residence.

While thus employed, Mr. James Stack arrived from New South Wales. He was a native of Portsmouth, and his family was well known in that town. Having experienced considerable reverses in their circumstances, James and his elder brother resolved, in the spirit of self-sacrifice, to emigrate to Australia, under very encouraging auspices. His brother, who held a tutorship in a respectable academy at Portsea, had embraced religion, and become a member of the Christian church. He persuaded James to go with him to his place of worship on the Sunday evening before they sailed. Here the gospel was preached with perspicuity and power. The text selected on this occasion was Zechariah ix. 12: "Turn you to the stronghold, ye prisoners of hope: even to-day do I declare that I will render double unto thee." This discourse made an imperishable impression upon the mind of the younger brother. On his arrival in the colony he was engaged in the surveying service of the government, and circumnavigated Australia. While pursuing this hazardous occupation, he experienced many remarkable deliverances both by sea and land. Those displays of the Divine goodness led him to decision; and, after due consideration, he united himself to the Wesleyan church. In the year 1822, the condition of the Heathen world excited much commiseration, and the cause of missions was ably pleaded both at home and abroad. Mr. Stack, feeling an intense desire to be employed in some department of missionary service, mentioned this desire to the colonial chaplain and the resident missionary. He wished, above all things, to go to New Zealand to assist his friend Mr. Leigh. Those gentlemen approving of his determination, and a wealthy merchant offering him, at the same time, a free passage to those islands, he regarded this concurrence of circumstances as a call of Providence. After encountering many difficulties, he reached the Bay of Islands in safety. "I am come," said he, "from a sense of duty, to share in your labours and trials, and intend to make myself useful in any occupation for which you may consider me to be qualified. My first business, I suppose, will be to learn the language; for then I can work on the week-days, and preach Christ on the Sunday." He applied himself assiduously and successfully to the study of the native tongue, for which he seemed to have a great natural aptness. In subse-quent years he was employed as the steward of the establish-ment, and kept an accurate account of every thing that occurred in connexion with the mission. After due trial and examination, he was received as an assistant, and afterwards as an accredited missionary.

Mr. and Mrs. Leigh had made considerable progress in the native tongue. They wrote prayers and hymns in English; and then, by the assistance of the brethren of the Church mission, with whom they still resided, they translated them into Maori. They taught the natives to repeat those prayers and to sing those hymns; and "while thus engaged," said Mr. Leigh, "in the open air, the Lord frequently poured His bless-ing upon our own souls."

Being informed that several extensive and populous villages were situated near the harbour of Wangari, and that Europeans might visit them without much personal risk, Mr. Leigh hired a fisher's boat and five natives, and left home for the purpose of examining that part of the country. For some time they had a moderate breeze; but, as night advanced, a storm came on, which drove them out to sea. The violence of the wind, the strength of the current, and the heavy waves with which they had to contend, carried them out of sight of land. The natives yielded to despondency, lay down in the bottom of the canoe, and left Mr. Leigh to manage the sail. After being tossed about till near midnight, the moon arose; and land was dis-tinctly seen in the distance. They bore down upon it, and found themselves near the harbour of Wangaroa. They were compelled, by stress of weather, to enter, and seek protection from the sanguinary tribes inhabiting that coast. Dr. B., of Edinburgh, had previously called, and humanely rescued the survivors of the massacre of the crew and passengers of the ship "Boyd;" but missionary Leigh was the first European that had placed himself in the hands of those cannibals since that bloody catastrophe.

As the night was far advanced, and the people were asleep, Mr. Leigh's natives fired off their muskets, to let them know that strangers had arrived, and that they were armed. The savages were roused from their slumbers, and, seizing their arms, came out to defend themselves, and take vengeance on their invaders. Mr. Leigh sought an interview with the chief who was present. He told him of their disastrous voyage, and begged that a hut might be appropriated to himself and his boatmen for the night. This was readily granted; and when the hut was pointed out to him, he crept into it, and was instantly followed by his five natives. He lifted his heart to God in prayer, sat down in a corner, and fell asleep. He had been asleep but a short time, when his people awoke him by pulling his legs. They were all awake, and lay quaking with fear; while the clamour outside was tremendous. "Do you hear?" said one of his men; "they are quarrelling about the time for roasting and eating us to-morrow." Mr. Leigh was so exhausted, that he felt quite indifferent to either life or death: he merely replied, "They cannot touch us without the permission of the white man's God; and I am sure He has not, as yet, consented to our being either killed or eaten: lie still and sleep." He himself slept till eight o'clock next morning. At that hour he rose and breakfasted. He then read the scriptures and prayed in the open air, being surrounded by one hundred and fifty natives, who presented a wild aspect, and seemed bent upon mischief. He felt uncomfortable, and was anxious to leave the place; but how to accomplish that object he could not conceive. He knew that his safety very much depended upon his own prudence and self-possession, and that the slightest indications of either fear or haste, on his part, would lead to his instant destruction. Appearances seemed to indicate that the savages were preparing to attack himself and his men on their attempting to unmoor their boat. Under those circumstances, he wisely asked the chief, whose name was Te Arā, called by the sailors *George*, if he would step into the boat with him, as he was anxious to see a little more of their spacious harbour. He consented; and, after sailing a short distance, they passed the hulk of a ship deeply embedded in the sand.

"That," said Te Arā, pointing to the wreck with his finger, "is all that remains of the ship 'Boyd.' The captain no good. Myself and another young chief met him at Port Jackson. He told us that he was going to our country for spars, and wished us to accompany him, and assist him in getting good ones. He was very kind at first; but after we had been a few days at sea, he insisted on our working with the sailors. We refused to work, and told him that we were chiefs. He did not believe us, and ordered us to be flogged. We told him that, on arriving in New Zealand, we should convince him that we were chiefs. We conducted the ship to Wangaroa; and, on landing, I told my father, who was principal chief, of the disgrace to which we had been subjected by Captain Thompson. He and the other chiefs resolved to have satisfaction; but, as there were seventy-four Europeans and five natives on board, armed with great guns and muskets, we could not, at first, conceive how it could be successfully demanded. At last it was suggested to request the captain to go on shore and select his own timber. He manned three boats, which I piloted up the River Kaio until out of sight of the ship. I then led the captain and his people into the woods, where I detained them until the tide turned, and left their boats dry upon the bank. While Captain Thompson was looking up a lofty spar, and admiring its beauty, I cut him down with my tomahawk. The natives who were with me struck the other Europeans at the same instant, so that all fell without being able to offer the slightest resistance. They were well armed; but no one had time either to fire his musket or draw his sabre. We carried the bodies to the boats, and took them to the village, where they were roasted and eaten. We continued our course down the river until we came within sight of the ship. At a given signal which the natives on board well understood, they rose up and murdered the remaining portion of the crew and passengers, excepting five, who escaped into the rigging, and were not killed until the following morning; and two children, who, on seeing the blood flowing on the deck, became quite frantic, and, before they could be caught, touched a chief, were made sacred by the touch, and could not be killed. In plundering the ship, my father set fire to the gunpowder, which exploded, killing himself and many others, and setting the ship on fire, which was burned down, as you see, to the water's edge." Having been repeatedly at Port Jackson, this chief could speak broken English, and entered into a detail of the above transaction without the slightest emotion.

After sailing about for a short time, Mr. Leigh landed with Te Arā, and walked towards the village. He desired his natives, who refused to leave the boat, to keep near the shore, and to pull quickly in when he should give the signal. The villagers came down upon him in considerable numbers; and, from their fierce, tumultuous, and ferocious appearance, he expected nothing less than personal violence. Any man, however strong his mind, or bold his natural disposition, must have felt his unprotected and perilous situation, on seeing a numerous body of naked savages rushing upon him with spears, brandishing their clubs, assuming the most terrific attitudes, and uttering the most discordant and unearthly yells. After a short but anxious interview, Mr. Leigh took his leave of them, and began to move towards the beach. They closed in upon him, formed a compact body, and almost surrounded him. The chief looked on with apparent indifference, and declined to interfere. Believing the crisis to have arrived, Mr. Leigh cried out, "Stand back! I have fish-hooks." Taking from his pocket a handful of fish-hooks, he threw them over their heads. They were taken by surprise; and while they turned round, and scrambled for the fish-hooks, he ran towards the beach, and succeeded in getting into the boat. Being persuaded that these fish-hooks were instrumental in saving the life of this intrepid missionary, we have much pleasure in recording the names of the donors: they were presented to him by Messrs. Turner and Co., of Birmingham. His boatmen soon cleared the harbour, and sailed with a gentle breeze and grateful hearts for the Bay of Islands.

Though he believed his life to have been in imminent danger on this occasion, yet, when Providence shut up his way in every other quarter, he cheerfully returned to those barbarians, and succeeded in establishing amongst them the first Wesleyan mission. On reaching home, their friends of the Church mission, and especially Mrs. Leigh, who did not expect to see her husband again till " the resurrection of the just," were affected to tears. Just at this season of severe trial, the Lord was eminently with them in all the means of grace.

But although Mr. Leigh was fully and usefully employed in studying the language, and in visiting and conversing with the natives, he yet felt deeply solicitous to form an enclosure of his own, that he might apply to it his own principles of cultivation. As 'Hongi had recommended Ho-do-do as being likely to form a suitable centre for a missionary settlement, he resolved to pay a visit to that neighbourhood; but as no European had visited that part of the country, it was impossible to anticipate the consequences of personal intercourse with the natives. The Church-mission boat was placed at his service; while the Rev. J. Butler, two other Europeans, and five natives voluntarily offered to accompany him.

They sailed from Rangahoo in April, at eight o'clock in the morning, and reached Doubtful Bay at midnight. One of the natives, who had assured them that he was well acquainted with the coast, reluctantly admitted that he knew nothing about it. In this state of uncertainty, they were obliged to go on shore, where they lighted a fire, and gathered themselves around it. After taking some refreshment and uniting in the worship of God, they stretched themselves upon the ground for the night, and soon fell asleep. At the dawn of the morning they arose, and, after breakfast and prayer, prepared to resume their voyage. They had not been at sea above an hour, when they discovered an opening inland, which they resolved to explore. They landed at the junction of a considerable river with the sea. Here they met with a native, who informed them that the place they were seeking lay a long way up the river. After ascending the stream for about twelve miles against an ebbing tide, they landed at Ho-do-do. This was the residence of 'Hongi's sister. On seeing the missionary party, she and her people burst into tears, and wept for joy. The news of their arrival spread with surprising rapidity; and the natives came from a great distance to see the strangers. The best provisions which the village afforded were set before them; "and the barbarous people showed them no little kindness." After this friendly repast, the Rev. J. Butler desired the assembled tribes to sit down, which they instantly did, when he addressed them in the most soothing and impressive terms. He described the object of their visit, and the gratification they felt in seeing them in their own country. At the close of his address, they pressed him to say what he thought of their bay, their river, their land, and their village, and whether he and his tribe would remain with them. On these topics Mr. Butler and his friends found it necessary to speak with extreme caution. Mr. Leigh stated, that it was necessary they should leave them for the present; and expressed a hope that they would offer no objection, as, should the weather change, they might be lost at sea, or, at any rate, would be prevented from seeing their families for several weeks to come. To conciliate their good feelings, he distributed amongst them a number of fish-hooks; presenting, at the same time, an axe to the principal chief, and another to 'Hongi's sister. They then moved towards their boat, which they reached without interruption, and descended the river with the falling tide.

Before launching out to sea, they held a consultation respecting the primary object of their visit to this dark region of the country. The conclusions to which they came were, "1. There is no convenient harbour for shipping. 2. There is no river of sufficient depth of water for the purposes of trade. 3. The whole district seems to be but thinly populated. 4. On these and other grounds, it is our deliberate judgment that Ho-do-do is not, at present, eligible as a mission-settlement."

They sailed from Doubtful Bay at three o'clock in the afternoon, passed the Cavalles, under a severe gale and heavy sea, at one o'clock A.M., and arrived at Rangahoo just as their families were assembling for morning worship. After recording these circumstances, Mr. Leigh adds, " Blessed be God for His preserving mercies to us, from the day we left home to the period of our return! We have sailed four hundred miles, in an open boat, on the wide ocean, and placed ourselves, for Christ's sake, in the hands of the dark sons of the forest, many of whom never before saw the face of a white man, and have been brought back in safety. May God give us success in our endeavours to reclaim the inhabitants of this land!"

The following extract may be interesting to some of our readers. "Expenses incurred by a visit to Ho-do-do, to examine its harbour, ascertain the condition of the people, and the number of adjacent villages:—

"One piece of salt pork, seven pounds; one piece of bacon, seven pounds; three quarts of rice; one and a half pound of tea; three and a half pounds of sugar; six bottles of porter; two bottles of brandy; three hundred fish-hooks; twelve knives; four razors; six pairs of scissors; and two axes. To four natives who navigated the boat, one hundred and fifty fish-hooks."

On the 13th of July, 1822, the ship "St. Michael," commanded by Captain Beveridge, sailed into the Bay of Islands, having on board the Rev. Walter Lawry, Mrs. Lawry, and several mechanics, on their way to establish a mission at Tongataboo.

The London Missionary Society sent nine missionaries to this beautiful and fertile island in 1797. Three of the nine fell victims to the intestine commotions and ferocious disposition of the inhabitants, instigated by a convict who had escaped from Botany Bay: the remainder, after enduring great hardships, were taken off the island in 1800. For several years no ship could approach its shores with safety. In December, 1806, the ship "Port-au-Prince" arrived in those seas, and was treacherously seized by the natives. Of her crew, consisting of sixty men, twenty-six were inhumanly massacred; seventeen fled from the island; and seventeen more concealed themselves in the different islands around. For some time after this period, the difficulties attending a mission to those islands appeared extremely formidable.

Captain Beveridge, who had frequently touched at Tonga, had made a favourable report of the disposition of the natives. Mr. Lawry had volunteered to go; and, when Mr. Leigh was in London, he obtained the consent of the committee to another attempt being made to bring the savages of Tonga to an acquaintance with civilization and Christianity. Preparations had been made for commencing this mission before Mr. Leigh left New South Wales; but Mr. Lawry remained to complete the arrangements. The "St. Michael" brought fresh supplies to Mr. Leigh, and the most cheering intelligence as to the state of the work of God both in the colony and in Van-Diemen's Land.

TONGAN DOUBLE CANOE.

On the following Sunday, Divine service was celebrated on board the "St. Michael." The devotional parts of the service were conducted by Mr. Hall, of the Church mission, and by Mr. Lawry. Mr. Leigh preached from Psalm cxxiv. 8: "Our help is in the name of the Lord, who made heaven and earth." A solemn service was held on shore in the afternoon, the officers and crew of the "St. Michael" increasing the usual congregation. Messrs. Hall and Lawry officiated. The sermon, which was listened to with deep attention, was founded upon Luke xii. 32: "Fear. not, little flock; for it is your Father's good pleasure to give you the kingdom." There was reason to believe that, before the "St. Michael" sailed, some of her officers received on board both pigs and potatoes, in exchange for powder and fire-arms. Those articles were not to be used, as in other countries, for the purposes of self-preservation, and of procuring the necessary means of subsistence, but were to be employed generally in revenging personal or conventional injuries. Mr. Leigh was of opinion, that every person putting those instruments of destruction into the hands of a savage, knowing that they would, in all probability, be used in shedding the blood of man, was an accessory before the fact, and responsible for all the acts of violence that might be perpetrated by them.

Any practical deviation from the instructions of the committee at home, on the part of its agents, he regarded as a criminal act of unfaithfulness. The obligations under which he had voluntarily placed himself to the Society, he felt to be binding upon him at home and abroad. He never lost sight of the great fact, that the Omniscient Eye, that witnessed the solemnities of his ordination, exercised a vigilant inspection over his motives and actions, though removed sixteen thousand miles from the scene of those solemnities! He looked upon the transaction in which the officers of the "St. Michael" had been concerned, as being opposed alike to the dictates of humanity and the authority of the magistrate. Submission to legitimate authority, whether civil or ecclesiastical, constituted part of his religion. "The British people," said he, "complain of the expense of civil government: let them come here, where there is not only no protection for property, but where any member of the community may wound, or even take life, with impunity; and they will soon be convinced that the benefits of civil government can scarcely be purchased at too great a price." The mission family had been for months without animal food, because they would not give muskets and gunpowder in exchange for it; and when these commodities were obtained from the officers of the "St. Michael," the disgraceful traffic was only calculated to exasperate the natives against the resident missionaries.

After the "St. Michael" sailed, Mr. Leigh and several others paid their first visit to the timber-country. They slept the first night in a native hut. Before retiring to rest, they had a long discussion with the priest of the tribe respecting the true God and the Christian religion. He was a man of great shrewdness and influence, and combined, in his own person, the offices of priest, sorcerer, juggler, and physician. He returned in the morning, but was less talkative. Deep mental anxiety was depicted in his countenance, while he said, "Your God appeared to me in the night, and spoke good to me."

After some conversation and a short religious service, Messrs. Leigh and Hall hired a canoe, and ascended the adjacent river. Observing a considerable number of natives and huts, they landed. The people came hastily down to the river-side; and the priest, stepping into the canoe, demanded an axe. Mr. Hall having refused to give him one, he quietly withdrew, but returned, in a few minutes, armed with an old European sword. Addressing himself to Mr. Hall, he exclaimed, "If you do not give me an axe, I will strike your head off, and take what you have got in your canoe." Mr. Hall took no notice of his threat; but, pushing him aside, stepped on shore, leaving Mr. Leigh to settle the affair. After some altercation, the priest left the boat in a passion, and went in pursuit of Mr. Hall. In the mean time, Mr. Hall returned by another path, and thus eluded his pursuer.

Having no confidence in those savages, they hastily unmoored the canoe, and sailed quickly up the river. Observing numbers of natives approaching the river-side, they again landed. The people were wild and clamorous for muskets and powder. They refused to allow them to reside amongst them, alleging that their God would kill all the natives. Mr. Hall addressed them, in Maori, from Psalm cxxxvii. 1: "By the rivers of Babylon, there we sat down, yea, we wept, when we remembered Zion." About eighty persons attended the service; but as one of them, a hideous-looking fellow, had got possession of a gun, and seemed, by his gesticulations, to challenge an antagonist, that he might show his dexterity in using it, he excited more attention than the preacher. After distributing a few fish-hooks, the missionaries entered their canoe, and, gliding down the river, reached home without interruption.

On the following Sunday, August 25th, 1822, Mr. Leigh attempted, for the first time, a regular discourse in the native tongue. Having ascertained that the people had left the village, and gone into the fields to plant potatoes, he and Mrs. Leigh followed them. Assembling them on their potatoe-ground, he preached a short sermon explanatory of the fourth commandment; and urged the reasonableness and necessity of devoting the seventh day to the worship of the true God. He said, in conclusion, "Mind what you do; for our God made heaven and earth, and will punish you if you break any of His commandments." Instead of waiting to controvert his statements, they threw down their implements of labour, and went home. As they were returning, they met the priest, who was coming out to know his reason for sending the labourers from the fields; when Mr. Leigh gave him a summary of the ten commandments. On alluding to the sixth, "Thou shalt not kill," the priest interrupted him, and, calling his attention to some bones that lay in a pile at a short distance, observed, with an indignant sneer, "These are the bones of a young woman whom *I killed* because she displeased me. I gave her body to my friends, who baked and ate it: I also put up that mat as a warning to others. These," said he, pointing in another direction, "are the bones of a young man whom *I killed* for stealing potatoes."

While Mr. Leigh was expostulating with him respecting these atrocities, he observed a promiscuous multitude of men, women, and children running towards the woods. "What is the occasion of that commotion?" inquired Mr. Leigh. A person present replied, "One of our natives was killed a short time since with a *maree* at the River Thames. The persons you see have got hold of a slave from that place, whom they are killing in revenge." This was quite enough for Mr. Leigh, who started off at the top of his speed, and came up with the moving mass as they were entering the wood. He now perceived the body of a human being, which they were dragging by the legs along the ground. They paused; but he pressed through the crowd, and reached the slave just as a tall athletic savage was lifting his axe to cut his body, which he had previously marked, in two. Without a moment's hesitation, Mr. Leigh rushed upon this formidable ruffian, and, seizing his arm, prevented the instrument from descending upon his victim. But while he was struggling with the murderer, the natives carried off the body of the young man, which they cooked and devoured at no great distance. The humane but perilous interference of the missionary was, on this occasion, unfortunately defeated.

Being informed that one of the chiefs was ill, he went directly to see him. He found him in great pain. "No doubt," said Mr. Leigh, "you have been praying to your gods to restore you to health." He replied, with vehemence, "I have not. Why should I pray to them? We have no *good* gods in this country. My god makes me sick. He is a bad spirit. He is killing me. Your God hears you, and gives you many good things. Pray to your God for me, and I shall get better. New-Zealand men know nothing : too much fight, too much eat men.   Europe people no eat men ; that be very good.   Pray for me."   After a long conversation, during which the aged warrior evinced much humility and teachableness, Mr. Leigh prayed with him; but the scene was peculiarly affecting.   There lay the barbarian, upon his mat, on the margin of the grave; turning with evident disgust from his cruelties and massacres, and feeling after the true God in the darkness and uncertainty of a bewildered intellect !   Who can describe the probable consequences of this last interview between the dying chief and the missionary?

On the 26th of May, the ship " St. Michael " called, on her return from Tonga, and gave an encouraging account of the reception of Mr. Lawry, and the commencement of the mission in that island.   The period for which the " St. Michael " had been chartered not having yet expired, Mr. Leigh resolved to detain her, for the purpose of assisting him to examine certain parts of the coast which he had not been able to visit.   It being commonly reported, that great numbers of natives had been seen in the vicinity of Wangari, Mr. Leigh, in company with several of his friends of the Church mission, sailed from Rangahoo to ascertain, by personal observation, the number and condition of the people in the bay and along the banks of the river.   The sea being calm, and the wind fair, they reached Wangari on the following day.   On landing, they were informed, that, only three years before, there were thousands of natives in the neighbourhood; but such had been the desolating effects of the late war, that within a circumference of twenty miles there were now but few villages and few families.   Next day they visited several creeks and bays, and penetrated as far into the interior as was judged prudent or safe, without having seen more than a few scattered inhabitants.   After dark they arrived at a small village, where they agreed to remain all night.   After a slight repast, they laid themselves down upon the ground, in the open air, and slept unmolested till morning.   After breakfast and prayer, they resumed their journey ; and about mid-day came to a considerable village in ruins.   The few natives that lingered about the desolate residences of their fathers, complained bitterly of the tribes who had invaded them.   They had burned the village, killed the people, and carried off the little property they possessed.   Such as survived those calamities had fled far into the interior, and were afraid to return. The chief showed Mr. Leigh, with evident satisfaction, the skull of one of his children, which, as he said, " he had been fortunate enough to preserve."   After mutual consultation, the brethren were of opinion, that Wangari did not afford facilities for the establishment of a permanent mission.   The natives said they were "a broken people." They were shy, dejected, and apparently destitute. When they saw Mr. Leigh and his friends preparing to leave, they evinced no hostile disposition, but sat down and wept.

In endeavouring to clear the harbour, the "St. Michael" took the ground, where she lay, in extreme danger, till after midnight. When the tide was near its height, the oscillation of the vessel indicated that the next half-hour would decide their fate. The capstan was now manned; and, by great exertion, aided by a slight swell in the river, the ship was worked into deep water. When the natives first saw the "St. Michael" upon the rocks, and observed that the captain and crew could not get her off, they assembled upon the shore, and vociferated, "*Te Tani 'wa*, 'the god of the sea,' is killing your ship: she is dying: the ship is ours, *Te Tani 'wa* has sent her to us!" According to their maritime laws or customs, the "St. Michael" had become the property of their chief, being stranded upon his territory. They would have boarded and taken possession of her; but, having no canoes, they could not reach her in sufficient numbers to overpower the crew. When the vessel began to move, Mr. Leigh made his appearance; he had been engaged, for several hours, in prayer to God for protection and deliverance. On ascertaining that the "St. Michael" had sustained but little injury, all hands were assembled on deck, and united in hearty thanksgivings to God.

The Rev. J. Butler, and Messrs. Shepherd and Hall, of the Church mission, now recommended another visit to Wangaroa. Mr. Leigh having consented, they sailed by the break of day on the 5th of June, passed the Bay of Islands at eight o'clock in the morning, and stood off Wangaroa at four in the afternoon. The entrance to the harbour is singularly beautiful and romantic. Near the northern head is a large perforated rock, presenting the appearance of a deep Gothic archway; the sea rolls through it, and the canoes find it a safe passage in moderate weather. The entrance is not more than half a mile wide, and it is impossible to discover it from any distance at sea. But it is deep, quite close to the land on either side, which is bold and steep; and, when once entered, is one of the finest harbours in the world. The largest European fleet might ride in it; nor is there a wind from which it is not completely sheltered. The interior is lined with lofty hills, richly wooded; and close to the western shore is a series of huge rocks, rising in the most fantastic shapes to an immense height; from the tops of which tumble many cascades that lose themselves among the innumerable trees and shrubs, with which the bases of those stupendous piles are profusely covered. The site of the *pa*, or "fort," of the natives, is an insulated rock, three hundred feet high, excessively steep, and in some places perpendicular: yet the natives ascend it without much inconvenience, and find sufficient room upon its extreme summit to form in considerable numbers. Its appearance is imposing; and, before the use of fire-arms, it must have been impregnable.

At an early hour on the morning of the 6th, the "St. Michael" was surrounded by native canoes, filled with men, women, and children. Mr. Leigh unhesitatingly landed amongst the people, who were called, by their own countrymen, "the man-eating tribes," and ascended the river to the residence of the principal chief. Along the banks of the river were seen several portions of the wreck of the ship "Boyd," and three of her carronades. The cabbages, turnips, parsnips, and carrots, sown by Captain Cook, were here and there to be seen, but much degenerated. The surrounding hills, which from their height and diversity of shape form a very splendid piece of scenery, are covered with wood; and the *kauri*, whose loftiness and richness of foliage distinguish it from the other trees of the forest, flourishes here in great abundance. When Mr. Leigh stepped from the boat, he was greeted with the salutation of friendship, *Haere mai ra: haere mai ra!* "Welcome! Welcome!" When *Haere mai ra* is not used on the approach of a stranger, he may conclude that the feelings of the people are not favourable towards him. On looking earnestly at him for a few minutes, several of them recognised him, and exclaimed, "This is the white man that gave us the fish-hooks,"—adverting to his former visit. After a short interview, the chief returned with him to the ship. As an apology for mixing the English with the Maori language, in his conversation, George observed, "Since I left the sea, my English has left me, and gone into the bush; but, now that you are come into the country, it will soon return to me again."

On the following day the natives became very troublesome, demanding muskets and gunpowder, and offering as much as one hundred baskets of *kúmara* for one musket.

On Sunday the 8th, Mr. Leigh conducted the first religious service ever held in this part of New Zealand. All present, both Europeans and natives, behaved well, and such as understood the English language felt "it good to be there." A tremendous thunder-storm came on, which deepened the solemnity and heightened the interest of the scene. The text selected for the occasion was 1 Samuel vii. 12: "Then Samuel took a stone, and set it between Mizpeh and Shen, and called the name thereof Eben-ezer, saying, Hitherto hath the Lord helped us!"

Early on Monday morning, a boat was manned; and, after

taking on board Mr. Leigh and the friends of the Church mission, they sailed up the river to the residences of George and Tepui his brother. They were situated in a beautiful and fertile valley, which was named "Wesleydale," about seven miles from the point where the river empties its waters into the harbour of Wangaroa, thirty-five miles north-west of the Bay of Islands, and twenty miles from Kiri-Kiri, commonly called Kiddu-Kiddu, the nearest station of the Church Missionary Society. The natives, numbering about two hundred souls, belonged to the Ngá-té-hura tribe, and occupied four villages within sight of each other. At the distance of five miles there dwelt, in the adjacent valleys, another tribe, called the Ngá-té-po; and to those two tribes, numbering about one thousand savages, Mr. Leigh proposed extending his labours. Having more confidence in Te Pune, chief of the Ngá-té-hura tribe, than in George, he claimed his special protection. Te Pune and his people had fled from the seat of war, and been located in this vicinity for some time past.

On the evening of the 10th, Mr. Leigh fixed upon an eligible site, on the sloping side of a low range of hills, and proceeded to erect a booth for the night, with branches of trees. During the erection of this frail and temporary dwelling, the natives frequently remarked, " Should the rain fall, you will be flooded, —you will be washed away:" but they took no notice of the observation. They had not, however, long retired to rest, before the "rain descended, the winds blew, and the floods came," and swept their booth, together with several boxes, containing carpenters' tools and various goods, which had been landed from the ship, into the river and the sea. The missionary party saved their lives by escaping at midnight to higher ground; but they suffered much from cold during this dreary and inclement night. This misfortune suggested the necessity of shifting their position; and after obtaining their canvass tent from the " St. Michael," they ascended to a more elevated situation, and pitched it in the name of the Lord.

On the day following, the foundation of a building was laid, of sufficient dimensions to serve the purposes of a dwelling-house and store-room. While Messrs. Butler and Leigh superintended the work, the ship's carpenter and the natives brought-in young trees, and cut them into equal lengths. Some of these were used as uprights, while others were placed lengthwise, and bound firmly together with cordage made from the native flax. The roof was thatched with grass and rushes. Calico was substituted for glass in the windows, but the building was without the protection of a door for several months. During the progress of this erection, the mission family slept in the tent, which, as it let-in the rain upon them, became very unhealthy, and induced general sickness.

On Sunday, the 15th, they were thrown into great confusion by the arrival of a war-canoe with slaves; one of whom was killed, roasted, and eaten in the village. The commandant wore a human scalp as a trophy and an ornament. Captain Beveridge could not be induced to place the slightest confidence in either of the chiefs, whom he regarded as treacherous villains, and became exceedingly anxious about the safety of his ship. He requested that no notice might be taken of himself or his men, while he made private arrangements for quitting the shores of this barbarous land unobserved by the natives. This he accomplished during the following week; and, at the same time, the friends from the Bay of Islands returned to their own settlement, with the exception of Mr. Shepherd, who was detained in consequence of the delicate situation of Mrs. Shepherd.

Mr. and Mrs. Leigh, being now left comparatively alone, felt the loneliness of their situation. The uncertainty that hung over the future was only relieved by the promise, "Lo, I am with you alway, even unto the end of the world." On the morning of Sunday, the 29th, one of the brethren expounded Luke xi. 13 : "If ye then, being evil, know how to give good gifts unto your children; how much more shall your heavenly Father give the Holy Spirit to them that ask Him?" In the afternoon they visited the residence of Tepui. His people attended in considerable numbers, and behaved well, while Mr. Shepherd addressed them on the character of the true Jehovah, the resurrection of the dead, and the future judgment. This was the first religious service they had ever attended; but, being addressed in Maori, they became wonderfully calm, and seemed to be overawed by a superhuman influence. Mr. Leigh preached in the evening, with much earnestness, from Mark xvi. 19, 20 : "So then after the Lord had spoken unto them, he was received up into heaven, and sat on the right hand of God. And they went forth, and preached every where, the Lord working with them, and confirming the word with signs following."

The invigorating services of the Lord's day prepared them, in some measure, for the varied trials of the ensuing week. As every article of food had to be cooked in the open air, Mrs. Leigh was under the necessity of protecting herself from the effects of almost incessant rain, by putting on her husband's great-coat and boots. During the process of cooking, the natives generally assembled and carried off every thing within their reach. Never having seen boiling water before, many of them plunged their hands into the pot to steal the contents, and, on being scalded, hastily withdrew them, exclaiming, "The water

NEW ZEALANDERS PREPARING FOR BATTLE.

has bitten our hands!" While Mr. Leigh dressed their wounds with ointment, he endeavoured to convince them that, in all their dealings with the missionaries, they would find honesty to be the wisest and safest policy. After this they used sharp-pointed sticks, which, with great dexterity, they thrust into the pot, and frequently succeeded in emptying it of the *kúmara*, pork, or fish, that might be in preparation for dinner; thus leaving the mission family without a morsel.

Still, with much that was trying and depressing were blended circumstances of encouragement. Religious services were held daily, morning, noon, and night, to which the natives were freely admitted. When any thing occurred to prevent the commence-ment of these services at the usual time, the domestics would call Mr. Leigh's attention to it, and inquire, "Why have you neglected prayer? Have you forgotten it? How can you expect us to learn, if you give it up?" If any one happened to retire to rest before evening worship, some of the others would follow the delinquent, and say, "You do wrong: you grieve the teacher: you be no good."

Their proceedings were again interrupted, on July 16th, by the unexpected arrival of a war-party from the Bay of Islands. They no sooner landed, than the Wangaroa tribes flew to arms, and mustered their forces in front of the mission premises. They commenced the war-dance, and became so excited that, in a few minutes, they were prepared to advance to either victory or death. One of the most conspicuous in these preliminaries was the principal wife of E Booas. She brandished a dagger, and made the most violent gesticulations. Mr. Leigh went down to salute the invaders, and spent two hours in earnest conversation with them. While thus engaged, Tepui impru-dently advanced and challenged them to the combat, stating "that he was ready to fight them, and that his warriors were not willing to be detained in the field, by their cowardice, till to-morrow." At the request of Mr. Leigh, the Bay-of-Islanders took no notice of this challenge. The chief George disapproved of the conduct of Tepui, and remonstrated with him. Tepui paid no attention to his remonstrance; which so exasperated George that, in order to mortify and vex his brother, he seized Mr. Leigh on his return to the mission-house, and threw him violently to the ground: he then attempted to lay hold on Luke, the servant, who eluded his grasp, and fled to the camp. No sooner had Mr. Leigh entered the house than Tepui, to be revenged on George, ordered his fighting men to attack the premises.

The journal written on the spot says, "The savages flew like arrows; they soon removed all obstructions, and entered our enclosure on all sides.   Mr. Leigh desired the door to be well barricaded, which was instantly done.   The chief, George, forced his way into the yard, and threatened to shoot the first person who should presume to venture within the range of his musket. The tumult and uproar that ensued led us to believe, that the hostile forces had met, and that the work of destruction had already commenced.   Our natives screamed; and Mrs. Shepherd, who was near her confinement, fainted, and lay for some time in a state of utter unconsciousness.   'See,' said Luke, 'they are robbing us of every thing: we shall all be murdered!' Having, as we supposed, but a few minutes to live, we knelt down, and commended our souls into the hands of God.   After repeated assaults, they were unable to force open the door; and, towards evening, the Bay of Islands' chief desired an interview with Tepui; when, after mutual explanations, they became friends, and ratified the agreement by an exchange of muskets.   This day has proved to us the necessity of living above the fear of death. There was much disturbance about our dwelling during the night; but we rested in peace.   Blessed be the name of the Lord!"   Next day the warriors took possession of the tent; and, as they refused to give it up, it was taken down.   On distributing a boxful of axes amongst them, they quietly withdrew, and returned home.

When Mrs. Leigh left the Bay of Islands, one of her domestics, who had evinced some concern about her soul, wished to accompany her to Wangaroa.   Being informed that to take her with them would, in all probability, be the occasion of war between the two tribes, they judged it best to leave her behind.   They were much attached to her, and made her several presents at parting; but nothing seemed to mitigate her sorrow.   After they left, she retired to her hut, which she set on fire during the night, and burnt herself to death.   Mrs. Leigh learned the fate of this interesting young savage from the Bay-of-Islanders, who had just left Wesleydale.

Having happily got rid of those troublesome and dangerous visitors, the brethren resumed their ordinary occupations, and carried forward their improvements with energy and perseverance.   It being found necessary to expostulate with a chief for an act of great cruelty inflicted upon the person of one of his slaves, he was instantly roused to a paroxysm of rage and indignation.   "What!" said he, with the voice of a lion; "do you talk of crime and cruelty to me?   I have been in New South Wales, and witnessed the amusements, drunkenness, and riot of white men.   They curse, they steal, they kill: go and teach your countrymen your religion.   Your own people will not embrace your Christianity.   You speak of cruelty: I saw them hang a white man at Sydney; and never did I witness so horrible a spectacle. They kept him in prison several days after they told him he must die: was not that cruel? They brought him out alive, and hung him up before all the people: was there no cruelty in that? We have no such custom in our country. When we intend to kill, we watch for a convenient opportunity, and, when the person least expects it, we bring him to the ground in a moment with one blow of the *maree*." Being reminded that the New-Zealanders put people alive into their ovens, he replied, "Never, unless there has been a fight or a quarrel; but there was no fight or quarrel when the white man was hung at Sydney."

Mr. Leigh had, for some time, felt anxious to have the property which he had purchased and built upon secured to the Society. Anticipating the colonization of the country by Great Britain as a probable event, and an official inquiry into the transactions that were taking place between the Europeans and natives at the Bay of Islands, he resolved that no persons coming after him should have it in their power to charge him with either duplicity or injustice. He had marked off about five acres of land, taken possession of it, and promised to give a fair price for it. The contract had not yet been ratified, owing to the difficulty of ascertaining who were the rightful owners of those acres, all claiming an interest in them who had at any time lived upon them. When the chiefs had settled this point amongst themselves, they made their respective demands upon missionary Leigh. Each was prepared to sell his interest in the land for so many spades, hoes, blankets, and pairs of trousers. The articles were taken down as enumerated, and the whole list read over to them. They were then asked, "Is this all you demand for the land?" They answered, "Yes." "Then I tell you," said Mr. Leigh, "that I should be doing wrong, were I to give you no more than you have asked: in justice to you, I must give you twice the quantity that you have demanded."

On the following day the chiefs came for payment, when their goods, which had been done up in separate bundles, were delivered to them. They ratified the bargain by transferring the distinctive mark of their respective tribes, from their tattooed faces, to a document which had been previously prepared. In subsequent years, when the equity of all such documents was tested, by order of the British government, and such as had purchased four or five miles of coast-land for a musket were obliged to relinquish their estates, it was declared in open court, that the Wesleyan property at Wangaroa had been settled on the most honourable terms.

As the wooden chimney which they had put up in the new house soon gave way, subjecting them to great inconvenience and some danger, it became necessary to contrive a more substantial erection. As they had no instruments for quarrying or dressing stone, and were fourteen hundred miles from the nearest brick-kiln, they were led to a careful examination of the soil in their own immediate neighbourhood, when a small bed of indifferent clay was discovered. Mr. Leigh prepared a mould, and soon produced bricks, which he dried in the sun. Beyond this, however, they could not proceed, as they had neither lime nor any substitute for it. Sailing up the river one day in pursuit of timber, they passed a vast heap of shells lying on the bank. "What is that?" said Mr. Leigh. The natives replied, "Cockle-shells." He landed, and, assisted by his boatmen, laid alternate layers of shells and wood, until he had raised a large pile, to which he set fire. Returning home a few days afterwards, he found the pile consumed, and as much lime as filled his boat. He made a square box of thin boards; and formed a sieve, by stretching the fibres of the native flax across the bottom of the box, through which he passed the lime. With a trowel made of wood, he commenced bricklaying; and built a chimney, which stood a monument of European ingenuity and industry long after the hordes of 'Hongi had cleared the country of its tribes, and reduced the adjacent buildings to ashes.

These laborious occupations had worn the shoes from off the feet of the missionary, and rendered another exercise of his inventive powers indispensable. He took a piece of wood, and shaped it into the form of a shoe-sole: while his wife cut the upper part of the shoe from a dog-skin, which had been dressed with the hair on. This was nailed down to the wooden bottom, which was sawn across, so as to form a hinge. The native earths were employed by the natives for tanning and dyeing the dog-skin in several colours. Their stock of soap, salt, and candles being exhausted, Mrs. Leigh manufactured those articles from tallow, wood-ashes, and salt water.

Those secular employments, forced upon them by circumstances, were not allowed to interfere with their more appropriate and religious duties. Devotional and exhortatory meetings were regularly held; and, in their daily intercourse with the natives, the brethren endeavoured to communicate useful knowledge, and at the same time acquire a more accurate acquaintance with the Maori language. They found the Lord's day, when they could worship in peace,—which, however, was seldom the case,—to be peculiarly elevating and invigorating to faith and hope. It was their practice to prepare discourses in short sentences, on the creation, the fall of man, redemption by

Christ, and future rewards and punishments, and to deliver them in the native tongue.

Mrs. Leigh commenced an institution for training native females, and formed a small class of the daughters of several chiefs. One of the conditions of admission into the class was, that they should submit to be washed with soap and water. As none of them had ever been washed before, they submitted to the process with great reluctance. Being assured that the washing made their complexion more like that of the Europeans, which was really the case, they became more reconciled to it. We subjoin a brief description of the first lesson, that the reader may be able to form a just estimate of their intellectual condition.

These interesting young persons being seated, Mrs. Leigh exhibited a small needle, and handed it round, that they might see and examine it. They expressed their surprise at the beauty of its polish, and the sharpness of one end, which they said "bit them," as often as they touched it. Their astonishment was increased when they saw a thread put through the eye of the needle. They were told that the artisan who made the needle had struck a hole in the end of it for the very purpose of receiving the thread. That so small a hole could be made in iron, exceeded their belief, until, by taking hold of the thread at both ends, and moving the needle backwards and forwards, they had ocular demonstration of the fact. The needle being returned to Mrs. Leigh, she put a knot on the end of the thread, and began to sew a piece of calico. A needle was then threaded and given to each, with a request that they would imitate Mrs. Leigh. After a few abortive efforts, they were all in confusion. One complained, that the thread would not stay in the cloth; another said, that she could not pull her needle through. The cause was soon ascertained: the one had not knotted the end of her thread; while the other had tied her thread to the eye of the needle! It was necessary to show them where the knot was to be placed, and how to make it.

This, then, is a sample of the first instructions ever given in the country in the arts of dress-making and millinery. Yet those young women, so totally unacquainted with the use of the British needle and scissors, could, in a few months, under the maternal supervision of Mrs. Leigh, cut out and make several articles of clothing for themselves and families. These mechanical and industrial exercises were commenced and closed with singing and prayer. Had the statesmen of Europe looked in upon this humble instructress and her swarthy pupils, what a lesson they might have learned! This was the commencement of a new era in the history of woman in that barbarous country!

Mrs. Leigh opened her mission by enunciating those principles and forming those tastes and habits which were destined, by their prevalence and moral power, to elevate the females of the country to an equality with the most intelligent and refined of their sex in the islands of Great Britain. It is true that we are here presented with civilization upon a very small scale, and in an incipient form; but we have it in God's order,—heaven before earth; religious before secular duties; the worship of God, and then the needle, the plough, and the steam-engine! Several of these young females displayed great quickness of apprehension, and, where attention and application could be induced, evinced intellectual powers in no way inferior to the youth of England. A spirit of emulation sprang up amongst them, and greatly facilitated their progress in the various useful occupations in which they were engaged. The change effected in their persons and manners soon became apparent, and excited the admiration of their respective families.

One of the most interesting of these pupils, who had often been affected during domestic worship, was unexpectedly sent for by her father. Several of the principal men of the tribe arrived, with orders from their chief to bring her home immediately. When Mrs. Leigh demanded a reason for so hasty and peremptory a proceeding, they replied: "Our chief is angry: he has been told that his daughter has given up the customs and gods of New Zealand, and is living like the Europe people." Expostulation was out of the question; and the poor creature, after adjusting her few articles of dress, walked off with them, under suppressed emotion, and with evident reluctance. After an absence of three weeks, she returned, much altered in appearance. On being introduced to Mrs. Leigh, she said, "When I got home, my father was very angry, and declared that I should remain at home. I had a hut built for myself, and so placed that I could look through the door to Wangaroa. Still I was unhappy. The last sermon I heard from the teacher was about heaven. I could not recollect any part of it but this: 'Yet there is room.' I could not stay at home any longer; so I have come to inquire whether there be 'room' for me in heaven." She had suffered much in her mind. "After some negotiation with the father," said Mr. Leigh, "he gave her up like a savage, saying, 'Take her, she be no good to me!' We received her joyfully; and, in a very few weeks, she obtained a scriptural assurance of God's mercy, and became an example of Christian consistency."

We do not write for the purpose of vindicating Methodism from the aspersions of its enemies; but all who understand its economy know that this is one of its peculiarities,—that, wherever it sets up its institutions, it establishes a barometer by which to determine the progress of its disciples in religious knowledge and Christian experience. At its weekly class-meetings, incipient conviction is detected, and continues to be deepened and strengthened until it terminates in faith in Christ. Yet this arrangement has been the subject of uncharitable criticism and severe censure. And, after all, it only carries into the organization of the church a principle universally recognised in all our schools of science and of arts. Even the men of commerce mark the developement of their schemes; and the husbandman himself is not indifferent to the progress of vegetation, and the ripening of his crops.

The want of such a criterion was a great defect in the teaching of the lay and clerical agents of the Church Missionary Society in New Zealand. They had their domestic services, and wrought industriously in the field or in the workshop on the week-days. They expounded the scriptures, and conversed religiously with the natives, on the Lord's day. But they had no catechetical exercise for ascertaining the moral results of their well-intentioned labours. Yet are we bound, in justice to those early labourers, to vindicate them from an implied censure published in "The Church Missionary Intelligencer" so recently as June, 1851. "The missionaries," it is said, "landed on the shores of the Bay of Islands in December, 1814. Not until the year 1825 was a first convert given to them, and a second in 1827. In the year 1832 we had no communicants amongst the natives of New Zealand." Let it be observed, 1. That from 1814 to 1822 the Society was represented by a few mechanics, who had no authority to form a church, nor even to preach. 2. After the arrival of the first clergyman, the Rev. John Butler, the secular and spiritual systems were perpetuated, which contemplated civilization first, and conversion as an ulterior object. "In the year 1824," says Mr. Butler, "I have ploughed and sown eleven acres of land, with my own hands, at our settlement on the Kiddu-Kiddu River. My son Samuel and myself had previously prepared the land." 3. Yet, notwithstanding the imperfections of the system, and the unfaithfulness of some of the agents employed, much spiritual good had been done. Possessing as we do manuscript journals of their proceedings, written upon their own establishment by disinterested parties, we are enabled to assure the contributors to the Church Missionary Society, that the preceding statement is not in exact accordance with ascertained facts. Long before the period specified, these brethren had witnessed the softening and subduing power of evangelical truth upon the minds of the living, and the sufficiency of the grace of God to impress the warrior as he lay dying upon his mat. The paucity of church-members, up to a later period than 1832, is thus easily accounted for. We regret to witness the attempt that is being made to depreciate the labours of these men, and to attribute the good that has been done in New Zealand to the appointment of a bishop, and the establishment of an ecclesiastical hierarchy.

We advance no claim in behalf of the first missionary agents that is not absolutely due to candour and truth. They served their generation according to the will of God, and, with one exception, left the world without personally making any demands upon the gratitude of posterity. Yet we affirm, that they laid the foundation of those measures that have issued in the commercial elevation of New Zealand. In their heroism and teaching originated the noble collegiate and educational institutions that now adorn the country. The statesman may smile at the assertion, but these were the pioneers who won those beautiful islands to the British crown. What did the natives care for the naval and land forces of Great Britain? They knew perfectly well that, though the artillery might damage many of their magnificent *kauri* trees, they could not reach the people; and that there would be as much sense in sending the troops into the dense forests of the country to catch the *kukupa*, as to kill the natives. What company of commercial speculators ever thought of establishing themselves in New Zealand, for the purpose of testing the quality of its soil, or of ascertaining its mineral resources, until the artisans of Marsden, and the missionaries Butler and Leigh, had demonstrated to modern scepticism, that, under the guardianship of the God of Daniel, good men could live amongst lions? Up to that time, the mariner whose ship was stranded upon its shores yielded to despondency, and felt that his days were numbered. Like a lighthouse in the midst of surrounding darkness and desolation, the first missionaries repelled the waves of savage violence, and maintained their position. Their co-adjutors and successors have been subjected to the misrepresentations of Colonizing Companies, whose cupidity they checked, and the insinuations of a vacillating local government, against which they felt obliged to appeal; yet have they done more to consolidate the peace of the country, to promote public confidence, (without which there can be no permanent prosperity in any state,) and to improve the social condition of the people, than all the civil enactments, the military establishments, and fiscal regulations of the politician.

CHAPTER VII.

CRUEL CUSTOMS OF THE COUNTRY—ILLNESS OF MR. LEIGH—SAILS WITH
THE REV. S. MARSDEN FOR THE COLONY—IS SHIPWRECKED—LANDED
ON A DESOLATE ISLAND.

THE Indo-Americans and the South-Sea Islanders have uniformly entertained the same ideas in regard to the necessity of revenging injuries, and of receiving what the latter call *utua*, or "satisfaction." In short, revenge is considered the most sacred passion and duty by both communities; while the forgiving of injuries is utterly unknown. No time can blot out the remembrance of an injury which has once been sustained: no distance can secure the unfortunate victim from the consequences of this passion. In the pursuit of vengeance, wiles and stratagems have been adopted by both nations. The Indian springs from his covert, on the object of his resentment, with his tomahawk: the New-Zealander cleaves his skull asunder, in some unsuspecting moment, with his deadly *maree*. The former scalps his victim, and makes a drinking-cup of his skull; the latter bakes his head in an oven, and preserves it as a trophy to future generations. The following incident may be adduced in illustration of those principles:—

The brethren received intelligence that a considerable body of natives were on their way, from a remote part of the country, to fight the tribes of Wangaroa. They soon arrived: they were numerous, and well armed. The natives of Wesleydale had made the best use of their time, and were prepared to give them battle. One division of the invaders was posted on the side of the hill, while the other was drawn up on the margin of the valley below. The Wangaroa chiefs were advancing to the attack, when Mr. Leigh ran to a piece of rice-ground which lay between the contending parties, and made a sign for the chiefs to meet him. They did so. He commenced an address to them on the mischiefs of war and the benefits of peace; but had uttered only a few sentences when one of them interrupted him · "You say too much," he observed: "*utua*, 'pay thou the price.'" Before Mr. Leigh could reply to him, the furious savage seized him by the collar, and threw him down the hill. He rolled over several times before he could regain his footing, and rose up much shaken, and covered with mud. Mrs. Leigh, having witnessed this act of violence, ran to the chief who commanded the strangers, and inquired, "What *utua* do you require?" Assuming an angry and menacing attitude, he replied, "Nothing less than a *kahu pai*, 'a good garment.'" Having bound over the belligerents to keep the peace for a few minutes, she hastened to the mission-house, and, taking the coverlet from off her own bed, returned immediately, and presented it to the enraged warrior as the gift of reconciliation. He received it with evident satisfaction; and, wrapping it round his body, exhibited the symbol of peace. His fighting-men expressed their assent by jumping simultaneously off the ground. On witnessing this unanimity, the chief exclaimed, *Kakahu Pakeha wahene rangatira*, "This European lady has slain our hearts."

Friendship being now restored, the foreigners wished to inspect the white teacher's residence, and insisted on seeing every thing inside and out. As they remained on the ground all night, the family was obliged to sit up and watch their property. Hearing much noise and confusion in the back yard, Mrs. Leigh went out to ascertain the cause, when she discovered one of the chiefs attempting to break open a cask of pork. She laid hold of him, and cried out, "If you don't desist, I will give you a fearful shake." He did not understand what she said, but seemed to think that it was a cabalistic utterance of awful import. "If you desire it," said he, in an agitated manner, "I will *tapu* this cask." "Yes, do," said Mrs. Leigh; and, after hastily putting on the *tapu*, he withdrew.

A chief can *tapu* any thing he chooses, so that no person of inferior rank will afterwards touch it: he can also, at his pleasure, remove the *tapu*, with all its consequences. The chiefs are fully aware of the advantages of the *tapu*. It confers on them, to a certain extent, the power of making laws, while the superstition on which it is founded insures the observance of them. The will of the chief is generally the law of the tribe; but on any emergency he calls the heads of the tribes together in council. Were they to transgress the *tapu*, the natives believe that the *Atua* would kill them; and so universal is this belief, that it is very rarely any one is found daring enough to commit the sacrilege. A delinquent, if discovered, would be stripped of every thing he possessed; and, if a slave, would in all probability be put to death: many instances of which have occurred. The ceremony of taking off the *tapu* is performed by cooking some food, generally *kúmara*, which is given to the chief. After eating a little of the food himself, he throws the remainder away: this is eaten (so it is believed) by the *Atua*, or at all events it appeases him. If a man imagines that he has offended his *Atua*, he generally offers a payment to appease his anger,—such as throwing a favourite object into the water, burning his house to the ground, or even killing a slave. Parents not unfrequently betroth their children in infancy; and a woman in such a case becomes *tapu* to her future husband, and to him alone: nor can any other person make proposals to her, even though he should die. This is a law which has had considerable influence on the population.

The chief who had thrown Mr. Leigh down the hill, while he was endeavouring to adjust their differences, now came to him in tears, and, with all the indications of profound sorrow, expressed his regret for having committed so unprovoked an assault upon the white teacher.

The enemy having retired from Wesleydale, the brethren proceeded with their fence. They broke up a portion of their land with spades and hoes, and sowed it with wheat. Most nobly did nature respond to this first call of the husbandman, and presented him in autumn with an abundant crop. The natives were induced to cultivate patches of their land, which they did with sharp-pointed pieces of wood; and, being supplied with seed, they also sowed them with wheat. The grain soon sprang up, and they had the happiness of seeing the corn in the ear; but, yielding to impatience, and believing that, like the potatoe, the wheat would be found in clusters at the root, they pulled up the whole crop. This total failure excited their surprise and disappointment. They were encouraged, however, to make another experiment, and advised to allow the grain to ripen on the ground: they did so; and were gratified beyond measure when they found that their wheat was not inferior in either size or quality to that of the missionary. When they reaped it, they brought it to the mission-house, to know what they must do with it. "O," said Mr. Leigh, "it was truly grand to see the chiefs approaching our residence, carrying some eight sheaves, some ten, being the first crop reaped by the aborigines from the virgin soil of Wesleydale." It awakened in the minds of the brethren delightful anticipations of that period when the prophetic vision of Micah shall be realized by these noble tribes of barbarians: "They shall beat their swords into ploughshares, and their spears into pruning-hooks: nation shall not lift up a sword against nation, neither shall they learn war any more. But they shall sit every man under his vine and under his fig-tree; and none shall make them afraid." The wheat was beaten out of the straw, winnowed, ground in hand-mills, made into dough, and baked in the presence of the natives. When the loaves were taken out of the oven, they looked at each other, and expressed their surprise at the effects which the fire had produced upon them. The Indian corn, which Mr. Leigh introduced, grew luxuriantly. The people parched or roasted the grain, and ate it. The fruit-trees and vegetables which had been sown and planted in the garden made rapid progress, so that their establishment began to assume the appearance of European comfort.

Mr. Leigh was frequently struck with the near approximation of some of the national customs to those of the ancient Jews. I shall only advert at present to the fact, that·their infants are baptized, if possible, about the eighth day after their birth. The priest fixes the time and place for the ceremony. It is usually performed by the side of a running stream. The priest takes the child into his arms, and demands its name. Having selected two very small smooth pebbles from the sea-beach, he puts them into the child's mouth, and makes it swallow them. He dips the infant three times under the water, and returns it to its parents and attendants. He then addresses the *Atua*. He prays, "that the child may become a great warrior; that he may never faint; that his heart may be as hard as the stones he has just swallowed; that he may be strong to eat the flesh and drink the blood of all who oppose him in war; and that when he performs the *haka*, his enemies may be seized with convulsions, and thus fall into his hand, like the *kukupa* into the hands of the fowler." A feast is given on the occasion, and a present of pigs or potatoes made to the priest. The priest is a sacred person. He prescribes no religious creed, nor any form of worship. From the prevalent belief that he can bless or curse, he has great influence in promoting peace or war. Their sons are brought up in strict conformity with the principles enunciated at the time of their baptism by the priestly juggler.

If children are not treated with intense affection in New Zealand, they are, at least, the subjects of great consideration. Boys are generally under the care of their father, who will talk with them and behave towards them as if they were full-grown men. Mr. Leigh has known the chiefs carry their sons upon their shoulders a distance of thirty miles to their assemblies. During the discussion of any subject, the children sit as quietly, and listen as attentively, as their parents. They are permitted to ask questions, and are replied to with as much respect as if they were old men. This treatment renders them very precocious, mentally as well as physically. Boys not more than three or four years of age, may be seen managing their canoes with great dexterity. They can use the musket with expertness at ten or twelve, and are made familiar with scenes of cruelty and suffering from infancy. It was not unusual for a chief to call out a slave, about the age of his own son, and order the boy to load his musket and shoot him. If he missed his object, his father would desire him to reload his piece, and fire until the slave fell. If, after receiving the shot, he lay upon the ground in dying agonies, the chief and the youthful sportsman would advance and examine the wound. His father would then show him how, by elevating or lowering the muzzle of his gun,

he might have killed him at once. He would then request him
to dispatch the sufferer with a blow on the head. They would
return from this tragedy to eat their *kúmara*, with as little
emotion as if they had only shot the *kiwi*.

In Wangaroa, and, indeed, all over the country, infanticide
prevailed to a melancholy extent. "I have reason to believe,"
says an author who had resided several years in the country,
" that at least every fourth woman with whom I was acquainted,
and had borne several children, had been guilty of this unnatural
crime. In vain I told the circle of women to whom I was addressing myself on the subject, that the Creator was too just to
allow a murderer to escape punishment. They only burst into
a shout, exclaiming, ' Your mother would have acted perfectly
right in so serving you!' A young girl sitting by, who had
dispatched her infant only the week previously, said it was useless to try to change their opinion : her own mother had several
times attempted to deprive her of life, having often commenced
the *roromi* on her nose, but that her father always interfered.
Various means were employed to deprive the child of life; such
as strangling, drowning, pressing its temples when newly born;
but the method in most general practice was that of suffocating
the infant by pressing its nose between two of the fingers."
"It has been my lot," says Yates, "to be an eye-witness of
several cases of infanticide, the mother being the destroyer of
her own child. I have seen the helpless infant strangled in a
moment, and then cast into the sea, or thrown to the dogs or
the pigs. Not unfrequently, a few days after its birth, has the
little sleeping baby been enclosed in the death-grasp of an
infuriated woman, who, but for the jealousy which raged within,
would have given her own life to save that of her infant." It
is not true, as represented in a recent publication, that they eat
their own children. Polygamy has been the fruitful source of
much social evil and of many domestic murders. "Why should
my infant live," said a woman indignantly, when being remonstrated with for having just deprived her child of life, "to dig
the ground, to be a slave to the wives of her husband, to be
beaten by them, and trodden under their feet? No! Can a
woman protect herself *here* as among the white people? and
should I not have trouble enough to bring up girls, when they
can only cry and make a noise?"

Being assured, from personal observation, and the testimony
of the young people in her own household, that infanticide prevailed amongst the tribes with whom she lived, Mrs. Leigh felt
anxious to discover some expedient by which to check, and ultimately to subvert, a practice that, while it gave greater intensity to the sinning principle, was gradually diminishing the

population of the country. To call infanticide *murder*, and dwell, as one of the above writers says he did, on the "justice of the Creator," was not the way to correct the evil, because it supposed a mental condition that did not exist. Your moral theory must be known and embraced, before there can be any practical acknowledgment of its authority. The New-Zealanders were wholly unacquainted with the first principles of revealed religion, and regarded the customs of their country as embodying the only code of laws entitled to the homage of the people. In endeavouring to deal with the atrocious crime of infanticide, Mrs. Leigh inquired, "Is there any mental peculiarity or maternal tendency on which I can lay hold, and, by giving it a moral and religious direction, make it the instrument of destroying this Moloch?" Observing that the native mothers were proud of seeing their children with any article of dress peculiar to the *Pakeha*, she employed her scholars to make several sets of baby-dresses. With those dresses she clothed the infants of the families to which her young people respectively belonged. These little ones were carried from hut to hut, and excited much attention. She then desired that it might be generally known, that any mother bringing her infant to the mission-house, not earlier than a fortnight after its birth, would be presented with a similar dress. In a short time several mothers arrived with their infants: placing them on the floor, they said, "These are your children, Mrs. Leigh; you must dress them like the Europe people." Mrs. Leigh would take the little creatures one by one on her lap, and dress them. On returning them to their mothers, she would say, "What beautiful children these are! See that you take great care of them: I will call occasionally, and see how they thrive." It was generally found, that when a native woman could be induced to preserve the life of her child for twelve or fourteen days, the strength of maternal affection was sufficient to save it afterwards from destruction. "In this way," said Mr. Leigh, "at a small expense, and in a short time, we saved scores of lives."

The rain had lately fallen almost incessantly for several days and nights; and as yet they had no building so far advanced as to be able to protect them from the inclemency of the weather. The fatiguing labours of the day, and exposure to rain during the night, combined with deep mental anxiety, induced a severe illness, which brought the missionary almost to the gates of death. "If I cannot be protected from the rain," he observed, "I shall undoubtedly die." Fortunately some of their goods had been packed in an empty wine-pipe: these goods were removed, and, one end being taken out of the wine-pipe, the sick missionary crawled into this homely hospital on his hands and knees. As there was no medical attendant to interfere, the question of life or death was pending, for some time, between the violence of the fever and the strength of his constitution. A more trying situation than his can scarcely be conceived. There he was, in the solitude of a strange land, at the ends of the earth, surrounded by a people who ate human flesh, and said, "The blood of man is sweet;" and having no earthly power to which he could appeal for protection. Nor was it less trying for his beloved wife, whose cup of sorrow was nearly full; for, to the prospect of increasing difficulties and dangers, there was now added that of an early widowhood. The only mitigation of their affliction arose from the contemplation of the wisdom, the goodness, and the sufficiency of Divine Providence. They could both say, "Being justified by faith, we have peace with God through our Lord Jesus Christ: by whom also we have access by faith into this grace wherein we stand, and rejoice in hope of the glory of God. And not only so, but we glory in tribulations also: knowing that tribulation worketh patience; and patience, experience; and experience, hope: and hope maketh not ashamed; because the love of God is shed abroad in our hearts by the Holy Ghost which is given unto us." The fever ran its course, and gradually subsided; but it left a chronic ailment that subjected the missionary to frequent and acute suffering for twenty years afterwards.

On the 6th of August, while all hands were busily employed in making some alterations about the premises, the natives shouted, "Europeans!" On looking down the valley, two gentlemen were seen slowly approaching the mission-settlement. The brethren ran to meet them, and were rejoiced to recognise, in the strangers, Messrs. Turner and Hobbs, Wesleyan missionaries. They had arrived on the 3rd, in the Bay of Islands, by the ship "Brompton." The same vessel had brought the Rev. Samuel Marsden, with additional labourers and fresh stores for the Church mission. The natives collected in considerable numbers, and evinced much anxiety to know who the strangers were, and what was their object in visiting Wangaroa. So soon as they were satisfied on those points, they quietly dispersed, when the mission-family united in thanksgivings to God for having brought their brethren in safety to their appointed sphere of labour.

The chief George called on the 10th, to inquire when Mr. Marsden and the ship "Brompton" might be expected in their harbour. Being informed that the captain was afraid, though well armed, to bring his ship into their harbour, he rose up in a rage, and exclaimed, "Tell Mr. Leigh to write immediately, and let them know, that if they come not, you must all go." Observing one of the brethren rising to reason with him, he said, in a menacing manner, "Sit down! Am I come here to be dictated to by a boy?" He remained a short time, until his passion subsided, when he went home.

On the following Sunday morning the service was conducted by two of the brethren: in the evening they went out to a native village, where they had an attentive audience. On afterwards alluding to this assembly, one of them said, "I felt exquisitely distressed when I looked round upon the dignified persons of those barbarians, because I could not address them with ease and fluency in their own language. Never did I more sincerely wish that the gift of tongues might again return to the church."

On Monday forenoon, part of a building in course of erection fell suddenly upon the two newly-arrived missionaries, and bruised them severely; while Mr. Shepherd, of the Church mission, who was on a visit, had a narrow escape from being blown to pieces by gunpowder. He was lighting a piece of dry fern, when the fire was communicated to his canister. An explosion took place: fragments of the canister were carried to a great distance; but Mr. Shepherd himself escaped with some slight wounds about his hands.

On the 15th, the government sloop, "Snapper," sailed into the harbour, bringing the Rev. Samuel Marsden and Mrs. Turner and family from the Bay of Islands. The natives of Wesleydale hastened to pay their respects to their great chief Marsden, and kept the district in an uproar all the afternoon. Mr. Marsden inspected every thing,—the buildings in progress, the garden, the fences, the cultivation, and the furniture. After this general survey, he expressed his astonishment that such an amount of work should have been accomplished in so short a time, and by so few hands. His astonishment would have been heightened, had he known how often that work had been interrupted. In the evening he inquired into the conduct of the natives, the situation of the tribes and villages, the state of the schools, and the progress which the brethren themselves had made in the knowledge of the Maori tongue. They enjoyed his cheerful and edifying conversation till a late hour, when the venerable man lay down for the night upon a rude sofa, or couch, of Mr. Leigh's manufacture, in the same apartment with Mr. and Mrs. Leigh. He arose early in the morning, and spent the day with the chiefs and their people.

On Sunday, the 17th, the sermon was founded upon 2 Peter ii. 9: "The Lord knoweth how to deliver the godly out of temptations." Mr. Marsden afterwards administered the Lord's supper, baptized the child of Mr. Shepherd, which was born during their visit to Wesleydale, and delivered an animated address on his first connexion with New Zealand, its present hopeful condition, and its future prospects.

He was affected on witnessing the change which had taken place in Mr. Leigh's health, declared it to be his decided opinion that he could not recover without medical aid, and urged his removal at once to New South Wales. After mutual consultation, the brethren gave it as their deliberate judgment that "brother Leigh should go, by the ship 'Brompton,' to Port Jackson, and secure that medical treatment he so obviously requires, but which cannot be obtained in this country." When their decision was communicated to Mr. Leigh, he exclaimed, "Lord, what wilt thou have me to do?" He keenly felt this dispensation: as there had been a marked improvement in the attendance of the natives on public worship, the class and prayer meetings had become edifying, and the children in the adjacent villages were assembling for instruction with increasing punctuality, he was reluctant to leave the mission at such a crisis. The chief Tepui was in deep distress when he heard that Mr. Leigh was going to Port Jackson. He inquired, with intense emotion, whether they had been praying to Jehovah for his recovery, and whether, should he die, the others would leave Wesleydale. Turning to Mr. Leigh, he said, with a faltering tongue, "Go to New South Wales. Get better, and come back to me soon: if you do, I will not go to war any more; I will stay at home and plant *kúmara*.

All being in readiness, the Rev. Samuel Marsden, Mr. and Mrs. Leigh, Mr. and Mrs. Shepherd, a servant and two children, went on board the "Snapper," and sailed, at eight o'clock on the morning of the 19th, for the Bay of Islands. After they had gone, Tepui called again, and said that he was restless and unhappy. "My heart," he observed, " is *kuamate*, 'bad,' on account of my love to Mr. and Mrs. Leigh, and my daughter, who has gone with them to Port Jackson. I am sick, very sick, very sick!"· They endeavoured to sympathize with him; for his distress of mind was great.

A variety of circumstances occurred to prevent the " Brompton " from sailing at the time appointed. During this unexpected detention, Mr. Leigh wrote an account of the state of the Church mission, which was transmitted to the secretaries, and subsequently printed in the " Missionary Gazetteer." Mr. Marsden was occupied with the general business of the mission, and in constant endeavours to convince 'Hongi of the advantages of peace, and of the commercial ruin in which war involves a people. To these observations he replied, " My chiefs tell me that they want no more war; and I have suffered so much myself, during the late fighting, notwithstanding my victories, that I am satisfied *hore rawa he painga i te waenga hore rawa rawa*, 'there is no good in war, none, none at all.'" Mr. Marsden, on the supposition that certain circumstances should arise, inquired how, in such a case, he would deal with the missionaries. With the savage curl of dissatisfaction upon his lip, he remarked, "'Hongi has said, long since, that the missionaries at the Bay of Islands and Wangaroa shall be protected."

The sons of several chiefs having died on Mr. Marsden's establishment at Paramatta, their fathers expressed a wish to go to the colony to recover their bones, and bring them to the sepulchres of their ancestors. They were to provide their own sea-stores, and Messrs. Marsden and Leigh agreed to give them a free passage. All were ordered to be on board on Saturday night, September 6th, 1823. Early on Sunday morning, Mr. Marsden proposed to Mr. Leigh that they should read and expound the Epistle to the Romans on their passage to Sydney. Mr. Leigh acceded to this request; and, after a delightful service, they retired to their respective cabins. In a short time, the chiefs entered Mr. Marsden's cabin in a state of great excitement. "What is the matter?" inquired Mr. Marsden. "The chief of the ship," they exclaimed, "has ordered the anchor to be lifted. You have taught us not to sail our canoes on the sacred day. Your God has ordered the ship to rest: then let it rest." Mr. Marsden told them that he, like themselves, was but a passenger, and that the captain was the great chief on board. They shook their heads significantly, intimating that, in their opinion, there could be no greater chief than himself. On retiring from the cabin, one of them said, sharply, "You do wrong, Mr. Marsden! and if your God be like the New-Zealand god, he will kill the ship. If your ship should die, you must not blame our god for killing it." Mr. Marsden spoke kindly and soothingly to them, in the hope of allaying their apprehensions; but they continued in a state of excitement, expressing their regret that their stores were on board, otherwise they would have quitted the vessel and returned home. Soon after the ship had got under weigh, an easterly gale sprang up, and baffled all their efforts to clear the bay. While tacking, in the hope of working the vessel out of danger, she missed stays, and struck upon a sunken rock with such violence, that a portion of the rock penetrated her bottom. She began to fill immediately. "Let the boat be manned!" cried the captain; "and let the officer in charge take on board the Rev. Samuel Marsden, and the Rev. Mr. and Mrs. Leigh, land them upon the nearest island, and hasten back to assist the ship." In two minutes they were seated in the boat; but the tempest had become so furious, that there was not the remotest prospect of their reaching the shore alive. Putting their trust in God, they committed themselves to the elements, and steered away from the vessel. She was in a perilous situation; oscillating between two rocks, with the sea rolling over her decks. After sailing four miles, they discovered land rising to view through the mist that hung over it. After reconnoitring the beach, and fixing upon a landing-place, they resolved to run the boat at all hazards through the foaming surge. They were landed in safety, and the boat returned immediately to render assistance to those on board the wreck, whom they found in a state of great excitement. Their arrangements were soon completed; and, after a brief consultation with the chiefs and officers, and looking at the difficulties in which they were placed, the captain judged it best, upon the whole, to sail in the boat, at once, to New Zealand. Soon after they left the "Brompton," she went to pieces and disappeared.

In the mean time the party on the island were looking about for shelter and the means of subsistence. The confusion on board the ship, when they left, was so great, and the command to clear the deck so peremptory, that they were hurried into the boat without being able to secure a single biscuit, or any article of clothing but what they had on at the time. On examination, the island was found to be desolate, some convulsion of nature having heaved it up from the bottom of the sea, without investing it with either beauty or fertility. The storm continued with increasing severity, the wind sweeping over them with amazing violence, and the waves lashing the surrounding shores until the island seemed to rock in the midst of the ocean. As the night advanced, their situation was such as to awaken deep solicitude; for, if the captain and his people should be lost on their way to New Zealand, which was not unlikely, or, if they did not send help as soon as they got there, the consequences would, in either case, be equally fatal to them. But no persons could have been selected, better adapted to meet the extraordinary vicissitudes to which their enterprise exposed them, than these missionary heroes. They were all of a sanguine temperament, and had an unbounded faith in God; while two of them had exposed themselves to the spear and *boomerang* of the Australian savage, and all of them to the *háni* and *maree* of the New-Zealand cannibal. Having sung a hymn, and commended themselves to the protection of God, they left the issue with Him.

"I see," said Mr. Marsden, as he looked wishfully across the great waters, "a dark speck floating upon the ocean: what can that be?" All eyes were directed to the same point, and all agreed that it had the appearance of a canoe. The storm that had proved so disastrous to them, had driven this canoe out of her course, and compelled her to run to this island for shelter. On nearing the land, they ascertained that the canoe was manned by two New-Zealanders, one of whom instantly recognised Mr. Leigh. After securing their canoe, they assisted the missionary party in collecting materials and building a hut. They had no instrument of labour but their hands, and no material but such as the wind and the rain were likely to penetrate and derange; yet they succeeded in constructing a rude hut which, in their circumstances, proved a source of great comfort to them. The canoe-men had left home to procure potatoes for their families. After taking the potatoes on board, they were returning home, when the storm bore them off the land, and obliged them to take refuge in the island. The weather moderated towards evening, when these friendly barbarians launched their canoe, and sailed homeward. They could not take Mr. Leigh and his companions in their small craft; but they presented them with four baskets of potatoes, and engaged to apprize their friends of their dangerous situation.

The missionaries dressed their potatoes, thanked God for having sent them, and crept into their hut. They had been for several hours in their wet clothes; and as the illness of Mr. Leigh prevented him from taking much exercise, he suffered severely from the cold. Their hut was so small that they were under the necessity of placing themselves in a sitting posture. Poor missionary Leigh! he had expatriated himself from his country and friends, for the sake of Christ and the Heathen; had hitherto sustained the cross with a noble bearing; had been " in labours more abundant," and " suffered the loss of all things ;" and now he is shipwrecked!

Reader, will you man the life-boat, or stop the supplies? You say, that the missionary lives in ease and affluence : stoop down, and look into this hut, and then say what pecuniary consideration would induce you to change places with him! Now, move softly : they are all asleep : there he sits, with the venerable Marsden on one side, and his faithful wife on the other, to preserve his body, attenuated by disease, in an erect position. See how his chest heaves ! how his manly countenance is crimsoned over with the hectic flush ! and how his legs, enlarged by dropsical swellings, lie exposed, without a blanket to cover them ! And what a contrast between Marsden associating with the officers of state, or at the head of his own princely establishment at Paramatta, and Marsden gathering the fern to roast potatoes for his breakfast, and then assisting " brother Leigh " to pull his shoes on his swollen feet ! As for Mrs. Leigh, her situation was too delicate and touching to be described. The

imagination of the female collector will, we doubt not, represent
in vivid colours what the feelings of a lady must have been in
such circumstances. To all appearance, they were destined to
suffering and death in the midst of the Pacific Ocean. But
why call it *Pacific* Ocean, when its waves, instead of wrapping the
shipwrecked in their oblivious mantle, seemed to have conspired
to prolong life—only that they might enhance its bitterness?

But how difficult to reason justly from outward appearances!
The objects of our present sympathy were as happy as princes.
When they awoke in the morning, and recollected where they
were, and through what they had passed, they thanked God
and congratulated each other. Mr. Marsden crept out of the
hut first, and was followed by Mrs. Leigh; and while they were
preparing the potatoes for their morning's repast, Mr. Leigh
went in search of water to quench his burning thirst. After
wandering about for some time, he discovered a small pool of rain-
water in the hollow of a rock. To this little reservoir he afterwards conducted his wife and Mr. Marsden, who, not anticipating
any scarcity, emptied the natural basin of its contents. They soon
had reason to regret their imprudence; for, not being able to find
any more water on the island, they suffered much from thirst.

But what pen can adequately describe the privations and
trials through which the missionaries had to pass, who laid the
foundation of the numerous churches that now flourish in the
islands of the South Seas? Yet Marsden and his two friends
were, like John in Patmos, emphatically "in the Spirit." They
had no book of any kind; but they reviewed their sufferings
and triumphs, related their Christian experience, and consulted
together as to the best means of spreading Christianity over the
populous islands of the Pacific.

They continued here for the space of three days and three
nights, in a state of suspense; but on the fourth day they saw a
small vessel nearing the island. It contained a few friends from
the Bay of Islands, who received them on board joyfully, and
bore them away, under an agreeable breeze, to New Zealand.

The report of the wreck of the ship "Brompton" was soon
carried to Wangaroa, with many exaggerations; which created
a great sensation there amongst the brethren. The intelligence
was brought by the chief George. Addressing himself to Mr.
Turner, whom he found working at the fence, he exclaimed,
*Kati ta koutou, mahi! kua puta oku roima-ta meake koutou
tangi ano hoki. Kua pakaru te kaipuke o ta koutou papa a te
Matenga raua ko te Ri. Kua tai hae tea nga kaho e te tangata
Maori. Kua pau te Matenga i Te Taniwa. Na Te Taniwa i
mate te kaipuke no te mea.* "Cease working: my tears are
burst forth; presently also you will cry. The vessel of your

parents, Marsden and Leigh, is broken! The cargo" (or casks) "is stolen by the New-Zealanders, and Marsden is devoured by the sea-monster. Te Taniwa broke the vessel because Marsden took flax from his *wahi tapu.*" Alluding to the captain, who had refused to bring his vessel to Wangaroa, he added, with a peculiar sneer of satisfaction, *Ka tai ano taku tau reka reka ka hari toku ngakau no te mea kahore ano i waka tere mai torea kaipuke ki taku wahapu. He pai ra kia mate tona kai puka.* "I have just now seen a slave." (A mode of speech indicative of contempt.) "My heart is glad, because he did not sail his ship to my harbour: it is good that his vessel should be destroyed." On the 24th, they received letters from Mr. Leigh, containing authentic information relative to the total loss of the "Brompton," his own sufferings, as also those of Mrs. Leigh and Mr. Marsden, and their deliverance by the good providence of God. The chiefs desired that Mr. Leigh might be informed, as soon as possible, of their continued love and sympathy.

On Sunday Mr. Turner preached from, "For this purpose the Son of God was manifested, that He might destroy the works of the devil." After dinner they visited Tepui's village. He pointed out his father's burying-place, gave them the history of his ancestors, and showed them the bones of one of his brother's children. His views of God and futurity were confused and irrational. He entered into an argument to prove, that the native lizard was God, and that sickness and death were occasioned by its getting into the inside of a person, and gnawing his vitals. Hence the uneasiness evinced by the natives on seeing these animals. One of the friends, having one day found a beautiful lizard, carried it to a native woman, to ask her the name of it. She shrank from him in a state of terror that exceeded description, and conjured him not to approach her, as it was in the shape of the reptile which he held in his hand that the *Atua* was wont to take possession of the dying, and to devour their heart and bowels. Tepui was an animated speaker, and urged the claims of the lizard to divinity with much force and variety of argument. "O," said the missionary, "that I could speak with the same ease and fluency in the native tongue! My soul heaves with emotion, and is agitated with alternate feelings of pity and indignation: but my tongue fails me." Turning to George, who stood by, he observed, *Ka mamae toku nga kai,* "My heart is sore, because you will not believe in the Lord Jesus Christ!" He replied, "I cannot see Him!" "But the natural man receiveth not the things of the Spirit of God: for they are foolishness unto him: neither can he know them, because they are spiritually discerned."

On the 29th, while they were erecting a saw-pit, on the very spot where the bodies of the officers and crew of the ship "Boyd" were cooked and eaten, some of the labourers ran to the mission-house, and reported, that one of the teachers had just been killed with an axe. On inquiry, it turned out that one of the brethren had been severely wounded with an axe in the leg.

Their time was now regularly divided between out-door work, studying the language, teaching and catechizing the children in the several villages, preaching to the adults, and visiting the sick. "I called in the evening," says Mr. Stack, "on a man that was dying. I asked him, 'In case of death, where will your soul go?' He replied at once, *Ké té po*. I told him about the true God and Jesus Christ, and urged him, with much earnestness, to embrace the true religion. As he manifested the utmost apathy and indifference, I assured him that unless he did so, he would go to hell. When I thought that I had made an impression upon him, he turned over upon his mat, and cried out, *Ehi kai ana, a hou*, 'I want food.'"

Sunday, October 5th.—The morning text was, "And they all with one consent began to make excuse." (Luke xiv. 18.) Tepui's village was again visited in the afternoon, and the adults and children instructed and catechized. The text in the evening was, "Pass the time of your sojourning here in fear." (1 Peter i. 17.) After service one of the chiefs called, and stated that he had been informed that a pewter pot had been stolen from the premises the night before; that he suspected a person, who was known to be a great thief, and was going away to kill him. The missionaries endeavoured to convince him, that the contemplated punishment was too severe, especially as there was no direct evidence that the individual suspected was connected with the theft. Their arguments, being regarded as contrary to the national customs, made no impression upon the chief, who hastily withdrew. After family prayer, they heard an uproar in the village, arising from some misunderstanding between Hururu and George. During this disturbance the devoted victim escaped, and bounded past the mission-house, exclaiming, *Ka nui taku mataku!* "I am horribly afraid!"

The noise continued till a late hour. After again commending the disputants and themselves to the mercy of God, the family retired to rest. They were roused from an agreeable slumber, at two o'clock in the morning, by the chief George, who, being assailed by the dog, was obliged to retire. He returned again at daylight, and informed them that his brother had gone to bring Te Peri, the chief of the harbour, and his tribe, and that there was going to be a fight. After breakfast the tribes assembled, armed with tomahawks, spears, and clubs, of various sizes, and otherwise equipped for the field. They made a sally over the hill behind the settlement, and seized a number of pigs: they killed them, cut them up, and returned about noon, stained with their blood, and carrying their carcasses. As they passed the missionary brethren, they shouted, *Ka pai Nuitirani!* "The conduct of New-Zealanders is good." At four o'clock in the afternoon, the war-whoop and firing of muskets brought together again a great number of armed men. They drew up at the end of the mission-house, and commenced fighting. The battle was fierce and noisy, and continued to rage for an hour and a half. One of the domestics got hold of George's muskets and concealed them, so that he was prevented from shooting any one. All at once the clashing of arms ceased, the hideous yells subsided, and the chiefs and their undisciplined hordes rushed within the enclosure, and filled the house. Some came to get their muskets repaired, and others to get food.

When they dispersed, the brethren went out, and laid the foundation of a new house on the rising ground, and near a fine broad stream of water. At the usual examination of the servants in the evening, several questions were asked on Christian doctrine, to which they replied with an encouraging readiness. Addressing a boy abruptly, and pointing to him at the same time, one of the brethren said, "Jesus Christ died for you." "What!" said the boy, with astonishment, "did He? What! for me?" They united in singing the evening hymn, with pleasure and devotional fervour, and thus peacefully closed a day of distraction and danger.

On Sunday, the 12th, Mr. Turner again conducted the morning services; the afternoon was spent in Tepui's village, both adults and children behaving with propriety. They commemorated the death of Christ in the evening; when He signally verified His promise, "Where two or three are gathered together in my name, there am I in the midst of them." At this period there were eight Europeans on the establishment; besides three male and three female New-Zealanders. The natives were fed principally on rice, and occasionally with pork and potatoes. The family was divided into two classes, and assembled for mutual instruction every night.

On November the 15th, they received a message from the brethren of the Church mission at Kiddu-Kiddu, to say, that the ship "Dragon" had called at the North Cape, on her way from Tahiti to New South Wales; that the Rev. S. Marsden, Mr. and Mrs. Leigh, and the shipwrecked mariners, were ready to go on board, and would sail with the first fair wind; that Mr. Leigh's ancles were still much swollen, while the pains in his head and chest were incessant and excruciating.

On the 26th, George offered a pig for sale, and expressed his willingness to dispose of it, at a moderate price. Mr. Turner laid down its full value, without making a single observation. Being dissatisfied with the articles offered in barter, this ungrateful savage insulted him. After dashing in pieces an iron pot, which had been given him as part of the price, he pushed him along the bank with his hands, and twice levelled his musket to shoot him. Mr. Turner, seeing him foaming with rage, said, "If you kill me, I am not afraid to die." Mr. Turner's colleague came quickly up, and addressed the chief, who was uttering the most wicked language. George was offended by his interference, and repelled his reproof, observing, *Hoi ano ta koutou homai-tanga maku E Thu te tamiti nei.* "This is all I can get from you, 'O Jesus the Son,'" alluding to a native hymn which they frequently sang. "We love your people," said Mr. Hobbs, "and are endeavouring to do them good." He replied, with much asperity of feeling, "If you love me, give me something."

He then walked off in a sulky mood. He had not been gone above a few minutes, when a loud scream was heard from the *raupo* house. On hearing this cry for help, Mr. Turner, who had been much excited and exhausted, almost fell to the ground. On reaching the *raupo* house, they found that the chief had gone in upon Betsy, and frightened the girl almost into fits. He left the premises without taking any thing, but returned again after dinner. His daughter Charlotte, who lived with Mrs. Turner, having cut her finger, was crying. When he saw the tears, he was so enraged that he seized the little creature by the head and feet, and doubled her body. As she fell to the ground, he lost his hold of her; when she scrambled into the house, and escaped from him. In conversation with Mrs. Turner, he remarked, "Anger rises first in my breast; it then goes into my heart; then it ascends to my head; and when it gets there, I could destroy any thing. It was this passion that prompted me to shoot your husband to-day." The journal adds, "It is of the Lord's mercies that we are not consumed. We assembled the family as soon as possible, and thanksgivings were offered to Israel's God, whom we found to be 'a very present help in trouble.'"

Early on the following morning, while they were employed in the field, one of the labourers said, carelessly, "They are roasting a slave in the village." Several other natives confirming this statement, three of the brethren set off to inquire into the facts of the case. On entering the village, they observed a large fire, surrounded by a considerable number of the people. On approaching this group, they discovered a human body, lying between two logs of burning *kauri* trees. The lower extremities were burned almost to a cinder ; but although the features were entirely obliterated, yet the head and trunk were but partially consumed.

He had been murdered by his master, because he was sick, and not likely to recover. The brethren solicited permission to bury the remains of the poor creature; and, while a hole was being dug in the ground, they spoke to the persons assembled respecting their accountability to God, and the final judgment. Before the body could be quite covered over with earth, a signal was made from the hill near the mission-house that the fight was come. The people fled, the fighting-men grasped their instruments of war, and darted forward in a body in the direction of the settlement. As the brethren had incurred the displeasure of the chief the day before, it seemed probable to them that he had taken advantage of their absence, fallen upon the family and domestics, and was sacrificing them to his rage. They approached their residence with apprehension, and found their enclosure filled with natives, running about in the wildest confusion; but they had committed no act of personal violence. It turned out to have been a false alarm; and as soon as the natives were convinced of this, they quietly dispersed.

On the evening of the 1st of December, a devotional meeting was held, at which accounts were read of the progress of Christianity in Western Africa. Those accounts were remarkably animating, and all present felt their hearts drawn out in earnest and protracted prayer for the Divine blessing upon their own mission. The next day a formal reconciliation took place between the chief George and the missionaries. After a mutual and hearty salutation, they all signed the treaty of peace by eating fern-root with the chief in the bush where he usually resided.

On the 10th Tepui demanded an axe as wages for his son 'Hongi, whom the missionaries were boarding and training gratuitously. Being refused so unreasonable a demand, he became quite furious, and threw the things about in all directions. A body of his men advanced, and placed themselves in readiness to enforce his claim. One of them, with a countenance distorted, and indicating all the malignity of a fiend, kept repeating, "An axe for 'Hongi." The brethren desired Tepui to restrain this savage, and they would talk with him. He ordered the ferocious fellow to be silent. They then reminded Tepui, that they were far from home, that they looked to him for protection, that their stores were nearly exhausted, and that before their friends could send them a fresh supply they were likely to be without food. This calm appeal touched the old man, and the tear started in his eye. He could not conceal the acuteness of his feelings, while, with a sort of growl, he muttered, " You shall not want food. But you have been more liberal to your servants, to whom you have given something every month, than you have been to Tepui." At the close of this altercation, one of the brethren

TANGI, OR MEETING OF FRIENDS, NEW ZEALAND.

remarked, "Little do our friends in England know of the exquisite trials we are daily called to experience from the ingratitude, treachery, and violence of this barbarous people."

On Sunday, December 14th, after the morning exposition of scripture and prayer, the missionaries crossed the river, and found, to their surprise, that the chief of Mudi Wai and a numerous retinue had just arrived. They seemed to be peaceably disposed. A great concourse of people soon assembled, to whom the brethren explained the love of Jehovah in the gift of His Son Jesus Christ, and a future judgment. Profound attention was paid to those addresses; and the strangers seemed quite surprised with every thing they saw and heard. From this interesting scene the teachers went to the residence of Tepui. They found him and his principal wife stretched upon the ground near their hut. Those huts were more like dog-kennels than habitations for human beings; and in hot weather they were intolerable. When not excited by war, the natives spent their time in sloth and idleness, living more like hogs than rational beings, and manifesting a great repugnance to all kinds of intellectual exercise. Tepui was in good temper, and appeared pleased to see them. They held a long service; at the close of which the chief desired them to take some native wine. This is a beverage made by squeezing the berries of the *tu pakihi*, a tree resembling the elder, and mixing the juice in a calabash with the root of the *kôrau*, which in taste resembles the sweet turnip. The wine was served up in a tin basin; and each guest was furnished with a spoon, made of a muscle-shell inserted in a wooden handle. This interview was equally gratifying to all parties. On returning home in the evening, they found Ranghee, one of their lads, who had been absent for some time to assist his widowed mother to plant her potatoes, awaiting their arrival. After answering some inquiries about his mother and other relatives, the lad said, "I found that the longer I stayed away, the more quickly did the things that I had learned here get away from my head. I have returned that you may bring them back to me again."

On the 19th, the first *te hakari*, or "fair," ever held in the country, was opened in Wesleydale. Numerous natives arrived from the mouth of the harbour, and adjacent villages. Various articles of foreign and domestic manufacture were exhibited, and exchanged hands. Christianity, producing "good-will to men," and habits of industry, would soon unite those warlike tribes in friendly and profitable intercourse. During the first day of the fair, Tepui's wife was confined. The mission-family went in the evening to pay their respects. They found the lady in the bush, cheerful, and apparently quite well. The infant lay beside her, with its legs tied together to make them grow straight. The chieftess intimated, that a European garment would much improve the appearance and comfort of her child. Her request was so moderate, on such an occasion, that it was readily complied with.

On the following Sunday, they visited Jakey's son, who was ill, and an old man of sixty years of age, whose symptoms were very similar. Their sufferings were peculiar and severe: both maintained that their lizard-god had insinuated himself into their chests, and was preying upon the substance of their hearts. They were supplied with medicine and rice, and exhorted to pray to the true Jehovah. The brethren observe, in reference to these and other cases: "Age and affliction are indeed calamities in this country. There are no outward circumstances of comfort to relieve exhausted nature; no attached friends to soothe the spirit in its deepest sufferings; and no blessed hope to animate faith with sweet foretastes of that joy 'which is unspeakable and full of glory.' O ye Christians of other lands, will ye not shed a tear over this misery? Will you not breathe to heaven a prayer, that God may reveal His mercy to these benighted islands of the South Seas, the inhabitants of which are living 'without God in the world,' and dying 'without hope?'"

Thursday, December 25th, was duly observed as Christmas-day. A prayer-meeting was held before breakfast, an appropriate sermon was preached in the forenoon, and the day was concluded with the usual evening exercise. Contrasting the state of things in England and New Zealand, one of the brethren said, "While multitudes in our native land are going up to the house of God to celebrate the festival of our Redeemer's birth, we are amidst cruel and benighted Pagans, who have no knowledge of the benefits of the incarnation: but 'hitherto the Lord hath helped us.'"

On the last day of the year, the missionaries assembled the people, and addressed them on the end of the world and the general judgment. They afterwards held a watch-night, when they renewed their covenant, and received the sacrament of the Lord's supper. The recollections of home, their present situation, and the stillness that reigned around them, all tended to give peculiar solemnity to those services. They could say, with David, "If it had not been the Lord who was on our side, when men rose up against us: then they had swallowed us up quick, when their wrath was kindled against us: then the waters had overwhelmed us, the stream had gone over our soul: then the proud waters had gone over our soul. Blessed be the Lord, who hath not given us as a prey to their teeth. Our soul is escaped as a bird out of the snare of the fowlers: the snare is broken, and we are escaped. Our help is in the name of the Lord, who made heaven and earth."

CHAPTER VIII.

DOMESTIC STATE OF THE SAVAGES OF NEW ZEALAND—'HONGI INVADES
WESLEYDALE—ATROCIOUS CONDUCT OF TABRA AND TEPUI—STATE
OF THE SCHOOLS.

THE year 1824 opened upon the brethren without any remarkable change in the moral aspect of things in Wesleydale.
On balancing favourable and opposing circumstances, they found
their minds at about an equal distance between hope and despair. Of the validity of God's promise they had no doubt; but
whether they were to be the favoured instruments of its developement, still appeared to be questionable. They had just
strength and courage sufficient to enable them to prosecute their
plans of usefulness, faintly anticipating a favourable result.

On the 6th of January they had a long interview and discussion with Tepui on the general condition of his people, and the
necessity for some more stringent regulations relative to the cor-
rection and instruction of their children. They assured him,
that there existed a criminal negligence and apathy on those
great branches of parental duty; and that the difference, which
he himself admitted to exist, between young Europeans and
New-Zealanders was owing chiefly to the sedulous attention of
the former to the teaching and governing of their children in
early life. This he absolutely denied, and maintained that their
conclusions were the result of ignorance, on their part, of the
native character. "I have myself," he remarked, "paid some
attention to the subjects and parties to whom you refer, and
have arrived at directly opposite conclusions. The difference
which you have pointed out as existing between the two races,
arises from an inherent principle of goodness in the European,
and not from the causes which you have assigned. It is a bad
thing to beat children, and must not be done in our country.
We are an *i'wikéno*, 'a bad tribe;' and were we to correct our
children, they would retire into the bush and hang themselves.
Were a son to hang himself because of ill-treatment at home,
the relatives would at once assemble, and not only strip the
father of all that he possessed, but also spear him, or beat his
brains out with a club. This is the custom of our country. It
is a bad thing to correct children." The customs of the country
could not be violated with impunity; and yet the audacious
behaviour of the children formed one of the most productive sources of domestic unhappiness, often issuing in polygamy
and murder.

On the following evening the friends were roused by a loud
and discordant noise coming from the river-side. On going

down to inquire into the cause, they learned that the Bay-of-Islanders had brought a present of a new boat to Tepui, and that he was preparing an entertainment for them. They had dug a large trench in the sand, and partly filled it with hot stones and leaves. Upon the leaves they had placed vegetables and the carcass of a pig, which they had killed and cut into pieces. Having covered the carcass over with leaves and a good coating of sand, they were cooking it. The young people had a cooking establishment at a short distance, where they were busily employed in roasting and eating the entrails of the pig.

While the mission-family were at dinner on the following day, they heard a mournful cry, that seemed to descend from the top of the hill opposite their residence. They thought that the natives were only following their usual practice of wailing on parting with the Bay-of-Islanders, and took no further notice of it; but, in a short time, a messenger arrived to inform them that E Kau, the principal wife of Hururu, had just hung herself. On hearing this statement, one of the native servants said, "Then she is gone to *kapúra nui*, 'the great fire!'" The brethren hastened to her hut, and found her surrounded by the principal chiefs and her own children. The body of the infatuated chieftess was wet with their tears; while the surrounding woods echoed to their cries. Finding it to be still warm, the brethren ordered the body to be removed to an airy situation on the side of the hill. There they employed the various methods prescribed for restoring suspended animation, and persevered until a frothy *mucus*, tinged with blood, issued from her mouth, and she began to respire. Having placed her in a favourable position for recovering, they left her. On returning, in the evening, they found her much improved and tranquil. They laid hold of this melancholy occurrence, and endeavoured to impress upon her mind, and upon all present, the awful consequences of self-destruction. On returning home, the family united in a hymn of thanksgiving to God, who had enabled them to pluck another "brand from the burning."

The 12th of January, on which they gathered-in their wheat-harvest, was a day of peace and rejoicing. Towards the evening, Mr. King, of the Church mission, arrived on a visit from Rangahoo, and gave them an affecting account of the massacre that had just taken place at the *Tawiti-rahi*, or "Poor Knights' Islands." "Our natives," said he, "got possession of the sails of the ship 'Brompton,' in which Messrs. Marsden and Leigh were wrecked. They cut up the canvass, and fitted their own canoes with sails. After taking a sufficient force, with arms and ammunition, on board, they steered for the above islands. When they landed, the natives, knowing that the invaders had muskets, were panic-struck, and fled in all directions. Numbers threw themselves from steep precipices into the sea, and were drowned. Our people pursued the fugitives, and continued the work of destruction until they had depopulated the islands. They fed like vultures upon the bodies of the dead, and returned home laden with slaves and the flesh of men. We could not go out without seeing numerous portions of the human body, baked and raw, lying in the open air. Seven of our own tribe have also been killed for stealing potatoes." After pausing a little, he added, "Lord, have mercy upon New Zealand; for the habitations of the people are habitations of cruelty!"

On the 19th, E'i Too, hitherto regarded as being a respectable man, was reproved by his wife for a gross act of unfaithfulness. To be revenged on her, he vented his rage upon a favourite slave. Understanding that the slave was still alive, the missionaries hastened across the river, where they found her sitting near her mother. One stroke of the tomahawk had cut deep into the hand, and almost separated one of the fingers; another blow, aimed at the head, laid bare the jaw-bone, but had not fractured the bone itself. She had also received a flesh-cut in the back; but it was neither deep nor dangerous. They bound up the mutilated hand and face, but entertained no hope of ultimate recovery. Her father was killed in battle; her mother, herself, and a brother fell into the hands of a cruel villain, who evinced no remorse for the crimes he had perpetrated. Mr. Shepherd addressed the people in Maori with great fluency and obvious effect.

The Lord's day, February 1st, was such a sabbath of rest and blessing as the settlement had not experienced for several months; but, on the following Wednesday, while they were working in the brick-field, a person came running to say, that the chief Rua Tarra had killed a little slave. They quitted the brick-field, and, following the messenger, were approaching the scene of the murder, when they met Rua Tarra. He had a bill-hook in his hand, stained with blood; while portions of the flesh and hair of his victim adhered to several parts of the hook. Assuming an air of ferocity, he demanded, "What brought you here?" They replied, "To see the body of the slave killed by Rua Tarra." Turning round, and walking before them, he said, "Then come and see it." After conducting them a short distance, he pointed to a pool of blood, observing, as they looked at it, "I struck him there: that is his blood; but the body has been carried off to be interred." The charge against the deceased was, that he had stolen a few *kúmara*. Without extenuating the offence of the slave, the brethren laboured to convince Rua Tarra and the natives who were present, that it was cruel, unjust, and, consequently, displeasing to Jehovah, to take away life for such an offence; that, in fact, there was no proportion between the crime and its punishment. The people, however, justified the conduct of the chief, and vindicated the customs of the country. It afterwards appeared, that what they said on the occasion created uneasiness in the mind of Rua Tarra; for he visited the missionaries the next day, and inquired, with some anxiety, whether they had told Jesus Christ in their prayers about the death of the slave.

Sunday, 9th.—The children were examined in the school-room. They repeated the Catechism with great readiness and accuracy. Some of the lessons were long, and afforded the brethren such an opportunity for testing the intellectual powers of the native youth, as had not previously occurred. Generally their memories seemed to be vigorous and retentive; but the wild restlessness of the eye, and their rapid utterance, showed that they neither understood the meaning, nor felt the importance, of what they said.

On the 12th of March, Mr. and Mrs. Fairbourn and three children, Mr. and Mrs. Williams, and Mr. Kendall, of the Church mission, arrived at Wangaroa at three o'clock in the morning. They found the settlement in a state of unusual tranquillity. The principal chief had received a present from His Excellency, the governor of New South Wales, which put him in good temper with all the other chiefs. Mr. Fairbourn and his friends examined the buildings, the garden, the land that had been cultivated, and the surrounding scenery, and expressed their satisfaction with the plans and labours of the resident missionaries. Mr. Williams preached, on the morning of the Lord's day, from Matt. xv. 28: "O woman, great is thy faith: be it unto thee even as thou wilt." In the afternoon Messrs. Fairbourn and Williams accompanied their Wesleyan brethren to the mouth of the river Wai Tangi. Mr. Fairbourn addressed the chief with admirable simplicity and fervour; but the savage soon became irritated, and interrupted him with questions about muskets, gunpowder, and fighting. Mr. Williams then turned round, and spoke to the people, for some time, on God's omniscience. They seemed astonished and impressed. The friends of the Church mission attended the class-meeting in the evening: the Lord answered their united intercessions, and "baptized them with the Holy Ghost, and with fire."

<blockquote>
"They all were of one heart and soul,
And only love inspired the whole."
</blockquote>

The following week was occupied in secular and religious duties, and on Sunday, the 28th, Mr. Williams again preached from Rev. ii. 10: "Be thou faithful unto death, and I will give thee a crown of life." They walked to Mangaiti, Jakey's, in the afternoon, where the natives assembled in considerable numbers, and appeared to understand and feel the touching appeals of Mr. Williams. When he had done, they said, *E ranga tira núi I' a nei?* "Is he not a great gentleman?" After the public service in the evening, the mission-family commemorated the death of Christ; and thus closed one of the happiest sabbaths they had spent in the country. Having occasion to go some distance by water on the following Thursday, they went on board Mr. Williams's boat. They had not proceeded far when, as Mr. Fairbourn was fastening the sail, a gust of wind caught the boat. The brother who held the other rope continuing to hold on, instead of slackening it, the boat was upset, and the whole party plunged into the water. By the good providence of God, and the assistance which they rendered to each other, they got the boat righted, and reached the shore in safety.

Sunday, April 4th.—They were fully employed at the settlement of Mangaiti. The people were assembled to gather-in their *kúmara*. The brethren told them that the *kúmara* was the gift of *Atua* to *Te Pakeha;* that the white man's God loved them; that he called to them to forsake sabbath-breaking; that they had come to show them the way to heaven; and that, if they did not believe and obey, they would go to hell. While they were endeavouring to impress those truths severally upon their minds, the chief said, *Kurakía:* meaning that they were to sing, pray, and have done. They concluded the service, and set out for Toropapa. On their way they met great numbers of natives dancing and shouting as they moved along, "The chief Hudi Wane's sister is dead!" On reaching her residence, they found the relatives and others assembled to express their respect and grief. The body of the deceased lady was wrapped in a native mat, and placed in a sitting posture, as when alive. The upper part of the head, which was covered over with oil and red ochre, was exposed. Near the body sat her aged father, and before it two of her slaves. The missionaries introduced and discussed the doctrine of the resurrection and its consequences; but had no reason to believe that what they said made any favourable impression upon the persons present.

Returning home at night, they observed a body of strangers dancing within a sacred enclosure, where the bones of their ancestors were deposited. The brethren crossed the river, entered the sacred place, sang a hymn to Jehovah, and spoke to the strangers on the gospel method of salvation. They were a body of fine men, and listened with profound attention to all that was said. To the brethren themselves this was a season of deep interest and encouragement. "What may we not now expect?" said one of their number: "Ethiopia herself is ' stretching out her hands unto God!'"

Several canoes filled with warriors sailed from Wesleydale on Friday, April 23rd, to join 'Hongi, in his expedition against Hwā Roā. Tepui, an elegant and promising youth, son of Hudu, was anxious to distinguish himself in battle, and could not be persuaded to remain at home. After the fighting-men had left, a number of suspicious-looking persons from a distance were seen loitering about the mission-premises. Their movements were closely watched; and, as the night advanced, they were asked what they wanted; they replied, *Ki te mataki taki ano matou*, "To look about only are we come!" As they remained till a late hour, it was necessary that the missionaries should also "look about," to prevent their taking away several farming-implements, and other valuable articles that were lying about.

While they were preparing, on Sunday, May 9th, to go to Toropapa, it was announced by signal that 'Hongi and his war-riors were on their way to Wangaroa. Not knowing what might happen, they judged it prudent to remain at home. The natives of Wesleydale were soon in arms, and appeared in their richest attire. They were not long kept in suspense, as the canoes were seen advancing at no great distance. The brethren went down to the river-side, and awaited the arrival of the illustrious general and his forces. As they approached the landing-place, the wife of one of the chiefs stood upon the west side of the *pa*, and waved her garment in token of friendship; at the same time several of the principal fighting-men advanced, brandishing their weapons in the most dexterous manner. Before the canoes, which drew up in regular order, were moored, 'Hongi jumped upon the shore, which was the signal for a general debarkation. He formed his men in a few minutes, and ordered them to advance. They had not proceeded far before he commanded them to halt: they then performed the war-dance, with much clamour and agility. The tribes of Wesleydale having returned the *háka*, or dance of welcome, there was an end to hostilities. 'Hongi and Taniha, who was supposed to be the largest man in New Zealand, were invited to the mission-house, and dined with the brethren. After dinner the chiefs were each presented with a small hatchet, which they handed to their sons, and requested that they themselves might be furnished with bill-hooks. Feeling their situation to be somewhat critical, the brethren deemed it prudent to comply with the unreasonable demand. 'Hongi seemed friendly, but reserved. Those of the friends who had never seen him before were astonished, that a person who had passed through so many perils and hardships should be so buoyant and vigorous. "But," said Luke, "if he was a perfect gentleman in England, he is a perfect savage here!" On the following evening he and his people quarrelled with the natives, and, during the scuffle that ensued, they loaded their canoes with potatoes, and then sailed for the Bay of Islands.

The mission-family removed to their new house at midnight, and took their goods with them: yet, notwithstanding the lateness of the hour and the vigilance of the servants, a valuable box of tools was carried off. Search was instantly made for it; and, on going into the bush, they discovered, by the light of the moon, the robbers dividing the spoil. Several fled; but three of the chiefs remained near the box. Tepui said, "I am *tapu:* I cannot touch it." The others had portions of the stolen property under their mats. Nearly the whole of the articles were recovered.

On the following morning, while the brethren were conducting family worship, there was such yelling in the yard that they hastily rose from their knees, and went out to ascertain the cause. The natives were observed to be much excited, all armed, and evidently intending to surround the house. Amongst the foremost were the chiefs who headed the plundering party the night before. Tepui, who was so "sacred" on the previous evening that he could not even "touch" the stolen property, forced his way through the fence into the yard, and struck a washing-tub that obstructed him with his *maree.* There being some wet clothes in the tub, he threw them amongst his followers, who eagerly picked them up, and concealed them about their persons. He then got into the house, and was immediately followed by George, who was armed with a bill-hook, which he brandished over his brother's head, threatening him with instant destruction. They then commenced an attack upon the new house. The missionary's wife, her little infant, and a European girl, were alone in the house. They were not, however, able to force the door; and, after securing several articles that lay about, they quietly retired. George returned almost immediately; and, after rubbing noses, had the audacity to sit down at the breakfast-table, and not only help himself, but also his friend Tara Tahe, who had that morning taken from the premises a large iron pot. After adverting to these circumstances, the journal adds, "Love endureth all things."

At four o'clock in the afternoon, George again entered the enclosure. Observing a number of natives in the old *raupo* house, searching for needles, nails, or any thing else that might have been lost in the confusion occasioned by removing at midnight, he ordered them to be gone! As they did not instantly comply with his mandate, he grasped a blazing firebrand, and applied it to the thatch, declaring that, if they did not leave at once, he would burn the house about them. As the stick burned his hand, he was obliged to throw it to the ground before the thatch became ignited.

No sooner had those troublesome pilferers gone than Tepui

came to make friends. He was not observed until he had entered the house, having narrowly escaped being bitten by the watch-dog; and because one of the boys, who saw him, did not run to restrain the dog, the infuriated savage seized the lad by the neck, and bent his body until his head touched the ground. The brethren expressed their disapprobation of his conduct by taking no notice of him. Not receiving the *haere mai,* or " salutation of peace," he retired, muttering his displeasure. " After a day of extreme difficulty and trial," say the missionaries, " we all assembled in the evening for the first time in our new house, and united in the worship of Almighty God. ' Surely goodness and mercy have followed us all the days of our lives.' We will trust in God, and praise Him for ever and ever."

Having heard of the turbulent behaviour of the natives, Mr. Fairbourn came by sea, from the Bay of Islands, to inquire after the health and safety of his Wesleyan brethren. He landed on Friday, May 1st; and, before night, a report was spread over Wesleydale, that he had brought his boat, for the purpose of removing the teachers and their families, in consequence of the rude and barbarous behaviour of the people. This report reached Tepui, who hastened to the mission-house with a hog, which he begged might be accepted as a reconciliation. George, coming in at the time, joined earnestly in his brother's request : both expressed considerable anxiety lest their "bad conduct should be published in Europe, as, in that case, it would affect their trade with the Europe people." A formal reconciliation took place, to the mutual satisfaction of all present.

On the following Monday the brethren finished and opened a school-room, which they had built in the village of Tepui. Seeing one of the natives present with a pair of trousers on, which had been stolen from the station, they ordered him to give them up. Instead of delivering up the trousers, he withdrew; but returned in a few minutes, armed with a *háni,* and presenting a countenance expressive of the deepest malignity. After a glance at the countenance, the instrument, and the trousers, the brethren observed, " You have spoiled them with oil and ochre, and may now keep them." His passion cooled; he was evidently ashamed of his conduct, and offered them a sucking-pig, which they refused.

Sunday, June 6th.—"This day," says the journal, "being the anniversary of this mission, the text selected for the morning service was Acts ii. 39 : 'The promise is unto you, and to your children, and to all that are afar off, even as many as the Lord our God shall call.' Our afflictions have been various, of long duration, and of great severity; but the Lord has been with us, and His outstretched arm has hitherto preserved us from the

rage and malice of the man-eater. Glory be to God, we are
'the living, the living to praise Him this day.'"

Mr. Shepherd came over from Kiddu-Kiddu on the 11th, and
visited the schools at Toropapa. He catechized the children,
addressed the adults, and prayed sweetly in Maori. The people
were attentive, and, at the close of these religious exercises,
gave expression to their convictions, by observing, "It is true,
very true! It is good, very good!"

On Saturday, 19th, they received a message from Kia Roa
to say, that he was ill, and wished to see the teachers. This
chief had been guilty of a gross act of fraud, in a business
transaction with the brethren, a short time before. On reaching
his residence, they found him in a fever, lying in the open air,
and exposed to a heavy dew. They had him removed, and covered with a mat. On inquiring into the nature of his illness,
his friends informed them, that the spirit of a departed friend of
his had returned from the invisible world, entered his body, and
was killing him, that he might take his spirit to the regions of
happiness. "If you are so sure of happiness hereafter, as you
profess to be," said the missionaries, "how comes it that you
are all so afraid of death?" They preached Christ to the
afflicted chief and his family, as "the way, the truth, and the
life."

Early on Monday morning George entered the mission-yard
like a fury, tossing into the air the instrument of death which
he held in his hand, and exclaiming, "Where is Huki? I
will kill Huki!" He jumped through the window into the
new kitchen, and, perceiving Huki's mat lying on the floor, he
caught it up, and chopped it to pieces with his hatchet. The
domestics fled from the incensed brute to the upper parts of the
house. He was passing from the kitchen to another apartment,
ordering Huki to be delivered up to him that he might kill him,
when the brethren met him. They spoke softly to him, and he
became calm. It appeared that one of the brethren had removed
some boards from the end of a rush-house, in which they permitted this chief to live, which so exasperated him, that he
determined to express his dissatisfaction by killing the boy.
The boy, however, could not be found; and before George left
the house he professed to be reconciled. "Surely the wrath of
man shall praise thee: the remainder of wrath shalt thou
restrain."

While visiting the village of Tepui, on the 1st of July, they
paid their respects to the old chief, whom they found sitting
near his own door. "I understand," said he, "that you have
put a blister on the neck of E Héde: I wish you to know that,
should any serious consequences ensue from it, I will hang

you." He raised his hands and grasped his own neck, to show them, by signs, what he meant. He concluded by saying, "The blister is a bad thing: the blister is a very bad thing!" Having no doubt as to the intentions of Tepui, they went to E Héde's and removed the blister. They returned home discouraged and vexed by the insensibility and ingratitude of the people. E Héde soon afterwards became deranged, and remained in that state for some time. The brethren continued to visit and to pray with him, until it pleased God to restore the use of his reason. His relatives said that his spirit had left him, and gone to the *po*, the region of darkness; but that the spirit of a departed brother had met him, and told him to go back again to *te ao*, the realms of light. This, they said, was the true cause of his recovery. The brethren asserted, that Jesus Christ, the Son of the true Jehovah, the Author of health and life, had restored him. When they had made this statement, they heard the natives whispering to each other, "Did you hear that? It was Jesus Christ that healed E Héde."

On recovering the use of his reason, this chief recognised the missionaries with great affection, shaking hands and rubbing noses in the kindest manner. On being pressed to take some medicine, he requested that it might be delayed, as the native priest was coming. The priest was received on his arrival with every mark of respect. The chief then rose up, and, taking a small basket of *kúmara* in his hand, which had been prepared for the occasion, walked backwards and forwards in front of his hut. His countenance was serene; but his lips were not observed to move as if he were praying. In a short time he sat down, and, taking from the basket a few *kúmara*, which he wrapped up in the leaves of a particular shrub, he handed them to the priest. The priest rose, with an air of seriousness, and retired into the bush, taking with him the parcel of *kúmara*, which he placed on the top of a low wide-spreading shrub, in the immediate vicinity of the chief's residence. He then returned; and, having seated himself, delivered a long harangue; at the close of which, the basket, with the remaining *kúmara*, was placed between them, and the priest and chief ate together. After taking a mouthful or two, E Héde said, " I will eat no more. I will now take medicine from the white people." The brethren sighed over this ceremonial, and, addressing the true Jehovah, exclaimed, " O God, when shall these superstitions terminate, and the enlightening power of thy gospel emancipate this people from doing service to them who by nature are no gods?"

On the 11th, the brethren went to the residence of Tepui, situated at Pú Púké, to the westward of Wesleydale. On ascending the high ground, they observed that the country on the south side was well wooded and beautifully diversified; while that on the north presented a long range of bare hills, which opened upon the harbour of Wangaroa. This situation afforded an extensive view to the eastward. As far as the eye could reach, the country seemed to be level, swampy, and covered with mangroves. The scenery was picturesque and sublime; but the moral condition of the people threw a gloom over the enchanting landscape. Alas! these beautiful regions are still pervaded by darkness, cruelty, and cannibalism! For many generations the inhabitants have been

> "As far removed from God and light of heaven,
> As from the centre thrice to the utmost pole."

On descending from these heights, they called at the village of Whau Puké, where they met with several persons who had visited the mission settlement, and amongst the rest Kia Roa. He remarked, that there was great sickness in the land; that it was now evident to him that the white man's God wanted their country; and that He was killing the people to make way for the *Pakeha*, or European. The brethren showed them, that all lands belonged to Jehovah; that He created New Zealand; and that, consequently, it was His before it was inhabited. In regard to the relation in which they themselves stood to Jehovah, they proved that He gave them life, clothed them, made the flax and fern-root to grow, and was now willing to save them. The natives seemed to be much interested by these discussions.

The brethren reached Tepui's in the evening, and met with a kind reception; but they had scarcely crossed the river, before their ears were assailed with the obscene language of the females. All the people, excepting the slaves, had gone to Toropapa to cry for the dead. A decent-looking woman, dressed in a white mat, assembled the people. As this was the first religious service that these natives had ever attended, the missionaries introduced and discussed the character of the true God. But, alas! they might as well have attempted to reason with the lightning as it glided past them. The men evinced a total indifference to every thing that was advanced on the subject of religion; while all sense of propriety, or feeling of shame, seemed to be extinguished in the bosom of the females: young and old appeared glad when the service closed. As the brethren were leaving the village, they were offered two baskets full of beautiful fish, as an expression of the respect and friendship of the people. After encountering many difficulties, they reached home in safety, and found the settlement and their families in peace.

The ship "Endeavour" sailed into the harbour of Wangaroa on the 15th, having on board the Rev. Daniel Tyerman and George Bennett, Esq., deputies from the London Missionary

Society, with several other gentlemen. " The ship was soon surrounded with canoes, and filled with native men, women, and children.   On the following morning so many natives crowded on board, that, to prevent confusion, the captain ordered a bar to be placed across the quarter-deck.   The natives beginning to practise their pilfering habits, the captain became angry; and while he was endeavouring to clear the deck of the intruders, one of them, a chief, on being jostled by him, fell into the sea. This was seized instantaneously as a pretext for commencing hostilities.   The natives took possession of the ship, and made the officers and crew prisoners.   Tremendous were the howlings and screechings of the barbarians, while they stamped and brandished their clubs and spears.   The captain was surrounded with spears, Mr. Bennett's arms were pinioned to his sides, while Messrs. Tyerman and Threlkeld were in custody in another part of the ship.   One of the cookies pushed off Mr. Bennett's cap, and stood with his axe, which he had sharpened on board, gleaming over him.   They had handled the arms, sides, and thighs of Mr. Tyerman, who understood the meaning of those familiarities. In this condition they had remained nearly two hours when they heard the cry, ' A boat, a boat !'   The boat contained one of the Wesleyan missionaries, and the chief Te Ara, who had come to invite the gentlemen of the deputation to visit Wesleydale.   When the natives saw who were in the boat, they liberated the prisoners, and quitted the ship."*

Under the above date we find the following record in the journal of the mission, which, although it does not invalidate any statement contained in the preceding narrative, certainly softens some of its sterner features; and justice to all parties and interests requires that it should be subjoined :—

"Thursday, 15th.—Just as we were retiring from family prayer, our domestics shouted, 'Mr. Leigh and a ship have arrived in the harbour !'   In about an hour afterwards, R. Dacre, Esq., a Sydney merchant, arrived.   We were all rejoiced to see him. He informed us that Messrs. Tyerman, Bennett, and Threlkeld and son, were on board the 'Endeavour,' on their way from Otaheita to Port Jackson.   His interesting conversation kept us up till a very late hour.   While he regards the state of things in Otaheita as not being quite satisfactory, he yet gives the most cheering accounts of the progress of Christianity in the islands generally.   About half-past seven o'clock on Friday morning, one of us went down in our boat to bring the gentlemen of the deputation to our settlement.   They did not, however, arrive till four o'clock in the afternoon.   We learned with deep concern that the lives of our Christian brethren had been placed in jeo-

* Tyerman and Bennett's Voyages, pp. 183, 184.

pardy, by a furious attack made upon themselves and their ship, by a body of Tepui's people. It appears that when our boat came alongside the 'Endeavour,' it was ascertained that, for the last two hours, our countrymen expected every moment to be their last. The *petulance of the captain occasioned this rupture.* Our friends were eager to obtain information respecting our circumstances, the state of New Zealand and its inhabitants, and our prospects of ultimate success. On these topics we spoke freely; while they gave us such accounts of the glorious things which the Lord is doing elsewhere, as strengthened our hope of seeing the slaves of sin around us 'turning from darkness to light, and from the power of Satan unto God.' In consequence of the conduct of the natives to-day on board the 'Endeavour,' Messrs. Tyerman, Bennett, and Threlkeld intend to leave our shores so soon as their departure can be effected. They purpose sailing, if it be possible, to-morrow. It is our opinion that the gentlemen were not in such imminent danger as they apprehended; but that the whole scene was a stratagem of the natives, intended to intimidate the strangers by horrid grimaces and frantic yellings, in which they excel all other people in the world. We did not, however, succeed in our efforts to persuade our brethren that all that they had witnessed might have occurred in consequence of the violence of the captain, without any real intention, on the part of the natives, to do them any serious injury. After breakfast, on the morning of the 18th, the deputation left Wesleydale, accompanied by two of the resident missionaries, who went on board, and remained with them until the 'Endeavour' had cleared the heads of the harbour."

On the evening of the 27th, the whole population was roused and put in motion by a report that a party of strangers was coming to rob their *kúmara* and potatoe stores. All that could carry arms turned out, some with muskets, others with spears, not a few with bill-hooks, while several had *marees*, and carpenters' chisels tied to the end of poles. George appeared almost naked, armed with two muskets; while his wife, who accompanied him, a woman of a mild disposition, entered the field with a bill-hook. George was suffering from a sore throat; and, at the request of the brethren, he reluctantly gave up the fight, and returned home. The strangers did not make their appearance, so that the chiefs and their men were much disappointed.

Next morning George sent a private message, requesting that all the mission-property might be made secure, as a strong party was coming from Hokianga; and report said, they intended to raise a quarrel with the missionaries. The mission-house yard was speedily cleared of every portable article. After breakfast, George came down again, carrying two loaded muskets, which he discharged, and then made a long oration.   One of the brethren, who had gone over to Tepui's school, found the Hokianga fighting-men entering the village.   They soon filled the school-room, and sat down quietly, while the children repeated their Catechism, and united in singing the praises of the true Jehovah.   They seemed utterly at a loss to comprehend the meaning of those remarkable exercises.   Tepui, who was present, delivered an address, in which he said many things in commendation of the missionaries, dwelling particularly upon the cures they had effected, and the surprising efficacy of the blister.   He concluded by recommending the teacher to present the *ranga tira* or chief of the tribe with an axe or a hatchet.   The missionary went up to the chief, and shook hands with him.   He gave them a brief account of the nature and objects of his mission, to which they listened with evident surprise and satisfaction.   Addressing the teacher, they inquired, "Have you heard that the god of the Bay of Islands is about to visit you at Wangaroa?"   "I have not," said the teacher: "who is he?"   They replied, "*Who is he?*   He is none other than 'Hongi; we call him a god because he has eaten so many men."   One of the villagers having been married during the day, his neighbours assembled in the evening and robbed him and his friends of their potatoes.   By this barbarous practice these poor people were left without food.   "It is a common custom," says Brown, "to rob a new-married couple immediately after their nuptials, and not unfrequently to give them a good beating into the bargain."

The weather having been wet and stormy, the missionaries had not been to the school at Toropapa for several days.   When they went over, on the 6th of August, the natives were anxious to know why they had been absent so long.   On hearing the reason, an old man said: "I am satisfied: but *E nui te hia hia o toku ngakau kia haere mai koe hei, wakako i an i nga kupu o tou puka puka*.   'Great is the desire of my heart'" (or has been) "'that you would come and teach me the words of your book.'"   "*Learn to read?*" said the missionary.   "Yes," he replied, "I want to read about Jehovah."   The teacher having expressed his surprise that he should be inquiring about Jehovah, a young man who stood by observed, "The teacher evidently thinks that we do not believe what he says: but, if we did not regard his instructions, would there be so many inquiries into the cause of his long absence?"

On his way home the missionary called on Tepui, who was laid up with a bad leg.   After dressing his leg, and conversing freely with him on various topics, he drew from his pocket a piece of bread, which he presented to Tepui, in the hope of inducing him to violate the *tapu*, and thus, by his example, weaken the force of this national superstition.   At first he appeared agitated; but after a moment's reflection, he seemed to overcome his fears, and, taking the bread from the hand of the teacher, placed it by his side.   He seemed to feel the more acutely, because an aged chief from Hokianga was present on the occasion.   Turning to this aged companion in arms, Tepui said, "These Europe men say boldly, that our *tapu* is of the devil."   The chief George, who was present, was dissatisfied with the conduct of the missionary, and remarked, in an angry tone, "I will permit you to dress my brother's leg; but I prohibit you from visiting any other sick person."   The teacher replied, "I am afraid of Jehovah; He has commanded me to visit the sick.   If you kill me, I must visit the sick."   "If, after this, you attempt it," said George significantly, "I will tie you fast, and keep you in your own house." It was extremely difficult to deal with these capricious savages.

The brethren, who had not heard from their friends for a long time, received both British and colonial letters on the 21st.   After perusing these affecting memorials of intimate and indissoluble friendships, they recorded the solemn effect produced upon their minds in the following appropriate terms: "O what motives to renewed action are here presented!   What a spirit of love do the people of God every where breathe!   What earnestness do they evince for the establishment of Messiah's kingdom!   What steady zeal do our countrymen manifest in promoting the salvation of the New-Zealand cannibal!   O Sun of Righteousness, arise upon this people with healing in thy wings!"   On September 3rd, all farming and teaching operations were again suspended, by the sudden irruption of a band of warriors from Toropapa.   Tepui, having ascertained that one of his wives had violated the marriage covenant, killed her; and as she was related to some of these fighting-men and their families, they had come to demand satisfaction.   By the interposition of a few friends of peace, a reconciliation was effected without bloodshed.   On the following Sunday the brethren went over again to Tepui's.   The chief, his family, and a large body of natives attended public worship, and conducted themselves with becoming seriousness.   At this season of the year, the missionaries generally worked in the fields in the morning, preparing the ground, and chipping-in the wheat; in the afternoon and evening they visited the schools, and instructed the natives.

Sunday the 12th was a memorable day in the annals of this mission, for the unprecedented encouragement it afforded to the brethren.   On their way to the residence of Tepui in the afternoon, they met considerable numbers of the people coming out to bid them welcome.   The son of the chief informed them, that his father was awaiting their arrival with some impatience.   On approaching Tepui, he rose up, and received them courteously. They stood upon the banks of the river, and addressed the assembly on the character of the great Creator, and on the guilt and punishment they would incur if they should live and die in ignorance of Him. After the service, Tepui said, "I and my people have been planting *kúmara* all this morning. But the teachers themselves are to blame for it. It was their duty to have sent one of their boys to inform us that it was *te ra tapu no te Pakeha*, 'the sacred day of the white people.' Still I am afraid we shall suffer loss in consequence; for I hear, from several natives, that those who have worked on the sacred day have had bad crops." After some further conversation, the brethren returned home, calling on their way at the village of Whau Puké. Here the mission lads related what had been said about sabbath-breaking, and its consequences, at Tepui's. In conclusion, they added, *Me he mea ka mahi koe ka mahi ou tangata ra nei i te ra tapu o a Ihowa e tau kai kore tenei.* " If you work on the sacred day of Jehovah, or allow your people to work, this will be a year of no food !"

Having promised to teach E Takka and Tara Kidi to cultivate wheat, they left home for that purpose, accompanied by those chiefs, on the morning of the 16th. After entering the woods, and ascending several rugged steeps, they came to a piece of ground, about the tenth of an acre, which had been previously prepared for the seed. The brethren sowed the wheat, while the chiefs and the persons attending them covered it with earth, with small pieces of wood, shaped like the paddles of their canoes. The natives regarded the proceeding as a foolish experiment, likely to end in nothing but disappointment. Rua Tarra, having prepared a small portion of land near Toropapa, requested them to go over in the afternoon and sow it with wheat. They complied with his request, and left him joyfully anticipating the reaping time.

After a careful inquiry into the progress of the children attending the schools, they remark: " We find several children here, who have spent one hundred and twelve days in the school, and cannot even now write the letters of the alphabet." Having visited their parents, and accused them of inattention to the education of their children, they vindicated their conduct, and said, " Give them rice to eat, and it will strengthen their minds; and pay them for attending, and they will come more regularly." On the 22nd the mission journal was duly forwarded to New South Wales, to Mr. Leigh.

While attending the school at Toropapa on the 29th, the brethren were called to witness the wife of a chief undergoing the process of tattooing. The place selected was the fleshy part of the arm. The incision was so deep that the blood flowed copiously from the wound. They inquired into the utility of the practice, when the person performing the operation threw aside his dress, and showed them how much his own person was improved by tattooing. Though the blood was squeezed out of the wound, and a stick dipped in charcoal run along the groove to insert the colouring matter, no complaint escaped from the lips of the lady.

While visiting George on the 3rd of October, he gave them an animated description of the first landing of Mr. Marsden upon their shores at Mutandi; and imitated his voice and manner so perfectly, that the whole scene seemed to be passing before them. The brethren called the attention of the natives to the resurrection of the body and a future state. The impression was deep and general. One of the chiefs of Hokianga was present, and said, that now he understood clearly the difference between good and bad men in the world to come. Their being able to preach, though imperfectly, in the native tongue, was already producing the most satisfactory results.

From this place they went on to Toropapa, where the public service was interrupted by Kia Roa, who insisted on hearing again what they had said the week before about Jesus Christ. When they adverted to the resurrection, he said, "That I cannot, at present, believe." He contended that, as the event was future, they could not know it certainly. He denied that the spirit of man is immaterial, and maintained that it carried in substance hands, head, and legs into the invisible world : "For, how else," said he, "can it feed on *kúmara ?*" In replying to him, allusion was made to the crime of polygamy and its consequences. He desired the speaker to pause, and, rising up, defended the practice with a graceful and manly eloquence. The gist of his argument is expressed in the following sentence : "A numerous offspring is the glory of man : a number of wives is the only means by which he can rise to that distinction." Witiki strengthened his case by observing, that their chiefs set them a noble example in this respect ; and were they not to follow it, and reject the doctrine and example of the *Pakeha*, their country would soon be without an inhabitant. Those discussions brought out the cheering fact, that the native mind was moved and interested on questions relating to religion and morality. But the reasonings of those acute Heathens assumed, that no authentic revelation had, as yet, been given to man; and that the dogmas of their teachers were, like their own, of human origin, and sanctioned only by human authority, or national "custom." The time had not yet arrived when the missionary could put into the hand of an inquisitive native a tract explanatory of the grounds of the Christian faith, or a New Testament, in Maori, saying, "Take this and read, 'in your own tongue, the wonderful works of God.'"

A little before midnight on Friday, the 15th, the mission-family was disturbed in their first sleep by the yelling of the natives and barking of the watch-dogs. On getting up to ascertain the cause of the disturbance, they learned that the ship "Endeavour" had sailed into the harbour, and that Mr. Dacre was at the door. After taking a little refreshment, the captain delivered his letters. "As snow waters to a thirsty soul, so is good news from a far country." A letter from the Rev. D. Tyerman informed them, that the public mind had been much agitated in New South Wales, by the report of the desperate attack of their natives upon the "Endeavour," her passengers, and crew. On the following day Messrs. Davis and Shepherd, of the Church mission, paid them a visit, and experienced much of the grace of God at the class-meeting in the evening.

At the close of the service on Sunday morning, they received information that, in consequence of some misunderstanding with the captain, there was likely to be mischief on board the "Endeavour." They ordered the boat to be manned ; and, taking the gentlemen of the Church mission with them, hastened down the river, in the hope of preventing bloodshed. They found the captain, officers, and seamen in a state of extreme irritation ; while the natives, being excited, presented a wild and defiant appearance. "On Friday last," said the captain, "Tepui and his people came on board the 'Endeavour,' and stole one of our boats. Yesterday morning they had the audacity to bring it back ; and, after rowing it round the ship a few times to show off its sailing qualities, offered to sell it to me for a musket. The chief himself set the example of stealing, by seizing every thing he could lay his hands upon in the cabin. But for you missionaries, I would get my ship under weigh, shoot those savages, and clear their harbour." All parties being at length reduced to order, one of the brethren preached from 2 Cor. v. 10 : "We must all appear before the judgment-seat of Christ." The contemplation of a future judgment had, at least for the time, a tranquillizing effect upon their minds.

After dining on board, they went on shore, and assembled the natives on the west side of the harbour. Just as they were commencing the service, a person came, and informed them that the captain threatened to bring a ship of war to fire upon them, if they did not give up his boat. This intelligence produced such commotion, that it was found necessary to give up the service. The people affirmed that they found the boat adrift, and that, according to universal custom, it had become their property. This the captain as positively denied, and charged them with having cut it adrift and stolen it. Though acts of violence had been prevented, yet the brethren returned home at night considerably depressed by the occurrences of the day. After partaking of the Lord's supper, they retired to rest. They returned to the ship early in the morning, and remained on board all day. The natives voluntarily gave up the boat, and the "Endeavour" sailed. The brethren close their accounts of these transactions with a devout and grateful recognition of God's goodness in preventing the destruction of either property or life.

CHAPTER IX.

EXTENSION OF THE MISSION—'HONGI AND A FLEET OF ARMED CANOES ARRIVE—THEY BURN THE MISSION PREMISES—THE MISSIONARIES ESCAPE TO NEW SOUTH WALES.

FROM various causes the missionaries' stock of provisions at Wangaroa was nearly exhausted; and no potatoes could be procured in Wesleydale, those on hand being barely sufficient for seed. After due consultation, it was agreed that as many as could be spared from the settlement should go by sea as far as Ho-do-do, and, if possible, obtain a supply of potatoes from that district. The boat was accordingly manned, and cast off from the wharf at five o'clock, on the evening of November 2nd, 1824. They passed the Heads at sunset, and fell in with a canoe, which furnished them with plenty of fresh fish. A light breeze springing up, they hoisted their sail, and stood out to sea. About nine o'clock the wind changed, and compelled them to run for the land. Finding good anchorage off a sandy beach, they landed. The wind freshened, and the rain fell; but, having made a temporary tent of the boat's sails, and lighted a fire, they lay down upon the ground, covering themselves with some native mats and a coarse hair blanket, where they slept more soundly than the "effeminate libertine." They got up a little before sunrise, and, for the first time since the creation, the solitude of the desert around them resounded with thanksgivings and prayers to the true Jehovah. While preparing their fish for breakfast, two natives joined them, who evinced a friendly disposition, and assisted them in procuring ballast for their canoe. This place was called "I' de Au;" the brethren named it "Recreation Bay." When sailing out of the bay, they perceived that they had passed the night in the immediate vicinity of a considerable village; but the darkness of the night prevented the natives from observing them.

They bore away for the north head of Doubtful Bay, which they passed at eleven o'clock A.M. As the wind had become boisterous and the sea heavy, they were obliged to take down their sail, put the boat under the lee of the land on the north-east of the bay, and pull into Tai ma roa Bay. Here they met with a few natives, and a fresh supply of fish. Having been con-tending for eight hours with opposing elements, and in their wet clothes, they felt tired and drowsy. After spreading their clothes upon the bushes to dry, and taking some refreshment, they col-lected their mats, lay down in the open air, and slept till the evening. After invoking the blessing of God upon themselves, and the protection of Providence for their families, whom they had left exposed to the caprice of the Heathen, they again launched their boat; but the sudden gusts of wind which descended upon them from between the mountains, rendered it perilous to carry canvass. They used the oars till midnight, when they raised their sail, and, with a beating wind, entered Ho-do-do River, a little before daylight, on Thursday, November 4th.

They landed, lighted a fire, united in the worship of God, and prepared their breakfast. After breakfast they ascended the river, but had not proceeded far before they were boarded by a chief and his family. He informed them that, by the light of the moon, their vessel had been observed floating on the great waters the night before, and created no small stir, as it was supposed they were warriors coming from the Bay of Islands to fight them. "As ye have come peaceably," said he, "ye shall rest in peace." They ran the boat ashore on the very spot where Mr. Leigh and the Church missionaries landed, when they came to ascertain the fitness of Ho-do-do to become the head of a mission settlement. They found a small village of rush-huts, and but few inhabitants. They went several miles into the country, to pay their respects to the chief Tai Happa. Here a female presented a book, which they found to be a New Testament, and which Mr. Shepherd had lost when he accompanied Mr. Leigh to this place on the occasion to which reference has been made. She demanded a reward for having preserved it. They told her that it was the book of Jehovah, a sacred book, and that she must take great care of it. She said, "I never before heard of Jehovah. If the book be sacred, I cannot keep it; for, in all probability, your God will be angry with me for having it." "Who do you sup-pose made the first man?" they inquired. She replied, *Ko wai hoki nei ka kite?* "Who can positively tell that?" The brethren stated the object of their visit, and asked the natives whether they had any pigs or potatoes to dispose of. They expressed their regret that they could not meet their demand, as they were short of provisions themselves, and had scarcely reserved sufficient potatoes for seed. "Do you suppose," said the missionaries, "that we shall be likely to succeed at Hwā Roā?" a place distant about a day's sail. "In reference to the people there," they observed, "their stock of provisions is as low as our own."

There being now no prospect of obtaining relief from either of those sources, the brethren resolved to return to Wangaroa. They had had no sleep during the previous night, the day was now far spent, and it was considerably past high water; yet they determined to attempt the descent of the river. The tide fell so rapidly that they were obliged to get out of the boat, cut a channel in the sand, and drag her along. After immense labour, they reached the mouth of the river, where they lighted a fire, took some food, dried their clothes, and gave God thanks for all His mercies. "Ho-do-do," they remarked, "possesses many advantages; the valley is extensive, the country around is agreeable, there is plenty of water, and the banks of the river are covered with flax; but the navigation is bad, and the harbour too open to afford good anchorage for ships." They sailed from the river with a fair wind, and reached home on Friday, November 5th, at six o'clock in the evening. Though they had not been successful in procuring either pigs or potatoes, yet they heartily embraced each other, and home seemed to all to be more than ever home. The chiefs were surprised that they should have ventured so many hundreds of miles to sea in an open boat, and concluded their remonstrances by observing, *E i wi porangi koutou ora woa parano:* "You are a mad-brained tribe, you have narrowly escaped drowning."

On the following Sunday, after a discourse on 2 Tim. i. 10,— "Christ, who hath abolished death, and hath brought life and immortality to light through the gospel,"—they went over to Tepui's. The people would not allow them to proceed, until they had given them an account of their voyage to Ho-do-do. When this was done, the natives listened with interested attention to a description of the general judgment. At the close of the address, one of the persons present rose up and inquired, " Is it your opinion that the condition of the soul is so fixed after death, that it cannot return again to this world?" They answered, "Yes: and will you tell us whether you desire to be found upon the right hand or upon the left, on the day of which we have been speaking?" Kia Roa sprang upon his feet; and, seizing his right hand with his left, exclaimed, with deep emotion, *Ki terei! ki terei!* "At this! at this!" He added, " Last night, while asleep, I saw a great pole, very high, very high indeed! On the top of it there was a flag, and, a little below the flag, a man was nailed to the pole. He looked down very lovingly upon me, and a white man asked me to go up to him. But as I did not know the white man, I refused to go. If you wish me to go up to him, should I have such another sight, I will go. Was this your Jesus Christ? If so, who was the white man that wished me to go to Him?" They informed him that, while they could give him no information respecting the white man to whom he referred, their sacred book enabled them to give him all necessary instructions as to how he was to go to Christ. They endeavoured to show him the distinction between the actual manifestation of Christ to the senses, and the revelation of the truth and grace of Christ in converting the soul.

On Thursday, the 11th, an expedition was suddenly equipped, and sailed for Hwa Roa. There were several canoes laden with men, women, children, provisions, and muskets. Tepui's was the most conspicuous, and contained his family, ammunition, and fire-arms. While they professed to be going on a trading and fishing voyage, there were strong grounds for suspecting that their real object was to fight and plunder other tribes. The chiefs Hudu and George delivered each an oration before they left. So large a body of their people having left Wesleydale, the brethren resolved to extend their labours, and seek elsewhere for converts.

Next Sunday, after the forenoon service, they set out, in a north-easterly direction, in search of a place called Hwai Nui. After a fatiguing journey through brakes, and over hill and dale, they arrived at Taka Pau. As soon as the chief, whose name was Tupi, saw them, he turned, ran home, fired off his musket as a token of respect, and then returned, and gave them a cordial welcome to his residence. They immediately opened their commission, and revealed to these barbarians, for the first time, the character of the true Jehovah. In speaking of the origin of things, they remarked, "All men sprang from one God and one parent." On uttering this sentiment, the natives smiled, and, interrupting the speaker, begged to remind him that the difference between his own complexion and theirs refuted his argument. After settling this point, they resumed their description of the creation of all things. The stars, they declared, were not, as they supposed, the eyes of New-Zealand warriors looking down upon them, but bodies of great magnitude, situated at vast distances from each other, and from this globe. From creation they proceeded to describe the fall of man; and, while they were speaking on that subject, the chief issued instructions to prepare fish and potatoes for the strangers. After a lengthened service, during which the natives paid marked attention, and seemed to comprehend what was said, they were presented with broiled fish, and about a gallon and a half of hot potatoes. The potatoes were served up in a native basket; while the water, the smell of which sickened them, was drawn from an old calabash. But the frankness and hospitality of the people made every thing pleasant.

After this repast, they ascended the hill on which the chief's residence stood, that commanded an extended view of both sea and land. Between this hill and the ocean there lay a beautifully diversified country; several islands were seen lying off the shore; the atmosphere was remarkably clear and serene; while the setting sun threw a softened glory over the whole scene, that rendered it truly magnificent. Observing, at no great distance, another *pa*, they set out to visit it also. Here the people received them with satisfaction, and behaved well while they spoke to them about the true God and eternal life.

They returned to the former village, as they had promised to spend the night with their new acquaintance, Tupi. In the mean time, he had set his house in order, and arranged every thing with a view to their comfort. The house itself was nothing more than a thatched roof, supported by stakes let into the ground. He had placed some burning logs at the further end of it, that produced such smoke and heat, that, but for a fresh breeze which passed through it, they would have been in danger of being both suffocated and roasted. Some green *raupo* was placed upon the floor for a bed, a bundle of dried mat-grass was provided for a pillow, and two coarse blankets which they had brought with them served for under- and over- covering. Having read the sixth chapter of St. John's Gospel and sung a hymn, they prayed in Maori, and lay down in peace. They rose in the morning at the break of day, and, after reading the scriptures and prayer, again breakfasted on fish and potatoes. After distributing fish-hooks amongst the principal men, they commenced their journey homeward, accompanied by Tupi, who engaged to conduct them to Matandi.

They took a north-easterly direction, and, after passing a plantation that skirted the sea-shore, turned into a rich valley of arable land. They crossed this valley, meeting with but few natives, and ascended a hill called Kidi Pukā, from the top of which they had a distant view of the *pa*, or fortification, of Hwa Roa. Passing through a forest of magnificent timber, they emerged into a barren region wholly covered with fern. They arrived at Matandi at ten o'clock A.M., and, after resting a little, assembled the natives, and spoke to them about Jehovah. These natives regarded with suspicion every thing that was advanced, as they "had never heard of this God before." Their surprise was evidently increased while they listened to a description of the fall of man. At the conclusion of these exercises, a pot of potatoes and some crisped fish were placed before the missionaries. Here they parted with Tupi, who, as an expression of friendship, made them a present of a small mat.

In travelling from Matandi to Wesleydale, they experienced a sensation which they had not felt in any other part of the country, and for which they were not able satisfactorily to account. In ascending the hills, they were seized with such a numbness in their limbs, that it was with difficulty they reached Wangaroa. After mutual congratulations, and devoutly acknowledging their obligations to Divine Providence, they entered the following record in the journal: "This journey has convinced us that travelling from place to place, assembling the natives wherever we go, and explaining to them the first principles of revealed truth, will be the most successful plan that we can adopt for diffusing the knowledge of Christ in this land of spiritual darkness."

On the following night, just before the family retired to rest, the chief Te Ara entered the yard in his shirt, with a bill-hook in his hand, and foaming with rage. He stamped with his feet, tore to pieces every thing that came in his way, and ordered the lads to be given up to him immediately. "I will kill them," he exclaimed: and then, distorting his countenance, expanding his jaws, and gnashing his teeth, he added, "and eat them too." They begged him to assign a reason for killing the boys; but he would assign no reason "until their blood was shed." After a little persuasion, he said, "My wife tells me that your boys have beaten my daughter, and that she now lies groaning in your house." He was informed that one of the young women was moaning, but that it was not his daughter; nor was the moaning occasioned by beating, but by a temporary illness. The girls were then introduced to him: and, when he saw them, the savage assumed the most pleasing aspect; confessed, in the softest forms of language, that he had acted rashly; and went home deeply mortified. His daughter, having expressed a wish to go home, took her things, and followed her father, to the no small gratification of the family.

On Thursday the mission-journal was prepared for transmission to Mr. Leigh.

After an early service, on Sunday, November 27th, they went on board a canoe, and paddled to Tepui's. The missionaries here asserted, as they had done before, "that their God was the true God, and the kind Parent of all." To this dogma the natives objected; for, while they admitted that their gods were bad spirits, they yet maintained that the God of the white people was but partially good. They declared that the statements that were being advanced were contrary to fact. "See," said they, "how the God of the white man gives him good food and all other good things; while He gives to us only fern-root, fish, and *kúmara*." These observations afforded the brethren an opportunity for explaining the connexion between cause and effect. They proved that, while the "good things" to which

they referred were the gifts of God, they were, at the same
time, the legitimate fruits of industry. Where there was indolence, there was the fern-root: where there was industry, there
were *kúmara*, wheat, and rice. They appealed to their own observation: When the natives cultivated their land, and planted
or sowed it, they saw that their crops were as early and as
abundant as those on the mission-settlement. After listening
to this reasoning for some time, they were at last convinced,
and observed, " It is very true ; it is very good."

Having sung and prayed, the brethren took to their canoe,
and sailed down the river to Motu Wai or Boyd's Island, a
small rocky islet close to the wreck of the " Boyd." Here they
landed, dined, read the fourth chapter of St. John's Gospel,
and prayed. After mutually expressing their admiration of the
goodness and mercy of God in establishing a mission amongst
such a nation of murderers and man-eaters, they seated themselves at the oars, and sailed for Hwai Tapu, which lay nearly
behind the high hill called, by Englishmen, " the Dome of St.
Paul's." They were surprised and disappointed in meeting
with so few natives, and so little encouragement.

After much labour and fatigue, they landed at Wangaroa at
twenty minutes to twelve o'clock at night. They had not been
long in the house before there came on the severest storm they
had experienced in the country. It raged, with uninterrupted
violence, during the following day. The wind, rain, lightning,
and claps of thunder, resembling parks of artillery playing upon
each other, combined to render the scene sublimely terrific.
When at its height, they expected, for several hours, that their
buildings would be swept from their foundations, and themselves and families placed in jeopardy by the falling materials ;
but Divine Providence preserved them. It required several
days' labour to repair the damage done to the premises by this
tempest.

George, who had suddenly withdrawn with a body of his
fighting-men, returned on the 11th of December. He said that
he lay concealed in the neighbourhood of Pārra till near midnight: he then rushed upon the forces of his brother Tepui and
the natives with such impetuosity and yelling, that they were
all panic-struck, and fled. Before they could be rallied, he had
taken their potatoes, gathered up their fishing-nets, and was on
his way home. He looked upon the execution of this daring
exploit as an evidence of his own superiority and that of his
warriors ; but, as the tribes whom he thus robbed were his own
allies, the whole proceeding was characterized by treachery and
injustice.

The brethren had a considerable gathering of natives at

Tepui's on Sunday, December 12th. In their addresses they had specified several crimes that were peculiarly displeasing to God, and declared that such as were guilty of those crimes would be inevitably and eternally punished. "They richly deserve it," said Kia Roa; "for they have eaten the people of Ho-do-do, where you have lately been; and, perhaps, by and by, they will come over and eat us also." It soon became evident that they had applied the whole discourse to their enemies at the Bay of Islands.

On the evening of the 20th, the ship "St. Michael," Captain Beveridge, entered the harbour. She brought stores, foreign letters, and several friends from the Bay of Islands. Captain Beveridge and four Europeans arrived at the settlement, Wesleydale, on the forenoon of Wednesday, the 22nd. An interesting prayer-meeting was held in the evening. After the meeting closed, a native said, addressing himself to the missionary, "Surely we are not so likely to go to hell, now that we have made peace with you and with one another? You must intercede with Jehovah, that we may not be cast into hell." *Panga ki te kapura o te po:* "Cast into the fire of the invisible world!" said an aged woman that stood by; "what has been said about the resurrection of the dead and hell is false. The *réinga*" (or state of the dead) "is a good place, where they eat *kúmara*, pork, and fish. While I was asleep last night I saw my father there. He hailed me in the most friendly manner, and gave me some of his food, which was sweet, very sweet." She was told, that it was no doubt the devil that appeared to her, and endeavoured to persuade her that hell is a fine place, that he might deceive her. "*The devil!*" she exclaimed; "you say that he is a wicked spirit: if so, is it likely that he would have used me so well, and given me such good food, the food of the invisible world?" She then altered her tone, and observed, "Jehovah will, perhaps, kill me in the evening for what I have said this afternoon." After some remarks on the infinite mercy of God to man, the natives were dismissed.

December 25th, being Christmas-day, Divine service was performed on board the "St. Michael;" and the whole was solemn and profitable in a high degree. They returned to Wesleydale, and dined upon roast beef, sent as a present from the brethren of the Church mission at Kiddu-Kiddu. On the Lord's day the congregation was increased by the attendance of several officers and men from the ship "St. Michael." The sermon was founded upon 2 Cor. iv. 5: "For we preach not ourselves, but Christ Jesus the Lord." All yielded to the impressions of truth; and the tear fell from every eye.

The natives raised such a disturbance on Tuesday evening,

the 28th, that the mission-family supposed some dreadful calamity had occurred.   On inquiry, they ascertained that, in some business-transaction with the "St. Michael," the chief George had obtained a quantity of gunpowder.   On examining his purchase, he supposed that he had been imposed upon, and roused the natives to demand satisfaction.   After much threatening, rage, and tumult, their passions cooled to a more moderate temperature.   On passing a woman that was sacred, who was lying down and eating in conformity with their national custom, one of the brethren said to her, "You ought not to do so : your custom is of the devil!"   She said nothing; but a sick man who was lying near her, replied, "You say this is of the devil, and that is of the devil; but do tell us if there be any thing of Jehovah about us."

These incidents, occurring as they did from day to day, clearly showed, that the truths of the gospel were leavening the public mind, and that, although the "kingdom of God" had not yet "come with observation," there was a great preparatory work in progress.   Up to a very recent period, the missionaries and their families had been subject to continued alarms, to noisy intrusions, and, in two instances, to personal violence ; but latterly the turbulence of the people had somewhat abated ; and a year which had been replete with evidences of God's all-sufficiency, was closed with the usual solemnities.

As it is a common practice with commercial men to balance their accounts once a year, or more frequently, to ascertain whether they have been trading to profit or exhausting their capital; so it is fitting that those who are employed in conducting the affairs of any branch of the universal church should occasionally pause and mark with discrimination the depression or elevation of Christian truth.   In applying this principle to the New-Zealand mission, we observe :—1. That at no former period had the mission assumed a more encouraging aspect than at the close of this year. The whole of Wesleydale presented a peculiarly interesting and beautiful landscape.   Such portions of it as were under cultivation, whether by the missionaries or natives, were laden with the bounties of Providence, while the copious rains that had lately fallen had revived and refreshed the verdure of the fields and the diversified foliage of the woods.   The kitchen and flower garden, on which the brethren had bestowed much labour, and which was well stocked with fruit-trees and European vegetables, while it yielded no small gratification to the eye, contributed much to their domestic comfort, by affording them a daily supply of green peas and new potatoes.   2. Considerable progress had been made in the acquisition of the native tongue.   When Mr. Leigh commenced his labours at Wangaroa, there was no written or printed book in the language; and his co-adjutors and successors were for some time without the assistance of any book. The brethren were now, however, so far advanced in their studies, that they could hold conversations with the people, and pray extempore in Maori. "No person can conceive," they remark, "what our feelings have been when we have gone amongst the natives, with our hearts yearning with pity, and burning with earnest desire, and have been obliged to return, from time to time, without being able to reprove them for their cruelty, or tell them of the love of God to men. Now, we can say a little to them in their own language, and but a little; but we hope to be able soon, by diligence and perseverance, to unfold to the barbarians around us some of the inherent beauties of the scriptures. We are anxious that a language hitherto employed in promoting crime and death should henceforth become the consecrated medium of enlightenment to the numerous tribes of savages spread over this extensive country." 3. The effects of their labours amongst the adults, and of the system of instruction introduced into the schools which they had established, were becoming more and more apparent. Looking back from this date, they observe, with equal surprise and gratitude, "What a change has taken place in Wesleydale! More respect is shown to us now, both by chiefs and people, old and young, than at any former period. We now live in comparative tranquillity, while the natives live at peace amongst themselves. Who could have supposed that, since the first landing of Mr. Leigh, so much could have been effected? How comfortable we could make him now! And, if it were the will of God, how desirable it is that he should return to this country!" Rays of evangelical light were falling upon the minds of the natives; and even the children in the schools were beginning to reason amongst themselves about their accountability to God, and the doctrine of future rewards and punishments. Such, then, was the state of things at Wangaroa when the January of 1825 invited the brethren to resume their work of faith and labour of love.

Several years prior to this date, one of the Wangaroa tribes had killed two of the brothers of the chief Patu One in battle. Patu One's resources had been so exhausted, that he had not till now been able to demand satisfaction; but, during the present month, he had succeeded in manning and equipping twenty canoes for the war. These forces were to assemble in a small bay within four miles of the harbour of Wangaroa. One of the brethren had left Bahia at eleven o'clock on the night of the 31st of January, accompanied by the Rev. Mr. Williams, of the Church mission. The next day, about eleven o'clock in the forenoon, they were boarded by three of Patu One's war-canoes, under the command of Nene, a chief from Hokianga. The chief stepped into the mission-boat,

and said, "We wish you to go on shore and eat some *kúmara*
with us." The brethren begged to be excused, as the tide was
beginning to flow, and they were anxious to ascend the river
with it. Nene said, *Kahore he wa kia rongo ki nga waka kahore :*
"There is not time for us to listen to objections," and ordered
his men to man the oars and carry the boat in-shore. The missionaries were surprised, on landing, to see such a formidable
array of warriors. They lifted their hearts to God in prayer for
His protection of themselves and property ; for they had valuable
stores in the boat, which was likely to be seized. They were
conducted into the presence of Patu One, who told them that he
was going to fight their people ; but that, not being able to commence the attack before day-break to-morrow morning, he had
intercepted them, lest they should carry the intelligence of their
approach to Wangaroa. Finding themselves prisoners in the
hands of a powerful army, the brethren resolved to make the
best use of their circumstances. They spent the whole of the
afternoon in conversation with the chiefs. In the evening all
the chiefs assembled in council. When the assembly broke up,
it was stated that they had agreed as to the best mode of attack ;
and that, instead of deferring it till daylight, they should sail
almost immediately. At ten o'clock in the evening, the missionaries proposed singing and prayer. The chiefs assembled the
warriors, when the brethren sang the following verses :—

> "Sing to the Lord! exalt Him high,
> Who spreads His clouds along the sky!
> There He prepares the fruitful rain,
> Nor lets the drops descend in vain.
>
> "He makes the grass the hills adorn,
> And clothes the smiling fields with corn:
> The beasts with food His hands supply,
> And the young ravens when they cry.
>
> "What is the creature's skill or force?
> The sprightly man, or warlike horse?
> The piercing wit, the active limb?
> All are too mean delights for Him."

Mr. Williams prayed, with much simplicity and fervour, in Maori.
The hour of the night, the peculiar circumstances under which
they were met, and the prospects of a battle, terminating, perhaps, in the destruction of themselves and families, all conspired
to render this an occasion of interest and deep feeling.

In ten minutes after the orders were given, the baggage was
on board, the men seated at the paddles, and the fleet in motion,
Patu One's canoe taking the lead. The night being calm with
moonlight, the sea smooth and unruffled, and absolute silence
observed throughout the fleet, the effect was solemn, and the

spectacle imposing. The fleet passed the mission-boat, on entering the harbour, and enjoined the strictest silence on all on board.
The brethren landed at Wangaroa on the evening of February
3rd.   After a sermon by Mr. Williams, several hours were spent
in profitable conversation and prayer. The fight was not attended
with much loss of life, as, after a few skirmishes, they settled
their differences.

On the 5th of March, a large body of natives assembled, without any apparent cause, about the mission-premises. Their
numbers and appearance awakened some uneasiness in the minds
of the brethren.   Presently Ahoodoo, one of the principal chiefs,
got over the fence, and went up direct to the house. He was
met, and informed that he had done wrong; that his example
would, in all probability, be followed by his people; and, if so,
the consequences might be such as he himself would have reason
deeply to regret.   In a moment he became furious, and ran up
and down the yard, foaming like a mad bull, and threatening
destruction to all in the most alarming manner. During this
confusion, some of his people stole a favourite young dog. One
of the brethren going after them, the thief quietly delivered up
the dog to him.   Seeing the dog in the possession of the missionary, the son of the infuriated Ahoodoo seized the animal by
the leg, and broke it.   He then struck the missionary with his
spear.   Two of the brethren, who had been looking out of the
window, hastened to rescue their colleague from destruction. On
seeing them coming to his assistance, the savage rushed upon
Mr. Turner, and, without saying a word, aimed a blow at his
head with his spear.   The blow fell upon his left arm, which he
had raised to protect his head, and the spear was broken in two.
Laying hold of the broken piece of the spear, he tried to stab
Mr. Turner in the side; but did not succeed, as it was the blunt
end of it.   On seeing the teacher lying senseless on the ground,
another chief interfered, and prevented his receiving further injury.   In the mean time, the father of Te Booe had thrown another of the brethren down, and would, in all probability, have
murdered him, had he not been prevented by several natives.
By a stroke of his spear he had bruised his arm, and cut two of
his fingers.   The chiefs called off the natives, and left the family
without further molestation. After the wounds of the missionaries had been dressed, they "made their requests known unto
God, by prayer and supplication, with thanksgiving."

On this calamitous day, the brig "Mercury," of London,
entered the harbour for supplies. Early on the following morning, March 6th, intelligence was brought to Wesleydale of her
arrival, and of a contemplated attack upon her by the Ngá-té-po
tribe.   The hope of saving life, even at the risk of their own,

led the brethren to unmoor their boat, and sail at once to the scene of danger. They were accompanied by Tepui. They found the ship surrounded by canoes, the deck crowded with natives, and the captain and officers bartering various commodities. After surveying the vessel, Tepui walked up to the brethren, and inquired, "Do you know this tribe?" meaning the ship's company. They replied in the negative. He further inquired, "Is this *their* sacred day? I know it is yours!" "They acknowledge it to be their sacred day," was the reply. He then exclaimed, with equal astonishment and indignation, "See how they trade! They must be a mean tribe!" The missionaries, perceiving, from the excited state of the natives, that they intended to create a disturbance, advised the captain to get out in the night, with the ebbing tide, when it was probable that the people would go on shore. As the vessel was on her way to Port Jackson, they wrote a hasty letter to Mr. Leigh: then, stepping into their boat, they drew off Tepui and the natives of Wangaroa from the ship. They had no sooner left, than the captain ordered the anchors to be lifted, the topsails to be set, and the decks to be cleared. In executing these orders, several of the natives were thrown overboard, and young Tepui, the chief, was nearly drowned. This was the signal for a general rising. The glittering and clashing of hatchets, and other weapons, together with the loud vociferations and deadly struggles of the contending parties, rendered the scene truly terrific. The brig, being at the mercy of the elements, was driven by a baffling wind, with her stern close to the shore. According to national law or custom, she became the property of the chief owning that part of the sea-coast; and, as he was present, he instantly ordered a general plunder. In a few moments the dead-lights were torn out, and the sails cut down; while boxes, chests, and other moveable articles, were seen flying over the sides of the vessel in all directions. The crew, being driven from the deck, took to their boats, and fled for their lives. The missionaries turned their boat, and, not without some apprehension for their own safety, steered for the ship. On observing them approaching, Tepui, who was armed with a musket, beckoned to them to come on board. The confusion on deck, and the general appearance of the brig, were singular and distressing: the rigging was cut away, the hatches were all off, and the decks swimming with oil. The savages were quite naked, and, having washed themselves over with oil, it ran so copiously from their heads, that they were nearly blinded by it. The chiefs having ordered silence, the brethren addressed them. They admitted that the captain had acted improperly in doing business on the sacred day, and in using violence in removing the natives.

from his ship; but maintained that they had given much provocation, and were deserving of blame for the way in which they had treated these foreign strangers. They pointed out the probable consequences of this outrage upon their own trade and social condition. They advised them to deliver up the ship, and retire.

In less than ten minutes the ship was surrendered to the missionaries, and the chiefs and their tribes retired. The brethren, having got the mate and three seamen on board, cut the cable, leaving thirty fathoms and the anchor, hoisted what canvass remained, and stood out to sea. They steered for the Bay of Islands. As the evening advanced, the wind changed, the sea rose, and they began to move to leeward, with every prospect of a storm. At midnight the storm abated, the wind died away, and a dead calm ensued. At ten o'clock on the following morning, they ascertained that they were twenty miles from the nearest land, that the heavy swell was carrying them rapidly out to the main ocean, and that they had no compass, chart, or quadrant, while the hatches were all off, and the dead-lights out. In these circumstances they agreed to abandon the vessel, and endeavour, if possible, to save their own lives. The mission-boat, which had been hoisted upon the ship's quarter, was now lowered, and the land reached, by the mercy of God, at half-past four o'clock in the afternoon.

The strength and spirits of the party were nearly exhausted; but, while they were preparing refreshments, a body of armed natives came suddenly upon them. The chief snatched the watch from the hands of one of the brethren, and refused to give it up. He insisted on seeing the inside of a box, containing wearing apparel, supposing it to be full of gunpowder. The portmanteau had also to be opened, that he might examine its contents. Had they attempted to go to sea, an immediate attack would have been made upon them. For two hours the number of natives continued to increase, so that the situation of the missionaries was becoming more and more critical. They did not, however, betray any fear, but went on with their cooking.

Amongst the last arrivals were a chief and his wife from Wesleydale. When the chief made his appearance, the mission lads said, "Now our hearts are well." His presence was quite enough to secure protection; and, at his request, a blanket was returned which had been stolen. After taking some refreshment, they read a chapter, sang a hymn, and united in prayer. Their natives, not being satisfied with these exercises, sang and prayed by themselves. They erected a tent with the boat's sails, against a perpendicular rock, and retired to rest; the chief taking a place at one end of the tent, and his wife at the other. The lads stretched themselves upon the sand, with only one blanket to cover four of them.

They rose at daylight on the morning of the 9th. The sky was serene, and the wind fair. They had no sooner left the tent, than the natives, who had assembled in considerable numbers, entered it, and carried off both the trunk and portmanteau. The friendly chief, having offered to see them safe home, went on board with them; and they had the unspeakable happiness of reaching Wangaroa a little before midnight.

About eight o'clock, on the morning of April 2nd, David, one of their native boys, came up to the gate, accompanied by the persons from whom he had been redeemed. A considerable number of natives assembled about the gate at the same time, armed with harpoons and lances which had been stolen from the ship "Mercury." Their conversation respecting the lad, who, they said, had injured them, increased in vehemence until it became a complete clamour, and he was in danger of being torn to pieces and devoured. Their plan, as it afterwards appeared, included the death of David and the plunder of the mission-house. While the brethren were engaged in prayer, they heard the report of a musket in the front of their dwelling. On opening the door, they observed Te Pune approaching them, with a countenance indicating friendship. He restored peace, and delivered the boy from destruction. "My heart," he said, "is sick, because I fear you will all leave, and *take your property with you.*" Believing that their goods could not be removed but at the risk of their own lives, they assured him that, whatever might become of themselves, the boxes should not be taken away. "But," said they, "should we remain here, perhaps the natives will murder us." He instantly replied, "No, no; 'Hongi has said, 'Do not hurt the white people.'"

On the following day, Sunday, 3rd, Kia Roa called to say, that the people had manned the boat stolen from the "Mercury," and taken it round to sell it, if possible, to a ship at the Bay of Islands. "We are sorry to hear that," said the brethren; "for some of them may lose their lives in attempting to sell the stolen boat to Europeans." "If they should," he remarked, "then yourselves and the missionaries at the Bay must die as a satisfaction." "But what evil have we done," they inquired, "since we came here, that you should fall on us, and take our lives as a satisfaction?" He said, thoughtfully, *Ko wai hoki nei ka matau i te mahi puku o te ngakau Maori?* "Who can fathom or understand the secret work of the native heart?" This was not the first evidence they had had that the people were beginning to trace many of their personal and social crimes to the depravity of their own hearts.

The friends of the Church mission at the Bay of Islands, having heard of the peculiarly trying circumstances in which their Wesleyan brethren were placed, hastened to Wangaroa, to render all the assistance in their power. It was their deliberate judgment, that the females and children should be removed to one of their stations immediately. Their arrangements were soon completed; and the party quietly left Wesleydale, and arrived in safety at Kiddu-Kiddu. Here the brethren of the Church mission held their quarterly-meeting on the 6th. The state of affairs at Wangaroa engaged their attention the whole of the afternoon. The result of these anxious deliberations was embodied in a resolution, to the effect, "That the Wesleyan brethren be advised to remove from Wesleydale as soon as possible, and not to endanger their personal safety by any injudicious effort to bring away with them the property of the mission." On receiving this communication, the brethren retired to consider what was to be done. After much conversation and prayer, they agreed to abandon the mission for the present; but, as the ship "Endeavour," from Sydney, was expected daily, they resolved to await her arrival, in the hope of being able to save her from destruction. In the evening they succeeded in getting on board their boat a cask of flour, and another of pork, and in removing them, during the night, to Kiddu-Kiddu.

On the 7th, they visited the chief George, who had been declining for some time; but, though it was the "sacred day," he would converse about nothing but ships, muskets, and war. He was now incapable of executing a scheme which he had seriously contemplated against the Bay-of-Islanders. "Should they molest us," he observed, "we will form an alliance with two other tribes, march to the Bay while 'Hongi is absent on his war expedition, and kill the wives and children of the fighting-men who have gone with him." They visited this chief again on the 17th, and were of opinion that his end was near. He was reduced to a skeleton, and able to converse only in broken sentences. But there were no indications of remorse for the atrocities of his past life, and no apprehension expressed in reference to his future safety.

At seven o'clock, a great cry was heard: George had ceased to breathe. The domestics fled from the mission-house, and set off at full speed to conceal themselves amongst their friends in the village. The brethren, having reason to apprehend the worst, walked hastily up the bank, locked the yard gate, and ascended the hill to listen whether the tribes were assembling to attack the settlement. Here they stood a considerable time, expecting every moment might be their last. No eye beheld their loneliness but His who never forsakes His people. After waiting some time, they returned home, and prepared for flight. At midnight two natives passed the gate, and informed them that the body of the chief was removed to the *wahi tapu*, or "sacred ground," and that Tepui desired to see them at the *wahi tapu* immediately. He had prevented any attack being made upon their families, and gave them a kind reception. They returned home, and enjoyed, upon the whole, a good night's rest. Next day they mingled freely with the natives, who evinced a friendly disposition, and seemed pleased to see them. Still they considered their situation to be perilous; for they knew that Te Ara, or George, had reflected upon himself, during his last illness, for not having taken satisfaction of the Europeans for the loss of his father on board the "Boyd," and had enjoined his people to demand that satisfaction after his decease. In compliance with the dying request of their chief, the people assembled round the mission-premises; and, while the brethren were uncertain as to whether they had come to claim life or property, they jumped over the fence, and bore off a fine duck, with the blood of which they were content. They now learned from unquestionable authority, that, notwithstanding his professed regard for them, Te Ara had been the principal cause of nearly all the assaults that had been made upon themselves and their property. He had, on one occasion, sold some pigs belonging to the brethren for a musket, and then accused his people of having stolen them.

The settlement now enjoyed a short interval of repose, during which the natives assisted the brethren to lay down such a breadth of wheat as was likely to afford a supply of flour for a whole year. Things thus presenting an encouraging aspect, and the ship "Prince of Denmark" arriving at the same time with fresh stores from New South Wales, it was judged prudent and safe to bring the females and children back from Kiddu-Kiddu, and to remain, for the present, at Wangaroa. They travelled overland, and reached the settlement of the Church mission on the evening of Monday, June 27th. The family united, with emotions peculiar to persons in their circumstances, in singing :—

> "And are we yet alive,
>   And see each other's face?
> Glory and praise to Jesus give
>   For His redeeming grace!
>
> "What troubles have we seen,
>   What conflicts have we past,
> Fightings without, and fears within,
>   Since we assembled last!
>
> "But out of all the Lord
>   Hath brought us by His love;
> And still He doth His help afford,
>   And hides our life above."

By the assistance of the friends at Kiddu-Kiddu, the children were safely conveyed back again to Wesleydale. The entire country had been kept, for some time, in constant excitement by the rapid movements of 'Hongi and his army. He was now engaged in war with the Koipara tribes, and forced them to a decisive battle. Those tribes mustered eight hundred fighting-men; seven hundred of whom were supplied with native weapons, and only one hundred with muskets. 'Hongi commanded not more than three hundred troops; but they were picked men, and all provided with fire-arms. Those forces met; and long and deadly was the conflict. Many fell on both sides, and 'Hongi's son was left dead upon the field.

On returning to the Bay of Islands, with the broken fragments of his little army, 'Hongi ascertained that, during his absence, the tribes of Wangaroa had seized and plundered the ship "Mercury." These acts of violence had been of such frequent occurrence, and accompanied by such circumstances of cruelty and injustice, that few European ships could be induced to enter their harbour. Being apprehensive lest their bad name should affect other ports in the country, and thus limit his opportunities for obtaining muskets and gunpowder, and check his ambitious career, he resolved to strike a fatal blow at the "man-eating tribes" of Wangaroa. The news of his coming, and a knowledge of his avowed object, produced a deep and general sensation amongst the people. He was coming, they said, like a whirlwind; "he will kill and eat *us* in the morning; proceed to the heads of the harbour, and eat the natives there for dinner; then conduct the multitude of his fighting-men to the North Cape, and eat the people there for supper. *A pare ho katou ratou o era wahi ekure ra a 'Hongi ratou ko ona i tangata e makona,* 'When all the people of those parts are consumed, even then 'Hongi and his warriors will not be satisfied.'"

'Hongi transported his warriors to Wangaroa, and landed in Wesleydale on the forenoon of July 23rd. They halted at Maitipara, about one half-mile north-east of the mission-house, and completed their arrangements for the attack. When drawn up in line, they presented a formidable appearance. When all was in readiness, they advanced upon the huts of Maitipara, which they levelled with the ground; then, crossing the river, they cut down a large *kumara*-house belonging to Tepui. The principal men approached the foot of the *pa*, which had been well fortified and provisioned, and performed the *hàka*, with convolutions resembling, one would suppose, those of incarnate fiends from hades. The great captain concentrated his men, and ordered them to erect booths for themselves of whatever material they could lay their hands upon. While they were thus employed,

'Hongi and Tariha, who was second in command, entered the mission-premises, and dined with the family. After dinner, they were each presented with a blanket.

The next day, being sabbath, the friends assembled, as usual, for religious worship. Their neutral position, while it gave intensity to their solicitude, increased the fervour of their devotion. To be suspected of a friendly feeling towards his enemy, by either party, was sure to involve them all in destruction before the close of the day. The text selected for the occasion was appropriate: "And now I exhort you to be of good cheer." (Acts xxvii. 22.) After the service, they felt calm and resigned.

Early on Monday morning, 'Hongi and Tepui were brought together, and had a friendly interview. When their differences were amicably settled, 'Hongi assembled his fighting-men, and, after addressing a few complimentary words to them, ordered them to march overland to the Bay of Islands. During their stay at Wangaroa, the brethren were obliged to watch their premises day and night. To prevent their sacred huts from being polluted, the warriors set them on fire before they left.

A formal meeting of the brethren took place on the 29th, at which it was resolved to complete, without delay, several buildings then in progress, re-organize the schools in the adjacent villages, and, by a simultaneous and vigorous effort, endeavour to bring the young people to an acquaintance with Christ. "If we shall succeed," they observe, "in this undertaking, these young people will become the most efficient instruments of instruction and salvation to their families and to the country." The importance of the schools was becoming more apparent every day, while the children were evincing an increasing interest in the main facts of revelation. The following is but a sample of the questions which the more intelligent children were beginning to propose while under instruction: "Could not Jehovah have prevented Satan, the bad spirit, from overcoming our first parents?" "Had the antediluvians no canoes in which to take refuge from the waters of the flood?" "Would our first parents have continued happy, if they had not sinned?" "If Jesus Christ had not died, what would have become of mankind?" "Would the Jews not be ashamed to see Jesus Christ, after what they had done to Him?" "Do you think that, if Satan had not got proud, all would have been well?"

On August 24th, Shari, a little girl who had been long on the establishment, behaved well, and had made an encouraging progress in civilization and general knowledge, was married to a boy who was her first cousin. The ceremony was simple: The parties met, and, after mutual explanations, signed a document in which they bound themselves to live together when they should come of age. A sick woman, who was dissatisfied with the visit of her native priest, sent for the white teacher. On arriving at her hut, he inquired, "What did you say to the priest?" "I asked him," she said, "'Whence is my sickness? What trespass have I committed? Have I touched a sacred head? Have I eaten any forbidden thing? Or is the *Atua* eating me? Tell me, shall I die, or shall I recover?'" The missionary adds: "The conjuror shaped his answer according to appearances, received his present, and retired to carry his prediction, if possible, into effect." Truly, "gross darkness" covers the mind of the people, while "destruction and misery are in their ways: the way of peace have they not known: there is no fear of God before their eyes."

Considerable sickness having prevailed in the mission-family, and Mrs. Turner being now dangerously ill, they wrote to the Church missionaries, requesting that, should any ship call at the Bay, having a medical officer on board, they would direct him to Wesleydale. Those brethren, with their wonted promptitude and kindness, pressed the doctor of a whaler into their service, and brought him themselves overland to Wangaroa. His advice and prescriptions were of great benefit to the whole family.

The watch-night was held December 31st. After an exposition of Matthew xxiv. 44, "Therefore be ye also ready: for in such an hour as ye think not the Son of man cometh," the Lord's supper was administered, and the year closed with devout thanksgivings to God.

On the 17th of January, 1826, they gathered into their new barn, not yet finished, a plentiful harvest, in good condition. Their stock of salt being quite exhausted, and there being no prospect of an early supply, they were obliged to relieve themselves by attempting the manufacture of that article. For this purpose they launched their boat, on the morning of the 26th, and, after taking on board five natives, three days' provisions, and several iron pots, sailed for a small creek not far from the wreck of the ship "Boyd." Meeting with several large stones upon the beach, they rolled them beyond the tide-way, lighted up their fires, and placed their pots between the stones, filled with salt-water. While some were engaged in superintending the salt-boiling, others were gathering wood, supplying fresh water to the pots, and sustaining the fires. "We continued thus employed," they say, "till midnight, when we laid ourselves down under the open canopy of heaven, with our domestics around us. The serenity of the sky, the rural spot we had selected for our operations, and the peaceful solitude that reigned around us, all tended to solemnize the mind, and strengthen that sense of security which faith in Providence can alone supply." They kept up the fires during the whole of the following night, watching and sleeping alternately. After much labour and fatigue, they reached home at a late hour on Saturday night.

Those secular occupations have been represented, by one class of writers, as being agreeable recreations; while another class, such as Dr. D. Lang, has insinuated that "they were more in accordance with the tastes and early habits of missionaries generally, than exercises of a more intellectual character." I will place before the reader what the missionaries themselves have said on the subject, and then leave him to form his own judgment. "Temporal things," they observe, "unavoidably occupy much of our time. Either we have laid our plans on too extensive a scale, or are short of hands, or we are unskilful in the application of our resources; for a large portion of our time is occupied in merely secular duties. It has been the grief of our souls, a real affliction to us, and has no doubt retarded, in some degree, the success of our primary object. But we must have houses to live in; and who is to build them ? preaching-houses and schools; and who is there here to provide them ? If we subsist at all, the land must be cultivated; and who will do it here even for hire ? These, with us, are not labours of choice, but of necessity. Yet we are not unmindful of the higher duties of our office. We have had much difficulty with a barbarous language, but have so far succeeded that we can now converse and preach in it: we have translated the first Wesleyan Catechism, and trained twelve boys and six girls upon our own establishment, who have made a satisfactory progress in reading, writing, and arithmetic. Some of the sons of the chiefs are very promising, while several girls excel in various kinds of needle-work. We are daily instructing the adults in the great doctrines and duties of the Christian religion, and visiting the schools we have set up in the adjacent villages. We have translated hymns for those schools, which the children sing delightfully. We are, no doubt, preparing the way of the Lord amongst the savages of this distant land." The Church of England sent out mechanics to teach the arts and religion, but no clergyman to form a church; the Wesleyans sent out missionaries to form a church, but no artisans. Nor was this possible in their case, with the small means which the Wesleyan church at home supplied. It was a happy circumstance that their agents were not ashamed to work with their own hands, while they discharged the duties of evangelists.

During the first half of the current year they passed through a succession of trials and of triumphs; being alternately elevated with hope, and depressed by discouragement. On the 15th of October, the chief Teuna, who had been ill for some time, expired. Just before he died, he sent for a slave, and ordered him to be shot, that he might accompany him as his servant into the invisible world.   Waikato, who happened to be present, ordered the slave to be set at liberty.   The dying chief, being thus disappointed, seized his muskets, and, pressing them to his breast, expired, carrying, as he supposed, their fiery spirits into eternity.

Much uneasiness was occasioned on the 17th, by the following message from 'Hongi:—*He houma koutou hei wahi kei! Me he mea ka kite i au i o koutou kanohi e nga te uru, ka patua katoa tea koutou e au pau rawa:* "Fly all of you to another place!   If I see one of your faces, O Ngate Uru," (the name of the Wesleydale tribe,) "I will kill you all, and devour you utterly!"   Tepui became almost frantic.   He shot a relation dead in a quarrel, and almost killed a slave with a hatchet. Inflamed with rage, and perhaps stung by a feeling of remorse, he made the valley ring with his vociferations.   "Let us have a general massacre," he exclaimed; to which the people coolly replied, "You must go to it alone."   On going to dress the wounds of the slave who had been struck with the hatchet, the brethren learned, with sorrow, that he was dead, roasted, and devoured.

Mr. Williams, of the Church mission, being with them on November 12th, preached from, "Do this in remembrance of me," and afterwards administered the sacrament.   In the afternoon they formed a party, and crossed the hills to Pu Puke. The 'natives, however, were so wild and turbulent, that it was found impossible to arrest their attention.   During their absence, a distant tribe entered Wesleydale, and took up their residence near the mission-premises.   After some annoyance and explanation, they were induced to withdraw; which they did without doing much mischief.   On the day following the brethren finished a new house for their European man-servant and his wife, and completed the desks and benches in the school-room adjoining.

After the service, on the morning of the 19th, a messenger arrived to inform them that the *taua*, or "fight," which had been expected overland, was coming by sea, and had actually sailed into the harbour; that, finding three of the natives gathering shell-fish, they had made prisoners of them.   The people fled to the *pa*, believing that the next tide would bring the warriors up to the settlement.   The mission-family assembled in the evening, and were much blessed under a sermon from Titus ii. 11–13: "For the grace of God that bringeth salvation hath appeared to all men, teaching us that, denying ungodliness and worldly lusts, we should live soberly, righteously, and godly, in this present world; looking for that blessed hope, and the glorious appearing of the great God and our Saviour Jesus Christ." They retired to rest about the usual time, and left themselves and the events of to-morrow in the hands of God.

The army appeared in the morning in due time, bringing with them the corpse of a fine young woman they had killed by the way. The body was baked and eaten near the mission-house. A detachment, of about three hundred men, spread themselves over the plantations, and pulled up by the roots the corn and *kúmara*, which were just rising above ground. They broke into the boat-house, and were carrying off several articles of value, when the brethren ran down and interrupted them. In the scuffle, they took the hat of one of the teachers, and threatened to spear or shoot him if he did not retire. They tore down the fences, entered the grounds, took whatever was within their reach, and then retired to their camp. The resident natives were shut up in the *pa*, and durst not come to the assistance of the brethren. Late in the afternoon a chief, with a band of warriors in his train, broke into the yard, and demanded a slave-girl, whom they had redeemed about eighteen months before. As the strangers were well armed, and quite peremptory and furious, the poor girl was reluctantly given up to them. Understanding that the mission-house was to be attacked during the night, the children were put to bed with their clothes on.

The circumstances of the missionaries had now become extremely embarrassing : they saw themselves, their families, and the property of the Society, placed in imminent danger. As they sat watching at midnight, the annalist took his journal, and made the following entry : "How little do our friends in Europe know of the insecurity of our condition! Before day-break we may be plundered, murdered, and eaten. O that, with the Psalmist, we may be always enabled to say, 'God is our refuge and strength, a very present help in trouble! Therefore will not we fear, though the earth be removed, and though the mountains be carried into the midst of the sea. The Lord of hosts is with us ; the God of Jacob is our refuge!'" Early in the morning they learned, to their great joy, that, peace having been made during the night, the hostile tribes were preparing to leave the settlement. It cost them much labour to repair the damage done to the fences and out-buildings.

In conformity with their resolution to extend education and Christianity simultaneously, they opened a school, on the 30th of December, upon a new principle. The children were to attend two hours in the morning, receive a little rice, or some other refreshment, and afterwards return home. Eighteen children attended on the first morning, and the scheme appeared likely to be productive of the happiest results.

This season of comparative tranquillity and success was but of short duration. For some time there had been prevalent rumours of the intention of 'Hongi to abandon the Bay of Islands, and take forcible possession of Wesleydale. Those reports were rendered the more probable, by the domestic calamities that had lately befallen him. His son-in-law, who had been detected while carrying on an improper connexion with one of his wives, shot himself, and soon after died of his wounds; while the woman strangled herself. Another of his wives was killed, as a satisfaction for the life of the former. In consequence of these occurrences, 'Hongi, it was said, was determined to leave Wai-mate, the scene of so many misfortunes, and remove to Wangaroa.

On Thursday evening, January 4th, 1827, while the brethren were engaged in Divine worship with their own natives, they were interrupted by the announcement of the actual arrival of 'Hongi and a fleet of canoes. As his intentions were involved in mystery, all was commotion, and the settlement rang with the cries of the natives. The chiefs, several of the principal men, and their slaves, fled to Hokianga, a place about forty miles dis-tant. 'Hongi sent his daughter and the wife of Taria to say, that he did not intend to visit the settlement, and to request that their fighting-men would go down and assist him to drive the Ngá-té-po tribe from their fortress. The men soon mustered, and descended the river. The fort stood upon the summit of a hill, almost perpendicular. After being repulsed with the loss of several lives, 'Hongi succeeded, at last, in reducing the place. The Wesleydale warriors returned on the following day, and removed their wives and families to the camp of 'Hongi; thus leaving the missionaries at the mercy of any marauding party that might be disposed to take advantage of their defenceless condition.

It was now deemed necessary to acquaint their brethren of the Church mission with these circumstances, and to solicit their assistance. While preparing the letter, twelve armed savages landed from a canoe, got over the fence, and proceeded towards the house. The brethren went to meet them, and inquired what they wanted. They replied, "We are come to take away your things, and burn your premises: your place is deserted, and you are a broken people." One of the native boys heard them say that their number was too small, but that to-morrow there would ·be a general plunder. At day-break on Wednesday morning, January 10th, they were apprized of the near approach of a small detachment of 'Hongi's men, armed with muskets, spears, and hatchets. They dressed themselves, and went out to meet them. The missionaries asked their business: they said, "We are come to fight." "But why do you do this?" it was asked. They replied, "Your chiefs have fled, all the people have left the place, and you will be stripped of all your property before noon; therefore instantly begone!"

Oro, the chief, ordered his men to proceed to the work of

destruction. They fired off signal-guns, and the natives were seen coming from various quarters. After breaking into the out-buildings, and completely gutting them, they commenced an attack upon the dwelling-house. While the assailants were forcing their way through the back door and windows, the family escaped through the front door. They ran down the garden, made an opening in the fence, and passed over the wheat-field. The party consisted of missionaries Turner and Hobbs; Mrs. Turner, who had been confined only five weeks; Miss Davies, who was on a visit; a European servant and his wife; five native boys, and two native girls. They had before them a journey of twenty miles, over a mountainous country, and under a heavy rain. They met a war-party from Hokianga, about two hundred strong. They ordered the mission-family to move to the side of the road, and go down upon their knees. They did so, and expected to be killed every moment. To their inexpressible joy, the chiefs assembled around them, and then desired the warriors to pass on. One of these friendly chiefs, fearing lest they might fall into the hands of some stragglers in the rear, accompanied them for some distance. The Church missionaries, with their accustomed promptitude and kindness, met them twelve miles from Kiddu-Kiddu, bringing with them twenty natives to carry the children, and assist several who were sick. They reached the station about seven o'clock in the evening, after a day of excessive toil and appalling danger, thankful to God for their miraculous preservation, and feeling deeply indebted to the brethren of the Church mission for their sympathy and seasonable assistance.

The destruction of the mission-property at Wangaroa was complete. The out-houses, including the barn, which contained a supply of grain and flour for twelve months, together with the dwelling-house, were burned to the ground. The cattle, goats, and poultry were all killed, and nothing remained but the brick chimney. 'Hongi destroyed or dispersed the " men-eating tribes," at the heads of the harbour: only twenty, it was supposed, escaped. In the vicinity of his camp, the ovens were crowded with victims of war; while all parts of the human body, those of the mother and sucking infant, lay in undistinguishable masses. He pursued the flying enemy as far as Hunahuna, a village near the Maunga Muka, where they made a stand. During the fight, 'Hongi stepped from behind a tree to discharge his musket, when a ball struck him : it broke his collar-bone, passed in an oblique direction through his right breast, and came out a little below his shoulder-blade, close to the spine. This shot interrupted his career. The wound never closed; and the wind whistling through it afforded amusement to the sinking warrior.

The brethren left New Zealand, for New South Wales, on the 31st day of January, 1827. The Church missionaries, expecting soon to follow, shipped their property to the colony by the same conveyance.

Thus terminated, for the present, one of the most noble, best sustained, and protracted struggles, to graft Christianity upon a nation, savage and ferocious, which the history of the church of Christ supplies.

CHAPTER X.

STATE OF THE MISSION IN THE COLONY—DISCOVERY OF NATIVE TRIBES —ARRIVAL OF THE REV. D. TYERMAN AND G. BENNETT, ESQ.

THE New-Zealand missionaries, being obliged, under the circumstances detailed in the preceding chapter, to leave that country, arrived in New South Wales, in February, 1827; and, by incorporating their labours with those of the resident missionaries, gave a fresh impulse to the cause of God in the colony. We must now call the attention of the reader to the condition in which Mr. Leigh found the mission, when, in an indifferent state of health, Mr. Marsden, Mrs. Leigh, and himself, arrived in Sydney, from New Zealand, on the morning of Sunday, November 30th, 1823. On the evening of that day he makes the following observations: "Through the mercy of God, I am once more amongst my old friends in New South Wales. I think I am not worse than when I left the shores of the 'man-eater.' I have been prevented by illness from attending public worship this day; but have been delighted with the accounts I have received of the largeness of the congregations, and the interesting and impressive nature of the services. There are now four missionaries, having in connexion with their societies one hundred and twenty-three communicants." The congregations had been improving, for some time, in number and seriousness throughout the colony. The influence of religion was spreading: many were being awakened to a serious concern about their salvation, and several conversions had recently taken place. The Sunday-schools were vigorously conducted; and a considerable proportion of the juvenile population of the country were experiencing their salutary effects. Several devout and intelligent young men had been admitted to various departments of usefulness, and were proving valuable auxiliaries in conducting the mission. Two of the most respectable and talented of them had been selected and sent to the Friendly Islands, to assist the brethren in those stations. A very general interest had been awakened in favour of Christian missions; and several missionary societies had been formed, for the avowed purpose of extending the kingdom of Christ at home and abroad. Some of the aborigines had begun to inquire, "What must we do to be saved?" and one, at least, had gone, as the first-fruits, to glory. For nearly twelve months Divine service had been conducted in Sydney Harbour on Sunday afternoon: it was well attended, and had led to a marked improvement in the general deportment of the sailors.

Having secured the vantage-ground by great personal sacrifices and labours, the missionaries felt anxious to maintain their position. Knowing the printing-press to be an engine of immense power in working out any extended scheme for the secular or spiritual advantage of a people, they solicited the committee to supply this grand auxiliary, and place it under their own direction. The lofty claims of some zealous Churchmen had provoked the hostility of those who held the principles of Dissent; and as the Wesleyans assumed neutral ground, they were frequently made the common object of attack. A press, in the opinion of the brethren, would enable them to vindicate their principles, expound their church-polity, counteract prevalent errors, multiply works of general utility, and publish rudimental books in the various languages of the southern islands. An additional argument in favour of this proposal was drawn from the rapid increase of the population, and the growing importance of the mission. An experiment had already been made, by the publication of a periodical, entitled "The Australian Magazine." To this work the governor extended his patronage, and several persons of distinction had promised their co-operation.

But while the committee admitted the importance of the objects proposed, they reminded the brethren of the abstraction of their time and talents from the more direct and spiritual objects of their mission, which the working of such an establishment would necessarily occasion. Nor did any practical inconvenience result from the refusal of the committee to accede to the earnest solicitations of the missionaries, as there was then a prolific provincial press, conducted, upon the whole, with considerable ability and impartiality.

The zeal, energy, and success with which the work had been carried on in New South Wales, during the absence of Mr. Leigh in New Zealand, afforded him great satisfaction; and mitigated, to some extent, the severity of his sufferings. During that period, however, the aspect of Methodism had been somewhat changed. In the opinion of several of his brethren, he had not, in his first organization of the Wesleyan church, claimed for it an independent *status*, but had assigned to it a subordinate position, and made it, in some degree, subservient to the interests of the Church of England. Under this impression, the brethren had drawn a broader line of demarcation between themselves and the colonial clergy than had previously existed; but this well-intentioned change had created much difference of opinion, and some prejudice against Mr. Leigh. Looking at the whole case, we may observe: 1. That Mr. Leigh, having been in early life a member of an Independent church, cannot be suspected of having had any particular predilection for episcopacy. 2. The colonial clergy had no antipathy to Methodism; on the contrary, the two senior chaplains avowed a grateful recollection of their early connexion with its societies. 3. Had Mr. Leigh set up a system antagonistic, even in appearance, to the Church, he would have been sent out of the colony. The governor doubted the propriety of giving him permission to preach at all, assigning as a reason, " that it might lead to religious controversies and divisions, and ultimately to a disturbance of the public tranquillity." "I am a member of the Church of England myself," said His Excellency, "and wish every person in the country to be of the same communion. To be candid with you, Mr. Leigh, I would rather you had come from any other body of people than the Methodists. It is true, that it matters but little by what name we are called; but while I govern this country, I must protect it from religious strife and party warfare. If you will see the colonial clergy, and put yourself on a friendly footing with them, it will tend much to promote your comfort and success."

What, in those circumstances, did Mr. Leigh do? Did he remind His Excellency that the Toleration Act was in force, and that he intended to claim and to exercise all the prerogatives of the colonial clergy? No. Did he shape Methodism to the taste of the clergy, and place himself and his system under their supervision? He did not. He set up Methodism in all the integrity of its doctrines, its disciplinary laws, and fiscal regulations, and placed the whole in a friendly, and yet not more friendly than Christian, attitude towards the Church. In acting as he did, he neither compromised his ecclesiastical system, nor his ministerial independence. They are spurious notions of independence, however plausible they may seem, that would place us at variance with good men of other denominations, or prevent our uniting with them in working out any general scheme for the social or spiritual elevation of the people. We are not able to perceive how Mr. Leigh could have adopted a wiser or more Christian policy, had there been no interference on the part of the civil power. Without any more particular reference to this case, we may say generally, that missionaries, on entering upon new spheres of labour, should speak with caution and reserve respecting the plans of their predecessors; nor should those plans be rashly tampered with. New ones may be suggested, and appear to be more enlightened, more comprehensive, and better calculated to consolidate and expand the work of the mission; but it will generally be found that the old ones resulted from experience, and were well adapted to existing circumstances. Sudden changes are the more to be deprecated, when the missionary finds that societies or churches have acquiesced in the former administration, and given it a hearty and united co-operation. If the new system, intended to supplement or supersede the old one, were a manifest improvement, still it would be unwise in him to force it upon a reluctant community. Even when it is indubitable, that his predecessor has erred in judgment, in conducting the affairs of the mission, he must guard against imputing that error to obliquity of intention, lest he should impeach the moral and religious principles of an absent brother. It was a rare case indeed, if Mr. Leigh, in alluding to the names or labours of his co-adjutors in his correspondence, did not speak of both in the most respectful terms.

About this time a young chief, having arrived in Sydney from Tonga, for the purpose of verifying, by actual observation, the incredible accounts that had reached his country respecting the Europeans of New South Wales, claimed the particular attention of the brethren. As the mission in Tonga had to struggle with formidable difficulties, it was judged desirable to make such an impression upon this young man as might lead him to give a favourable report of the effects of Christianity, should he be spared to return to his own land. The governor received him with obvious satisfaction; he was conducted to various objects of public interest, and seemed to be particularly struck with the process of education in the public schools. After gratifying his curiosity, he returned to Tonga, when he assembled the chiefs, and gave them an account of his travels by sea and land. His remarks upon the stone walls, large houses, articles of barter in the shops, number of ships in Sydney Harbour, exercising of the military, variety of fruits, enormous sizes of the horses and horned cattle, extent of the country, and, above all, the unbounded liberality and kindness of our friends, produced an electrifying effect upon the chiefs, who sat amazed and overwhelmed to hear such reports from their own relations, whose veracity they never questioned. He also informed them of the schools, especially Sunday-schools, and the sacred attention which the people paid to the sabbath-day; and added, "The people of Tonga will never be wise until they adopt the same measures." The condescension, attention, liberality, and advices of His Excellency the governor were detailed with uncommon eloquence and extraordinary effect. "In short," said the missionary who was present, "I never witnessed a scene which excited a greater variety of grateful and delightful sensations in my mind than this, in which the best interests of our missions are involved."

Although the disease of Mr. Leigh had not assumed any more aggravated form, it yet wholly incapacitated him for public duty.   Dr. Bland communicated to him the result of a medical consultation on his case.   "In our judgment," said the doctor, "the disease under which you labour may be effectually subdued by judicious medical treatment, and attention on your own part." Mr. Leigh's views and feelings, at this period, are expressed in the following abbreviated extracts from his journal :—

"December 1st.—The doctor encourages me to expect a perfect cure ; but without God we can do nothing. 'God is my refuge and strength, a very present help in trouble !'

"2nd.—I am much reduced in strength ; but I have great peace of mind. I have been much exercised about the New-Zealand and Tonga missions ; but 'is any thing too hard for the Lord ?'

"3rd.—My affliction increases : the remedies prescribed seem to aggravate all the symptoms of my complaint. Lord, thy blessing will make all well !

"6th.—I am a little better. I can hear the service going on in the adjoining chapel. What a privilege is this ! Lord, bless New Zealand !

"8th.—I was not able to attend public worship last Lord's day ; but I can say, 'My soul cleaveth unto the Lord.' 'Hold thou me up, and I shall be safe : and I will have respect unto thy statutes continually.'

"9th.—This day we removed to our new house. How like strangers and pilgrims we are ! Lord, give me the spirit of holy zeal."

10th.—The Rev. William Cooper called to see him. He held a long conversation with Mr. Leigh on the state of the natives ; during which he explained his plans for their civil and religious improvement. Mr. Leigh concurred in his views generally, and expressed a hope that he might live to see his benevolent wishes consummated. On his retiring, Mr. Leigh observed, "What a spiritually-minded man this is ! He is always longing for the salvation of men. How deeply he feels for the poor natives, and with what earnestness he wrestles with God in their behalf ! He seldom parts with any one, without saying something in commendation of Christ and religion. May the Lord breathe into me the same spirit, and fill me with zeal for the glory of Christ in the spread of His gospel !"

"12th.—I feel a little better. I have peace with God, and my soul longs for the salvation of the Heathen.

"13th.—This is a time of trial and discouragement. The mission amongst the natives declines, and our brother has felt himself obliged to withdraw from Tongataboo; but 'if God be for us, who can be against us?' The account which the senior chaplain gives of the New-Zealand mission, in this week's 'Gazette,' is, upon the whole, encouraging. Without holy, zealous, and self-denying men, those missions cannot be successfully prosecuted. I have received several visits from the Rev. Messrs. Cooper and Hill. How cheering to have intercourse with the excellent of the earth!

"14th.—My missionary brethren called. Their conversation was truly profitable. I have recommended them to preach in different parts of this populous city. Here are vast fields of usefulness, especially amongst the black natives, and in Tonga. New Zealand must yet be supplied with a few zealous and holy missionaries."

On Tuesday, 16th, he was enabled, for the first time since he left New Zealand, to conduct family prayer. He read and prayed; but his voice was tremulous and indistinct. In prayer he expressed his anxiety respecting the New-Zealand mission, and entreated God to display His truth and grace in saving that country.

On the 19th, it was found necessary to apply twenty-two leeches, to arrest the progress of inflammation in his throat. "I can endure all the sufferings to which I am now subjected," he remarked, "as I hope to give up my account with joy on the last day. The Lord is my comforter."

"23rd.—Through the mercy of God, I am better. 'I had fainted, unless I had believed to see the goodness of the Lord in the land of the living.' The Rev. Samuel Marsden called to-day: he has always been to me a friend and a brother. May God sanctify our Christian intercourse!

"January 1st, 1824.—This is the first day of another year. On looking over the last year, what mercies! what sufferings! what deliverances! what consolation! Mrs. Leigh and myself were on board the 'St. Michael,' when she struck upon a rock, and remained for six hours in imminent danger. By the goodness of God, and the combined efforts of the crew, she floated with the rising tide, and sustained but little injury. The Rev. Samuel Marsden, Mrs. Leigh, and myself, were shipwrecked in the 'Brompton,' and landed upon a desolate island. Here we suffered many privations for several days, but were at last taken off the island by a boat from New Zealand. Here I lost £40 in money, and every thing else but the clothes I wore at the time. And are we alive this day? 'What shall I render unto the Lord for all His benefits toward me? I will take the cup of salvation, and call upon the name of the Lord. I will pay my vows unto the Lord now in the presence of all His people.'

"5th.—I have just received good news: a glorious work is in progress in several of the islands. Many are renouncing idolatry, turning to the true Jehovah, and singing the praises of Christ in their own tongue.

> 'Jesus shall reign where'er the sun
> Doth his successive journeys run;
> His kingdom stretch from shore to shore,
> Till suns shall rise and set no more.'

"6th.—The sittings of the district-meeting terminated on Saturday evening. The brethren kindly and frequently visited me; and, while they were engaged in united prayer, the Lord gave us an abundant blessing. I find that, though deprived of the public means of grace, the sabbath is the best day of the seven.

"13th.—I am somewhat better; but my complaint is exceedingly variable. The conversation and prayers of the clergy, and of my own brethren, are exceedingly refreshing. The New-Zealand mission lies near my heart: Lord Jesus, look upon the wretched savages of that country!

"25th.—I have been suffering from inflammation of the chest. A large blister has failed to relieve me, and recourse is being had to bleeding. I am very weak, but quite willing either to die or live. My wife is indeed a valuable companion.

"28th.—The seton in my side has afforded me considerable relief, so that I am now improving. Bless the Lord for any signs of returning health!"

These extracts, brief as they are, may suffice to show the severity of the trial through which Mr. Leigh was passing, and the state of peaceful resignation in which he was preserved.

In a letter, written at the close of this month, and addressed to Joseph Butterworth, Esq., M.P., he gives that gentleman a general view of the Church and Wesleyan missions in New Zealand, and of the state of things in New South Wales; and adds, "You will peruse, I doubt not, with much interest, the enclosed extract from a communication I have just received from the Rev. William Cooper: 'I have the pleasure of informing you that the journal of a recent expedition of discovery to Moreton Bay, latitude twenty-seven or twenty-eight degrees south, and the narrative of two Europeans who were found there, exhibit some very favourable traits in the dispositions and habits of the aborigines in that part of New Holland. This journal and narrative, I understand, are to be published immediately, under the direction of Mr. Justice Field. With the perusal of both, in manuscript, I have been kindly favoured: to me they have been very interesting, and to the missionary cause they are most encouraging. Herein we may perceive that the natives, six or seven degrees to the northward, are in a condition much superior to that of those in this neighbourhood. They seem to be endued with stronger sociability and affection, and with more intellect and invention, than any we have seen. The tribes there form little villages of huts; they have a king or chief, whom, with his queen, or wife, and a concubine, they both honour and maintain. For the support of the king, they give a portion of what they have taken in fishing or hunting; and when this is done, and they themselves left without a morsel, they murmur not. Their humanity and honesty appear to be real. The Europeans who had been cast away on the coast, and had for several months resided among them, they treated with every mark of respect, kindness, and hospitality in their power.' With such a statement of well-authenticated facts before us, may we not most reasonably and hopefully conclude, that missionaries who are duly qualified, and able to endure some privations, going to these people, might, under the Divine blessing, do them both present and everlasting good? May the Lord send forth more labourers into His vineyard!"

The missionary, however, found it extremely difficult to make any permanent impression upon the native mind in the colony. On the 15th of March, he observes: "Yesterday I visited the settlement of the aborigines, to whom I preached. As many of the wild natives were about the woods, I had an opportunity of conversing with them. Some of them were seriously hurt by fighting a few days before: the rest were lounging under the trees in a state of apparent torpor, waiting till the shades of the evening should assist them to hunt the opossum. In the institution there are thirteen children,—seven girls, and six boys. Four of the girls' fathers were white men, and three or four of the boys have the same origin. The natives have been engaged in a terrible conflict, in consequence of the death of Coke, a black boy who was baptized, and is since dead. A year has elapsed since he died; but his death was only avenged last week. The natives believe death to be occasioned by the malice and craftiness of some one of a hostile tribe, who, they think, unperceived and *unfelt*, perforates with a poisoned dart the side opposite the heart. No sign of puncture is left; but he dies in consequence of the poison. The discovery of the murderer depends upon some dreamer; and the individual who is the subject of the dream must pass through the usual ordeal. In the case of Coke's death, his aunt dreamed, twelve months after the event, that he was speared by his companion, who was ordered to stand punishment on Sydney race-ground, last Sunday but one. In a short time a spear penetrated his body a little above the hip; but it was extracted without having endangered life. The man who threw the spear which wounded the boy, had to stand in his turn, and three or four hundred natives assembled to do their utmost.   He defended himself successfully against a host of spears, with a shield about one foot broad and three long.   His friends then turned upon his assailants, and the result was, that one of them had his skull dreadfully fractured.   They then entered into mutual explanations, and made it up.   As many as had the means, afterwards intoxicated themselves, either with grog or peach-cider, and then began little less than a murderous scuffle. The strongest, of course, came off the best.

" If the friends of humanity at home could only witness those scenes of depravity, those desolating effects of sin, many tears would be shed in sympathy for the sufferers.   At a missionary meeting held last week, I related those circumstances ; and one of the speakers, in applying some of my remarks, and summing up the number of dollars which he would give on certain ac- counts, said, ' I will give another dollar a-year, because I am not a black man.' Had he *seen*, as well as heard, he would have given still more.   O, what a work there is to be performed in New South Wales ! It is a comfort to me to know that the arm of the Lord is not shortened.   God can save to the very uttermost."

Nor was the individual referred to the only liberal contributor at the above meeting.   Mr. John Lees, of Castlereagh, was pre- sent, and addressed the assembly.   After some animated remarks on the duty of supporting Christian missions, he said, " I will give twenty bushels of wheat as my contribution to this branch society.   I wish to encourage my friends at Windsor to give liberally."   On the following day a similar meeting was held at John's own settlement.   Reflecting upon the goodness of God towards himself and family, he was filled with devout gratitude, and expressed it by such spontaneous acts of benevolence as astonished his Christian brethren.   Before the close of the meet- ing, he said, " In addition to the twenty bushels of wheat I gave yesterday, I will now give forty more ; and, as my tobacco crop is good, I will also give ten pounds of tobacco."   After the meet- ing, he added a cow and calf to those noble contributions.   He sold the whole for £45, which sum he paid to the auxiliary trea- surer, as his subscription for that year.   Though a severe drought had occurred during the earlier months of the year, and affected vegetation in several districts of the country, yet to John it had been a prosperous year, both as it regarded his cattle and his crops.   The love of man, originating in supreme love to God, is like the mountain stream : you may obstruct its progress by fill- ing up its channel ; but its accumulating waters will find a new vent, and pour themselves upon the valleys below, spreading beauty and fertility over the whole landscape.

The ingenious method by which John Lees endeavoured to

meet a change of circumstances, without diminishing the amount of his subscription to the sacred cause of missions, has been well described in a paper drawn.up by missionary Carvosso. "One of those distressing droughts," he remarks, "with which New South Wales is not unfrequently visited, having occurred, John's crops, in common with others, entirely failed. After many painful exercises as to how his subscription of nine guineas should be paid, he resolved to sell one of his horses. For some months great pains were taken by himself, his wife, and children, to make it as marketable as possible. It was often seen tied under a shady tree, while the children were employed in the woods cutting grass for it. On the week immediately preceding our missionary meeting at Sydney, I happened, on the day of the fair, to cross the market-place, and saw John, my most benevolent friend from the Nepean, in the act of mounting his horse to return home. Not knowing his errand there, nor the state of his mind, I spoke cheerfully to him about attending the meeting; for we could not well afford his absence, 'having no man like-minded.' He returned no answer. I spoke a second time: he was still silent. On lifting my eyes to his countenance, as he sat on his horse, I saw that he was overwhelmed with grief. As well as tears and perturbed feeling would permit, he said, ' No, sir; I shall now be ashamed to be seen there. I can't pay my subscription; for I can't sell my horse.' More astonished at this speech of tried, disinterested benevolence, than any thing about 'giving' that had before dropped from his lips, or any other, I attempted to render him a word of consolation, such as, indeed, the occasion seemed to require; but his distress was too deep to be mitigated by any thing that I could say. He broke from me while I was in the act of speaking to him, and bore the burden of his painful disappointment back to his distant abode in the bush. Apologizing for his absence at the meeting, and non-payment of his subscription, the incident did not fail to draw tears from the audience. But improved cultivation, fruitful showers, and the blessing of God on grounds so peculiarly connected with the skies, gave him a very plentiful crop the following year. On leaving his lowly roof to go with him to the missionary meeting at his own chapel in the wood, his wife, in very homely attire, sitting on a stool with an infant on her lap, called loudly after us: ' John, mind, you did not pay your subscription last year: you must pay two years now.' Considering that Mary was not a member of the church, that she did not in every thing see eye to eye with her zealous husband, and that the *rate* of the subscription stood at a point *so elevated*, this word of exhortation I could but regard as being above things of common-place. John did his duty at the meeting. He put down various subscriptions *in kind*, the whole of which, when disposed of, amounted to, I think, £14. 'There is that scattereth, and yet increaseth.'"

On the 20th of August, the Rev. Daniel Tyerman and George Bennett, Esq., deputies from the London Missionary Society, arrived in Sydney. Every thing appeared at this season to disadvantage. "The neighbouring country," they said, "is good in soil, and diversified in feature; but its aspect is dreary from long drought, which has exhausted the springs, withered the herbage, and reduced the cattle to living skeletons. We have made various calls on, or received visits from, naval, military, and civil officers, to whom we had introductions, as well as to the Wesleyan missionaries, who are here carrying on a blessed work amongst all classes of colonists." Those gentlemen visited the barracks, hospitals, and schools in Sydney, and inquired particularly into the state of religion and morality in the city. They paid a visit to Paramatta, where they were hospitably entertained at the residence of the Rev. Samuel Marsden. They inspected the factory for the reception of female convicts, and found them employed in dressing flax, sorting wool, and spinning both, to be woven by the male convicts at their quarters. One hundred and eight females were thus occupied, and as many more were expected in a few days. A respectable matron superintended the establishment. The institution for the education of the orphan children of convicts, which is admirably conducted, excited their deepest sympathy. Upwards of one hundred young persons were in course of preparation for situations as servants and apprentices.

Considering the circumstances of the aborigines, and knowing what had been accomplished in the islands of the South Seas, by the preaching of the gospel in their own tongue, in all its diversity of dialects, the deputation were of opinion that some effectual means might be suggested for recovering the New-Hollander to civilization and to Christ. On their return to Sydney, they sought an interview with the governor on the subject; but the case of the natives was not understood, at that period, either by the missionaries who occasionally mingled with them, or by the government itself. His Excellency gave them a cordial reception, and instituted many inquiries respecting the islands they had visited, and seemed much gratified by the account they gave of the wonderful progress of Christianity, and the rapid change from savage to comparatively civilized life, which had taken place in many of those islands. They informed him that, after much deliberation, they were anxious to leave Mr. Threlkeld, who was returning from the South Seas, as a missionary to the aborigines. They proposed to station Mr. Threlkeld at the new colony on the river Brisbane, Moreton Bay, if the government would make a suitable grant of land for a missionary settlement. To this proposal His Excellency at once acceded, and assured them of his readiness to further so benevolent an enterprise.

The deputation then waited on Mr. Leigh, whose health was improving, and explained their plans relative to the settlement of Mr. Threlkeld, concluding with the observation, "If you can occupy the station we contemplate for our missionary, we will at once yield the preference to you." Being assured that the Wesleyans had no means nor agents for such an extension of their labours, the gentlemen proceeded to make arrangements for commencing their mission. They obtained an extensive allotment of land for their settlement at Newcastle, and secured the approval of the government to their plan for conducting the mission.

Before leaving the colony, they addressed a letter of admonition and direction to their agent; in which they say, "The novelty of an undertaking which proposes the conversion of the debased aborigines of this country to Christianity, and their instruction in the arts of civilized life, will fix upon you the eyes of the Christian world, and awaken at once a universal interest, and a peculiar curiosity in observing your operations, and in anticipating the results of the pending experiment. The liberal promise which the government of this country has given of the appropriation of ten thousand acres of land for the use of the natives at Reid's Mistake, and on which you will reside with your family, removes every impediment, and makes your way open to proceed to your station as soon as you can complete your arrangements. As a knowledge of the language of the natives must be regarded as essential to the success of your mission, you will deem it to be your duty to use your best efforts to acquire it; while it will greatly facilitate the progress of your work, to make yourself familiar with their customs, superstitions, and habits. By a knowledge of these, you will see what the principal difficulties opposing your success are; while an intimate acquaintance with their language will enable you to communicate that information respecting the gospel of Jesus, which will be the best adapted to remove obstacles, and insure success. Your knowledge of what has been done in these respects among the adults of other heathen nations, will forbid that you should despair of success among those who have reached the years of maturity: but your special attention will be directed to the children, and to the rising generation, as affording the best grounds of hope. Schools, for the instruction of all, it will be your first object to establish, and which you will superintend with indefatigable care and zeal. And while your best efforts will be directed to heal their mental woes, your knowledge of medicine will enable you to remove their bodily sufferings. A steady attention to these objects, together with a kind manner, a tender solicitude to promote their temporal happiness and comfort, and a glowing zeal to advance their eternal salvation, will not fail, we trust, to secure to you their love, confidence, and attachment. To accomplish all this, will be indeed an arduous task; but the confidence which we have in your talents and diligence, and in that Divine assistance which you will constantly implore, enables us to anticipate a period, not very remote, when this will be achieved."

The provincial press urged the claims of this truly difficult undertaking upon the government and the country with frequency and eloquence. "We understand," said the "Gazette" of October, "that the Rev. Mr. Threlkeld, from the South Seas, is on the eve of departing to Moreton Bay, in order to attempt reaching the understandings of the fine race of savages in that quarter, through their own language, which he is determined on acquiring, if within the compass of possibility. We are inclined to think that this attempt will be instrumental in performing wonders in the course of a few years. The natives are worthy of such attention, and the mission should be assisted in the most munificent manner by all classes in the colony. Wellington Valley presents another endless field for missionary labour; and we are warranted in announcing that the Wesleyan missionaries will enter it during the ensuing year. Thus the time appears to be at hand, when the long-neglected and degraded natives of this continent will be brought into a state of Christianity, and thus happily subjected to the control of civilization."

Messrs. Tyerman and Bennett having kindly offered their assistance at the fourth anniversary of the New South Wales Wesleyan Auxiliary Missionary Society, the public meeting was held in Macquarie-street chapel. Preparatory sermons were preached, on the preceding sabbath, by the Rev. Samuel Leigh, and the Rev. Daniel Tyerman. At the evening service especially, several of the first personages in the colony were present; and the sermon, which was grounded upon 1 Thess. i. 9, 10, "Ye turned to God from idols to serve the living and true God, and to wait for His Son from heaven," was such a display of cogent reasoning, exalted sentiment, and masterly eloquence, as produced the most salutary impressions on a large and attentive audience. George Bennett, Esq., presided at the public meeting. As might be expected, the edifice was quite full. The solemn and dignified appeals that were made to the noblest feelings of human nature were supported by the recital of striking and impressive facts. The meeting was addressed with great effect by the Rev. Messrs. Tyerman and Threlkeld: several distinguished lay-gentlemen also took part in the proceedings. In the course of a speech of great power, by the solicitor-general, he said, "On an estate, in the island of Tortola, belonging to myself, there were a number of slaves sunk in the lowest depths of ignorance and vice, and particularly addicted to every species of dishonesty. To the instruction of these slaves the Wesleyan missionaries were invited, and in a short time, so complete was the reformation, that thefts became unknown; one of the Negroes was appointed to the management of the estate, a post which he occupied with the most exemplary fidelity, and the annual produce of the plantation amazingly exceeded the amount of any previous year." An eye-witness remarked, "We do not remember any former occasion on which the claims of the millions of our fellow-men, who are yet without God and without hope in the world, were more effectually urged, or more cordially recognised; whilst the friendly union of persons of different religious denominations, in promoting the common cause of Christianity, was conspicuously exhibited." The contributions for the year amounted to £300.

A young man, who had been employed for some time in the instruction of the natives, was now dispatched to examine Wellington Valley. This was an extensive region in the interior of the country, of above ten millions of acres, lying, as a reference to the map will show, between the Macquarie and Lachlan rivers. The governor, who evinced a lively interest in the mission of this young man, placed him upon the government-stores, and under the protection of its officers. He was to find his way to the interior, present his credentials to the commandant of that part of the country, and claim, by the authority of the governor, his assistance. It was his duty to ascertain the number and state of the native tribes in Wellington Valley; the probability of bringing them to adopt the habits of civilized men; and to report, on his return, on those subjects. Travelling under the auspices of the governor, he was treated with much respect, and reached the place of his destination in safety. He attached himself to the wandering savages in the valley, and remained with them until he had acquired a knowledge of their social condition, and was able to converse with them, on common subjects, in their own language. On returning to Sydney, he presented his report, which was, upon the whole, highly satisfactory.

"I found," he remarked, "five tribes spread over the extended valley of Wellington; but how large those tribes may be, it would be hazardous to conjecture, a whole tribe having perhaps never been seen together. They are commonly divided into groups of sixty or seventy persons. They are, in general, taller, stouter, and more athletic than the blacks near the colony, and evince a slight superiority of intellect: in point of ignorance and immorality, however, both are on a level. They are perpetually roving from place to place, either as prompted by caprice, or in search of food. They build no houses, and their only covering is the skin of the opossum; but they generally go naked, and even in cold and wet weather sleep on the bare ground, without shelter, in the open air, with only a fire by their side to keep them warm. They live on kangaroos, emus, opossums, snakes, and fish. The women are not allowed to partake of the animals procured by their husbands, but left to seek their own subsistence, which chiefly consists of large grubs found at the roots of young trees. They have some notion of a Supreme Being; but they pay Him no worship. They have also some idea of a future state: they believe that, though they shall rise again, it will be as human beings in this world. Murder is the only crime which, in their apprehension, deserves punishment hereafter. Those sentiments, however, have no practical influence over them."

The brethren were so satisfied with the manner in which this young man had discharged the duties of his mission, that they appointed him to the office of assistant missionary, and assigned to him the above interesting field of labour.

The native school which had been established at Black Town was beginning to develope the mental capabilities of the youthful savages who attended it. Mr. Leigh, being improved in health, took a tour through the colony, visited this institution, and examined the children. He was accompanied by the resident missionary of Windsor. They found two boys and five girls, two of whom were mulattoes. These read tolerably well, and repeated portions of the scriptures, and hymns, which they had committed to memory: their needle-work was executed very neatly. When this school was opened, it was said, "The missionary may as well attempt to teach the kangaroos and opossums sense and industry, as the children of the New-Hollander." "In my opinion," said a magistrate at a public meeting, "the best use that could be made of the black population of this country, would be to shoot them all, and manure the ground with their carcasses." But how satisfactorily has it been proved, since that day, that the gospel of Christ possesses a singular adaptation to every variety of physical and mental condition, existing throughout the entire family of man!

The native teacher, having found his way to Jervis Bay, transmitted to Sydney some interesting details which throw considerable light upon the character of the aborigines in that part of the country. We can only afford room for two or three condensed extracts. The communication is dated October, 1826.

"At sunset I went on shore at Bowen's Isle, to see the blacks who were employed in fishing. I found their dialect had but very little affinity to that with which I am acquainted. I distributed

AUSTRALIAN GROUP.

a few fish-hooks among them, and went with them into a cave in a great rock by the sea-side. Here I addressed them on the doctrine of a future state. I observed that they were very careful in removing the scales from a fish; believing that if the scales are taken off before the fish is laid upon the fire, the waves of the sea will rise up, and prevent them from catching any more fish that day. They appear to be of a very litigious character, exceedingly depraved, and dissatisfied, give them what you will. A few of them accompanied me a short distance into the interior, through a thick wood. Being unable to return to the vessel, I lay down with the blacks, and slept soundly. They have no fixed habitation, and only seek a temporary shelter under the branches of a tree, the hollow of a rock, or two or three sheets of bark, laid in a reclining position against each other. They are seldom employed except in fishing and hunting the kangaroo and opossum. They use spears and clubs. In the use of these weapons they are very dexterous, and will hit a bird on the wing, at an amazing distance.

"14th.—We arrived at Bateman Bay. It is forty miles from Jervis Bay. On the following day a native came on board : I gave him a blanket and some biscuit, and dispatched him to bring his countrymen. This I was obliged to do by making signs, as he did not understand the language of the blacks of Wellington Valley.

"On the 20th we weighed anchor, and were leaving the bay, when we were hailed by a number of blacks from the south side of the bay. When the vessel was moored, I took with me a few presents, and went on shore. One of those blacks had been over to the *new country*, and could speak English sufficiently to interpret what I had to say to the rest of his countrymen. On first approaching them, men, women, and children raised their hands in token of peace. I stood for some time ruminating upon the affecting scene before me. The women separated themselves from us, and sat down, at a distance, by themselves. I sat down with the men, and explained, through my interpreter, the objects of my visit. At the close of this interview I wrote as follows :—
1. Those are the cleanest blacks I have yet seen in the country.
2. They are very kind to their women and children : the blankets I gave them they handed to their wives. A venerable pair, with white hair, came to me arm in arm. 3. The men appear to be of the middle size; some, however, are tall, and all seem to be athletic. The women are rather short; but I believe this generally arises from carrying immense burdens. Both men and women are remarkable for their docility. 4. My interpreter tells me that they are on good terms with the neighbouring tribes. 5. They are not so vagrant as the tribes at Jervis Bay; but it is

impossible they should be settled, as they have no means of subsistence but those of catching fish and seals, and gathering wild fruit in the woods.

"On the 25th, I discovered a site that will just answer the purposes of our mission, and sailed out of the bay, for the present, while the blacks waved their hands in token of friendship."

The missionaries, who had so providentially escaped from New Zealand, had been employed in the colony, in various departments of labour. On the 29th of August, the brethren were convened to consider certain communications that had been received from the Church missionaries at the Bay of Islands. Mr. Leigh informed the meeting, that peace was restored to New Zealand; that the brethren of the Church mission had no intention of leaving the country; and that the way was now open for the re-establishment of the Wesleyan mission. After a little discussion, it was unanimously agreed, that the missionaries should sail for the Bay of Islands by the first conveyance. In this arrangement, they anticipated the decision of the committee in London. On hearing of the destruction of the mission-premises at Wangaroa, that committee had held a special meeting, at which it was resolved, that New Zealand should not be given up while there remained any hope of reclaiming the natives to Christianity; and that the brethren who had left should be requested to return to the country without loss of time. In those conclusions the missionaries acquiesced, and sailed from Sydney soon after.

On October 20th, 1827, after recapitulating the principal incidents of his own missionary life, Mr. Leigh adverts to the state of the mission in Australia at that period. "It is now thirteen years," he writes, "since I first landed upon the shores of this country. What extraordinary events have occurred in that time! For several years I laboured alone. My privations and sufferings were great. My appeal for help brought out my esteemed friend and brother, W. Lawry. My health declining, I visited New Zealand, but derived little benefit from the change. I returned to England. The account which I gave of the savages of New Zealand induced the committee to appoint myself and two others, to commence a mission in that country. I sailed from England in 1821, with two brethren, one of whom, the Rev. William Horton, I left in Van-Diemen's Land, to establish, if possible, a mission there. Well and faithfully did he discharge his duty in that flourishing colony. On arriving in Sydney, I found my old round, of one hundred and fifty miles, divided into three ample circuits. Mr. Carvosso was stationed at Windsor, Mr. Lawry at Paramatta, while Sydney was favoured with the labours of an eloquent and able minister. After travelling with great acceptance and usefulness in each circuit in the colony, Mr. Carvosso removed to Van-Diemen's Land, where are abundant fruits of his ministry. Mr. Lawry's course of usefulness was interrupted at Paramatta, by his being appointed to form a mission in Tonga. I sailed to New Zealand, and, having formed the mission there amidst great dangers and trials, returned to New South Wales, broken down by affliction. At present I reside in Paramatta, one of the brethren is stationed at Windsor, two in Sydney, and one in Hobart Town. With those brethren I have been associated for years : we have prosecuted our work in harmony. New South Wales presents an encouraging aspect. In Sydney we have two chapels and good congregations; in Paramatta, three chapels, which are well attended; in Windsor, four chapels, and a good attendance. In Van-Diemen's Land there are two circuits, two chapels, and two societies, enjoying peace and prosperity. Several have been added to our churches, and this year the subscriptions to the mission-fund exceed £500."

At the district-meeting, which was held at Windsor, on Tuesday, November 6th, the whole question of the South-Sea mission and its management engaged the serious attention of the assembled missionaries. An elaborate statement on these topics had been prepared by one of the brethren, and submitted to the meeting. It was resolved, that, as this statement is " sound in its principles, correct in its facts, and judicious in its suggestions," it be forthwith printed, and transmitted to the parent committee.

In the following quotation, the extended field thrown open to the Society in the South Seas, is urged as a reason why the committee should send out immediately a large accession of labourers to that quarter of the globe. The reasons which led to this appeal have been acquiring accumulative force with the progress of every year since that period.

" You have in this part of the world one of the most interesting and inviting fields of missionary exertion any where to be found. Here are two extensive and flourishing British colonies, urging powerful claims on your Christian benevolence, and promising ultimately to yield a most ample return. Their inhabitants are almost entirely British, as well in their feelings and habits and general character, as in their origin. Here, therefore, we have no foreign language to learn, nor foreign prejudices to encounter. We labour amongst a people whose national genius and manners are similar to our own. This facilitates our undertaking; and their appeal for our help derives irresistible force from the circumstance of its coming from our countrymen; it moves our patriotism as well as our piety; and the consideration that many amongst them are the offshoots of those very families in Great Britain by whose liberality the funds of the Society are replenished, and by whose prayers its success is furthered, seems to render our exertions for their welfare a debt of justice as well as a call of mercy. To shut up our bowels of compassion towards those who are so closely allied to us by the ties of country and of kindred, whilst the streams of our charity are expending themselves in other directions, would appear to be an inexcusable inconsistency.

"The propriety of these remarks will be the more clearly manifested, by adverting to the deplorable darkness and debasement which characterize the moral condition of these colonies. They have been peopled chiefly by the very outcasts of society. Here the mother country has disgorged her most worthless and vitiated sons : here those children of misfortune and iniquity have been congregated together to form the rudiments of a new community. From those elementary seeds have sprung up a thick and diversified mass of depravity, whose exuberant growth and revolting character and deadly influence can nowhere be paralleled. It is, indeed, to a considerable extent, controlled and kept under the shades of secrecy, by the vigilance and coercion of civil authority, and the presence of some virtuous characters scattered here and there throughout the land ; but still it exists, and diffuses its destructive poison. In the case of perhaps one-third of the population, this awful degeneracy is fostered by the superstitious ignorance and hostile bigotry of Catholicism ; for in that proportion has the insurrectionary spirit of Ireland, coupled with her poverty and vice, contributed to crowd this place of exile.

"It need not be argued with you, that the desolating effects of this gross delusion and rank iniquity can only be counteracted by a full and faithful ministration of the gospel of Christ, or that this sovereign remedy is able to repair the mischief, and destroy the very stamina from which it springs. Of this you are fully aware. But perhaps you inquire, 'Are there not other ministers in abundance, whose labours in those colonies supersede the necessity of ours?' We answer, Their number is indeed considerable ; but the extent and effectiveness of their labours fall very far short of the exigencies of the case. Here there is an establishment of twelve chaplains, whose duties very much resemble those of a parochial clergyman at home, with an archdeacon at their head. We would not speak disrespectfully of this clerical body ; but we may safely affirm, that it is very incommensurate with the spiritual wants of the country. There are also some catechists employed by the Church corporation, in the distant and thinly-inhabited parts of the country. These are laymen, who are empowered to read the liturgy and a sermon on the sabbath, and to bury the dead. Perhaps the most efficient department of labour in which the Establishment is engaged, is that of schools. In imparting instruction to the young, and training them up to habits of decency, and to the external observance of religious duties, it is conferring a great and lasting blessing on the colony. We have also two Presbyterian ministers, both pious, well-educated men; one resides in Sydney, the other at Portland Head. Their ministerial labours are unquestionably useful; but we are not aware that they extend them much beyond their own flocks; so that there is still a great mass of the community on whom Christianity has made no aggressive movement. From those statements you may readily infer, that your attention to these colonies is not superseded by the zeal of others. Indeed, it is the opinion of many judicious persons here, that the greatest share of spiritual good which has already been effected is owing to the influence of your system; and we are persuaded that its continued and extended agency is urgently needed to saturate the whole land with the knowledge and love of God.

"It is also important to observe that, in our endeavours to bring on this glorious consummation, we meet with few obstacles, save those which arise from the moral corruption of the people. The higher classes of society, not excepting the civil and ecclesiastical authorities, treat us with respect, and almost every where we are received with civility and kindness. The whole land is thus open to us, and many are disposed to patronize and further our undertakings.

"Nor should the magnitude and prospective enlargement of these colonies be overlooked. Already do they comprise a population of Europeans, and descendants of Europeans, amounting to sixty thousand souls. This population is every year augmented, not only by natural means, but also by large accessions of prisoners and free emigrants; and there is little doubt that, as the immense resources of this part of the world become more fully known at home, the tide of emigration will be more generally and steadily directed toward these shores. And as the vast extent of our unoccupied territory affords unlimited scope for industry, and inexhaustible means of subsistence, New Holland is likely to be, for centuries yet to come, a receptacle for British felons, and an asylum for British settlers. We may, therefore, look upon our present settlements as the rudiments of a great and mighty empire, obviously destined, by a wise and merciful. Providence, to abolish the Paganism of this portion of the southern hemisphere, and to diffuse amongst the numerous surrounding nations and tribes the arts of civilization, and the blessings of Christianity. Already have we penetrated three hundred miles into the interior, and have formed incipient establishments on the east coast, at Port Macquarie and Moreton Bay; on the north, at Melville Island; and on the west, at King George's Sound and Western Port; thus encompassing this immense island with the ensigns of British authority.   It is true, the standards we have unfurled at those places betoken, at present, only the penal consequences of crime; but the prisoners banished thither will pioneer and prepare the way for adventurous settlers; and those spots, which now exhibit nothing but rigid coercion, compelling the reluctant labours of fettered bondmen, will hereafter assume the diversified form, and acquire the multifarious strength, of regular, industrious, and thriving communities.

"By this means is British power spreading forth its ramifications over this wild and almost untenanted wilderness, whose soil the ploughshare never touched before, and whose rich resources are, even yet, but partially explored.

"Now, it must appear to every one a matter of the highest importance, to impregnate with religious influence and energy these elements of the future greatness of Australia; to purify and sweeten those primitive sources of her future population. In doing this we confer a blessing on generations yet unborn; we deposit seeds whose fruitfulness will endure and increase to the most distant times.

"Nor will the influence of Australia's piety be confined to her own offspring.   She sits as the undisputed queen of the great South Pacific.   She already exerts a powerful, though not a political, influence over the numerous insular nations that are scattered over that mighty expanse of waters.   To her they look with reverence; the benefits of her commerce they have begun already to experience; and, pestiferous as has been the moral influence she has hitherto exerted upon them, yet she seems designated by Heaven to be the handmaid of dispensing to them the blessings of religion and science and law.   Her capability, however, of thus becoming the illustrious benefactor of those subordinate tribes, will depend entirely upon her own moral character; and this is another reason why all should be done for improving and maturing it that lies within the compass of our power.

"Having thus endeavoured to survey the extent, and display the peculiar claims and prospects, of that portion of our missionary field which comprises the colonies of New South Wales and Van-Diemen's Land, let your eye now glance at its Heathen division.   To the aborigines of those countries we owe a debt of deep compassion and national justice.   They are the most degraded of human beings, roaming in small independent hordes, nearly and often completely naked, without home or habitation, through trackless wilds and immeasurable forests, living on the spontaneous productions of nature, and distinguishable from brutes only by their form and speech, which are almost the only fragments of humanity they retain.   Men cannot sink to a lower level.   Nor have they taken a single step towards improvement.

Their intercourse with the colonists has had a deleterious, rather than a beneficial, influence upon them.   They have adopted none of our useful arts or civilized habits ; but have added to their original barbarism some of our most detestable vices.   The sad spectacle of wretchedness which their condition exhibits, is the most frightful and affecting proof of the debasing influence of sin which the world can furnish, and is enough to wring from the eye of the stoic the tear of pity.   And surely it is especially incumbent upon us, who have taken possession of the land which they first occupied, and driven them from its most fertile districts, not only to extend over them the protecting arm of our national laws, but to open to them the hand and the heart of our national benevolence.   This duty is so obviously binding upon us, that we cannot neglect it without incurring the displeasure of Him who judgeth among the nations.   Their case is, indeed, one of great and unequalled difficulty; but it is not beyond the reach of that wisdom and zeal which the gospel supplies ; and some means, we have no doubt, will yet be devised for raising them from their present debasement and misery.

"The islands of the adjacent ocean spread before us a less gloomy scene.   In some of them, Christianity has already achieved a splendid triumph ; in two others of them, the work has been commenced by your own agents ; and the tract which stretches before you, and through which there is nothing to obstruct your progress, is extensive and interesting.   The Society, Georgian, and Sandwich Islands, together with the Marquesas, are already occupied by the London and American Societies.   But there is open to you, in conjunction with the Church Society, the whole of New Zealand ; and, at present, yours is the only institution that has formed a settlement at the Friendly Islands.   From the station which you have there taken, may your labourers spread themselves over the whole of that large cluster ; and thence proceeding to the Navigators', the Feejees, New Caledonia, the New Hebrides, the Solomon Isles, New Britain, New Ireland, New Guinea, and numerous subordinate islets, might they reach the Carolinas, the Ladrone and Pelew Isles, the Manillas, and the vast number of other populous islands which crowd the great oriental Archipelago, and bring us to the frontiers of the Chinese empire.

"Such, then, is the vast and interesting field before us ; and you are doubtless as anxious as we can possibly be, to adopt the most wise and effectual means of diffusing throughout the whole breadth thereof the saving influence of the gospel of Christ."

They conclude by recommending,—

1. The appointment of one of their own number, "a man of sound experience, clear judgment, and conciliatory manners,"

to visit the churches of the colony, New Zealand, and Tonga, for the purposes of fraternal counsel and general inspection.

2. An increase in the number of missionaries. They do not plead for this increase with a view to the enlargement of their sphere of exertion in the islands, but that they may be enabled to complete, in a proper manner, their first establishments. They had arrived at the conviction that, without additional help, "no hopeful commencement could be any where made, nor any adequate success reasonably expected."

3. That a vessel be purchased, and employed to navigate the South Seas, and carry missionaries, stores, and intelligence from one station to another.

Those claims, restricted, as they believed, within the narrowest possible limits, they advanced with a becoming earnestness; but, alas! the liberality of the Wesleyan churches of Great Britain had not kept pace with those movements, by which Divine Providence had thrown open these great and effectual doors of usefulness in the South Seas. A paucity of means rendered it impossible for the committee to accede to the expostulations and entreaties of the brethren. But, indeed, this Society has been precipitated, from time to time, by the ardour of its zeal, into labours that could not have been sustained but by consummate prudence on the part of the directors at home, and the most rigid economy and self-denial on the part of its missionaries abroad. It may be confidently affirmed, that no other missionary institution, since the apostolic age, has achieved so many signal triumphs over idolatrous systems, ferocious men, and barbarous languages, with such insufficient means.

CHAPTER XI.

ABORIGINES—SCHEME FOR THEIR ELEVATION—SWAN-RIVER COLONY FOUNDED—NARRATIVE OF A VOYAGE TO THE ISLANDS OF THE PACIFIC.

WE have previously adverted to the condition of the aborigines of Australia, and to the means that had been adopted, by the colonial government and others, for the amelioration of that condition; but the subject must be reiterated until the British churches shall be induced to take it up with that consideration and gravity which its importance demands. The Rev. William Cartwright, who had paid more attention to the state of this unfortunate race than any other gentleman in the colony, estimated their numbers at considerably more than one hundred thousand souls; but accuracy cannot be expected, even now, with our defective knowledge of the interior of the country. If they had been a people constituted like the Kaffirs of Africa, the Indians of America, or the New-Zealanders, they would have long since awakened the attention of the civilized world; but having, after a few ineffectual struggles, surrendered their soil and the mineral wealth of their country to strangers, and quietly fallen back into the solitude of their immeasurable forests, the public mind in this country has never rested upon their social misery with either curiosity or compassion. The confederated churches of Great Britain must take up their case; and, in the unity of their wisdom, strength, and benevolence, proceed to discharge a debt, which has been accumulating for half a century.

The annual meeting of the Society for the Propagation of the Gospel in Foreign Parts, was lately held in London. That meeting was addressed by the Right Reverend Dr. Broughton, bishop of Sydney and metropolitan of Australasia. The right reverend prelate dwelt upon a variety of interesting topics at that meeting; but, from the beginning to the end of a long, able, and eloquent address, to which the people responded with enthusiasm, there was no allusion whatever to the aborigines, though his lordship had been seventeen years in the country. We do not mention this fact for the purpose of reflecting upon the bishop, but simply to show, that, amidst the boisterous demands and conflicting interests of the votaries of mammon in that country, there seems to be some danger, lest the very existence of the native savage should be blotted from the recollection of even good men.

In 1827, the period of which we now write, a deep feeling pervaded the colony respecting the lost, helpless, and depraved state of the natives. We subjoin an abbreviated account, sent to Mr. Leigh by the principal agent, of an experiment then in progress for their improvement. It is dated from Lake Macquarie, is signed L. E. Threlkeld, and throws some light upon the character and language of the people.

"The aborigines of Australia have no combined numbers, no political power, to render them the objects of either respect or fear. When the civilized hand comes to cultivate their soil, they are driven, like other wild beasts, from their districts without sympathy. Their existence as a people has been transferred to the king and parliament of Great Britain, who could prevent their speedy extinction, and induce them to become protectors of the emigrants, by appropriating a moiety of the sales of their hunting and fishing districts to the purchase of Indian corn to be distributed amongst the tribes, within the line of demarcation. Every enlargement of the colony might then be hailed by the natives with delight; and the murder of stockmen, the destruction of cattle, and the abduction of infants, be prevented. The present feeling existing in the colony would accord the equity of such an arrangement. An act of parliament, a glass of rum, or a loaf of bread, would most probably induce many here to be baptized, and thus become nominal Christians; but it is our office, as ministers of Christ, to teach them to '*think on these things;*' to '*persuade them*' to receive the truth, that they may 'be ready always to give an answer to every man that asketh them a reason of the hope that is in them with meekness and fear;' and it is the duty of the church to meet the expense incurred with cheerfulness; 'for God loveth a cheerful giver.'

"As it regards the occupation of our time, I would observe, that our mornings are generally spent with M'Gill, a black, who speaks English, in speaking and writing the native language. Our conversations generally arise out of inquiries into their customs and habits. Easy sentences, passages of scripture, and information on Christian subjects, are attempted. A few weeks since M'Gill said, 'I forgot to tell you, I was speaking last night to some blacks about what you tell me respecting Jehovah; and they would not believe what I told them. I saw some pictures in your book. They desired me to bring a *picture of Jehovah*, and show it to them to-night.' To one who, in these lonesome woods, watches for the least sign of intellectual life in the death-like stillness of the native mind, this incident gave encouragement and inspired hope. The apostle's description of the 'unknown God' was the only picture I could present to the barbarian; and his reply, 'Thus, Jehovah is a Spirit,' convinced me that M'Gill understood the representation. This led to a description of the incarnation of Christ and of some of His acts. The raising of the widow's son, which is affixed as a specimen of the language, was translated to him as an evidence of His power.*

* AN ATTEMPT TO RENDER LUKE VII. 11–16, INTO THE NATIVE DIALECT, AS A SPECIMEN OF THE LANGUAGE.

11. *Tahri tah   untah Purreungkah uwah noah Jesu Nain kolahng,*
     Another it it was   day   came he Jesus Nain towards,
kowwol ngekoung kahtoah uwah, kowwol ngiyah kora.
great   his   with came, great much man.

12. *Uwah noah pahpi gate ahko, kokere kahl kobah, tatteborahng*
     Came he nigh gate it for, house place of of,   dead man
kurraah wahrah tah ko, dunkahn kobah yenahl wah-korahkobah,
was carried outside it for, mother of   son   one only of,
mahbongun bountoah; kora yahntebo uwah bounnoun kahtoah   kokere
widow   she;   man thereof came her   with house (place)
kahl.
of.

13. *Nahkahlah noah Perrewollo bounnoun, minke kahn noah kahkahlah*
     Looked   he Chief the to her, sorry being he   was
bounnoun, weah bounnoun, Ngurran bahn korah.
to her,   said to her, Weep   not.

" The natives here have constant communications with each other, and even with tribes whose dialect differs so much from theirs, that they are unable to converse together. Their messengers travel with great speed, are always armed, painted red, and adorned with down in their hair. Lately a black messenger arrived from Sydney. He said, ' My wife was intoxicated, and met Munan, a black on the government domain, Sydney : Munan cut her mouth with a knife, split her head with a tomahawk, and then, with more blacks, jumped upon her body. I took her to Broken Bay, where she expired, and buried her at Pit Water. Her little daughter desired revenge; and Boongaree, the chief of the Sydney tribe, has sent me to collect the blacks, that the murderer may be punished.' As they demand blood for blood, such are generally the occasions of their public fights. As knowledge increases, messengers will as quickly convey religious intelligence, and excite distant tribes to seek Him ' whom to know is life eternal.' The European missionary will be the fountain-head, whilst the aborigines themselves will become channels to convey ' living streams ' into the remotest parts of this vast moral wilderness.

" I was with a tribe when two blacks were appointed messengers, to meet one who was supposed to be on his way from a distant part of the colony. That they might be thoroughly equipped, they were decorated with red and white paint, their persons ornamented with feathers, a bone was thrust through the *septum* of the nostrils, and their long hair tied up in a pyramidical form. Trousers and other encumbrances were cast away, and they moved with dignity and an agreeable consciousness of security. Their persons are sacred, so that they go into a hostile tribe with boldness. Just as they were starting on their embassy,

14. *Uwah   noah,   numah   noah,   mung-ah;   bakrur   kurretoahrah*
    Came   he,   touched   he,   covering;   they   carry-who
ngahrokaah korun.   Weah bohn noah, Allah! uhngngahrahbahn, weahn
stood   still.   Said to him he, (vocative)   Young   man,   say
bahnu, Boangkaleah.
to thee,   Arise.

15. *Newwoah tatte kah berung yallahwah, butobiyah noah weahleahlah.*
    He   dead was from   sat up,   began   he   conversation.
Ngutaah kahn noah bohn bounnoun dunkahn ngekoambah.
Gave   he him   to her   mother   of him.

16. *Kintah   bahrur   kahkahlah   yahnteyn,   petal mahn bahrur bohn*
    Fear   they   was *or* were   all,   rejoiced   they to him
Jehovah   nung,   weahleyn bahrur kowwol ngurahke noah pibaah kaan
Jehovah   to,   saying   they great wise   one   he appeared has
ngaurrun kin.   Uwah kaan Jehovah ko bahrun kin ngekoung kah tah
us   among.   Come has Jehovah for them among his   are that
kora kah.
people are.

the expected messenger appeared through the distant woods. They broke their spears, gave specimens of a sham fight ; and, as the exalted personage approached their camp, they squatted down at their fires, without noticing his arrival. One person told him to sit down, at a respectful distance, by a log, where he applied the firebrand, which they generally carry with them, and gravely lit his pipe, but spake not a word. The oldest man in the tribe now rose up, and, taking some broiled fish, went towards the stranger, and threw the fish at him, which the other condescended to receive, with every symptom of a keen appetite. Had the message been of special importance, it would have been first communicated to an old woman, who would have whispered it from hut to hut, until every fire-side became familiar with it.

" In the past year death has made sad havoc amongst our tribes ; nor have we escaped. Our men, our children, my wife, and myself, were all at one time laid up with the influenza. The cries of the savages in pain, the howlings of the living for the dead, and the circumstances in which myself and mission were involved, harrowed up our feelings, and painted the surrounding scene with the blackness of despair. But 'there is a Friend who sticketh closer than a brother.'

" When health and strength were in a measure restored, I went to visit my neighbour, some fourteen miles across the lake. On my return I was informed that the natives had burned a woman, whom I knew to have been ill. On the following day, accompanied by the son of the deceased, and the man who burnt her, I went about two miles into the bush to ascertain the fact. The column of smoke ascending from the remnant of the pile guided us to the spot, where, under two immense trees, amidst the smoking embers, the skeleton of the woman presented a painful spectacle : her tobacco pipe, purified by the fire, claimed the victory over softer clay in the devouring element. The skull, the thigh, and arm-bones, were discernible, but so much destroyed by the fire as to fall to pieces on the gentle touch of a stick. I asked, 'Why did you burn her?' He replied, 'The blacks ordered me, to feed the large hawks, who will come at midnight and feast on her roasted flesh.' 'But why should hawks be regarded?' I inquired. 'Because,' said he, 'they were formerly black men, and the blacks are afraid of them.' 'Was she alive when you burnt her?' 'No.' I then said, 'Her flesh is consumed, her bones are there ; but where is her soul?' He pointed with his finger to the east, saying, 'Out yonder, a great way off.' Her own son smiled, and observed, 'She go to England.' I then addressed them on the immortality of the soul, and the resurrection of the body. They declared that they had eaten no part of the body. They informed me that when a plump young

man was killed in punishment, by one blow on the head, it is
the custom of the tribe at Port Stephens to roast and eat the
body; but of the truth of this I have no evidence.

"A native, of the name of Purcel, died of inflammation. As
the blacks came for spades to bury the body, I went to witness
the ceremony. The body, which had been previously painted,
was wrapped in bark from head to foot. His spears were broken,
and, together with his hatchets, tied up in a bundle and placed
by his side. The body was borne upon the heads of two young
men, who supported themselves steadily with long staves. An
old man went to the head of the corpse, and whispered, 'Do you
wish to see?' then, turning round to the natives, said, 'He does
not.' An old woman came with a friend's hair, which she had
just cut off; she thrust it in through the bark to the head of
the deceased. Two old men brought a bunch of boughs of trees;
they made a feigned desperate blow, then, stepping up to the
head, repeated the question, 'Do you wish to see?' Each time
the blow was made, the bearers of the body voluntarily stooped,
as though compelled to give place by the violence of the stroke.
They then turned round, proceeded some yards, stopped, turned
round again, repeated the same ceremony for seven or eight
times, until they reached the grave, in which they deposited the
corpse, amidst the howling of the dogs, and the most horrid yells
of the assembly. The women smeared themselves with pipe-
clay, burned their thighs with fire-brands, and then limped with
pain, shedding abundance of tears.

"In a few hours after, the widow of the deceased came to my
house in a state of alarm, and claimed my protection. Inquiring
into the cause of so much excitement, she said, 'Two blacks,'
whose names she mentioned, 'were going to tie me to a tree,
spear me to death, and then roast and eat me, as a satisfaction
for the death of my husband.' On the statement of the woman
being corroborated by others, I determined to prevent, if possible, such a horrid piece of cruelty. On telling them that I would
write to the governor, they met in council. At the close of their
deliberations, they vociferated, 'Let her not be killed;' and the
oldest man present responded, 'Let it be so.' One of the intended murderers, on being informed of my interference, threatened to kill me in the woods. On hearing this, M'Gill coolly
said, 'Give me the loan of a gun, and I will go immediately and
shoot the fellow for saying so.'

"Thrice have we been visited by bush-ranging robbers; but
our natives assisted us, and we captured two of them. It often
happens that our greatest fears are excited when there is not a
black about our station. At this moment there is not a black
within seven miles of us. We are now armed to defend our-

selves, should any thing occur. It would be well if such as are enjoying the sweets of society, the security of cities and towns, the parlour and its concomitant comforts, would take these and similar considerations into their abstract speculations on the *expense of missions.* The annual grant from the directors, and the assistance rendered by His Excellency, have *established this mission on a satisfactory basis.*"

This scheme, supposed to be satisfactorily established, was, like that of the Wesleyan church to the same people, constructed upon too *narrow a basis* to be either efficient or permanent. To place one man in the interior of Australia with an allowance of only £250 *per annum*, and a few perquisites from the government, (and this was more than the Wesleyans could expend upon that particular mission, and the utmost which the funds of the London Missionary Society would allow,) was so wholly inadequate to meet the exigencies of the case, that a more accurate knowledge of the circumstances and habits of the natives would have foreshown the certainty of failure. Any scheme that would, even now, meet the whole case, and fully realize the contemplated objects, must comprehend, 1. A spiritual agency that shall impress the native mind with a sense of man's responsibility to God for every deed "done in his body:" 2. A system of means eminently calculated to draw those wandering savages to a common centre, and fix them in friendly and beneficial intercourse with each other: 3. To provide them with places of shelter or dwellings, and teach them the arts and habits of civilized life: 4. To supply the means of subsistence during the whole process. This latter provision is indispensable; for a community broken into hordes of from sixty to seventy persons, and living chiefly upon fish, roots, and wild animals, must, like the beasts that graze in the fields, be constantly moving from one locality to another. The want of such a provision, in the days of Leigh and Threlkeld, constituted their main difficulty. The Wesleyan and London Missionary Societies sought the secular improvement of the natives but as a means of leading them on to their ulterior object, the salvation of their souls; but their limited resources did not enable them to reach either of these desirable results.

Public attention has often, of late years, been directed to the practical working of the missionary institutions of Great Britain. They have been described, not as embodying the "kingdom of God," which is "righteousness, peace, and joy in the Holy Ghost," but as consisting chiefly in "meat and drink," material commodities, merely human arrangements, and conducted upon a low, interested, if not a mercenary, policy. The language of commerce has been taken from its legitimate application to the affairs of men, and applied to the work of God. It has been maintained that the machinery employed by those establishments is out of all proportion, in elegance and expense, to the amount of work done. The sum expended upon domestic management, the outfit of missionaries, and the current expenses of the respective missions, have been carefully contrasted with the small number of Heathen gathered into the foreign fold of Christ's church. A money value has been put upon each convert; and, because they have been comparatively few, the subscribers have been informed that their contributions have been laid out without any regard to either utility or economy. In many instances, where there has been a total ignorance of facts, these representations may have been believed. May we invite the attention of such as have been thus imposed upon, to the case before us? After the labour and expenditure of years, there was not, at this time, one native convert in the Wesleyan church of Australia; and at the end of the year the committee announced the "suspension of the mission to the black natives," assigning as the reason, "the numerous obstacles opposed to its efficient operation by the habits and circumstances of the natives themselves, and the very great expense that would be incurred by the adoption of any vigorous and extensive plan for localizing the tribes, and bringing them under constant and regular instruction."

However much such a result may be regretted, it will excite no surprise in the mind of any one at all acquainted with the extreme difficulty of dealing with the native population of New Holland. The government had employed various expedients, for a succession of years, to bring them into a friendly relation to civilized men, and expended many thousands of pounds upon experimental plans for their personal and social advancement, without any obvious advantage. The Rev. William Cooper, who had studied the native character closely for many years, was sanguine as to the success of an educational institution, that should combine the order and comfort of a European home with religious and secular instruction, and industrial occupations. To encourage this judicious undertaking, the government offered him £20 *per annum* for every native boy he might be able to induce to reside upon his premises, and submit to his mode of physical and mental training. Yet, with all the kindness and industry of this excellent clergyman, he could only obtain seven boys, who not unfrequently absconded, and spent the night with their friends in the bush. The native girls, under the Wesleyan teacher, were equally trying and irregular; fleeing occasionally into the woods, and only brought back after much trouble and persuasion. Can any thing be more unreasonable than to require the directors of missionary societies to give a guarantee that they will eradicate the prejudices of a nation of barbarians at a certain rate of expenditure, and change the customs of ages within a specified period?   In contracting for the erection of a national monument, those principles might be regarded as being fair and equitable; but, in the work of missions, where success is as much dependent upon the blessing of God as upon the honest and vigorous co-operation of man, we regard them as wholly inapplicable.

Mr. Leigh, feeling deeply interested in the success of every aggressive movement of Christianity, kept up a regular and rather extensive correspondence with the missionaries of his own church and of other denominations.   We insert the following communications, because they mark the commencement of a new era in the literary and commercial history of several of the South Sea Islands.   The original letters, which now lie before the writer, are neatly executed.   They were translated for Mr. Leigh by Captain Henry, to whom they were addressed.   They were all written early in the year 1828.   The first is from the chief of the north side of Tahiti, and signed Hitoti :—

"Health be to you and family, my friend.   I received your letter.   I am glad you have let me know of your intended voyage. What you request shall be attended to : don't make yourself uneasy.   Tati will take care of it, and we will support him.   I am now convinced that your compassion is real, because you write to me.   You request me not to be angry with you.   I am not angry with you; but I feel disappointed that I did not see you before you left in the boat.   Health be to you on your voyage to New South Wales.   This is my request to you, dear friend : I wish you to bring me some clothes.   I enclose a sample of the cloth.   I wish them to be made at Botany Bay : one coat, one waistcoat, and pair trousers.   If making them at Botany Bay will be a trouble to you, bring the cloth, and I will get them made here.   Bring little water with you : this is a country of rain.   This is all I have to say.   HITOTI."

The following letter bears the signature of the king of Raietea :—

"Health be to you, Captain Henry, through the true God, Jesus.   This is my word to you : bring me some canvass and six bolts, and we will settle on your return : also, bring nails, one cask; the nails to be of two sizes, large and small; and one cask of pitch.   Let the cask of nails and the pitch cask be large : we will settle when you return.   Don't forget my requests : if you neglect them, I shall feel disappointed and hurt with you. Remember my request.   TAMATOA."

A postscript is added to this letter by Tahitoe, who was related to the king :—"This is my little request," he observes : "bring me some canvass for my boat. I will be ready to pay you on your arrival. Don't behave bad to me; think of me, and bring me five bolts. Health be to you, through the true God, Jesus Christ. I have no more to say. TAHITOE."

Fareahee, the chief woman on the south side of Tahiti, and step-mother to the late king, being anxious to set an example of European elegance before her people, desired Captain Henry, whom she called her son, to procure for herself and family the articles enumerated in the following order :—

"Dear Teareotahi, health be to you through the true God, Jehovah, on your passage to Botany Bay. This is my request to you, my son: bring me some ribbons, red, yellow, and black; one shawl; some red cloth for a bonnet; one white jacket and coat for your father, and get a box that will hold the things. That will be well. Perhaps my request will not be agreeable to Teareotahi. FAREAHEE."

The last letter of this class that we shall introduce, is from the pen of Tati, chief of Tahiti :—

"Dear friend Teareotahi, health be to you through the true God, Jesus Christ. I have received and read your letter. According to your request, I have sent you three hundred and thirty-two shells, mats, cloth, and plantains. I hope you will receive them. You know Tahiti is a country of no property. I wish you would bring me a little ribbon for my family. Health be to you. TATI."

The information which Mr. Leigh was receiving about this period from several other parts of the mission-field, was eminently calculated to strengthen and animate the languid missionary. "Blessed be God," says the Rev. W. Crook, "we are in good health, and going on steadily in our work, at Taiarapa. We have nearly three hundred church members, and numbers are constantly applying for admission to the Lord's table. Though our people are correct in their behaviour, we are under the necessity of maintaining a strict discipline. One of the brethren has just returned from England, and brought two excellent men and their wives ' to the help of the Lord against the mighty.' Messrs. Simpson and Pritchard go to the Marquesas, and Mr. Buzacott joins Mr. Pitman at Raratonga. We all met last month at Papara, and found much comfort and edification. Our people advance slowly in civilization. I am obliged to attend to the garden, the forge, the cattle, and the boat. If I do not assist myself, I can get nothing done. The soil is rich, and would well repay the labour of cultivation. Our sons and daughters must labour, or live like the savages. Our numerous family creates some uneasiness, as we cannot expect to be long with them; but surely the Lord will provide. We are bringing them up in the fear of God.   I write this note in the midst of continued interruptions from the natives."

The Rev. J. Orsman, writing from Otaheita, observes, "We are yet in the land of the living; but my multiplied engagements and deep anxiety are pressing me into the grave. Here the laws are more respected, and the people more orderly, than formerly. An effectual check has been given to the corrupting influence of foreign shipping. Our churches are reviving, Sunday-schools are being multiplied, and our congregations are increasing. Last sabbath our place of worship was filled *all day*. It was truly an animating sight. One of the chiefs said, 'The words of the teacher have melted me. Neither the blows of the constable, nor the cords of the judge, could have made me feel so much. It is hard work.' God, who made the 'dry bones live,' can turn these lions into lambs, and make them monuments of His grace. I am blessed with five little children, and expect a sixth in a few months; but my wife is evidently sinking under the weight of her school and domestic duties. *We die labouring !* All is sweet while Jesus smiles; all is light while Jesus aids; and all is success while He blesses."

Missionary Darling remarks, in a letter from Tahiti,—"From your narrative, I learn how wonderfully the Lord saved your brethren from destruction in New Zealand. The printing of the word of God in that language, which you say is in progress at the Bay of Islands, is the most important event that ever took place in that country. The Lord prosper the brethren of the Church mission in that great undertaking ! We are getting on here as fast as we can. We are fully occupied in translating and printing the sacred volume. The Assembly's Catechism and several useful tracts have been already published; and a large collection of hymns is now passing through the press. Our churches increase, and every where there is an intense thirst for the word of God. We are commencing two new missions; one to the Harvey Islands, and another to the Marquesas. Two missionaries will proceed from hence to the Marquesas, with several Tahitians as assistants, and a number of Marquesans who can read, and who have been residing in Tahiti for some time past. We feel anxious they should get a footing; for the field is large. I will send you a complete copy of our published works by the first conveyance."

Under the same date, the Rev. T. Blossom writes from the academy, Eimeo :—"I pray that the Lord may administer support to your brethren who have fled from New Zealand. In these islands we have met with severe trials ; yet the Lord has not suffered the mission to fail. Our difficulties here have been great, and many of them still continue. The death of young king

FIRST MISSION HOUSE BUILT IN TONGA.

MISSION HOUSE AT HIHIFO, TONGA.

Pomare has been a great affliction to us. My time is much taken up with the duties of the institution. I am obliged to superintend the native schools, and work at the bench for five or six hours a day. We have just had a ruinous hurricane. It carried away all our outhouses; blew our bread-fruit trees down upon my joiner's shop, and crushed it to the ground. It has shattered our dwelling-house, damaged the institution, and laid waste our garden. The state of things here is now somewhat quieter than it was a short time since. For this we are truly grateful."

At the same time, the barbarous Tonguese were beginning to feel the softening power of evangelical truth. They had long and obstinately resisted the gospel, and even washed their hands in the blood of their teachers; but the following extracts, from letters addressed to Mr. Leigh, contain encouraging evidence that a new day was opening upon Tonga. "Mrs. Thomas and myself," says Mr. Thomas, "are at Hehefo alone, prosecuting the work of God, in dependence upon His promise and grace. We occupy a school-house that will contain about one hundred persons. We hold two native services on the Lord's day, consisting of singing, exhortation, and prayer. We have now about fifty hymns in the native tongue: our prayers, of course, are written. We read the most striking parts of scripture, and endeavour to explain them in their own language. We hope soon to be masters of this rude tongue; and then we may expect the word of God to renew the face of this moral wilderness. I shall have no fear of our chief Ata, when I shall be able to address him in his own language. I shall then deal faithfully with him, and leave the issue with God. His known hostility to us prevents hundreds from attending our ministry. With your counsel and prayers, we shall be able, I trust, to subvert the walls of Jericho. September 20th, 1829."

On the same day Mr. Turner wrote from Nukualofa. "Hitherto," he remarks, "we have succeeded beyond our most sanguine expectations, and ere long we shall be able, I doubt not, to gladden your heart with the tidings of many conversions in Tonga. The work is unquestionably begun. Many have entirely laid aside their heathen customs and superstitions. They are athirst for the word of life; and, according to their light, sincerely worship the true God, and feel anxious to understand and practise the Christian religion. I can hear them pray to Jehovah, in their little communities, with such a solemnity of spirit and propriety of expression as quite affects me. Observe, I do not say that any are evangelically converted; but we expect soon to witness this consummation of our hope. From amongst those stones the Lord is raising up sons unto Abraham, whom we shall joyfully initiate into His church by baptism. Our trials are serious and severe; but they are swallowed up in our mighty concern to instruct and save this interesting portion of the human race. There is a great difference between the Tonguese and New-Zealander. The former are far more docile and teachable than the latter : their disposition is less restless and turbulent, while their intellectual powers are, in my opinion, in no degree inferior to the New-Zealander. We have above one hundred natives under daily instruction. Our congregations on the Lord's day average from three hundred to four hundred, and their eager attention leads us to exclaim, 'Surely the kingdom of God is come nigh unto you.' My colleagues, who are laborious and diligent, make great progress in the language. Thousands in the neighbouring islands are crying aloud to us, 'Come over and help us!' They are, indeed, 'perishing for lack of knowledge.' To their incessant inquiry, 'Will you not come and teach *us* the way to heaven?' we are compelled to say, 'We cannot!' O may the church at home pity and help those Heathen! Brother Leigh, pray for us!"

The sanguine hopes expressed by Mr. Thomas in his former communication, were being realized in Hehefo. "A young chief," says he, "who from the first attached himself to our mission, and was, after due instruction, received into the church by baptism, was soon afterwards seized with severe indisposition, and died in great suffering in the beginning of this year. He has gone to glory, as the first-fruit from Tonga under the Christian dispensation. This one soul is an ample recompense for all our expenditure and hardships here. The continued hostility of the chief exposes us to constant danger. Those of the natives who do attend our instructions are making a pleasing progress in learning. Such has been their eagerness to improve, that many of them can read whatever we put before them. The light is spreading rapidly amongst them; but still it has much to contend with. The enemies of the gospel are strong and united; but 'the weapons of our warfare are not carnal, but mighty through God to the pulling down of strong holds: casting down imaginations, and every high thing that exalteth itself against the knowledge of God, and bringing into captivity every thought to the obedience of Christ.' The missionaries here are comfortable together, and are bending all their energies to beat down Satan's kingdom, and build up that of Christ."

The results of these combined efforts were detailed to Mr. Leigh, in a letter from Mr. Cross, written two months after the above date. "The proficiency we have been enabled to make in the language exceeds by far any thing we had expected. We have already translated the most important parts of the Old-Testament history, the miracles and parables of our Lord, and a considerable part of the Acts of the Apostles. Many of the natives have become truly enlightened, and a goodly number of them have been converted. We have formed a church of twenty-seven members, with ninety-one on trial. Our congregations become so inconveniently crowded, that we have been obliged to enlarge our chapel. Our schools are also prosperous. We have four hundred and ninety-five men, women, and children, under constant instruction. Many of the people now read and write with a fluency and elegance that would astonish you. Having no printed books, as yet, to put into their hands, we are, of course, much employed in writing. We have applications every day for books. They say, *Misa Kolosi, o mi ha tohima akei,* 'Mr. Cross, give me a book to myself.' Our time is fully occupied; but our duty is our delight. Mrs. Cross unites in love to yourself and Mrs. Leigh."

This excellent young woman was brought to the knowledge of the truth by Mr. Leigh's ministry in New South Wales. She was, up to the time of her marriage, an efficient teacher in the Paramatta Sunday-school. She perished at sea, with nineteen others, in the prime of life, and while removing with her husband to a new station.

At the close of the month in which the above letter was written, Mr. Turner spoke in more decisive and expressive terms respecting the change that was taking place amongst the people of Tonga. "The work which the Lord is carrying on here, is almost incredible to ourselves, who are eye-witnesses of the facts. The deep and almost universal desire for religious instruction surpasses all that I have ever before seen. All the chiefs seem now to be almost ready to abandon their gods and embrace Christianity. The whole island will, no doubt, follow their example. The ability we feel to address them, is matter of astonishment to ourselves. As missionaries, we enjoy God's favour, and labour in perfect harmony. We are endeavouring to get our little works through the press as soon as possible."

Should any missionary peruse these pages, who, in consequence of his having entered into the labours of other men, finds himself in comparative comfort, and is tempted to self-indulgence; or, should he be isolated from his brethren, brought into circumstances of extreme difficulty, and urged to extricate himself by betraying the trust confided to him by the church at home; O let him remember that the least part of the penalty of yielding is official death. The following note is from the pen of one who, for many years, was in " perils by the Heathen." Nobly did he risk his life, by night and by day, by sea and by land, for Christ's sake : and neither the spear nor the club of the savage, though often brandished over his head, could move him from the steady discharge of his missionary duty.   And yet, just as he was passing into a state of outward tranquillity and personal safety, he perpetrated an act of great unfaithfulness, was dismissed by the Church Missionary Society, and became, through life, the subject of deep mental anguish.

"My dear Mr. Leigh, when I was with you last Saturday evening, my heart was so full that I could not give expression to either my sentiments or feelings: for while I felt thankful to God that I had ever known you, I had, at the same time, a distressful impression on my mind, that we should never meet again on earth.   You have laboured many years in this remote section of the globe.   Your Christian patience has been wonderfully tried; but the Lord has strengthened your hands.   You have seen great improvements in the temporal and spiritual condition of the people.   Considering the subtile attempts that are being made to undermine the Wesleyan church in New South Wales, your services here cannot, I am sure, be dispensed with.   May the God of your salvation still continue to bless, support, and preserve you, in your endeavours to promote the eternal interests of perishing men!   Through plenty or poverty, good report or evil report, may you follow the steps of Him who said, 'The foxes have holes, and the birds of the air have nests; but the Son of man hath not where to lay His head!'   And, should you be called to greater dangers than any you have yet encountered, though this is scarcely possible, may you not count 'your life dear unto yourself, so that you may finish your course with joy, and the ministry, which you have received of the Lord Jesus, to testify the gospel of the grace of God!'   May the Lord bless your excellent wife, that, with yourself, she may continue to be useful for many years!   Ah, my dear sir, I cannot refer to my own case: it is too painful.   You are aware that I have at this moment two rich and extensive estates in ——; but I am miserable.   In my rush-covered hut, where you used to visit me, I was happy: the pleasure I experienced in the service of God, the joy of a good conscience, and the approbation and prayers of Christian friends at home and abroad, mitigated trials, and made me indifferent to poverty and danger.   My children are well, happy, and dutiful."   The boat in which this gentleman was sailing to ——, to fulfil a mercantile contract, was upset, when he and several others were drowned.

Mr. Leigh having written to one of his ministerial brethren on the subject of mental improvement, a correspondence commenced between them, from which we select the following judicious observations on reading, in the hope that they will be found of service to the youthful inquirer after general knowledge.

"The plan which you have adopted, of making all your reading subservient to the important business of the pulpit, ought certainly to be observed by every minister of the gospel. We have solemnly consecrated to the service of the sanctuary all our time and talents ; and if we apply them to any pursuit not connected, either directly or indirectly, with its holy duties, we are virtually guilty of sacrilege. But it is encouraging to the clerical student to be assured, that art, science, and general literature are by no means incompatible with his sacred calling ; but may all be rendered tributary to the full and effective discharge of his spiritual duties. They unfold the wonders of the Creator's power and skill, and shed instructive light on the words of inspiration. They tend to make the man of God ' a workman that needeth not to be ashamed.' Life is so short, knowledge is so extensive, and the faculties of the mind so limited, that to every aspirant after wisdom it must be obvious,—whatever can retrench his expenditure of time, strengthen his intellectual powers, and permanently fix the new ideas and sentiments which he accumulates by study, is more precious than rubies. My own reading and experience suggest, that, before we enter on the examination of any work, we should inquire, 1. 'Is it worth reading?' On this question we should consult the two recognised ends of reading,—*pleasure*, which must be innocent to the conscience, and refreshing to the mind ; and *profit*, which is either the informing the understanding, or the amendment of the heart. A book from which we have no reason to anticipate either this pleasure or this profit, it would be a waste of money to purchase, a waste of time to read, and a waste of room to accommodate in the library. 2. 'Is this the *best* book on the subject ?' It would be a pity to read an author whose views are inaccurate, or partial, or badly expressed, when we might obtain one who is free from those defects. 3. ' Is this the very time and order in which it should be read ?' Study should be systematic. Books stand in the same relation to each other as the stones of a building : some form the bases, some the corners, some are key-stones, some are ornamental, while others are top-stones. As it would be preposterous in architecture to overlook this natural order, it would be equally so in literature to neglect the relative character of books. Hence there are many works well worth our careful perusal, but which it would be injudicious to read now : we must first study those which lead the way to these, by developing first principles and settling the meaning of terms. 4. 'Should it be read slowly and thoughtfully, or cursorily ?' Much of time and improvement depends upon this single point. Some books, such as ' Locke on the Understanding,' would be useless, if not read with the closest attention : others, such as the ' Spectator,' or the greater part of it, would be hurtful to the mind if dwelt upon. A knowledge of the reputation of books, and the opinions of enlightened men respecting them, are much to be regarded on these points."

The usual time for holding the anniversary of the New South Wales Auxiliary Missionary Society having arrived, the public meeting was held in Macquarie-street chapel, Sydney, on October 5th. The audience was numerous and respectable : the honourable the colonial secretary presided on the occasion. In the report then submitted to the meeting it was observed, " On looking on the few years that have revolved since the foundation of your Society, the committee see much that demands renewed acknowledgments of the goodness of the Most High. Within that period, limited as it is, the cross of Christ, borne by devoted men into the regions of pagan idolatry and superstition, has multiplied its peaceful triumphs beyond the most sanguine expectations of many of its servants. That holy combination in which the Christian church has concentrated its best energies for the spread of the gospel ' in the regions beyond,' has defeated the calculations of its scornful enemies; for, instead of consuming itself, as they sagely predicted it would, by the intensity of its own enthusiasm, it has continued steadily to increase, from year to year, in the number of its patrons, in the ardour of its zeal, in the boldness of its enterprises, and in the extent of its successes. Every year has brought fresh proofs that the cause of missions is the cause of God, having His command for its warrant, His glory for its end, His strength for its support, and His promises for the foundation of its hopes. Not alone in the countless treasures that have been offered at its altars,—nor in the increasing multitudes that have thronged to its anniversary assemblies in all parts of the civilized world, nor in the lengthening train of candidates for the honourable dangers of its service in heathen lands,—though these are delightful proofs that the missionary feeling is not the fitful impulse of fanaticism ;—yet it is not in these that we read the surest tokens that ' God is with us,' but in the actual conversions from darkness to light, and from the worship of idols to the worship of the living God, which have been accomplished by missionary instrumentality. Since your auxiliary was established, nine years ago, we have on record every possible evidence that thousands have been brought to embrace the sinner's only refuge; and that multitudes, having ' washed their robes and made them white in the blood of the Lamb,' have passed into the heavenly world, adding new gems to the Redeemer's crown, and causing angelic legions to sing with higher rapture, ' Glory to God in the highest : on earth peace, good-will towards men.' These are the true sources of our joys and encouragements; these fill our hearts with gratitude and our lips with praise; and while, in recounting these trophies of missionary warfare, we 'thank God and take courage,' it becomes us to enter with redoubled energy into the spirit and execution of this sublime undertaking, resolving that, seeing 'our labour is not in vain in the Lord,' we will, in humble dependence upon the Master we serve, be 'steadfast, unmovable, always abounding' in His Divine work."

In presenting the cash-accounts, Mr. Leigh, who was treasurer, remarked, that the receipts for the last year amounted to three hundred guineas, and that, since the commencement of the Society, there had been raised in the colony, for missionary purposes, not less than £2,655. 11*s*. 11*d*.

The demands for the services of the missionaries multiplying on all hands, Mr. Leigh made a strong appeal to the committee, pointing out the necessity for immediately strengthening and extending the missions in the South Seas. With a generosity and promptitude characteristic of the proceedings of that committee, and in the face of the most formidable pecuniary difficulties, did they respond at once to that appeal. The reply, bearing the signature of the Rev. George Morley, was as follows :—"Your own very interesting letter, one from Captain Henry, and one from Tonga, arrived by the same post, were read to the committee on the same day, and produced a most electrifying effect : for, though they had voted away all the money they had received, or expected to receive, and had even gone beyond their most sanguine expectation as to the annual income of the Society, they at once resolved to send four additional missionaries to your quarter of the world. One is to be a surgeon; another a printer. They have been induced to pass this resolution, 1. Because they hope that, when our people shall be made acquainted with the case, they will increase their subscriptions : 2. Because, from the accounts now given of the friendly disposition of the natives, they think that the expenses of supporting missionaries will be small, compared with what they have been. At any rate, we must say that sending out four missionaries to your islands is a bold undertaking. We are looking out for the men; but have not yet found them. No time, however, will be lost, and I hope we shall soon succeed. As your labours are wanted in the colony, the committee wish you to remain until you hear from them again. I trust that your remaining a while longer will be a great blessing to others, and not disagreeable to yourself. We pray for your health, happiness, and usefulness."

But, alas ! those fresh and seasonable auxiliaries were scarcely able to meet the pressing necessities of Tonga and its dependencies; while an entire new province, which was being established in Australia, was wholly unprovided for, or left to the mercy of contingencies.

It was during this year, 1829, that the Western or Swan-River colony was founded. Captain Stirling, who had previously surveyed the coast, was appointed governor. The western province is a vast region, extending twelve hundred and eighty miles from north to south, and eight hundred miles from east to west. It is farther from Sydney to Perth, the capital of this colony, than from London to Constantinople. As might be expected in a country of such extent, there are large tracts unavailable for the support of civilized man; but within its circumference are millions of acres of the greatest fertility, adapted to the growth of all kinds of grain, and the sustenance of flocks and herds, which may be multiplied for centuries without any apprehension of exhausting the provision which nature has made for them. The profit of sheep-farming, combined with the means of extending indefinitely the number of sheep-farms, must attract, in the course of years, a large amount of capital to this part of Australia. Many parts of the colony are rich in minerals. The climate is salubrious, warm, and dry; but, of course, in a country of such large dimensions, considerable variety may be expected to exist. Swan River discharges its waters into an extensive bay, called Melville Water. The river is subject to disastrous floods, which at times inundate the lands in the vicinity, and cause considerable damage.

At the close of the first year, there were twelve hundred persons on this new settlement. Many of these settlers, never having been accustomed to manual labour, were unequal to the difficulties and dangers incident to an infant state, and, after maintaining, for a short time, a feeble struggle, descended into indigence and an early grave. The town of Freemantle had been founded at the entrance of Swan River; Perth, the seat of government, is situated on a rising ground about nine miles inland; and Guildford, about seven miles further east, at the junction of the river. Fifty miles east of Guildford, stands the town of York. Augusta and Albany lie upon the sea-coast.

The number of aborigines cannot be ascertained with any degree of accuracy; but seven hundred and fifty have been known to visit Perth from the surrounding districts. The colony is rising in importance, commerce, and population; and yet the Wesleyan body has but two resident missionaries and an assistant in the entire province. The country has been examined for three hundred miles, and is every where accessible to the Christian teacher. The town of York and its neighbourhood present a fine sphere of ministerial usefulness. Within a range of a hundred miles people are found scattered, in all directions, like sheep without a shepherd. The government has offered land

SWAN RIVER FEMALE AND CHILD.

for the establishment of a mission ; and there is every probability, that, if there were a resident teacher, many of the natives
would be gathered in and taught to labour. There is also an
extensive tract of country stretching along the side of the river
Murray, peopled more or less by British and other emigrants.
"Men of Israel, help !" Unless your resources are entirely
exhausted, hasten to send at least one additional teacher, to
proclaim, amongst these perishing outcasts, "the unsearchable
riches of Christ !"

The district-meeting of 1830 was held in Princes-street chapel,
Sydney, when the state of the mission and the claims of Australia were carefully investigated. On reviewing the labours of
the year, it was gratifying to find that they had resulted in an
increase of church members, and the addition of one hundred
and forty-two children to the schools. Their places of worship
were well attended; religious truth was steadily permeating the
public mind; and, as might be expected, the habits and pursuits
of the people were becoming more conformable to the precepts
of the gospel. At the same time, the Lord was pouring out His
Spirit upon the brethren of the London Missionary Society, so
that, during the current and following years, they were enabled
to plant Christianity in many islands, the inhabitants of which
had not previously heard either of the white man's God, or of
His sacred book.

The Rev. John Williams, the "Martyr of Erromanga," was
the chosen instrument in promoting this extension of the kingdom of Christ. After accomplishing a long and perilous voyage
of observation in this service, he stated the result in an interesting communication to Mr. Leigh. We copy the following
particulars from his manuscript journal :—

"I mentioned to you my intention of taking a long voyage,
and settling as many native teachers as possible in several important groups of islands that lie to the westward. That voyage
I have now completed, in company with my friend the Rev. Mr.
Barff. We carried with us twelve teachers, fitted out by our
different churches in the Leeward Islands. We were obliged to
settle one of the best at the island of Aitutaki, and another at
an old station, judging it imprudent to sacrifice the interests of
existing stations for the purpose of commencing new ones. At
the latter island the people presented me with £103 in money,
as an offering to our Society. This was the aggregate of many
contributions, and was realized chiefly by the sale of hogs and
other commodities. Two natives and their wives, also, offered
to go and live on some heathen island, to prepare the way for
better-instructed teachers. We gladly accepted their offer, and
took them with us. We then sailed for Roragua, where we

found the mission families in a very distressed condition, owing to the prevalence of a disease that was raging like a plague. Nearly one thousand of their afflicted people had been suddenly carried off. After a short absence, we touched again, and found that the malady had subsided, and that the stations were prospering greatly. They had about nineteen hundred children in their schools. Flat stones, obtained from the mountain-quarries, and ground smooth, served them for slates, and the prickle of the sea-egg was used as a substitute for slate-pencils. With this rude apparatus there were some of them writing very prettily.

" After visiting several other islands in their neighbourhood, we proceeded to Tonga, touching on our way at Savage Island, intending to leave our Aitutaki teachers there; but the natives were so exceedingly wild, that we did not think it prudent to land them amongst them. After much difficulty, we succeeded in bringing two young men from the island. Having treated them kindly, we are now sending them back with a missionary, in the hope that their good report of us will insure him a kind reception. We then proceeded to Tonga, and were joyfully received by the resident missionaries. You will be pleased to hear that your Wesleyan brethren and their families are well. We spent ten days agreeably with them. Their patience is much tried; but they are getting on well, and must ultimately succeed. I am much mistaken, if some great event be not at hand that will give a general turn to the minds of the people here. Their fine new chapel stands on the top of the hill, within the intrenchments; in which the natives took refuge when they were attacked by the Vavouans, with the great guns which had been taken from the ship 'Port-au-Prince.' On that occasion the flower of Tonga was cut off. I examined the place with deep interest. Your brethren and their wives seem to be truly devoted to their work.

" It was our intention to have gone to the Feejees and the New Hebrides; but the information we received at Tonga induced us to abandon that design, a series of distressing disasters having occurred to a number of ships that had gone down there to procure sandal-wood; and we directed our whole energies to a group near home, leaving other groups for a subsequent voyage. After taking counsel with your brethren, we left the Haopais, and steered for the Samoas, or Navigators' Islands. La Perouse, the French circumnavigator, describes them well : he says, ' They vie with the Tahitian group, in extent, fertility, and population.' We were struck on beholding such fine extensive islands, two of them being considerably larger than Tahiti. This group is formed into windward and leeward, four islands in each group : the windward group we did not visit, as war was raging furiously at the time. We providentially met with a Samoa chief at Tonga, who wished to return home. He was related to the reigning family, and was of the utmost importance to us. By his representations the chiefs and people received the most favourable impressions respecting us and our teachers. We ventured on shore amongst them, and were treated with the greatest respect. We made presents to the old king at a public assembly of the chiefs and people. In acknowledging our presents, the king said, 'Although English property be invaluable to us, yet I value your friendship far more than your property. I have ever been a great man: I am now a greater man than ever; for here are two great chiefs come from England to unite themselves to me, and form one family with me.' He gave us the large dancing-house for a place of worship, and three or four houses as residences for the teachers. He was fetched from a neighbouring island on our arrival, where he was engaged in war with the natives. We urged him to go and settle his differences with them amicably. He said, 'I will go immediately, and put an end to the war, fetch my people home, and begin to learn this new thing. I have driven my enemies to the mountains, and another battle will insure victory; and then the conquered party will give me no further trouble.'

"On the morning on which we landed the teachers on the large island of Savai, the opposite shores of Upolu, the seat of war, were in flames, an engagement having taken place: the conquered fled to the mountains, and the conquerors, native-like, set fire to their dwellings and plantations. We hope that, by the time we return, which will be in a few months, this war will have closed. I never saw a mission commenced under more promising circumstances. Although we did not go to the Feejees ourselves, we sent three teachers, who were kindly received. The king said, when they landed, 'You may remain; but I cannot embrace your religion until I have called my people together, which will require time.' The teachers commenced building a large store *marae*, which they carried so high, that it has fallen down three times. The natives have not overlooked this catastrophe, which they attribute to the power of their god. Let us rather hope that it is the forerunner of the downfall of their entire system of superstition and idolatry. 'Alleluia: for the Lord God omnipotent reigneth!'"

CHAPTER XII.

AN EPIDEMIC VISITS NEW SOUTH WALES—MRS. LEIGH FALLS A VICTIM
—MR. LEIGH LEAVES THE COLONY—THE COLONY OF VICTORIA
FOUNDED—DESCRIPTION OF THE COUNTRY.

DURING the year 1831, New South Wales was visited with an epidemic of unusual malignity. It extended its ravages beyond the frontiers of the colony, and, after sweeping off thousands of all classes, broke out in Paramatta, where Mr. Leigh then resided; and scarcely a family in the town entirely escaped the calamity. Mrs. Leigh, who had always devoted a large proportion of her time to the visitation of the poor, the afflicted, and the dying, felt it to be especially necessary to meet the crisis by a more general and sedulous attention to this important branch of Christian duty; and many obtained the blessing of God by her instrumentality, in the last moments of life. This heroic woman, who never quailed before death, even in its most appalling aspects, approached, without hesitation, the most aggravated forms of the prevailing malady. Of a kindly and social disposition, unobtrusive manners, and unaffected piety, she was to be seen at all hours passing silently along the streets to the "house of mourning." But, in her solicitude to comfort the sorrowful and save the lost, she imposed upon herself an amount of labour which her constitution could not long sustain. Inhaling the miasma in the contaminated chambers she visited, she fell a victim to the common scourge, which, combined with several other diseases, soon terminated her valuable life. After enduring much suffering in the true spirit of calm resignation, she died peacefully. The following inscription marks the place of her interment: "Sacred to the memory of Catherine, the beloved wife of the Rev. Samuel Leigh, the first missionary to these colonies and New Zealand. She followed her blessed Master's example, in going about doing good, deservedly loved and esteemed by all who knew her; and died in peace on the 15th of May, 1831."

As might be expected, Mr. Leigh felt this bereavement acutely. He was for some time wholly incapacitated for public duty; and nothing but the grace of God, and the warm sympathy of Christian friends, carried him through so severe an ordeal. From New Zealand, where her worth was duly appreciated, he received many letters of condolence. They all breathe the same spirit of Christian love that pervades the following brief extract: "Although we are unable to estimate the greatness of your loss, or materially lessen the distress it has occasioned, we can sympathize with you in your present circumstances. Permit us to remind you of your own beautiful hymn:—

> 'Beyond the bounds of time and space,
> Look forward to that heavenly place,
> The saints' secure abode:
> On faith's strong eagle-pinions rise,
> And force your passage to the skies,
> And scale the mount of God.'

Here, in your 'Father's house, there are many mansions.' You can say with Job, 'I know that my Redeemer liveth, and that He shall stand at the latter day upon the earth: and though after my skin worms destroy this body, yet in my flesh shall I see God: whom I shall see for myself, and mine eyes shall behold, and not another; though my reins be consumed within me.' No wonder if, in an ecstasy of faith and love, you exclaim, 'Thanks be to God who giveth us the victory through our Lord Jesus Christ!' 'Therefore, beloved brother, be you steadfast, unmovable, always abounding in the work of the Lord, forasmuch as you know that your labour is not in vain in the Lord.' We hear that you intend returning to England as soon as you can be relieved by the arrival of additional labourers. May you be preserved on your passage, and blessed in your native country! The missionaries on this settlement, and their families, are well, and the work of the Lord prospers." This communication is dated from the Bay of Islands, and signed by the brethren of the Church mission.

Just before Mr. Leigh left the colony, the eighth anniversary of the "Australian Tract Society" was held. It has been already observed, that, soon after Mr. Leigh's arrival in the colony, he formed a tract society, employing as distributors five pious soldiers and three reformed convicts. The labours of those individuals, humble as they were, excited much public attention at the time; and, several rather remarkable cases of usefulness having occurred, a few respectable persons came forward to encourage and assist them. The utility of the society becoming more and more apparent, a public meeting was held in Sydney, in 1823, for the purpose of forming a society that should extend its benefits to all Australia. Being thus placed upon a wider basis, it gained a more liberal patronage, and was enabled to extend the sphere of its usefulness. It is always interesting to the philanthropist to mark the progress of public institutions in infant colonies. In the report, submitted to the above meeting, it was stated, "that 15,052 tracts and books had been gratuitously distributed during the year; 1,250 amongst the Europeans in New Zealand; 1,000 amongst the convicts on the penal settlement at Moreton Bay; 1,000 amongst the labourers employed by the Australian Agricultural Company at Port Stephens; 1,596 amongst the stockmen, settlers, and others at

Hunter's River; 250 amongst the patients in the hospital and prisoners in the jail at Newcastle; 1,250 amongst the convicts employed on the roads, and poor settlers about the Lower Hawkesbury; 1,000 amongst the widely-extended and various population at Bathurst; 1,500 amongst the stockmen and labourers in the county of Camden; 500 amongst the settlers in Airds and Appin; 500 amongst the convicts and inhabitants in and about Windsor; 125 amongst convicts and others in and about Paramatta; 3,950 amongst the Sunday-schools, prisoners· in the jail and on board the hulks, the sick in the hospitals, and the poor in and about Sydney."

Let the reader pause, and examine the limits of this field of operation; contemplate the light which these few lines throw upon the actual condition of the people, the singular diversity of character they present, and the prodigious accumulation of degradation and suffering they disclose. Surely the establishment of such an institution, and the maintenance, from year to year, of such an agency as we have described, was the very climax of Christian benevolence. Let us hope, that, while the stockmen in the bush, the patients in the hospitals, and the convicts in their cells or in the chain-gang, were perusing those valuable publications, the Spirit of the Lord was present, to expound the truth to their understandings, and apply it to their consciences and hearts.

As soon as Mr. Leigh could be relieved from his official duties, he left the colony, carrying with him the best wishes of the public at large, and the earnest prayers of religious people of all denominations. In consideration of the state of his health, the ensuing Conference (1832) was induced to place him at Liverpool in the capacity of a supernumerary.

The agencies and institutions of the Wesleyan church were fully organized, and in efficient operation, before Mr. Leigh left New South Wales. Its political importance was felt by the civil authorities, and its claim to be regarded as one of the principal instruments in promoting public order and colonial regeneration was generally admitted. While it looked upon the Church on the one hand, and the nonconforming bodies on the other, with a friendly eye, it yet maintained its neutral position, and attended industriously to its own department of duty. Its members were few in number; but they were evidences of the transforming power of the Divine truths which were taught, and showed the country that it was prepared to shape in the same mould the entire mass of society, as soon as it should possess the means of doing so.

In 1815 Mr. Leigh was the only Wesleyan missionary in the South Seas. He was patronized by two schoolmasters and their wives, ten or twelve soldiers and reformed convicts, and a few disorderly children in a Sunday-school. When he returned to England, he left in those islands nine circuits, fourteen missionaries, seven hundred and thirty-six communicants, and one thousand children in the schools. The supervision of the infant churches of Australia devolved upon the Rev. Joseph Orton. The labours of the brethren were as systematic as those of the ministers at home, and they went on peacefully; breaking up the " fallow ground," sowing it with the " incorruptible seed," watering the rising blade, and occasionally, at least, reaping the reward of the spiritual husbandman. The paucity of labourers was still felt and complained of, by all who had just views of the growing importance of the mission. The chairman, in an official communication to the committee, observed, " Be pleased to take into account the description of character peculiar to the greater proportion of our population, and the infantine state of our colony, together with the encouragement which is now afforded by the emigrants who are flocking to our shore, to make a rallying effort. May I hope that these and other considerations, arising out of circumstances which will, no doubt, suggest themselves to your minds, will induce you to send us additional assistance at this juncture of importance to the future prosperity of this mission? Three more missionaries might at this moment be usefully employed in the colony. In Sydney there should be, at least, two resident ministers : here is a population of more than fifteen thousand, and there are but two churches and one dissenting place of worship besides our own. We have two chapels, besides several other places, and but one preacher, whose time is much taken up with matters referring principally to the islands, and which will increase upon the person who has the charge of the district, in proportion as this colony rises in commercial importance, and our island stations improve and extend. I have endeavoured to possess myself of all possible information regarding the aborigines of this country. I have seen a little of them in my travels, and have discovered that every where they are a degraded race, but quite capable of receiving instruction. I am not aware of a better mode of accomplishing this object than that of forming a settlement at one of their principal places of resort, as far away from white men as possible; to acquire their language, and pay particular attention to the rising generation. Of course, such settlement, in its establishment and maintenance, would be attended with expense, say from £500 to £600 in the commencement, and at least £300 *per* year afterwards. The great obstacle to success will be found to consist in their wandering disposition. They are never long in one place; but they have generally a district for each tribe, and a rallying-point or place of general rendezvous within the limits of that district.   They are a miserable race of beings, and truly deserving the attention of the committee; and I have no doubt much might be done for them to advantage, if a mission were commenced with spirit, and carried on with energy; but feeble efforts, I think, would sink money to little purpose.   The credit of our Missionary Society in this colony is at this time suffering for want of such exertions in behalf of the natives."

Having heard that six or seven Wesleyans had commenced religious services, and formed a class-meeting, in the improving settlement of Bathurst, this able and vigilant missionary resolved to pay them a pastoral visit, for the purpose of directing and encouraging them.   This town, now the capital of an extensive county, stands on the river Macquarie, and is distant from Sydney about one hundred and thirty-five miles.   The Plains, a district of naturally clear land, commence near the town.   They are about nineteen miles in length, and from six to eight in breadth, containing a superficial area of about one hundred and twenty square miles.   These Plains consist of a series of gentle undulations, with intervening valleys of moderate extent, the surrounding forest and country being generally but thinly timbered, and patches of the forest stretching, at irregular intervals, into the plains, like points of land into a lake.   The Macquarie river traverses the whole length of the district.   These Plains are situated upwards of two thousand feet above the level of the sea; the locality is temperate and healthy, and is selected, as an occasional retreat, by the invalids of other less healthy districts.   Much of the land has been reclaimed, and is now under cultivation.

As this visit led to the permanent establishment of the ordinances of religion in Bathurst, we shall supply two or three particulars of the journey.   The road of the missionary lay over a broken and extensive range of hills, called the Blue Mountains. Those mountains consist principally of a succession of sharp ridges, intersected by remarkably abrupt and narrow ravines, or gullies, some of which are little less than two thousand feet in depth. Many of these ravines constitute the beds of rivers.   The scenery is of a singular and varied character.   After overcoming the difficulties arising from the heights, valleys, and swamps of this part of the road, being a distance of nearly seventy miles, he was gratified to find himself on the margin of a beautiful open country; the contrast of which, with the wild and limited view of sterile rocks, horrifying ravines, and dense thickets, was to him enchanting.

It was his practice, during the journey, to collect the people at the close of every day's march, whether at an inn or a private dwelling, and explain to them the way of salvation.   The people willingly assembled, and gladly listened to the word of God.

His attention was chiefly directed to road-parties and chain-gangs, consisting of men convicted of offences committed in the colony, who were sentenced to penal labour, and were employed in making and keeping in repair the interior roads. They were interspersed over the country, in parties of from fifty to three hundred in number. They were generally a most depraved body of men, having no one to care for their souls. If an important collateral object of penal infliction be the reformation of the subject, these poor outcasts were awfully neglected. Whenever the missionary addressed them, they listened with deep attention; and, in many instances, were melted into tears, while the mercy of God in Christ to the chief of sinners was being exhibited.

The missionary found the little flock at Bathurst firm and united, amidst circumstances of strong temptation, and the almost total destitution of the outward ordinances of religion. One gentleman offered an acre of good land, on which to erect mission-premises, and £50 towards the building. The people assembled and passed a resolution, in which they solicited the appointment of a missionary, and pledged themselves to meet all the expenses that might be incurred. The committee sent them a teacher; and such has been the success that has attended the preaching of God's word there, that now, while we are recording these facts, there are several resident missionaries, and nine hundred persons under their instruction every Lord's day.

Anterior to the establishment of this branch of the Australian mission, the settlers treated the natives with great severity. As actual hostilities had commenced, in several places in the district, between the colonists and the black tribes, a public remonstrance was addressed to the former through the medium of the "Sydney Gazette" of October 14th, 1835. In that remonstrance it was observed, "However outrageously the aborigines may have comported themselves in the neighbourhood of Bathurst, it is no less authentic than remarkable, that the same natives live on terms of perfect amity with our settlement at Wellington Valley. Whilst Bathurst and its surrounding neighbourhood are engaged in an exterminating war, peace reigns in the ever-verdant plains of Wellington Valley. What a contrast! For the last twenty months, constant intercourse has existed between the aborigines and this settlement; and it has invariably been found, that those miserable wanderers have been much influenced by kind treatment. But if humanity is outraged on the part of men who are, in name at least, Christians, can it be expected that the untutored Heathen will tamely submit to see his parent, brother, or friend murdered, and not resent the injustice? This has been the true cause of hostilities. Men professing to be more enlightened than savages, and having the death of no relative to revenge, have gone out on horseback to hunt the natives down, firing indiscriminately at all they could overtake. The sufferers have gone in agony to the next settlement, to solicit the Europeans to dress their gun-shot wounds. Just Heaven! it is horrible to think, that, at a moment when the whole civilized world is united for the abolition of the slave-trade, there should be found amongst us even one man cruel enough to think it necessary to exterminate the whole race of these poor misrepresented people! Bring hither a laborious missionary. Are not the fields white unto the harvest? If affection and gratitude be even now the inmates of their untutored nature, what would not the gospel accomplish amongst them?"

The writer of this humane and touching appeal might have added, "Look from your own shores across the waters to the Friendly Islands, and other groups in their immediate vicinity, and then contemplate the transformation now in progress by the instrumentality of Christianity." What an apposite illustration! Those several groups include about two hundred islands in the whole, many of which are thickly inhabited. Till very lately the people were living in the grossest idolatry; but the Sun of righteousness has arisen "with healing in His wings." The aborigines of these islands speak the same language, worship the same gods, acknowledge Tonga as their head, and bring an annual offering in token of their submission. "Tonga," says the superintendent of the mission, "contains about ten thousand inhabitants, who, with few exceptions, are worshipping dumb idols. Had the principal chief used his influence in favour of Christianity, hundreds would, before this time, have become worshippers of the true God. Several chiefs will not allow Christian worship to be established in their territories; yet religion is making progress, and some of the people are leaving the enemy's camp and joining us almost every week. The next of the Friendly Islands is the Habai group: eighteen of these are inhabited. They lie about fifty or sixty miles to the north of Tonga. It is judged that there are about four thousand souls on these islands, all of whom, with their king, have embraced Christianity. The Vavou group lies about a day's sail north of the Habais. The Haafuluhao group is by far the largest, as the islands are more numerous. The king received Christianity in 1831, and shortly afterwards the whole of his people renounced idolatry, and professed the Christian religion. The Keppel's Islands are two in number, and lie between Vavou and the Navigators' Islands. The Feejees are about a day and a night's sail to the west of Tonga. In several, if not in all, of the islands, they go quite naked, until they are seventeen or eighteen years of age. But a few years since they were cannibals. The friends of missions will rejoice to know, that from eight to ten thousand persons have abandoned their idols, and become worshippers of the true God, within the last six years, in these islands. Still there are six or eight thousand savages in Tonga alone, who are paying homage to birds, fishes, horses, and infernal spirits. They pray, cry, and cut themselves; cut off the fingers of their children and friends, and sometimes strangle their relatives, to appease their gods. Send them more missionaries: hold us up by your prayers, and God will bless us."

While the Spirit of the Lord was being thus poured out upon several of the Friendly Islands, Divine Providence was making arrangements for a sudden and remarkable enlargement of the work in Australia. On the 1st of June, 1836, it was ascertained that one hundred and seventy-seven persons had settled in the neighbourhood of Port Philip, and imported from Van-Diemen's Land sheep and other property to the amount of £110,000. In the following year, when the first governor arrived, he found five hundred colonists, with one hundred and fifty thousand sheep, and upwards of two thousand horned cattle and horses. Such were the materials with which he laid the foundation of the province of Victoria. It stretches from the river Murray on the north to Wilson's Promontory. In round numbers, it is about two hundred and fifty miles from north to south, and five hundred from east to west, with a coast-line of six hundred miles. It embraces an area of eighty thousand square miles, being about equal, in extent, to Great Britain. The climate of Victoria is superior to any other in Australia. From being the most southerly part of the Australian continent, it is naturally the most temperate; and its mountainous character supplies it with health-giving breezes in abundance. The clouds from the South Pacific, being thrown in fleecy columns against the high lands of the colony, are precipitated in copious showers, especially during the winter months. With the delightful temperature thus obtained, the summers are never intolerably hot, nor the winters cold. This province contains more fertile land near the sea than any of the other colonies, and great tracts of undulating pastures, lightly timbered, well watered with rivers and deep lagoons. The soil is rich, the climate genial, the rain abundant, and the crop certain.

Melbourne, the seat of government, is built on the banks of the river Yarra-Yarra. The site, abandoned a few years ago to forest-trees, kangaroos, and straggling savages, now possesses many commodious public buildings, government-offices, churches, chapels, hospitals, hotels, and banks; a court-house, botanical garden, mechanics' institute, and extensive warehouses. No colony has been so remarkably rapid in its progress as this. In 1851, there were 5,000 inhabited houses, containing a population of 23,070 souls. Here are Bible, educational, temperance, and harmonic societies ; circulating libraries, reading societies, and book-clubs. There is an efficient colonial printing-press, sending forth nine periodicals and three daily papers. In the above year there were 77,345 Europeans in Victoria, possessing six and a half millions of sheep, and 263,305 horned cattle and horses, and actually consuming as much British merchandise as does the whole kingdom of Spain, or one-fourth as much as the empire of Russia, with its sixty millions of inhabitants. Thus we see how valuable those new settlements are becoming to English manufacturers, merchants, and ship-owners.

At the end of two years from the establishment of the colony, there were but two Wesleyan missionaries in the province, with thirteen communicants. In 1852, there were four missionaries, having 1,630 persons sitting under their ministry, and 656 children in their schools.

Geelong, the second town in Victoria, lies on the western side of the bay of Port Philip ; and bids fair, in consequence of its maritime position, to rival the capital at no distant period. The situation of this important town is peculiarly picturesque, with beautiful park-like views immediately about it, and the Pyrenees towering in the distance. There are already above 10,000 inhabitants, who have supplied themselves with various religious, benevolent, and educational institutions. The scenery, throughout this fine province, is eminently beautiful. " Around me spread," says Howitt, " a spacious plain, with trees thinly scattered, and in clumps. On the boundary of the plain are knolls, slopes, and glens, all of the smoothest outline, crowned with the same trees. Beyond were mountain ranges, on which rested deliciously the blue of the summer heavens. Some of these mountains were wooded to the summits ; others revealed through openings immeasurable plains, where sheep were whitely dotting the landscape ; the golden sun being seen at intervals betwixt the long shadows of the trees. There only wanted a stately river to render the scene magnificent." Here is " a nation born at once ! "

The following note, addressed to Mr. Leigh, by the resident missionary at Windsor, and dated November 19th, 1836, refers to the state of things in the parent colony : " In reference to the work of God in New South Wales, I am happy to say that it is steadily advancing. In Sydney, Princes-street chapel has been enlarged and re-opened for Divine service again this week. We have commenced religious worship at the house of Mr. Landales, on the way to Botany Bay. At Liverpool a considerable sum has been subscribed towards the erection of a chapel there, exclusive of the magistrate Moore's subscription, which, I under-

stand, will be handsome. At Bathurst we have a chapel in progress. The congregations at Windsor have greatly increased
within the last three years : all the sittings are let, and a new
chapel is indispensable. Within the above short period, the
subscriptions to the mission-fund have increased fourfold. In
Windsor circuit alone there is plenty of work for three efficient
missionaries. One is particularly wanted at the Lower Hawkesbury. We are glad to hear that your health has improved, and that
you are using it in zealously pleading for the perishing millions
of mankind. Many, with ourselves, would hail your arrival
once more on the shores of Australia; but I am inclined to
think, from all I can hear, that you are serving the cause of
missions as effectually where you are. Your old friend John
Lees, of Castlereagh, died a few months since. At the request
of his family I attended his funeral. There was a large attendance of relatives, neighbours, and Christian friends. The clergyman delivered an appropriate address in the church, and I spoke
of the deceased at the grave. I afterwards dined with the Rev.
Mr. Fulton. Mrs. Fulton died a short time ago. She was
fully prepared for 'the inheritance of the saints in light.' The
last time I visited her, she spoke with confidence of her interest
in Christ, and said, 'For to me to live is Christ, and to die is
gain.' The Rev. W. Cartwright improved her death to a large
and affected audience."

This year closed with another division of this mighty continent, for the purposes of colonization. Our limits will only
admit of our marking the commencement of those communities
which are destined, in the progress of years, to "multiply,
replenish, and subdue" this great southern section of the globe.
The principal feature in the Act of Parliament constituting the
South Australian colony was, "that it should pay its own current expenses ; that the land should be so allotted as to be
improved ; and that it should, from its very nature, form a market for labour." On the 20th of December, the first governor
landed. He examined the coast, fixed upon the site of the
capital on an eminence about six miles inland, laid out the
streets, squares, and public buildings, and named it, at the
request of the king, Adelaide. This territory does not seem
large on the map of Australia, yet it comprehends three hundred
thousand square miles, being, in reality, twice the size of Great
Britain and Ireland, and three times as large as Prussia. The
sea-coast is about eight hundred miles in length, and contains
some fine gulfs and bays, easy of access, and safe as harbours
for vessels of a large size. The greater part of the province,
being nearer the line than Victoria, is somewhat warmer in
summer. The general face of the country is gently undulating,

dotted at intervals with patches of majestic trees, and wearing, on the whole, the appearance of an English gentleman's park. Vast plains of fertile soil abound ready for the plough, requiring no clearing from trees or brushwood. The principal river is the Murray, which for two hundred miles, at least, is as wide as the Thames at London Bridge. This colony possesses the richest copper-mines in the world. The discovery of this ore not only verified geological predictions, but revealed, at the same time, such an abundance of metallic veins, that their like has been unparalleled in the history of mining.

The city of Adelaide, now erected into a bishopric, is pleasantly situated, and contains a population of about thirty thousand souls. A college has been built in the neighbourhood, which is under the direction of the bishop. Here are commercial banks, assurance companies, a mechanics' institute, and public library. There are above six thousand children receiving secular and religious instruction in the day and Sunday schools. Seven newspapers are published, one of which is a daily journal. Small capitalists should peruse the history of this colony before they embark in any colonizing speculation; while the intending emigrant should acquaint himself with it, and consider well the probable consequences of landing his dependent family upon a foreign shore.

The affairs of the Wesleyan church in Australia, which was now divided into four colonies, were administered by the Rev. John M'Kenny. Mr. Leigh being regarded as the father of the mission, a regular correspondence was kept up with him by the official brethren in Sydney. In a note dated February, 1837, they remark, " Christianity is still advancing in the colony, notwithstanding the attempts that are being made to arrest its progress. We have the gospel faithfully preached to us in all our chapels. Our Sunday-schools are in prosperous circumstances, and experimental religion is being revived amongst us. The Protestant public is very much roused by the attempt that is being made to force the Irish system of education upon the colony. We have now two bishops in New South Wales; one presides over the established Church, the other over the Roman Catholic body. We have had a large influx of clergy, Episcopal, Presbyterian, Wesleyan, Independent, Baptist, Quakers, and Popish. We rejoice to hear of your improved health, and of the success with which you continue to advocate the cause of missions. The Rev. Samuel Marsden, and his daughter Martha, sailed last week for New Zealand. A missionary from that country officiates in his church during his absence. Mrs. Marsden died a short time since: indeed, the mortality has, of late, been very great. Many of your own dear and valued friends have gone to glory. One

HINDLEY STREET, ADELAIDE.

of your young converts, Miss Augusta Smith, married Mr. Cross, the missionary, and has gone with her husband and several others to Tonga, where the natives, in vast numbers, are embracing Christianity. The savages of Feejee are also turning to the Lord. Glory be to God!"

These statements respecting the hopeful condition of the mission generally, are fully borne out by the testimony of the brethren. The superintendent, writing subsequently to the above date, observes, "God in His good providence has opened the country before us in its length and breadth, so that we have only to go up and possess it. I am sure that our committee will be at once ready to avail themselves of the present state of things, and feel their obligation to enter the open door that Divine Providence has set before them. This is not a question of pounds, shillings, and pence; for it now assumes this form, 'Shall Australia be a Protestant or a Popish colony?' The number of priests who are being sent out is quite frightful: lately eight arrived in one vessel, and received from the home government £150 each for their outfit and passage. In Sydney our chapels are by no means equal to our congregations, and it will be my immediate duty to endeavour to get a large one in the centre of this extensive and beautiful town. A blessed influence attends our services, and the increase of religion is manifest. Come, or send soon to our help." "Our congregations at Paramatta," says the missionary, "are overflowing, and fresh inquiries are constantly being made for pews and sittings. We have not yet been able to commence the new chapel, but hope to do so in about a month. The plan and specifications are now complete, and we are just ready to receive tenders for the erection, which, it is presumed, will cost about £1,000: this sum, with the assistance of government, will, I think, be easily raised. In my opinion, Paramatta bids fair to flourish as a mission-station. I think it necessary to furnish the committee with an account of my public engagements, that they may know how my time is taken up. On Sunday morning, at eleven o'clock, I preach in the chapel here; in the afternoon I ride, on an average, eighteen miles, and preach in the country; I return again to town and preach in the evening, at six o'clock. On Monday I visit the female class at four P.M., hold a public prayer-meeting at seven, and frequently meet the juvenile class afterwards. On Tuesday I hold a meeting for prayer, in a private house: many attend. Wednesday, I go to Liverpool, visit the people, and preach in the evening. Thursday evening I preach in town. On Friday I meet a class. These engagements, with visiting the town members, and preparing for public duty, fully occupy my time. The Sunday labour is excessive, and frequently makes me ill on

the following day. I thank God I have no other object in view,
than to serve my generation according to His will:—

'Be they many or few, my days are His due,
And they all are devoted to Him.'

"Our Sunday-school is becoming more efficient than ever.
One hundred children were present last Sunday morning, and
eighty-five in the afternoon. The teachers are actively engaged,
and much good is anticipated. The public examination of our
children, a fortnight ago, gave much satisfaction. The attainments of the children far exceeded my expectations. The teachers, with several ministers and friends, afterwards took tea together, when the greatest harmony and Christian feeling prevailed.
The Rev. Samuel Marsden died on Saturday, and was interred
on Tuesday. His funeral was attended by an immense number
of the most respectable colonists, by whom he was much vene-
rated. He was seventy-three years of age, and had been senior
chaplain for upwards of forty years. Next Sunday morning we
intend to close our chapel, and, as a mark of respect to the
memory of this venerable man, go to church to hear his funeral
sermon."

The arrival of the first missionary, and establishment of the
worship of God, in Adelaide, the metropolis of South Australia,
is thus acknowledged by the stewards of the little society:
"Since the arrival of our missionary, we have been enabled to
introduce those parts of the regular Wesleyan discipline which
had not been previously brought into operation; and the results
are already highly satisfactory. We feel quite confident that, if
he be permitted to remain with us, we shall be fully competent
to meet all the expenses required for the maintenance of himself
and family. Since his arrival we have enjoyed peace and prosperity. We have already raised £500 towards a new chapel;
our small society has increased, and our prospects brighten.
Adelaide, October 27th, 1838."

At this date there was but one missionary and twenty members in the province: within thirteen years from the above date,
and within the same geographical limits, they had increased to
six missionaries, 1,215 communicants, 1,677 Sunday-scholars,
and a weekly attendance on their ministry of 5,900 persons of
both sexes and of all ages. Who can reflect upon these wonderful displays of the providence and grace of God, without feeling
constrained, like Moses and Miriam, to yield to the impulse of a
grateful heart? Looking at their own safety and the complete
overthrow of their enemies, these illustrious persons said to
Israel, in an ecstasy of joy, "Sing ye to Jehovah, for He hath
triumphed gloriously."

The attention of Parliament was at this time directed to the spiritual destitution existing in several of the British colonies, and the government was urged to act with greater liberality towards the colonial clergy, and to acquiesce in some financial arrangement that should greatly augment their number. While Popery was being patronized at home, and endowed abroad, an utter indifferency was evinced by the statesmen of the day to the interests of Protestantism. The Propaganda of Rome, duly appreciating the sympathy of England, was multiplying the agencies of their church, and sending them to confront Protestant missionaries in every quarter of the globe. Having set up ecclesiastical hierarchies in Australia and New Zealand, they had the audacity to claim, as members of their communion, all who had been baptized by the clergymen of the Church of England, or by the Wesleyan missionaries, though they themselves had neither baptized nor instructed one of them. They had brought several of the religious orders of their church into these colonies; and, having lately received considerable reinforcements from France, were making a determined attack upon Protestantism.

In the hope of counteracting their aggressions, and at the same time of strengthening and extending their missions, the Conference sent out four additional and very efficient ministers, together with the Rev. John Waterhouse, who was appointed general superintendent of the missions in Australia and Polynesia. That there was a simultaneous movement on the part of the directors of the Popish mission, is obvious from the following notes:—"The Romanists are evidently organizing a system to occupy, as far as they can, every part of the colony of New South Wales; and in those districts where the people are destitute of the means of grace, what is to prevent the ignorant from being imposed upon and carried away to Popery? Two persons were lately baptized by the Catholic priest in the Hawkesbury. The most painful apprehensions are entertained by all the Protestant communities in the country. By a late arrival the Romanists have got out six sisters of mercy, who have taken a house at Paramatta, and zealously commenced their works of charity. They do not remain at home like nuns; but are active agents, going into every open door, and visiting every family that will receive them, in order to promote their doctrines and practices. New South Wales never had such claims upon the commiseration of the friends of missions as at this moment. Here are a few missionaries in a new world, which is rising rapidly into immense importance, not only in a commercial, civil, and political point of view, but especially in a religious sense. This colony will form the centre of this new world, and become the fountain of legislative and executive authority to surrounding states. Hence must issue, either the 'law of the Lord,' which is the basis of national liberty, or the mandate of the despot, which binds men to superstition and idolatry. The occupation of this country by Protestant teachers is closely connected with the success of the gospel in the islands of the South Seas."

The other note is as follows : "The Roman Catholic bishop, and his co-adjutors in New Zealand, are ready to employ any means to advance and disseminate the influence of Popery. Notwithstanding all their efforts, they have not yet done much among the people, though with the utmost impudence they pretend to have proselyted to the 'Catholic' Church nearly one half of the entire population. As an antidote to their pernicious system, we have much to hope from an extensive circulation of the word of God, which is now eagerly received in every part of the land, but especially from the valuable addition to the amount of missionary labour which we are happy to hear you have so seasonably appointed. The present is certainly a very important era in the history of New Zealand: it is a momentous crisis, and its political condition assumes a very serious character. May the Lord in mercy save this land from the grasp of Popery!"

The "additional" labourers, referred to in the above note, had already arrived in Van-Diemen's Land. Mr. Waterhouse had met the brethren in that colony, and communicated the result of his inquiries and observations in an official letter to the committee. It is dated "Hobart Town, November, 1839." "I look upon this colony," he observes, "as being every way important in the southern hemisphere. Your mission here is enriching other colonies by the almost constant emigration of pious persons, as well as benefiting vast numbers of prisoners and others, who, but for the labours of your missionaries, would be entirely destitute of the means of grace. To judge of their success only numerically, would not be fair: immense good is being done incidentally and collaterally; and your missionaries must be kept at their post, or Popery, infidelity, and an anti-Christian liberalism, will destroy their thousands. There is no system better adapted than ours for meeting the wants of this people; and to see such great things accomplished in so short a time, especially in the interior and northern part of the colony, calls loudly for gratitude to God. The important opening at Melbourne, Port Philip, I hope, will not be overlooked. The want of more missionaries distresses me: it is so important to take possession of the new colonies that are springing up with such unwonted rapidity. Your mission to the natives will be greatly aided by that thriving town. Your men of commerce should help. Missionary labours prepare the way for commercial enterprise. The report which I have received from Adelaide has delighted me greatly. From New Zealand I have received cheering accounts, and hope in a little while to visit the brethren there. Several New-Zealanders are here: they appear to be a highly interesting people. There is likely to be a regular trade between Kaipara and Van-Diemen's Land."

But not only in the places specified in Mr. Waterhouse's letter were there special tokens of God's presence with His people, but also in other localities within the vast field assigned to his supervision was the Lord making bare His holy arm. The brethren in Sydney, describing the state of their own mission, remark, "A wonderful change has taken place here within the last two years, as it regards morals and religion. This appears not only by the increased attendance on Divine worship, but also by the general desire that is expressed for religious instruction and pastoral care. Many new chapels are rising up; new societies and congregations are in the course of formation; and loud calls are made for additional teachers. Those calls, which are from all parts of the colony, are earnest and repeated; but we have no labourers to send. At West Maitland a new chapel is ready for the roof. At Patnuk's Plains a gentleman has offered a site, and as many bricks as will build a chapel. A new society has been formed at the Five Islands, and both ground and subscriptions offered for a chapel. At Bathurst they require an additional minister. At Liverpool £200 have been already subscribed towards a new and larger chapel. Penrith is still almost destitute of the means of grace. We must have more missionaries."

The native Institution, established about forty miles from Geelong, was beginning to yield hopeful indications of permanent benefit to the aborigines. The government had granted an extensive tract of ground for the use of the Institution. Twenty-five natives had been induced to reside with the missionaries, who supplied them with food and clothing. They were regularly taught to work, and several of their children had already become perfectly familiar with the alphabet. Though the language be poor, in regard to expressions appropriate to religious subjects, yet they were beginning to understand some of the doctrines of Christianity. There were, however, difficulties connected with the mission, which nothing but self-denying, persevering, and energetic labour could overcome. The legislature had passed an Act, commonly called the "Squatters' Act," under which settlers might establish themselves in any part of New South Wales. As this Act did not recognise even the existence of the natives, it made no reserve in their behalf. "The result of this Act," says an intelligent writer, "is, that the natives who remain in the neighbourhood of the settled districts become pilfering, starving, obtrusive mendicants. After enduring incalculable deprivations, abuses, and miseries, they will, if no better system be adopted, gradually pine, die away, and become extinct, leaving an eternal blot upon the justice, equity, and benevolence of a *Christian* government, which made no adequate provision for them. Being driven back upon the territories of other tribes, they will be murdered and exterminated. Nothing less than the 'hue and cry' of Christian philanthropists will ever move the Imperial Parliament to the due consideration and adoption of measures so comprehensive and liberal, as shall at once secure to these children of nature their inalienable rights."

The missionaries had succeeded in ascertaining the principal haunts of several neighbouring tribes; in accomplishing which they had laboured hard and suffered much, particularly in a recent expedition, in the course of which they were drawn into an exceedingly rough country, and had well-nigh perished. Two gentlemen, friendly to the mission, had kindly volunteered to accompany them, and became their fellow-sufferers. In penetrating dense forests, crossing deep ravines, and passing over rugged rocks, two of the horses died from exhaustion. During the last three or four days, the party subsisted on one pound of damper (a cake made of flour and water) each, with a little fish which they casually caught. They, however, were providentially preserved, and succeeded in reaching their homes, though almost starved and naked.

This journey, though rather disastrous, was of great service, inasmuch as it led to the discovery of a tribe before unknown to Europeans, and who, it is believed, had never seen white men before. It also afforded the brethren an opportunity for witnessing new developements of the native character. "The appearance of the aborigines of Western Australia," they observe, "is certainly forbidding, besmeared as they are with grease and *wilga*, which are plentifully distributed over the head, face, and neck, and some other parts of the body. A bandage is tied around the forehead, which is decorated with feathers of the emu or cockatoo. A *booka*, or 'cloke,' made of kangaroo-skin, is their principal article of dress. The women have a bag, made of the same material, with a sling to throw over the shoulders, in which they carry their infants; and a smaller bag, in which they deposit their *wilga*, rice, and drinking-cup. The women generally carry a *won-no*, or 'digging-stick,' with which they dig up roots out of the earth for food. The men carry a throwing-board, a few spears, and a hammer of peculiar construction, made of stones and gum: this is stuck in a belt, and worn about the waist. The hammer is useful in climbing trees, and is a terrible instrument of attack on an enemy. These few articles constitute the wardrobe and kitchen-utensils of the natives. Thirty or forty tribes, amounting to upwards of two thousand individuals, were known to live within one hundred miles of

Perth.   They live by fishing, digging-up roots, gathering grubs, burning out the kangaroo-rat, or catching the opossum.   If fed to-day, they feel regardless about to-morrow.   Many of them are employed by the settlers in cutting wood, fetching water, and carrying messages; in return for which, they receive rice, sugar, flour, and bread, which they distribute amongst their families.   At night they erect circular huts, kindle a fire, place their spears in readiness for use, and sleep in the open air.   It' is customary for the head of one tribe to give all their daughters in betrothment to another tribe, and that tribe makes a similar return; and if a man dies, having one or more wives and children, then those naturally fall to the lot and inheritance of the next brother, if he is old enough to marry, who enters at once upon his new charge and cares; though of the latter he has but few, for it is the province of the woman to find food, and do all the drudgery of life.   This law, or custom, is the cause of great domestic suffering, and not unfrequently leads to bloodshed, and the destruction of life.   They are addicted to inhuman and barbarous murders.   At the death of any one, they have an idea, that the *goor-do-mit*, or 'spirit,' cannot rest until satisfaction is made by taking away the life of some one belonging to another tribe.   Thus they proceed from tribe to tribe, until many lives are lost.   The circumstances attending a last sickness or death are truly affecting.   When the sufferer is supposed to be near death, the relatives assemble around him, and begin the *me-rang-win*, or 'crying,' scratching their faces, putting their hands in their caps, betokening the greatest depression and grief.   On arriving at the place of interment, they scoop out a grave with their hands, and burn some brushwood inside.   They then pass the corpse one to another, and each takes a final farewell.   When the body is placed in the grave, it is filled up, and the natives, after the *me-rang-win*, retire.   When a man dies, he is interred in his *booka*, or 'cloke;' and his throwing-board, spears, and hammer are placed near him.   These tribes labour under no physical or mental defect.   They are universally ignorant of the true God, of their accountability to Him, and of future rewards and punishments.   They have no knowledge of the fact, that life and immortality have been brought to light by the gospel.   Men must be sent amongst them to reveal this astonishing mystery."

We can only further advert to the case of Paramatta, where a considerable chapel had been opened in the morning, and the foundation of a smaller one laid in the evening of the same day. The new chapel had been in progress eleven months, and was at last finished to the satisfaction of all parties.   Many persons of distinction expressed their admiration of the chaste and elegant style of the building.   It was agreed to open it on Thursday,

September 19th. The friends assembled for prayer at five o'clock on the morning of that day; at eleven the Liturgy was read, and an edifying discourse delivered to a numerous audience, from, "Thy kingdom come," by the Rev. John M'Kenny. Immediately after the morning service, the congregation proceeded to the site of the intended erection, which was distant about three quarters of a mile. It lay on the other side of the water, where there was a rapidly-increasing population, with no other place of worship than a Roman Catholic chapel. The allotment of land on which it was proposed to build, was presented to the Rev. Samuel Leigh, some years before, by Richard Rouse, Esq. The procession having arrived on the ground, the foundation-stone was laid by H. K. M'Arthur, Esq., a highly respectable member of the established Church. The principal topic in his address was, "The Church of England and Wesleyan Methodism, the grand barriers to the progress of Popery." A large concourse of people heartily responded to this sentiment. The Rev. Nathaniel Turner, who had just arrived in the colony, and several others, also addressed the people. The friends then returned home, and in the enjoyment of social intercourse awaited the evening service. It was conducted by the Rev. Joseph Orton, who preached an admirable sermon, from Balaam's exclamation, "How goodly are thy tents, O Jacob! and thy tabernacles, O Israel!" A most blessed influence pervaded the congregation, and many eyes were moistened with tears. The opening services were resumed on the following Sunday. The morning service was conducted by the Rev. Nathaniel Turner, who preached from Luke xv. 10: "There is joy in the presence of the angels of God over one sinner that repenteth." His touching appeals to the conscience moved the audience, and affected many hearts. An excellent sermon was delivered in the evening by the Rev. James Watkin, to a full and an attentive congregation. After the public service, the members of this missionary church partook of the emblems of the Saviour's dying love. The expense of the building was £1,400; but such was the liberality of a comparatively poor people, that, within three months from the time of its being opened, the whole sum was raised and paid.

CHAPTER XIII.

INTERVIEW WITH THE GOVERNOR OF NEW SOUTH WALES—THE STATE OF TONGA—PROSPERITY OF THE COLONIAL CHURCHES—DEPUTATION APPOINTED TO GIVE THEM A CONNEXIONAL FORM—DISCOVERY OF GOLD AND ITS PROBABLE CONSEQUENCES.

DURING the first six months of the year 1840, Tonga was in a state of political convulsion, arising from the malignant attacks of the Heathens upon the chiefs and natives who had renounced idolatry and embraced Christianity. Several unfriendly journals had, in their accounts of these painful occurrences, thrown a shade of suspicion over the characters of the missionaries, by insinuating that an imprudent interference on their part had led to fatal results. The chairman of the New South Wales district, being anxious to ascertain the facts of the case, sought an interview with the governor, in the hope of being able to obtain such information as would enable him to vindicate his brethren in Tonga from the aspersions of their enemies. The governor received him and his colleague, the late Rev. Joseph Orton, with much cordiality, and frankly acceded to their request. His Excellency entered into a minute detail of the transactions that had occurred at Tonga, as far as they had been reported to the government. In the course of the conversation that ensued, several pointed questions were proposed to His Excellency respecting the deportment of the resident missionaries ; in reply to which he was pleased to state, in the most unequivocal terms, that they were perfectly exonerated from all blame. It appeared that, in the midst of civil commotion among the natives, and when their persons, families, and property were in great danger from the attacks of the Heathen, the brethren had applied for protection to the captain of the ship "Favourite," which happened to appear off the island at this awful crisis of affairs ; but that they had in no wise dictated to Captain Croker as to what measures he ought to adopt : they with himself were anxious for conciliation. His Excellency conferred upon the brethren the favour of an introductory letter to the officers of the "Favourite," which had just arrived in Port Jackson, stating the nature of their business ; and further evinced the interest he took in the matter by ordering a government vessel to convey them on board. "We found the first lieutenant," they observe, "lying in a cot, suffering extremely from his wounds. He and the other officers received us with every mark of civility, freely entering upon a communication which, in all points, corroborated the representations which we had previously received from the governor, particularly in vindication of the conduct of our missionaries throughout the transaction ; assuring us of their readiness, if necessary, to give their united testimony to that effect."

The statements received on this occasion, as to the measures adopted by Captain Croker, varied in some trifling respects from previous reports. When the "Favourite" approached the island, the missionaries and their families were in jeopardy from the heathen natives, and had fled from their habitations for security to a small fort belonging to the Christian natives. Under these circumstances, they were induced to inform Captain Croker of their dangerous situation, and to solicit his protection.   Without delay the captain directed a number of volunteers from his ship to proceed with him on shore, carrying with them three carronades, besides their small arms, and ammunition.   The fortress, where the heathen forces had principally assembled, was about four miles inland, and was represented by the officers of the "Favourite" to be a well-constructed fortification, almost impregnable, formed by the butts of cocoa-nut trees, placed perpendicularly to the height of upwards of twenty feet, the wall being several feet in thickness; above this was a kind of network of cane or bamboo, to render the fortification more difficult to scale; round the outside of this barricade was a deep trench, about forty feet wide, with water in it; at certain distances there were loop-holes made, to afford those within the facility of firing upon invaders.   The only entrance was barricaded by cocoa-nut trees placed horizontally, with a carronade just within, pointing through an aperture made for the purpose; the whole presenting the appearance of having been constructed and superintended by persons well skilled in the science of military engineering: which there was too good reason to suspect, from the fact of there being, at least, two Europeans who evidently took a very active part in the business: one was said to have been an armourer on board a ship of war, and had resided on the island for many years, being well known as "Jemmy the Devil!"

By the orders of the captain, the carronades were brought within one hundred and six yards of the fortification, quite within the range of the enemies' musketry.   This position being taken, a native female, bearing a flag of truce, was sent to the fortress, conveying Captain Croker's wish that they would surrender, and come to amicable terms with the Christian natives. In a short time the messenger returned, bearing the intelligence, that the Heathen were desirous for peace; at the same time a flag of truce was displayed from the fortification; and the European, Jemmy, presented himself on the barricade.   The captain called to him, expressing his gratification at their willingness to come to terms, and informing him that the only condition on which peace could be obtained would be, the observance of certain propositions, the principal of which were, that all the fortifications on the island, those belonging to the Christians as well as those of the Heathen, should be levelled to the ground, and that both parties should quietly resume their avocations and friendly intercourse.   The European then appeared to communicate with the natives: the result of which was, that Captain Croker was invited to a conference with the chiefs; to which he consented, and proceeded within the fortification, accompanied by the second lieutenant, and two or three others, bearing a flag of truce and the British flag. When they were admitted, the entrance was again strongly barricaded, every thing around them presenting the most warlike appearance. There was a vast concourse of natives, with fire-arms and clubs, who assumed menacing attitudes of a terrific nature; so much so, that, at first, the Europeans were exceedingly apprehensive for their safety. They were, however, treated with courtesy; and, after a parley of three quarters of an hour, the natives required half an hour to consult some chiefs who were at a distance; which was granted by the captain, who with his companions was then allowed to retire from the stockade. A little before the half-hour was expired, the natives sent to say, that they were willing to come to terms, but could not hold intercourse with their enemies; the reply to which was, that the " terms proposed must be complied with."

When the time had expired, the command was given to make the attack, the captain himself leading the way to the entrance of the fortification. The sergeant of the marines was now ordered by the captain to scale the barricade, and to fire; which was no sooner executed, than returned by firing the carronade at the entrance, and a volley of musketry from various parts of the fortification, by which the captain and several of his men were wounded. He then exerted himself to the utmost to enter the stockade; but, feeling exhausted, he retired to a tree at a short distance, by which he supported himself until he was shot through the heart, and dropped lifeless to the ground. All this time the officers, seamen, and marines were within a few yards of the fortification, exposed to a hot fire from the natives, who themselves were perfectly screened from the attack of their invaders. The consequence was, that the captain and two other officers were killed, and the first lieutenant and nineteen men dangerously wounded. With the utmost difficulty they succeeded in carrying off the killed and wounded, and embarked on board their ship, taking with them the missionaries Tucker and Rabone, and their families, whom they conveyed to Vavou. The captain was buried in the island of Tonga; and it is singular that, previously to the affray, he pointed to the spot, and remarked, " Were I to die here, I should like my remains to be interred there." With this wish the surviving officers complied. The commander of this unfortunate expedition expected, no doubt, that the first fire would intimidate the Heathen, and constrain them to surrender. " He had often expressed a hope that no blood would be shed." .

The suspension of the mission was, however, but of short duration; for, though the country was in a disturbed state, and threatened with famine, the missionaries returned in a few weeks, and were permitted to resume their labours. The Spirit of the

Lord was shortly afterwards poured out upon Tonga, and Christianity waved her peaceful banner over the whole island.

The Rev. John Waterhouse, who had undertaken a series of hazardous voyages to the Polynesian Islands, returned to Hobart Town in September, 1841, after an absence of sixteen months. He had visited successively the stations in the Friendly Islands, Keppel's Island, Wallis's Island, Rotumah, and the Feejees. He brought a cheering report of the progress of Christianity in those distant and isolated spheres of labour. He was every where struck with the magnitude of the work, the paucity of labourers, and the insufficiency of means for carrying it on. It was obvious to him, that if the Society could not increase the number of its missionaries, more attention ought to be paid to the cultivation of native talent, and some competent training-institution set up for the education of such of their Christian converts as were likely, in future years, to fill the various offices of the church. Several of the brethren being impressed with the same views, an experiment was made, upon a small scale, in Feejee under the Rev. John Hunt, and in the Friendly Islands under the Rev. Francis Wilson.

The health of Mr. Waterhouse had experienced occasional interruptions, during his absence, in consequence of the severe labours, frequent privations, and imminent perils to which he had been exposed; and the business which awaited his return home made undue demands upon his mental and physical powers. Not six weeks after his arrival, he left Hobart Town, with the intention of visiting every place of importance in the interior of the colony, in order to strengthen the interest already existing in behalf of the South-Sea missions, and increase, if possible, the income of the colonial branch of the Society. The first day he travelled twenty-eight miles, and spoke at a public meeting. On Tuesday he proceeded to Oatlands, twenty-four miles further; and, at mid-day, addressed a large and respectable audience, on the state of the Friendly and Feejee Islands; after which he went to Somercotes, a distance of twenty miles. On Wednesday he attended a missionary meeting at Ross, and described the scenes he had witnessed during the preceding eighteen months. On Thursday he visited Campbell Town, where he spoke at length in reference to the South-Sea missions. Early on Friday morning he set out for Aovea, twenty-one miles through the bush; where he again spoke, with deep feeling, of the necessity for increased exertion and liberality in the cause of missions. He returned on Saturday to Somercotes, a distance of thirty miles, calling on his way at several residences, at each of which he read the scriptures and prayed. On Sunday he preached at Ross in the morning, met the society at Somercotes in the afternoon, and preached in the evening in a new room built by Samuel Horton, Esq., after which he made a collection for educating native teachers in the islands.   On Monday, November 1st, he descended the Macquarie River twenty miles, where a large assembly of settlers were met to receive an account of what he had seen and heard during his late voyages.   The day following he proceeded to Perth, twenty miles, where he spoke with much effect on the general subject of missions.   He reached Launceston on Wednesday afternoon, and, though much fatigued, preached in the evening.

On Sunday, November 7th, he closed his public ministry with a missionary sermon at Launceston, from Isaiah lv. 8–13 : "For my thoughts are not your thoughts, neither are your ways my ways, saith the Lord.   For as the heavens are higher than the earth, so are my ways higher than your ways, and my thoughts than your thoughts.   For as the rain cometh down, and the snow from heaven, and returneth not thither, but watereth the earth, and maketh it bring forth and bud, that it may give seed to the sower, and bread to the eater : so shall my word be that goeth forth out of my mouth : it shall not return unto me void, but it shall accomplish that which I please, and it shall prosper in the thing whereto I sent it.   For ye shall go out with joy, and be led forth with peace : the mountains and the hills shall break forth before you into singing, and all the trees of the field shall clap their hands."   On Monday he attended the sittings of the district all day, and spoke for two hours in the evening, in the most animated and impressive language, on the claims of the Heathen and the duty of the church.   He sat in the district-meeting on Tuesday, 9th, till one o'clock, when he set out for Longford, and travelled through torrents of rain, reaching the chapel just in time to commence the missionary meeting.   His heart warmed as he proceeded with his favourite theme; but, after speaking about an hour, he sat down quite exhausted. After the meeting, he walked with great difficulty two miles, through the rain and long wet grass, to the residence of G. P. Ball, Esq., where he was to lodge.   Next morning he said, "I must now return home, and make arrangements for visiting New Zealand."   He then added, "I fear I am about to have a serious affliction."   He left Longford, and reached home in four days, in a state of complete prostration.   He continued the subject of much suffering for five months, during which period he maintained a calm and cheerful resignation to the will of God.   Just before he departed, he raised himself up in bed, and, with the last effort of expiring nature, exclaimed, "Missionaries, missionaries, missionaries !"   So fell this noble standard-bearer !   O reader, hasten to assist in raising the standard that fell with him, and in carrying it forward until it shall float on the breeze as the signal of a consummated victory over all the idolatries of mankind !

Just four weeks from the date of this event, the Rev. Joseph Orton died at sea, on his way from New South Wales to England. This excellent Missionary, whose abilities were above mediocrity, and whose zeal could only be quenched by death, laboured for several years in the West Indies. He was apprehended, tried, and convicted of having taught the slaves to believe that they had souls, that they were as responsible to God for their actions as white men, and that if they embraced the Christian religion they would get to heaven. The court decided that such teaching was *contrary to law*, and sentenced him to imprisonment. He was removed to prison : we will not describe it : it is enough to say that it was a West Indian jail ! There he lay, like a vile miscreant upon whom the anathema of God had fallen, until his health failed, and his life was in danger. On obtaining his liberty he was sent to Australia, where for several years he distinguished himself by the able and conscientious discharge of his various official duties. His constitutional powers never recovered the depression they experienced in the West Indies ; and, illness again returning, he was obliged to leave the colony. He rapidly declined, and died peacefully off Cape Horn, on the 30th of April. He was buried in the sea, in the presence of his widow and seven children. Ought not the church, voluntarily, to discharge the full measure of its duty to the widow of such a man, and to his fatherless children ? Alas, how slow and tardy she has been to admit the validity of the claim of persons of this class to Christian sympathy and benevolence !

During the last ten years the Australian and Van-Diemen's Land missions had enjoyed a gratifying degree of peace and prosperity. From the year 1832 to 1842, ten new circuits had been formed, sixteen additional missionaries sent out, fifteen hundred and forty-seven communicants added to the church, and, at least, two thousand children to the sabbath-schools. A deep feeling of solicitude, on the subject of personal religion, had been awakened in all the colonies ; while a spirit of devotion, zeal, and liberality pervaded their churches and congregations. In Sydney, a new, but most efficient, body of labourers had been organized. Fifty or sixty of the most pious and intelligent members were selected, and divided into fourteen classes. Each class was appointed to a particular district of the city. They were to visit every dwelling, in their respective districts, on the Sunday afternoon, distribute religious tracts, and invite the people to some central house, where they themselves were to meet, for singing, reading the scriptures, exhortation, and prayer. The effects soon became apparent in the increase of their congregations, and in the multiplication of the members of the church. Such a system, judiciously conducted, in the populous towns of England, would be attended with the happiest results.

A revival of religion had been going on in Paramatta for more than nine months: five new preaching-places had been opened, and congregations formed in the Cow-pastures. Fifty members had been added, in a short time, to the church at Windsor, and a new chapel opened at Richmond. Four new classes had been raised up at Bathurst during the year, and all the sittings in the chapel were let. The demand for religious teachers had become so general in the neighbourhood of Geelong, that it was found necessary to employ a lay-agent to assist the missionary. The congregations had so increased in Perth, that every pew in the chapel was occupied.

This good work continued steadily to advance, so that when Mr. Lawry, who had been appointed to succeed the late Rev. John Waterhouse, arrived in the colony in 1844, he found the religious state of the societies to be very satisfactory. Notwithstanding the commercial depression which prevailed in the country, the Wesleyans of Sydney had succeeded in building a large and commodious chapel in York-street, which cost nearly £6,000. Mr. Lawry assisted at the opening of this beautiful edifice. The subscriptions of the people and the opening collections amounted altogether to about £5,000. As the ship "Triton" required to be re-coppered, he was detained for some time in New South Wales, and was thus furnished with an opportunity for acquainting himself with the religious condition of the colony, as well as making several arrangements deemed necessary to the more efficient working of the mission.

After a long season of labour, expense, and discouragement, the establishment at Swan River, for the secular and religious improvement of the natives, was slowly but satisfactorily unfolding their mental peculiarities, and its own adaptation to their circumstances. The report of the missionary will be read with deep interest by all who are acquainted with the history of this singular people. "The religious improvement of the natives," he observes, "is beginning to present a very encouraging aspect. Their occasional meetings for prayer amongst themselves before they retire to rest, the repeated invitations which the teacher has received to come and pray with them, their attention to private prayer, and the strict manner in which they observe the Christian sabbath, are circumstances sufficient to show that they entertain a regard for religion, and that the Spirit of God is at work upon their minds. It was gratifying

to hear, a short time since, Hoymonaneu, a young man, describe
the feelings of his heart, at the close of one of our aboriginal
meetings. He lingered behind the other natives, and appeared
as if he wanted to have some further conversation, and was
labouring under some unusual emotion. On being asked if he
were seeking the salvation of his soul, he said, with a very
heavy sigh, pointing at the same time with his finger to his
breast, ‘ I have two spirits within me, the good spirit and the
bad spirit; and they are talking to me every day : they never
stop. One of them tells me to be bad, and the other tells me
to be good.’ When asked if he ever prayed, his answer was,
‘ Yes, always pray. I am very sorry for my sins : and when I
pray, my heart is sometimes hard, and sometimes a little soft.’
That the spiritual warfare has commenced with this young man,
there can be no question. The temporal department of the
mission is at present carried on by one white man and the
natives, and is prospering well. They grow. sufficient wheat,
potatoes, and other vegetables, for the station : and it is gratifying to witness the rapid improvement of the men and boys in
almost all kinds of manual labour connected with the cultivation
of the soil. It is equally pleasing to see the women engaged at
their needlework, making clothes for themselves and families.
The children of the school, and the young men, have, during
nine months of the year, made considerable proficiency in reading; and it has been cheering to the mind of the missionary to
hear these children of the woods, who but a short time since
were classed, by some, among the higher orders of the brute
creation, repeating the catechism, and responding to the prayers
of our church.”

In 1846, the Rev. William B. Boyce was appointed to take
the general superintendence of these missions. He had been
honourably and successfully employed for several years in the
African section of the mission-field, and brought into his new
office a judgment sobered and matured by religion, reflection,
and observation. Leigh, like the first settlers, had cleared the
ground, quarried the materials, and laid the foundation of the
ecclesiastical homestead; and his successors had, with an equal
regard to utility and perpetuity, raised the building to its present respectable elevation. It now only required “a wise
master-builder” to preserve harmony and efficiency amongst
the labourers, multiply their number, and direct their operations, in order that the structure might be completed, and
become an “habitation of God through the Spirit.” Mr. Boyce,
combining zeal and intelligence with considerable experience as
a missionary, was peculiarly qualified to conduct the increasingly complex affairs of the colonial churches. If he has had

greater resources and facilities at his command for carrying out
the original purposes of the mission than any of his predecessors, he has proved his fidelity by their judicious appropriation,
and the prudence of his arrangements by the large amount
of practical good he has effected.   It was impossible for him to
take a survey of the spiritual domain assigned to his pastoral
oversight without deep emotion.   It was too wide to be taken
in at one view.   The natural eye can see nothing but blue land
stretching along the distant horizon; but by a closer inspection,
and the aid of the telescope, there rises up a charming variety
of fields, woods, spires, and villages.   In the colony, as in the
natural firmament, fresh lights were constantly appearing within
the field of observation.   The new states were expanding on all
sides; and, in consequence of the continuous stream of emigrants flowing in upon the country, society was passing through
a severe ordeal, and assuming every diversity of character and
form.

The cry for religious teachers was loud, earnest, and almost
universal; but, alas! it could only be met by an emphatic negative.   A short distance from their shores, there stood up, in the
midst of the waters, Van-Diemen's Land, now, comparatively
speaking, a Christian colony.   The principal incidents occurring
at this time, or spreading over several successive months, can
only be mentioned with an unsatisfactory brevity.

A new chapel had been completed in the Haymarket of Sydney, and the foundation of another one laid in Balmain, a populous and improving suburb of that city.   At Castle Hill, near
Paramatta, a neat stone chapel had been erected, and paid for
by local subscriptions; and at Duval, twelve miles distant, an
excellent temporary place of worship had been provided.   A
weekly service had also been commenced in Paramatta jail, which
was attended by thirty or forty prisoners.   The entire debt upon
the mission-property at Bathurst was liquidated, and a new congregation collected at Green Swamp, a country place in that
circuit, where several persons had experienced the saving grace
of God.   A new chapel had been built and opened in the town
of Morpeth, Hunter River station; while another was advancing
to completion in Campbell Town.   The Sunday-schools were being
conducted in a more satisfactory manner.   They were every where
exciting more public attention, and commanding a more liberal
and general support.

The first missionary visit was paid to Goulbourn in June.   This
town lay about one hundred and thirty miles south-west of Sydney, and was, from its geographical situation, rapidly rising into
importance.   Its buildings and population were equal to those
of Bathurst itself; while it formed a centre to several towns and

villages lying within distances varying from twelve to forty miles. The missionary found that two young local preachers, who had lately removed from Paramatta, and commenced business in Goulbourn, had fitted up a temporary place of worship, which held a hundred hearers, and had formed a class of six persons. The missionary held several public meetings, and the people evinced a deep and general solicitude to have a teacher. The government offered one acre of land for a chapel, one half acre for a Sunday-school, and one half acre for a minister's house. The missionary could only promise to use his influence to procure a teacher for them; but he had none at present to send.

Similar and numerous openings were presenting themselves in South Australia, that could not be entered for want of labourers. Missionary Draper, writing from Adelaide, in December, 1847, says, " I am happy to observe, that we are still favoured with peace and prosperity; and are desirous, above all things, to promote the glory of our Lord Jesus Christ. Our last quarterly-meeting was a very happy one: the increase of members was forty-five, and the financial income exceeded our expenditure. During the past year, about £1,250 were raised by voluntary subscriptions in the circuit for different objects. We are now about to erect a building for school-purposes and prayer-meetings, the entire expense of which will be £250. Two months since we opened a very excellent new chapel at North Adelaide, about a mile and a half from our Gawler-place chapel. The opening collections were £63. The congregations are good. We have just opened a chapel at the far-famed Burra-Burra Mines, one hundred miles north of Adelaide. There is no place of worship within seventy miles of the new erection. The building cost £240; which sum has been raised and paid. A day-school has been commenced, and there are already one hundred children in the Sunday-school. Next month Mr. Harcourt will go to Burra-Burra, and take under his care the mines within fifty miles of that place. Mr. Thrum will remove to Willunga, thirty miles south of this, and take under his care several places lying between Adelaide and his head-quarters. I shall then be left alone in town, with sixteen places to attend to, at eight of which we have chapels. This colony requires, at least, five ministers. Our hands are full,—as to our health, dangerously so. Our circuit is one hundred and thirty miles long, and forty miles broad. We have now four hundred and sixty communicants. We are not able to meet the claims of the people: send us help, and generations yet unborn will rise up and bless you."

At a later date, he remarks: " Our chapels are too small by half in and about Adelaide; and as building is very expensive, it almost distracts me to conceive as to how the spiritual wants of the people are to be supplied. £5,000, at the very least, ought to be spent in chapel-building, within five miles of Adelaide, during the next year; and a very large proportion of that sum *must* be spent in that period, or our work will suffer greatly. The chapel at Burra-Burra has been enlarged to twice its former size, and will now seat four hundred and fifty persons. The enlargement cost £470; £300 of which sum was raised on the spot by private subscriptions. It is now not half large enough, and a new one must be built. Willunga chapel has undergone alterations and enlargement within the last three months: it is becoming too small again. We have lately enlarged the premises at Walkerville; yet they are insufficient, and a very large chapel will have to be built soon."*

The religious assemblies of the Wesleyans in Melbourne were visited about the same time with special tokens of the Divine presence and blessing. The resident minister writes: "The cause of God is prospering in this circuit. We are at the beginning of a work here that will last as long as the sun and moon shall endure. Being persuaded of this, and feeling like the painter, who said he was painting for eternity, we are wishful that all things belonging to Methodism should be built up upon the firmest foundation. Almost every day gives us converts to Christ Jesus our Lord; whilst those who have believed seem to be more than ever careful to maintain good works. But we want more missionaries; men who can at once enter into the doors which Providence is opening, and minister the gospel and sacraments of the Lord Jesus Christ. Send suitable men, and send them without delay. In the mean time we shall labour on, and endeavour to fill the pages of life's volume with such memorials as shall not disgrace nor condemn us in the day of the Lord."

"The aboriginal mission," he remarks, "is rising above its pecuniary difficulties, while it is extending its limits and influence. Hitherto the expenses of the establishment have, for the most part, been met by the Wesleyan Society, the colonial government, and local donations and contributions; but at present it is expected that the mission is in a position to defray the expenses of one missionary and one tribe of natives, independently of the three sources from which supplies have hitherto been drawn. The flock of sheep which was formed by the generous donations of the friends of the mission, amounts at present to about two thousand: and the proceeds of the herd of cattle, which have been taken on terms, have already been laid out on cattle to

---

* In the late census, which gives a population of 22,390 for this province, 2,246 are returned as Methodists, while there are 11,961 Church of England, 1,958 Presbyterians, 1,524 German Lutherans, 2,888 other Protestants, 1,649 Roman Catholics, 58 Jews, and 52 Pagans.

form a mission-herd, which amounts to about one hundred and twenty head. Three thousand sheep have also been taken on terms, to graze on a portion of the reserve, with the view of getting it stocked as soon as possible for the benefit of the blacks: this arrangement will secure to the mission, in four or five years, six or seven thousand sheep. There is the prospect, therefore, of getting the reserve stocked with mission-property in a very short time; the proceeds of which, in connexion with the produce of the agricultural department, will supply, with economy, the temporal wants of the scattered tribes in the vicinity of the mission, and afford to the young the means of education. The plan for the extension of the mission, proposed to the consideration of the district committee, is as follows:— 1. That a school be opened, as soon as the necessary preparations can be made, for the youth of some other tribe, at a distance of from forty to sixty miles from the present station, where there is the probability of collecting the greatest number of children: 2. That application be made to His Honour the superintendent, for permission to erect the requisite buildings: and, 3. That the services of a suitable agent, as schoolmaster, be secured."

The lord bishop of Adelaide, being on a tour through the western province, evinced a lively interest in the Wesleyan mission generally, but especially in the progress of the native Institution at Gallillelup. Being exceedingly anxious to see that establishment, he rode out, with a few friends, in a very hot day, and examined the boys and girls in reading, writing, knowledge of the scriptures, Commandments, and Creed. He spent an hour in those exercises; and, after hearing them sing, expressed his gratification at the "knowledge they evinced of common and Divine things." "You have proceeded," he observed, "upon right principles, pursued right plans, and I now witness the efficiency of your operations: you want only one thing more, namely, good and suitable land, to make this a self-supporting system. Your present situation is not good: I advise you to fix upon some other, and state your wishes to the government." Arrangements had been previously made for marrying four couples of natives: his lordship kindly consented to perform the ceremony, which was paternal, imposing, and will long be remembered. The colonial secretary and several other gentlemen were present.

On the preceding evening, one of the first native converts departed this life. She had been married four years to a civilian, a carpenter by trade; and had conducted herself, both as a wife and mother, with the most exemplary propriety. As she resided with her husband's relatives, who made no profession of religion, her spiritual advantages were but few, and her piety declined.

While bathing one day, she caught a severe cold, which settled in her throat, and proved fatal, after a few days' illness. Her last days were embittered by the recollection of her unfaithfulness. She urged all about her to pray for her. In the most melting tones, she said to the missionary, "Good master, do pray for me! Good master, do pray for me!" She prayed herself with much simplicity and fervour, "Jesus, take away my sin! Lord, for Jesus's sake, take away my sin! Jesus, take all my sin away!" Her black sisters and brother were much affected, and looked upon the scene with astonishment. She gave her little infant to her brother-in-law, and took leave of her husband, her family, and the missionary; then, looking up towards heaven, she said, with much emphasis, "God loves me, God loves me,—takes me to heaven." She thus died in sure and certain hope of a glorious resurrection to eternal life. "What hath God wrought!"

In the May of this year, 1851, a discovery was made by a gentleman of the name of Hargraves, which, from its peculiar nature and probable consequences, may be regarded as being one of the greatest discoveries of the age. While we cannot wholly overlook so remarkable an occurrence, we would at the same time speak with brevity and diffidence respecting results which can only be developed by the progress of time. It may just be observed as a singular coincidence, that on the very week in which the Crystal Palace was opened in London for the exhibition of the products and industry of all nations, were the mineral resources of Australia revealed to the colonial government. It had been long suspected by Sir R. I. Murchison and other scientific men, that the precious metals were deposited in large quantities in various localities in New Holland; but, at the above date, Mr. Hargraves set the question at rest by actually producing a portion of gold, obtained from Bathurst, in the vicinity of the Blue Mountains. Should the mines that have been already opened continue to be as prolific for a series of years to come as they now are, yielding at the rate of £12,000,000 *per annum*, it requires no uncommon degree of sagacity to foresee that they must produce incalculable effects upon the trade, commerce, and social condition of the civilized world. No doubt the subject will be viewed differently by the men of commerce and the Christian philosopher; the one will contemplate its probable bearings upon mercantile interests, while the other will view it chiefly in its relation to religion and morality. The mercantile aspect of the case is of acknowledged importance; for so sudden and unprecedented an importation of foreign gold—that from California alone being estimated by Schier at £60,000,000—must, first, lead to the deterioration of the article in the general market; or, secondly, enhance the value of all other commodities; or, thirdly, gradually open a new market for itself, and thus become a blessing to mankind; and this process, we are happy to find, has already commenced in Australia. Many of the industrious and economical gold-finders have saved a few hundreds of pounds, and invested them in land. They are now building residences on their own estates; thus forming an entirely new class of settlers, and multiplying the demand for labour.

The religious aspect in which the revelation of this "treasure," hitherto "hid in a field," may be viewed, is still more interesting. We would not assume an acquaintance with the motives that give an impulse to the Divine will, or that influence an infinite judgment in its final decisions, neither would we rashly interpret the acts of the Divine government; but we think we see God as clearly in the reciprocal action now going on between Great Britain and Australia, as in the Exodus of the Hebrew lawgiver, accompanied by the visible symbols of the Divine presence. Will any person undertake to show, that either the policy of man, or a fortunate combination of circumstances, irrespective of a special interference on the part of Providence, has put this country in possession of the inexhaustible resources of the "great south land?" "Do not err, my beloved brethren. Every good gift and every perfect gift is from above, and cometh down from the Father of lights, with whom is no variableness, neither shadow of turning."

1. Was there not a peculiar fitness in making the English nation the recipient of this vast auxiliary to her wealth and greatness? Is she not, above all others, the "light of the world," "the salt of the earth?" Who could have calculated the consequences to national liberty, to the progress of intelligence, or to the institutions of Protestantism, had these treasures fallen into the hands of any of the states of Europe who have apostatized from the primitive and apostolic faith? Can it have been by accident that they have been placed at the disposal of the most religious nation in the world? in fact, the only nation upon earth possessing the disposition and ability to spread the knowledge and faith of Christ all over the globe. England has been preferred to other states; and we are inclined to think, that the reason for this preference will be found in the address of the angel to the church of Philadelphia : "These things saith He that is holy, He that is true, He that hath the key of David, He that openeth, and no man shutteth; and shutteth, and no man openeth; I know thy works: behold, I have set before thee an open door, and no man can shut it: for thou hast a little strength, and hast kept my word, and hast not denied my name. Because

thou hast kept the word of my patience, I also will keep thee from the hour of temptation, which shall come upon all the world, to try them that dwell upon the earth."   Since the commencement of the present century, " the heavens, and the earth, and the sea, and the dry land," have been " shaken ;" and yet, amidst the dismemberment of empires, the subversion of thrones, and the convulsions of states, God seems to have said to Britannia, " the queen of islands," " Because thou hast kept the word of my patience, I also will keep thee from the hour of temptation." Like the oak which, having ramified its roots in the ground, maintains its position after the tempest has swept over the forest, Great Britain is almost the only political stem that has survived and now stands erect, after change and revolution have altered the geographical limits, and affected all the interests, of continental Europe.   Why should not her offshoots be planted in other lands, rather than those of the sapless trunks that lie around her ? England has become to some extent the centre, the refuge, and the home of the civilized world ; and so far as real substantial happiness is concerned, she is blessed above all other lands. Surely it is a proof of consummate wisdom to send the sons and daughters of such a people to become the men and women, the fathers and mothers, of the new states that are rising up in the extended plains of Australia.   Like the fragrance that descended from the head of Aaron, and flowed to the skirts of his sacerdotal garments, so shall the evangelizing influences of Christianity diverge, and spread the beatitudes of salvation amongst the black savages in the interior of that continent.   What is this wonderful movement, but a new link added to the golden chain that is yet to encircle the world, and bind the men of all nations in one common brotherhood ?

At the time of the Reformation, England was obviously constituted the trustee of the " lively oracles " of infallible truth ; and nobly has she discharged the duties of her trustship.   However unfaithful she may have been in the exercise of her political power and moral influence, she has yet maintained her integrity as the " stewardess of the mysteries of God."   She has not only " kept this word," but also hired, at her own expense, the literature of Europe ; and by its aid translated the sacred volume, in whole or in part, into one hundred and forty-eight languages or dialects.   Her combined societies have, under her auspices, circulated about forty-five millions of copies of the holy scriptures, and rendered the inspired records accessible to about six hundred millions of the human race.   It is said of our Lord, that " God hath highly exalted Him, and given Him a name which is above every name; that at the name of Jesus every knee should bow, of things in heaven, and things in earth, and things under the earth; and that every tongue should confess that Jesus Christ is Lord, to the glory of God the Father." If the exaltation of Christ and the universal diffusion of revealed truth be the primary objects of the Divine government, then do we see a sufficient reason for putting the people of this country in the possession of more ample means of becoming " workers together with Him," in realizing those stupendous results.

It will be admitted, we presume, that Great Britain had arrived at a crisis in her history, when Providence gave her access to the golden deposits, which had been concealed in the mountains of New Holland since the foundation of the world. Her children had multiplied beyond all precedent, so that the paternal estate had become too limited for their accommodation, and wholly inadequate to their comfortable sustenance. If the mysterious but unequivocal acts of the Supreme Being, just referred to, had been enunciated in the language of man, it would, in our apprehension, have assumed something like the following form : "' Because thou hast kept my word, and hast not denied my name,' 'I have set before thee an open door, and no man can shut it.' I will draw, by a golden magnet, your surplus population to the shores of Australia, and open a bank there, from which you may provide the means of feeding and clothing some millions of your industrious artisans, for generations to come. 'Be fruitful, and multiply, and replenish' this part of 'the earth, and subdue it.'" Upon the government and people of England now devolves the responsibility of executing this high commission.

2. The selection of the time for laying open those inexhaustible treasures, and engaging the co-operation of the British people in accomplishing His purposes of mercy to man, compel us to acknowledge "the manifold wisdom of God." Supposing the events that have occurred in New South Wales within the last three years, to have taken place half a century ago, their effects, we doubt not, would have furnished materials for one of the darkest chapters in the history of civilized man. Within the colony, at that period, the population, the convict portion of which was ever ready to perpetrate the most atrocious crimes, was under the surveillance of a military police ; while, beyond it, lay multitudes of black savages, habituated to dishonesty and bloodshed. Even so late as 1816, there were but two clergymen in the country, and Leigh, the Wesleyan missionary. The settlers, who lived remote from the principal towns, never heard the gospel from the beginning to the close of the year. Even in the metropolis itself, there was but one Bible to every tenth family, and no means of supplying the deficiency. But what a change has God wrought in the character, manners, and social and religious condition of the people since that time ! They

always had a shadow of the government and jurisprudence of the mother country, with several of her other admirable institutions. To these have been added Bible and Tract societies, day and Sunday schools, infirmaries and hospitals. We can now teach these enterprising states to conduct their internal commerce by rail, to correspond with their distant citizens by the electric telegraph, and to multiply the Bible and other good books by means of the steam-press, until the inhabitants, both European and native, shall become acquainted with "all knowledge."

3. Surely the uncommon events to which we have just alluded, and which are still in progress, convey a distinct call to the Protestant churches of Christendom, and more especially to those of Great Britain, to adopt some appropriate means to meet this new state of things. Never did those churches possess so much political power, learning, or wealth, as at the present time; and never were the intimations of God's will more intelligible in summoning them to "the help of the Lord against the mighty." Look at the antagonism now going on in the colonies themselves. When Mr. Leigh opened his mission, there was not a Romish priest in Australia; now there is a Popish hierarchy, with swarms of foreign priests, religious orders of various descriptions, and sixty thousand members in the Catholic Church. During an emigration unparalleled in the history of nations, the churches of this country have done but little. It was unquestionably the duty of those churches to have confederated for the purpose of rendering this, to some extent at least, an emigration of good men. They should have put a religious teacher on board every emigrant ship. He would have struck up a light that would have revealed the Cross to many, thrown in a portion of evangelical "salt," that might have neutralized the corruption around him, or introduced the leavening principle which, by diffusing itself, might have leavened the "whole mass."

We are aware that numerous private individuals have done nobly; but we complain that the feeling of the church has been so superficial, and that hitherto there has been no combined action. But it is not, even now, too late; for competent authorities tell us that the mineral wealth of the country cannot be exhausted for ages; and that the tide of emigration may be expected to flow on for many successive years. And let it be observed, that this is not an emigration of childhood and age, but of men, for the most part, of energy and enterprise; the very class whom it is desirable to bring under the influence of Christian instruction, and who would become the most successful instruments in promoting the salvation of others. Let the churches do their duty, and we shall soon see the Holy Spirit going forth over "the far-off land," in His sovereign power, to brood over the Australian scene, and bring out of the chaos and confusion which now prevail there a new world of harmony, beauty, and moral grandeur. "One society alone, as far as we know, has done its duty, namely, the Religious Tract Society; and we hesitate not to say, that if it had done nothing from its first institution till now, the work that it is now doing, silently and unostentatiously, is more than a return for all that has ever been contributed to its support. One good man or more, we believe, is stationed at our several ports, going on board all emigrant ships, supplying emigrants with Bibles, emigrant families with a parcel of well-arranged books, and the ships with good libraries, for the use of the passengers and crew." Let other societies evince the same zeal and liberality, and what may we not yet expect? It is of the utmost importance, not only to the present, but to all future generations, that the foundations of the Australian empire be well laid. Believing, as we do, that Christianity alone can purify the character, comfort the soul, and elevate the hopes of man, let us seize the present opportunity to extend and perpetuate its blessings.

4. In the mean time, let it not be regarded as an unseasonable intrusion, if, while gold is convulsing the country, and the people are under a temporary delirium, we venture to remind them that the aborigines are not yet quite extinct! Speaking candidly of the conduct of the government and the colonists towards this unfortunate race, we would say to both, "'Ye are verily guilty concerning your brother, in that ye saw the anguish of his soul, when he besought you, and ye would not hear!' Your hands are stained with the blood of their fathers, whom ye shot in the woods. After driving their children back upon the hostile tribes of the interior, who treated them as 'sheep for the slaughter,' your musket enabled you to take possession of their hunting and fishing grounds; and now ye have broken in upon their storehouses, and are distributing the wealth of their mountains amongst strangers. You denied their manhood; but, after a death-struggle, maintained for half a century, they have succeeded in establishing their claim to the common attributes of humanity. According to the Rev. William Cartwright, the most competent authority in the country, they numbered, a few years since, 100,000 souls. In behalf of the surviving remnant of this nation of savages, we appeal to the senators of Great Britain, to the ministers of religion of every denomination, and to all men of reason and religion, whether some arrangement ought not to be made by the Imperial Parliament, by which a portion, at least, of the price of their lands and the produce of their mines, may be appropriated to the amelioration of their condition, and that of their degraded offspring. The European population now ex-

ceeds half a million souls, and holds property estimated at £120,000,000."

The following extract from the "Sydney Gazette" may be regarded as a near approximation to the actual state of things in New South Wales: "The population is not less than 200,000 persons, possessed of about 100,000 horses, 1,500,000 horned cattle, and more than 8,000,000 sheep, yielding an annual income of £600,000; and exporting, of their own produce or manufacture, to the extent of £1,000,000 *per annum*, independently of our gold. Coupling these figures with the great fact, that in ten months this colony has shipped a million's worth of the newly-found product, the fruit of a peaceful industry, and the earnest of a still brighter future, our friends in England must admit, that our shores have strong attractions to the industrious emigrant." Then let the friends of humanity at home, and the Christian colonists abroad, unite for the accomplishment of some comprehensive scheme that may issue in the elevation of the native blacks of Australia.

Should the question be proposed, "What class of emigrants is most likely to succeed?" we reply at once, that success in all countries mainly depends upon the principles and habits of the individual himself. In the present case, we record the opinion of Mr. Fairfax, editor of one of the Sydney journals, lately announced in a lecture, delivered in this country: "To the young man of industrious and sober habits, and of moral character, whose anxiety is to pursue a course of honest perseverance, unappalled by difficulty and danger, I say, 'Go.' To the idle, the dissipated, the drunken,—him who is reckless alike of his own peace and the sorrow he causes to others,—I say, '*Stay;* for if you go to a warm climate, and persevere in your present habits, you will be an outcast, you will die miserably, neglected by man, and perhaps unpitied by God.' To the masters or workmen who are doing well in England, I suggest the old motto, 'Let well alone.' But if you are struggling with difficulties which appear unconquerable, wind up your affairs, and try the colonies. There we are not so thick upon the ground; and with the primest beef at 2*d.* and mutton at 1½*d.* per pound, you need not, you cannot, starve. Not that I would hold out the expectation of success without exertion, of fortune without the application of industry, or of the quiet repose of old age without thrift and care in early and middle life. 'The battle of life' must be fought lustily and bravely on both sides of the world; and moral worth is as valuable and as highly prized there as here. In England there is a large class of young men who are well educated, but are not brought up to any business. Many of this class make their way to the colonies. They bring letters of introduction to respectable and wealthy people, often to the governor himself, and imagine their fortunes made.   Poor fellows!   Any well-instructed colonist may see that they are unfit for hard work, and therefore necessarily unfit for the colony.   Often persons such as these are returned home to their parents, like unsaleable bales of merchandise; and too frequently, alas! they remain to disgrace their name, to ruin their character, and to debauch their lives.   Ardour, intelligence, and industry, will do any thing for a man who is left to his own resources; and I have known cases where such persons have overcome almost innumerable difficulties. There is another and a large class, dividing itself into seamstresses and general female servants, to which I would briefly say, ' In Australia you are wanted; and if you land virtuous and respectable, you may soon settle down, the wives of honest and intelligent men.'"

As might have been expected, the discovery of gold loosened the whole framework of Australian society.   Men of all ranks and professions rushed to one common centre, and seemed to consider themselves as being freed from all their previously recognised obligations to God and to one another.   In their eagerness to "comprehend the dust of the earth in a measure, and weigh the mountains in scales, and the hills in a balance," they wholly overlooked all the interests of religion and commerce.   Christian communities, of all denominations, were paralysed, and in many instances great difficulty was experienced in finding a sufficient number of suitable laymen to fill the several offices of their churches.   In a short time the southern province was half depopulated. These new circumstances occasioned great additional labour and perplexity to the missionaries.   Their influence upon the general state of the colony, and the lamentable deficiency of religious instructors to meet the emergency, are well described in a communication, dated "Melbourne, January 21st, 1852," and addressed to the committee.

"From other sources you will have learned," says the superintendent, "that large portions of this vast country have been proved to be immense gold-fields of surprising richness, and that already several tons of the precious metal have been brought into Melbourne.   The news of our wealth has drawn thousands of persons from the adjacent colonies, who, with many of the inhabitants of our own towns and villages, are now congregated where the rich deposit is found.   It is impossible to imagine the wild excitement which has been induced, and the effects which have followed in every department of our work.   At the date of the discovery, every thing was in a healthy and flourishing condition: our chapels were filled to overflowing, our class and prayer meetings were well attended, our members in society

were steadily and rapidly increasing, our Sunday and day schools
were in great prosperity, our tract society was in vigorous and
efficient operation, and our members and office-bearers generally
seemed to feel that they were called to be co-workers together
with God and with us, in spreading scriptural holiness through
the land; but the gold has, for the present, sadly deranged our
plans.   Many of our members, and half our local preachers, are
scattered. over the length and breadth of these extensive gold-
fields.   Some of them have become suddenly and unexpectedly
rich, while others have been greatly inconvenienced by the
changes which have taken place; and there is manifest danger
lest the all-absorbing subject of the day should turn away their
minds and hearts from things unseen and eternal.   We confidently hope, however, that this state of confusion will soon pass
away, and that the wondrous events which are transpiring around
us will be made subservient to the extension and establishment
of the Redeemer's kingdom.   What the ultimate effects of these
discoveries may be, the shrewdest among us dare not guess.   It
seems reasonable, however, to expect that an immense population will be attracted to the place.   About one thousand persons arrived from Van-Diemen's Land and Adelaide yesterday;
and we are told thousands more are coming.   I suppose multitudes may be expected from the country which we still delight
to think and speak of as *home*.   If so, we shall require a proportionate increase of ministerial strength.   At our September
quarterly-meeting, held before any thing important in reference
to the gold was known, the propriety of requesting the committee to send out help was earnestly urged; and twelve of
those who were present engaged to contribute or collect £5 each
towards paying the passage and outfit of two missionaries from
England, if they can be sent at once.   The thousands that have
been added to our population since then have rendered the case
increasingly urgent.   This circuit requires, at least, four ministers.   Mount Alexander, about eighty miles distant, with a
population of from thirty to forty thousand souls, has no Wesleyan service but what we supply from Melbourne.   In consequence of an unexpected demand for help from another quarter,
I am now left alone.   Our chapel here is the largest Protestant
place of worship in the province; but it was overwhelmed with
debt.   A few evenings since, a number of friends met together,
and raised what, with amounts previously promised, was sufficient to pay off the entire debt, of something more than £1,300.
Several of our successful gold-finders gave nobly on this
occasion."

On the receipt of this appeal, the committee resolved to send
out four additional missionaries.   A similar appeal from the

western province was responded to by the appointment of two additional labourers to that colony.

The resident missionary of Bathurst writes, under date of May 18th, "I could wish that the effects of the discovery of gold had left us nothing to regret, as it regards the state of religion amongst us; but, upon the whole, we have much cause for thankfulness, in that the spiritual interests of the people have not suffered, as many of us feared. As I live in the midst of the Bathurst gold-mines, I suppose you may desire to know something concerning them. It would be impossible to state the number of persons employed around us, as on all sides of us gold is found. As to their earnings, many persons who before were in very humble circumstances have suddenly acquired much wealth; and, generally, gold-mining has been found to be a lucrative employment. I know very few persons who have steadily pursued its labours, and who have not greatly improved their circumstances. However, a large number of persons would have done much better by continuing at their former occupations, at the present advanced rate of wages. The copper-mines in this district are turning out to be very rich; and they seem only to want skill, and capital, and labour, in order to work them to great advantage. California, with its vice and immorality, its rapine and murder, contributed not a little to awaken our apprehensions of the horrors that might ensue in our own land, and lead us to seek their prevention by all the means in our power; and, by the blessing of God upon our labours, and the exertions of other churches, and the prudent regulations of the government, the mining population of this district, and others also, have been very orderly. Drunkenness and sabbath-breaking, with many other forms of vice and immorality, we witness to our grief; yet the general sobriety and sabbath observance which have obtained have been very gratifying; and the good effects of a vigorous effort to repress every outward form of sabbath desecration have now become apparent. We visit Ophir, and other places; but the largest population is found at the river Turon. Here, within the last twelve months, a considerable township has risen up, called Sofala. The appearance of this place, especially in its earliest days, was most singular: a city, built not of stone, nor brick, nor wood, but of calico. Calico might be seen stretched in all directions, forming abodes of all dimensions, assuming every variety of form, which, with the costumes of the people, serge shirts, blue and red being the most fashionable, girt with leather belts, with other varieties of apparel, and unshaven beards, made the whole affair to present as novel and grotesque a picture as could well be conceived; every point of observation affording a view as diversified, if not so orderly, as that of a kaleidoscope. Then, all around by the side of the winding stream of the Turon, the astonished observer beholds a scene the most animated that human strength and activity and the lust of gold could well produce; crow-bars, picks, spades, buckets, bags, and wheelbarrows, all in motion. What with the diggers, carriers, and washers, and the din of cradles, the stranger looks upon a spectacle such as he is never likely to witness again. The change which the face of nature has undergone is surprising; the very mountains have been embowelled in order to secure the precious metal. We preached for several months at Sofala, in the open air, and generally had large and attentive congregations. A large circular tent was raised by subscription, which soon became inconveniently small. Another subscription was commenced, and a weather-board chapel built, which cost £280. The building is sixty feet by twenty-five, ten feet being partitioned off for the minister's residence. The whole has been paid for. People of all denominations attend our ministry; and several very satisfactory conversions have already taken place. Regular open-air services are also held in various other places. By these services much evil has been prevented, and considerable apparent good effected."

Two months after this was written, the following document was transmitted to the Mission-house. It is dated " North Adelaide, July 14th :" " We are now favoured with such indications as lead us to believe that the days of our financial difficulties are numbered. The debts upon our places of worship are daily disappearing. We are, at the same time, favoured with such gracious visitations of Divine influence, as lead us to thank God and take courage. We are happy to say, there exists the utmost disposition, on the part of such as have been successful at the gold-fields, to contribute freely towards the support of the cause of God. Gold is brought into the colony to an enormous amount; and I should suppose that the great majority of the working-classes must become rich. We hope that, in a short time, this will operate favourably on the finances of all religious interests; but until the men themselves return, as well as their gold, our agencies will be inefficient. With trustees, local preachers, leaders, and the most active and enterprising members of the church away at the gold-fields, it will be obvious to you that our operations must be sadly cramped. Indeed, several of our best chapels have been shut up, because of the impracticability of supplying them with local preachers. You will not be surprised to hear, that these circumstances are by no means favourable to the spiritual interests of the people. The amount of worldliness is extreme; and our best people are lamenting the deadening influence of gold amongst themselves, as well as the spiritual privations endured by those who go to seek it. Our eyes cannot be closed to the fact, that the people of these colonies, many of whom belong to the working-classes, must become possessed of wealth to an unprecedented extent. O may it not be to their eternal destruction! We find it utterly impossible to supply the many places that are anxious to obtain the benefits of our ministry. Missionaries are wanted more than ever."

The exigencies arising out of that state of things which had sprung up, under the auspices of Divine Providence, could only be satisfactorily met by the establishment of a colonial authority, having a right to regulate the labours of the agents of the churches, and to adapt those labours to the ever-varying phases of society. If any person doubted the propriety of investing the Australian churches with the prerogatives of self-government, surely the new and altered circumstances of those churches must effectually remove that doubt. For several years prior to the gold discovery, they had enjoyed much temporal and spiritual prosperity. The funds which they drew from the parent Society were appropriated chiefly to the propagation of the gospel in remote and thinly-inhabited districts. They had been given to understand, long since, that, on their becoming independent of foreign aid, they should have rectoral authority conceded to them over their own affairs. All foreign missions should be conducted with an immediate reference to the same result, and all colonial churches should anticipate the same lofty elevation. In this case it was not a question of principle, but of time. There were many circumstances, however, arising out of the political and transition state of society in these colonies, suggestive of extreme caution in introducing so comprehensive a change just now. This, we presume, led the committee and the Conference of 1852 to decide upon nothing but general principles, and to send out a deputation to ascertain by personal observation and a free intercourse with the missionaries and others, whose interests were likely to be affected by the proposed change, whether this be the very best time to apply those principles. If, in the judgment of those competent and responsible parties, the " set time " is come for giving those churches a Connexional form, it is proposed to place them in a fraternal relation to the British Conference. The confederated churches of Australia will preserve in their integrity the doctrines peculiar to Methodism, and retain the same models as to organization and discipline, with such adaptations as the geographical positions of the circuits, spread over an area nearly as large as Europe, and the habits and tendencies of the members of those churches, may require. Should this grand experiment succeed, as we hope it may, no human foresight can calculate the results. Give to those churches an independent *status*, and show them how much is depending upon their Connexional unity, zeal, and benevolence, and the probability is that they will leaven with Christian truth the multitudes that are constantly arriving amongst them from Europe and America, and exert a salutary influence over the not very remote countries of eastern Asia, as well as upon the myriads of islands which extend eastward from Australia itself. All who are duly impressed with its magnitude will commend this momentous undertaking, and those to whom it has been confided, to the blessing of God.

Founding our reasonings upon present and ascertained *data*, we think we discover the outline of the future history of the "Great South Land." Let Australia be placed under a legislature solicitous only to maintain the ascendancy of justice, truth, and Protestantism, and let the clergy of every denomination act under a due sense of their obligations to God and their country, and ordinary difficulties cannot long retard its progress in political power, commercial greatness, moral grandeur, and national glory!

We place before the reader in figures the result of the labours of Leigh and his successors up to the year 1852. The Wesleyan census for that year shows that there were 30 missionaries and assistants in Australia, 237 places of worship, 4,276 communicants, 6,730 children in the schools, and nearly 22,000 persons sitting under their ministry.

CHAPTER XIV.

THE NEW-ZEALAND MISSION RE-ESTABLISHED—AFFECTING INTERVIEW BETWEEN PATU ONE AND 'HONGI—THE BATTLE OF HOKIANGA—PROGRESS OF THE MISSION.

IN a former part of this work, we have described the circumstances under which the New-Zealand mission was suspended in 1827. In that year 'Hongi invaded Wesleydale, and depopulated the district. A small detachment of his warriors burned down the mission-premises, and compelled the brethren to escape to New South Wales. Tepui, under whose protection Mr. Leigh placed himself when he commenced the mission, feeling himself unable to resist the aggression of 'Hongi, fled with his people to the Hokianga. Shortly afterwards, Patu One, the principal chief of that district, sent to the colony to inform Mr. Leigh, that if the teachers would return to New Zealand, he would protect them. Mr. James Stack lost no time in embarking at Port Jackson, and landed at Paihia, on the 8th of October, 1827, being followed soon after by Mr. and Mrs. Hobbs. They proceeded without delay to the settlement of Patu One.

Hokianga is situated on the western coast, about forty miles from Wangaroa, their former station, and about fifty miles from the Church mission-station at the Bay of Islands. The population of the neighbourhood was understood to be not less than four thousand souls. The land in the district was enhanced in value by the facilities which the river afforded for floating timber and spars to vessels lying at anchor in the main stream. Mangungu, which lay considerably inland, was fixed upon as the centre of operations. The situation was open and healthy, the soil good, and the adjacent country beautiful. From this central position they could visit all the tribes lying along the banks of the Hokianga by water, at any hour of the day or night. Ships of five hundred tons could approach within one hundred yards of the site they had selected for their establishment. The country was generally in an unsettled state, and the natives would render them no assistance but on condition of their being paid for their labour with muskets and gunpowder. The brethren, having often witnessed their cruel and reckless use of these instruments of destruction, declined purchasing their services with such dangerous commodities. On inquiry, they found five lads, who had formerly lived with them at Wangaroa, who expressed their willingness to receive instruction, and render them what service they could. Assisted by this little band of juveniles, they commenced, on the 19th of January, 1828, to make preparation for the erection of a wooden house for the accommodation of the family. After erecting a place of shelter, they proposed forming the general outline of their mission-premises, and, by subsequent and occasional labours, filling up and completing that outline. The tribes among whom they were settling were regarded as being amongst the most barbarous and sanguinary in the country.

The first ship that entered the harbour, and crossed the bar of the Hokianga, was the "Macquarie." Her arrival produced great interest and excitement amongst the natives along the shore, who considered her as being a great and certain prize. So soon as she dropped her anchor in the river, she was boarded by the natives in such numbers, that Captain Kemp and his crew could scarcely move about on the deck. Wainga, who combined in his own person the offices of king, priest, and physician, was an incorrigible cannibal. Mr. Martin, who was chief officer of the ship, paid such attention to Wainga's daughter, as effectually to secure her confidence and affection. This interesting young savage, being anxious to save Martin's life, told him, in confidence, that it was the intention of the natives to murder the Europeans and take the ship on the following day. Those crafty barbarians endeavoured, by an unusual display of hospitality, to lull the suspicions of the strangers; but at dusk, Captain Kemp placed a gun on each side of the deck, with their breeches against the taffrail, filled with grape, that, should any attempt be made to take the vessel, the parties might suffer for their temerity.

As the period approached, the master and mate alone remained upon the deck, close to the guns, and prepared to defend themselves. The natives, who had come on board in considerable numbers, suddenly commenced hostilities, by stripping off their only garment, yelling the war-song, and dancing the *haka :* on which the daughter of Wainga rushed before the guns, and implored the natives to fly instantly, or not one would escape death, by the discharge of *nga pu repo.* The terrified assailants jumped overboard, and swam on shore, leaving their garments behind them. Wainga was seized, and detained on board ship. He was treated with respect and kindness, and executed a treaty of peace and commerce, which proved highly beneficial to both parties. Mr. Martin married the young lady who had been thus instrumental in saving him: she abandoned the customs of her country, and was, some years afterwards, received into the Christian church by baptism. Mr. Martin remained in the country, and conducted the navigation of the Hokianga, being, with his wife, universally respected.

In the journal of their proceedings, which was forwarded to Mr. Leigh, the brethren complain of being again obliged to devote a large proportion of their time to manual labour. This necessary occupation of their time occasioned a deeper feeling of regret, because they could now speak and write the Maori language, and were not able to meet the demands which the adults and children made upon them for instruction. It became more obvious every day that their situation was one of great insecurity. Writing under date of February 19th, 1828, they remark, "Important events seem to be in embryo in this country. The whole of this side of the island have confederated against the south-east; but, in consequence of the severe illness of 'Hongi, they remain quiet. The death of 'Hongi, it is said, will be the ruin of the missionaries; but the 'keys of death and hell' are in the hands of the God of missions. The afflicted chief, generally amiable and social in private life, dwells, as he lies upon his mat, with impassioned eloquence on the prosecution of the war, and utter extinction of his enemies. In a letter, just received from the Bay of Islands, our friends of the Church mission say, that the expected death of 'Hongi had spread terror and despair amongst their people; that they anticipate nothing now but slavery or death; but that they themselves had made up their minds, if they should 'suffer the loss of all things,' to remain at the post of duty."

This great event, the expectation of which had created a deep and universal feeling of anxiety, took place on the 6th of March. As various and contradictory accounts of the last moments of this extraordinary man have been published in Europe, by travellers and others, we shall copy from the journal what was written at the time, from the lips of Patu One, who related what he himself had seen and heard. "I collected my people," said he, " and went down to Wangaroa, to pay our respects to 'Hongi, little thinking he was so near death. When we arrived at his residence, we found that he had lain down. When we entered into his presence, he sat up and saluted us: we all wept together; but, as he was still alive, we did not cut ourselves. When he had ceased crying, he talked cheerfully. Having raised himself up by the aid of his sound arm, he stood upon his feet, and wrapped his blanket around him. While he stood covered with a garment, he did not look so bad; but really he was quite wasted, except his face. He soon sat down, and moved as if in great inward pain. He then lay down and slept. When we told him that he was dying, he said, ' No, I am not dying: my heart is quite light: I am not dying.' The next day we determined to leave Wangaroa, and return home; but at an early hour 'Hongi fainted, and was supposed to be dead. When I found this, I said, ' We must not go: for should he die after we shall have left, we shall reproach ourselves for not having seen the last of him.' When he recovered, he seemed to think himself that he should die, but added, ' It will not be to-day, but to-morrow.' He ordered his powder to be brought to him ; and, when he saw it, he looked at it, and said to his children, *Ka ora koutou*, 'You are well,' or ' safe.' He called his sons to him, and, after presenting to one of them the coat of mail which he had received from the king of England, distributed amongst them his battle-axes and fire-arms. He then demanded, in a peremptory tone, ' Who will come to attack my followers after I am gone ?'

"Early on the morning of the third day, he was evidently going fast ; yet he ceased not to rally his friends, in case they should be attacked after his death, and concluded an impassioned address in the following words : *E aku tamariki e aku wanaunga ko nga Pakeha karakia kia atawaitia e koutou he hunga aroha ratou ki ahau. Otira ki te haere mai nga tangata Maori ki te patu i a koutou i hea ra nei i hea ra mi ina ka riro ahau kaua koutou hei mataku: Otera e aku hoa aku tamariki kia toa! Kia toa!* 'O my children ! O my relatives ! to the praying foreigners' (missionaries) ' be kind and affectionate. O my children ! O my relatives ! these are the people who have been kind to me. But should our countrymen come to fight you, from any quarter, when I am gone, do not give way to fear.   My children and friends, be brave ! be brave !' These words he continued to repeat until he ceased to breathe.

" We were all sitting in our huts when we received the first intelligence of his death.   Lest we should excite the fears of his people, we desired our body of natives to sit still, while we went to the *pa* to see the body of 'Hongi.   On our approach to the *pa*, the most alarming apprehensions were depicted in the countenances of 'Hongi's followers.   They ran to the several pass-ways to block them up, to prevent our entrance ; but we called to them, and assured them that their fears were groundless.   The chief Hudu Roa interfered, and desired us to enter the *pa*.   We perceived the people shivering and shaking with dread.   When we got to where 'Hongi's body lay, we found one of his sons binding him up.   His head, which had not yet been bound up, reclined upon his breast.   When the body was fully dressed, and his head richly ornamented with feathers, all the usual marks of respect were shown to him.   His family, fearing an attack from their enemies, wished to hurry his funeral obsequies.   They also detained a messenger, who should have carried the news of his death to the northward.   When I saw this, I said to them, ' What need of all this haste and reserve ?   You are the first that have proposed to bury their father alive : let him smell before you bury him : what, if he does smell ?' Yielding to my advice, the two following days were spent in repeating the funeral ode, cutting ourselves, crying, and firing off muskets.   In the mean time, many of the deceased's friends arrived from the Bay of Islands, who, with the Hokianga natives, formed a large procession, when 'Hongi's remains were borne to the sacred place, amidst the din of shouting and firing, dancing and crying.''

The journalist adds, " Alas ! what desolations this man hath wrought in the earth !   How are the mighty fallen !" No general movement took place amongst the natives, such as was expected, on the death of 'Hongi ; and the battle of Hunahuna, where he fell, proved to be the Waterloo of New Zealand, and led to a better understanding amongst the turbulent chiefs that governed the country, and a more general and lasting tranquillity.

While they were interring 'Hongi at Wangaroa, a party of natives marched from Te Waima, on the Hokianga, and not only robbed several neighbouring tribes, but also killed the son of the celebrated Pomare. This roused the Bay-of-Islanders, who assem-bled four hundred warriors, and sent them, under the leadership of Toi and Ware Unu, to demand satisfaction.   The chiefs of Hokianga were anxious to avoid war, and offered compensation for the injury which the natives of Te Waima had done to their property; but Ware Unu, or King George, would be satisfied with nothing but blood. Having no alternative, Patu One and Muri Wai placed themselves at the head of their fighting-men, and arranged their mode of defence. Patu One formed his men into a square, three deep: his front rank, kneeling, was armed with muskets, his centre with spears, and his rear with hatchets. His general orders were then issued: "Obey your chiefs ; maintain compactness ; do not fire until you receive orders ; we shall not fight unless they fire upon us." The Bay-of-Islanders advanced upon Patu One's square. They continued for a short time to brandish native weapons, when one of them fired his musket, and shot one of their own front-rank men. The contending parties were so near to each other, that the dead man fell upon the Hokianga front rank. "Never mind," said Patu One: "it is only one of their own men: be steady." A second and third shot being fired amongst Patu One's men, he said to Muri Wai, *Me pehea ekara?* "What shall we do further?" *Me pupuhi,* "Fire," said Muri Wai. Patu One instantly gave orders to fire ; Muri Wai exclaiming to his men, *Kawea nga nu a te Karaka!* "Bear away with Clarke's things," referring to the gentleman of whom their muskets were purchased. This discharge was so effective, that the Bay-of-Islanders turned and fled from the field. They ran about a quarter of a mile, when they rallied, and prepared to face their pursuers.

At this critical juncture the natives of Waima, who had been the occasion of the war, deserted Patu One, and fled, leaving him with only seventy-two men to renew the combat with three hundred and eighty. Patu One and his little band fell back about one hundred yards, when Muri Wai was shot through the thigh. This roused his men, who cried out as he fell, *Ka Muri-wai e—! ane—! Ka Muriwai e—! Ka mate rawa o tatou papa; a Muriwai e—!* "O, Muri Wai, alas! Muri Wai, our beloved father," (or head chief,) "is fallen!" and, instantly turning round, fired upon their assailants. A slave, before discharging his musket, singled out King George, and shot him through the neck. On receiving the ball, he was observed to jump up several feet, and then to fall lifeless to the ground. Their chief having fallen, the Bay-of-Islanders were panic-struck, and fled in all directions. Patu One would not allow his men to pursue them ; but, taking up the dead chief, he had his body bound up in the usual way, and made great lamentation over him. This was a disastrous day for Ware Unu and his family : his wife, who had come with him to the war, and carried her youngest child on her back, was shot, with her infant, in the morning by mere accident. This battle was fought near the mission-premises.

The brethren observe, "In these times, the name of the Lord

A NEW ZEALAND PA, WITH MEN, DANCING THE WAR DANCE.

is a strong tower, into which we run and are safe." It being of
the utmost importance that the gentlemen of the Church mission
should be apprised of these transactions, an account was prepared, and a young man offered, at the risk of his own life, to
carry it to Paihia. The messenger reached Paihia in safety, and
returned with the following note : "We have had a meeting for
consultation. The Te-nga-puis throw the whole blame of Ware
Unu's death upon your two chiefs, Patu One and Muri Wai.
This death, you may rest assured, will be avenged; and God
only knows what the result will be. The Ngapuis are assembling at our place and at Korararika, from all parts, and will
form a very large body indeed. They will clear your country of
its inhabitants, and, unless God interfere, Clarke's establishment
will be burned to the ground. Bury your best things. The
principal chiefs and the majority of the people are for war. The
Wangaroa party is thirsting for Te Puke's blood. Rawa, however, and a considerable number say they are in favour of peace.
These have applied to us to accompany them to Waima as mediators. The laws of the country admit of the interference of a
neutral party. We have determined to go with them, and, by
the grace of God, and at the hazard of our own lives, endeavour
to promote reconciliation. We expected that Patu One would
have insisted on removing you and your stores to his own *pa*.
If he should, let him take your stores; but for the world's sake
do not go yourselves, but come over at once to us. We requested Rawa, the chief, to keep his eye upon you. If they decide for peace, you will soon see us; if for war, we shall soon see
you. May the Lord of hosts be our refuge in this savage land!"
   The Church brethren, Williams and Davis, set out on their
mission, and entered the fortress of Waima on the 23rd of
March. After protracted negotiations, they secured a mutual
declaration of peace. The narration of these proceedings closes,
as might be expected, with devout acknowledgments of the
Divine goodness. "This prevention of hostilities," they remark,
"calls forth our gratitude to God; for had not affairs taken this
favourable turn, this would have been one of the most sanguinary contests ever known in New Zealand; for the parties were
inflamed with mutual resentment, and, like bloodhounds, longed
for an opportunity to devour each other."
   Having brought their negotiations to a successful issue, the
brethren H. Williams, Davis, Clarke, and Kemp, left the fortress
of Waima on the morning of the 25th. Finding the Wesleyan
mission-boat, from Mangungu, waiting for them, they went on
board, and reached that station at six o'clock in the evening.
They conversed together until a late hour, on the events of the
last few weeks, commended themselves and their cause, as they

had often done before, to the blessing of God, and hoped for peaceful times.

As the ship "Herald" was over-due from the Bay of Islands, two of the brethren went down the river, on the afternoon of May 5th, in the expectation of meeting her. As they passed along, a native hailed them, and presented a parcel which he had found upon the sea-shore. On opening it, they found that it contained the invoice of goods that had been shipped on board the "Enterprise" at Sydney for their station, and concluded that the vessel and all on board had perished on the coast. While reflecting on this melancholy affair, their own boat hove in view, having on board Messrs. Clarke and Hobbs, and the master of the "Herald." The captain told them that he had left his ship a complete wreck, and that all on board had barely escaped a watery grave: that Mr. Fairbourn, of the Church mission, and several others, had suffered so much in an attempt to swim to land during the night, that they were obliged to leave them behind. No sooner had Mr. Fairbourn crept out of the water upon the shore, than he was seized by a savage, who threatened him with instant destruction if he did not give him his shirt. The natives claimed the ship, cut away her masts and rigging, and attempted to set her on fire : the flowing-in of the tide, however, rendered the attempt abortive. Some portions of the wreck of the "Enterprise" were discovered soon after, a few miles from the North Head; but the officers and crew were lost.

Understanding that a native festival was to be held at Waihoa, on the 14th of April, in honour of the dead, one of the missionaries resolved to attend, for the purpose of explaining to the people the resurrection of the dead. On the day appointed there was a large assemblage of the natives; but they were wild, clamorous, and turbulent. The dead were placed in rows, in a sitting posture, under a shed made of the *nikau*, or "palm-tree," and presented a ghastly spectacle. The missionary, finding it impossible to fix their attention on any religious topic, withdrew, grieved to witness such utter indifference to the things belonging to their peace.

While explaining the parable of the rich man and Lazarus to several chiefs, on Sunday, May 15th, To-too-nui said, "We want evidence! When a spirit comes from the invisible world to the Horoke or Mangungu, and tells us that he has seen the things of which you speak, we will believe him; but all the accounts we have received as yet have been directly opposite to yours. Tell us plainly, are there no places to besiege in the other world? no people to fight with? and no guns? Have you yourself seen any persons who have been raised from the dead?" Being answered in the negative, he laughed heartily, observing, "O indeed! then you only heard it from some one else. You *nga Pakeha* are no better than old women!" This was regarded, by himself and his companions, as being conclusive; and here, for the present, the question had to rest.

Muri Wai, the chief, who was shot through the thigh in the late engagement with the Bay-of-Islanders, died on the 17th of July. The immediate cause of his death was inflammation of the lungs. He always treated the solemnities of religion with levity, and seemed amused when the subjects of death and eternity were discussed in his presence. He was a brave warrior; but died as ignorant of God as the beasts that perish. After death, he was wrapped in a blanket, and placed in a sitting posture, his head being well soaked with oil, and decorated with feathers. His powder-horn rested on his knees. On one side were placed his guns and a whalebone *meri parana:* on the other, sat his youngest wife, who had strangled herself during the night in a paroxysm of grief. Her body was also covered with a blanket, and her head adorned with feathers. His wives, children, brothers, sisters, and other relatives, sat near him weeping, and seemed to feel acutely. The missionaries were admitted into their presence, and addressed them, with much effect, on the way of salvation.

Four days after the death of Muri Wai, nine hundred warriors, chiefly related to the deceased chieftain, arrived in canoes. The fort of the Horoke saluted them with four great guns; which salute they acknowledged by firing two guns from their canoes, and a shower of musket-balls. They presented a formidable appearance, and were received with suspicion. They disembarked, and, after dancing on the beach, commenced lacerating themselves, and crying in the most frantic and distressing manner. Two of the missionaries approached them, and gave them, in English and Maori, an exposition of 1 Thess. iv. 13, 14 : "I would not have you to be ignorant, brethren, concerning them which are asleep, that ye sorrow not, even as others which have no hope. For if we believe that Jesus died and rose again, even so them also which sleep in Jesus will God bring with Him." A European who was present said, with much feeling, "If British Christians could witness this affecting scene, it would remove all doubt as to whether these savages need the gospel." After having, as they supposed, discharged their duty to the dead, they peaceably retired.

A season of comparative freedom from open hostilities ensued, which the brethren did not fail to improve by exerting their influence to soften down the mutual jealousies of the chiefs, and impress upon the people the inestimable blessings of prolonged peace, and increasing industry. In these respects, at least, they were successful. In reporting to Mr. Leigh their condition and prospects, they say, " You will be glad to hear that peace reigns amongst the natives generally throughout the country. The case of the Hawees may tend to throw a shade over the character of the natives; yet it is due to those who reside at this end of the island to say, that their conduct towards Europeans is quite as good as can be expected at present. Our sabbath labours are now extended to our countrymen, from whom we receive but little encouragement. In visiting the native villages, we meet with a friendly reception; but the higher objects of our mission are, as yet, but imperfectly understood. 'Faith,' however, 'is the substance of things hoped for, the evidence of things not seen.' September 11th, 1829."

Mr. Leigh, having collected several important facts, illustrative of the utility of this mission, submitted the whole to the consideration of the committee, accompanied by the following note, dated from New South Wales: " Several captains, who have lately visited some of the distant parts of New Zealand, declare, that the labours of the missionaries have spread far and wide in that country; that the prayers they have taught the people have been transmitted from tribe to tribe, until they have become well known by natives residing hundreds of miles from the mission-station. They tell me that the one desire of the chiefs, at the ports they have visited, is to have missionaries. Those chiefs have evinced their sincerity by offering to give those captains any quantity of pigs, potatoes, or flax, for a missionary who can pray, and teach them the way to the God and heaven of the white man. Such language and feelings I have heard and seen myself, at a great distance from the mission-station, in that country. I as firmly believe that the New-Zealanders are about to be converted to the Christian faith, as I believe that I am now alive upon the earth. I have seen a person lately, who has returned from Mangungu. He informs me that the brethren there have erected a good school-house, and have now a promising school. 'The tribes,' he says, 'are peaceable, the missionaries are fully employed, and their prospects are highly encouraging. The chiefs are increasingly attached to our brethren, and evince an increasing interest in the things of God. 'We shall reap, if we faint not.'"

Mr. Leigh forwarded, by the same conveyance, a letter he had just received from Captain S. P. Henry, on the religious state of Tonga, Habai, Niua, and Vavou. When these communications were laid before the committee, they unanimously resolved to send out four additional missionaries and a printing-press. This formed a new era in the history of those missions. As soon as possible the premises at Mangungu were so enlarged as to afford

accommodation for a considerable number of young natives, whom
the missionaries were anxious to subject to a thorough European
training, both in civilization and religion. That these young
persons might be removed from the corrupting influence of an
unrestricted intercourse with the natives, twenty-eight young
men and six young women were taken into connexion with their
own families. They were daily instructed in reading and writing: they were examined on various subjects on three evenings
in the week, and admitted to the exposition of the scriptures
and family worship twice a day. They soon displayed a taste
for mental improvement, and became thoughtful and serious.
Several of these young persons had formerly lived with them at
Wangaroa. One of these, whose name was Hika, was related
to the chiefs George and Tepui, and was taken into the mission-
family by Mr. Leigh. When the warriors of 'Hongi burned the
mission-house, and compelled the brethren to leave the country,
Hika sailed with them to New South Wales. When it was
determined to resume the New Zealand mission, he returned
with them to Mangungu, where he was of inestimable service in
protecting their property from the depredations of the natives.
He had resided with them six years, was remarkably honest, and
seemed to be influenced by the fear of God. Towards the close
of the year 1830, his naturally delicate constitution gave way,
and he was obliged to desist from all manual labour. His mind,
always active and thoughtful, having now full scope for reflection, came to the conclusion, that, in case of death, he should be
eternally lost. On several occasions, when pressed to tell them
what he thought about his own state, he replied, with deep emotion, *Ka haere ahau ki te kapura nui,* " I am going to the great
fire." He continued in this state for some weeks, complaining
of his want of feeling as a sinner, and of the weakness of his
desire for the mercy of God in Christ Jesus. After some time,
through exhortation and prayer, he began to entertain hope.
The scriptures now seemed to afford him comfort and relief; and
his earnestness increased in proportion to his confidence in the
Divine goodness. It was not, however, until a few days previous
to his death, that he found repose in Christ, and agreed to be
baptized. Having fully and decidedly expressed his desire for
that sacred ordinance, together with his entire resignation to the
will of God, it was agreed, on Sunday morning, February 16th,
1831, to admit him into the militant church, and publicly acknowledge him as a brother in the Lord, not doubting but Christ
would seal him His unto the day of redemption. He was accordingly baptized in the name of the blessed Trinity, in the presence
of several brethren and their wives, who had stopped a few days
on their passage to Tonga, and a considerable number of natives.

Some of the young people on the establishment appeared to be deeply affected, while the natives generally manifested much interest. About tea-time he sent for one of the brethren, who found him sinking, as it seemed, into the arms of death. He said, with much difficulty, *Hei ko nei rau koutou;* "Here abide all of you;" "I go away" being understood: to which they replied, *Kia mau, kia kai koe ki te hapa tapu,* "Wait a little, and take the sacred supper;" upon which he presently revived, and continued much refreshed until he had taken the sacred emblems of his Saviour's death, which he did apparently with much satisfaction. He afterwards spent the night chiefly in conversation with the two boys who attended him, giving them much good advice, and exhorting them to become Christians. He said to them, "Remain where you are: all your actions are observed from above: turn from your sins. You must also believe in God and Christ: His residence is above: it is far more happy than any earthly place: I shall be safely conducted to it." Thus he continued to talk to them till two o'clock in the morning, when he calmly fell asleep, to await the coming of the resurrection. Having become a Christian in every sense of the word, the brethren could not think of allowing his relatives to take away his body to the common receptacle of the dead. On Monday they made a coffin for Hika, and on Tuesday buried him with European and Christian solemnity.

"We have just heard from Mr. Turner," they remark, " of the death of Shukkee, who went to England, and afterwards to Tonga, where he has died in a hopeful state. He was also from Wangaroa. Mr. Turner likewise informs us that the boy Tungahe, who went from our station to New South Wales, and thence to Tonga, where he has been baptized, is doing well. It is matter of encouragement, therefore, to see three instances of the grace of God from Wangaroa. May we ever hear the holy apostle saying, 'Therefore, my beloved brethren, be ye steadfast, immovable, always abounding in the work of the Lord, forasmuch as ye know that your labour is not in vain in the Lord!'"

Towards the close of the year one of the brethren had occasion to visit Wangaroa. Wesleydale was grown over with bushes and fern. The well-wooded hills, surrounding the vale, deep ravines, and beautifully winding river, which to any other person, or in any other circumstances, would have been irresistibly enchanting, seemed to him clothed in gloom and melancholy. The roads he had assisted to make, with immense labour, were covered with bushes; he recognised the place where each building and fence had stood; but not a vestige of either remained, except here and there a half-burned post, and two or three heaps of bricks. Several fruit-trees and vegetables were observed in the garden; but all was confusion and desolation. The natives begged that the teachers would come back and take possession of their estate in Wesleydale. He informed them that Mangungu was such an extensive field of labour, and presented so many circumstances of encouragement, that no one could be spared from that station at present.

This period was distinguished by a remarkable movement on the native mind, all over the country. All along the extended course of the Hokianga, the people were loud in their appeals for missionaries. Several chiefs arrived, one sabbath morning, and insisted on taking the missionaries away by force in their canoe to teach their people. The first native class was formed in the December of this year. There were five members, one of whom had a distinct knowledge of the forgiveness of his sins, and all the others were " striving to enter in at the strait gate." One of these native converts was so far advanced in intelligence and piety, that he was considered competent to conduct the school and the public worship of God, in the absence of the missionaries. This marks the commencement, in New Zealand, of a native agency which has been increasing in strength and efficiency, with the progress of every succeeding year.

The pervading and awakening influence, to which we have alluded, was experienced on all the stations connected with the Church mission. Several blood-thirsty chiefs, who had always delighted in war, and repelled the missionaries with scorn, now came, from remote parts of the country, and demanded teachers. On having their attention directed to the contrast between the savageism of their people, and the peace and industry which prevailed within the territories of a neighbouring chief, one of them replied with vehemence, " They have teachers : can we believe through trees? Come and live amongst us !" The stations of the Church mission were rapidly multiplied, and a valuable staff of lay-helpers raised up. The Wesleyan brethren soon had above one hundred persons of both sexes in their schools. The demand for catechisms, and those portions of scripture which had been translated into Maori, could not be met. Three bushels of potatoes were offered for a slate and a few pieces of pencil, and five bushels for twenty-one chapters of the word of God, two catechisms, the Liturgy, and twenty hymns.

Cases of conversion continued to multiply throughout the year 1832. We can only notice that of Hae Hae, a chief of considerable distinction. Being taken ill, he began seriously to contemplate the probability of his being cast into " the great fire " after death. During his illness he was frequently visited by the brethren. After prayer, one evening, he inquired particularly into the nature of that faith in Christ. of which they were constantly speaking.   After explaining justifying faith, and the relation in which it stands to Christ and to all spiritual blessings, they left him. Next morning, while reflecting on what they had said the day before on the subject, he lifted up his heart to God in prayer. The Lord poured upon him " the spirit of grace and of supplications;" and he continued to seek the pardon of his sins, for Christ's sake, until he obtained an inward assurance of the Divine favour. He was baptized on the following Sunday in the morning, and in the evening received the sacrament of the Lord's supper. In the middle of the night he sent for the missionaries and his relatives. Addressing himself to his friends, he said, " Listen to me, for I am now dying: perhaps you will remember what I say when I am gone.   You are all in darkness and in the way to hell. This country is full of misery; who would live in it always? You see I have no fear. I am going to Jesus. Will you meet me in heaven? I am going: farewell." In a few minutes afterwards he ceased to breathe.

The public worship of God became more attractive and influential as the year 1833 advanced. It was remarked that many of the congregations were much affected when certain parts of the Liturgy of the Church of England were read, particularly, *Tapu, tapu, tapu, rama E I howa te Ana onga mano tuauriuri waioio ;* that is, " Holy, holy, holy, Lord God of Sabaoth ;" and the response, *E kiki Ana te rangi me te wenua i te kahanga O tau koioria,* " Heaven and earth are full of the majesty of thy glory !"   In conversation it was not uncommon to hear the natives reproving each other, by simply quoting a passage of scripture.   On witnessing indications of a haughty and disdainful spirit, they would say, *Kei waka, pehapeha te tahi kikokiko kitona aroaro:* " That no flesh should glory in His presence !"

Sedulous attention having been given to the schools, the brethren resolved to hold a public examination of the children and young people under their care in July. The announcement excited much attention, and drew together above four hundred persons. The examination brought out the interesting facts, that one hundred scholars could repeat the catechism *without a mistake,* nine could read the New Testament *without spelling a word,* and fifty could both read and write a little.

A great improvement had been going on for some time, in reference to the observance of the Lord's day. In some of the villages professing to have embraced Christianity, a hoe was suspended by the handle, morning and evening, as a substitute for a bell, and struck with a stone, to call the people together for family worship. The service consisted in singing a hymn, reading a portion of scripture, and then praying extempore. During

the late fighting on the banks of the Hokianga, both parties
agreed to suspend hostilities "on the sacred day."

The hands of the missionaries were much strengthened by the
conversion, and admission into the church, of Katia, a man of
considerable influence and of great energy of character.   He
became a most exemplary Christian; and, as an exhorter, superintendent of the schools, and class-leader, was the instrument of
extensive good to his countrymen.   The stability which characterized the native converts was likewise a source of much
encouragement.   Adverting to this gratifying fact, the brethren
observe, "The singing of the native professors, their prayers,
their attention to their classes, and other ordinances of religion,
leave no doubt on our minds as to their sincerity; and, for consistency and decorum in the house of God, they are a pattern to
many who have enjoyed greater advantages.   For a long series
of years, the servants of God laboured in this country with but
little success; but now a glorious change has taken place, and
they are amply rewarded for all their toil.   Hundreds are for-
saking their foolish and wicked customs and practices, and are
seeking the salvation of their souls.   We are by no means able
to supply their spiritual wants.   On the 9th of February, 1834,
six couples were married at Mangungu, and thirty children and
adults baptized.   The number of converts is increasing, and will
increase; for God is true, and God is love."

When the first edition of the New Testament, printed by the
British and Foreign Bible Society, arrived in New Zealand, the
natives looked at the boxes and observed, "These are full of
knowledge.   We have often had things come which we thought
good,—casks of rum, barrels of gunpowder, and boxes of muskets.
What is now come is to teach us not to drink rum, not to set
fire to powder, not to use muskets, but to do us good for ever
and ever.   Our hearts are sick for the word of God: we desire
it more than axes, hatchets, or blankets."

At the examination of the schools in 1835, fifty-three canoes
arrived, bringing to the station upwards of a thousand visitors.
Above two hundred children answered the questions in the catechism, and seventy-eight read the word of God.   This was a
day of sanctified rejoicing, as the triumph of Christianity seemed
to be almost complete.   Several chiefs, connected with the
Church and Wesleyan missions, had lately abandoned savage
life, received Christian baptism, and died in the true faith.

While the schools were multiplying readers, and creating a
thirst for knowledge on every hand, the seasonable arrival of a
printing-press, and of a gentleman capable of conducting it with
judgment and efficiency, awakened the most cheering anticipations of future and extended usefulness.   We transcribe the fol-

lowing interesting communication on the subject, from the pen of the above gentleman. It is dated "New Zealand, 1836," and addressed to Mr. Leigh. "I have been pleased to learn from the newspapers, that you continue to plead successfully, before the Christian public in England, in behalf of this and other missions. Knowing that you are specially interested in the New Zealand mission, I hasten to inform you that our printing-press is in full activity. A 'Harmony of the Gospels,' one hundred and twenty pages, 12mo., twelve pages of prayers of the Church of England, and twelve pages of hymns, have been entirely printed off, and are now in circulation amongst the people. We have nearly five hundred persons meeting in class : our places of worship are filled frequently to overflowing : the spirit of inquiry is spreading amongst the natives; and I trust that thousands will ere long be gathered into the fold of Christ. I heard the experience of two hundred aborigines lately, and feel persuaded that the salvation of God has, at last, visited this land. But, alas ! much is yet to be done. Several atrocious murders have been committed lately, and many of our people have been exposed to violence. Just before I commenced the service, a short time since, at Mangataipa, guns were heard in the distance. Concluding that an attack had commenced upon our Christian brethren, our friends formed a party, and hastened to the place. On their arrival, they found that two of our most interesting young men had been shot, and were dying, literally praying for their murderers. A fine young Christian chief had a narrow escape : the ball penetrated his garment, and grazed his shoulder. The young men had gone down to persuade the people to embrace Christianity. The murderers fortified themselves, and set justice at defiance. A body of natives, however, attacked them, killed fifteen, and dispersed the rest. The wife of a chief, and a man and child, were killed near our station. The chief delivered up the murderer, who was put to death. The native ovens at Tauranga and Rotorua have been literally filled with human flesh, and many have carried it away, to a distance, in baskets. Many a poor creature has been roasted and eaten of late, and hundreds have been cut off in war; yet a friend in London asks, with evident surprise, 'Are the New-Zealanders really cannibals?' You know they are, and this statement confirms it. Matangi and his people, while engaged in war, took several prisoners, whom they roasted alive on red-hot stones, and afterwards feasted on their remains. Matangi is now a class-leader and an exhorter ; and I have seen the tear trickling down his cheeks, when we have been singing a hymn expressive of the love of Christ. The printing-press of the Church mission, and ours on this station, are in active operation, disseminating truth.

The brethren at the Bay of Islands have proceeded as far as the Gospel of John, with the translation and printing of the New Testament. When completed, this work will pull down the strongholds of Satan in the land. 'Pray for us,' and continue to exhort your countrymen to support Christian missions, by their prayers, influence, and liberality. I subjoin specimens of the language, and of our work :—

"*I taua wa he mea motu ke atu koutou i a te Karaiti, ehara i te tangata whenua no Iharaira, he tangata ke ki nga kawenata o nga mea i whakaaria mai i mua, kahore he mea hei tumanako-tanga atu, he hunga Atua kone i te ao :*

"*Tena ko tenei i roto i a Karaiti Ihu ko koutou, ko te hunga i tawhiti i mua, kua meinga e nga toto o te karaiti kia tata.*

"'That at that time ye were without Christ, being aliens from the commonwealth of Israel, and strangers from the covenants of promise, having no hope, and without God in the world :

"'But now in Christ Jesus ye who sometimes were far off are made nigh by the blood of Christ.' (Eph. ii. 12, 13.)"

The chiefs who governed these distracted districts, instead of settling their differences by an appeal to the spear and musket, agreed to refer their mutual grievances to the missionaries, and abide by their decision. After spending ten days in endeavours to adjust their respective claims, the brethren succeeded in restoring harmony for the present, and returned to their families in peace.

At this time they were gratified by the arrival of a native of distinction from the river Thames, having a message from Patu One, 'the superior chief of the tribes in that neighbourhood. "I have come," said he, "to inform you, that Patu One and his people have turned from their evil ways, to worship Jehovah the true God : and they wish you to come over to counsel and teach them." Alas! this was impossible : for the labours of the school, the pulpit, and the press, were not commensurate with the urgent claims of the people connected with their own settlement. The messenger returned to Patu One disappointed and grieved.

The last Sunday in August, 1837, was a memorable day at Mangungu: On that day one hundred and twenty adults, of both sexes, who had been under instruction for some time, made a public "profession of faith in the Triune God, and were baptized in the presence of a crowded congregation."

The wife of one of the brethren had been the subject of a severe and protracted affliction. Her husband, having occasion to use the fire frequently in the night-time, had been in the habit of placing a fresh log upon it before retiring to rest. On the night of August 18th, 1838, the burning log, having rolled back, set fire to the chimney. About two o'clock in the morning the family were aroused from their slumbers by a roaring noise and a dense smoke. The flames spread so rapidly, that the afflicted woman had to be removed in her night-dress, without either shoes or stockings; while their five children were like "brands plucked out of the fire." The missionary escaped through a back window, and alarmed the settlement. The natives soon spread themselves over the premises, and saved every article of furniture, provision, or apparel, that came within their reach; but the building itself, the most valuable part of the furniture and stores, together with several public documents, were completely destroyed. Never was the depth and force of religious principle more strikingly displayed by the natives, than on this occasion. The loss was estimated at £800, and it necessarily involved much anxiety and labour to remove the consequences of so great a calamity.

But in the work of God there was no pause. Upwards of one thousand natives attended the public worship of God on the 18th of November, and seemed unusually impressed during the service. On this occasion, one hundred and thirty-eight adults were baptized, and forty-six children. Several of the adults were persons of rank, who had stood out for years against warning, entreaty, and every other means that Christian zeal could employ to bring them to Christ. Several of them had assisted in expelling the missionaries from Wesleydale : they had removed to Mangungu, and now submitted to the yoke of Christ.

CHAPTER XV.

STATE OF EUROPEAN SOCIETY—SCHEMES FOR IMPROVING THE COUNTRY —POLICY OF THE GOVERNMENT—BISHOP SELWYN—EDUCATIONAL EFFORTS.

JUST at the period when the fierce contest which had been going on between darkness and light, for above twenty years, seemed to be drawing to a close, savageism and its auxiliaries slowly and reluctantly retiring from the field, and Christianity standing forth to receive the palm of victory, circumstances arose that threatened the subversion of all the civil and religious institutions of the country. Considering the influence which those circumstances were calculated to exert over the peace, commerce, religion, and morals of the people at large, we feel compelled, however briefly, to advert to them.

The splendid harbours of New Zealand, and especially the Bay of Islands, had for several years been the favourite resort of the numerous British, colonial, American, and French whalers of the southern Pacific; while several establishments had been formed on the banks of its navigable streams, and along its numerous bays, for the purchase of flax and the cutting of timber. This originated a demand for European labourers; and sawyers and mechanics of various descriptions were attracted to the island, and induced to make it the place of their permanent abode. Several individuals opened stores, and became traders, in the Bay of Islands. Vast numbers arrived from the two penal colonies, and set up as retail dealers in rum and tobacco. With few exceptions, the European population consisted of the very refuse of civilized society,—of runaway sailors, of runaway convicts, of convicts who had served out their term of bondage in one or other of the penal colonies, of fraudulent debtors who had escaped from their creditors in Sydney or Hobart Town, and of needy adventurers from the two colonies, almost equally unprincipled. In conjunction with the whalers that visited the coast, the influence of these persons on the natives was demoralizing in the extreme. Their usual articles of barter were either muskets and gunpowder, or tobacco and rum. "Most of them lived in open concubinage with native women : and the scenes of outrageous licentiousness and debauchery that were ever and anon occurring on their premises, were often sufficiently revolting to excite the reprobation and disgust of the natives themselves." That scenes of lawless violence, injustice, and oppression should be perpetually recurring in a community composed of such materials, was naturally to be expected. There was no authority in the island to which application could be made, and no redress procurable for the most atrocious injuries, but by an appeal to physical force. It is true, there was a British resident; but he was provided with no adequate powers to enforce obedience to law. While the British and French journals were urging the necessity of some foreign interference with the existing state of things in New Zealand, and pressing the claims of their respective governments to the right of preemption in those islands, the Baron de Thierry arrived in the district of Hokianga, and issued a proclamation, beginning thus : "Charles, by the grace of God, sovereign chief of New Zealand." He claimed a large portion of the country, and showed his title-deeds. He had purchased the land from Mr. M. K. in London. The chiefs of Hokianga were anxious to have a teacher, and agreed to give Mr. M. K. the territory now claimed, if he would come and reside amongst them in that capacity. Having forfeited the confidence of the Church, he returned to England, and sold the property to the baron. The chiefs repudiated the baron as " sovereign chief," and told him that the land was promised conditionally; but that, as the condition had not been fulfilled, they could not allow him to take possession of any part of it.   He was an English adventurer with a foreign title, and brought in his train a number of servants and mechanics from Sydney.   But after the British government had avowed its readiness to afford protection to property, trade, and life in the islands, a difficulty arose as to the most equitable and efficient means of accomplishing that important object.

By the increase of fire-arms, the introduction of the most loathsome European diseases, and the use of intoxicating liquors, the aborigines were fast disappearing.   Wherefore, to arrest the progress of depopulation, "repress the crimes of British settlers, and prevent the further emigration of convicts and other desperate vagabonds," it was proposed :—

1. To colonize the country.   The earl of Devon suggested the appointment of a committee of the House of Lords, to obtain information, and examine witnesses, respecting the natives, climate, soil, produce, and harbours of New Zealand, and report to the House the result of their deliberations on that information. A large and influential committee was accordingly appointed, including several bishops, the duke of Wellington, and other distinguished members of the government.   The scheme of the New-Zealand Association was submitted to this committee, and urged by persons of great political influence.   On looking at the outline of the proposed plan, the committees of the Church and Wesleyan Missionary Societies were convinced that it was equally adverse to the interests of the natives and the progress of Christianity; and they combined to oppose it.   The opposition on the part of the Church was conducted by Dandison Coates, Esq., and on the part of the Wesleyans by the Rev. Dr. Beecham.   These gentlemen placed before the committee a series of incontrovertible facts, illustrative of the condition and claims of the natives; which, being corroborated by other witnesses, convinced them that to force any merely secular scheme upon the country would be attended with the most disastrous consequences.   This conviction was deepened in the minds of several of their lordships by the perusal of an able and seasonable publication, on the principles of colonization, by Dr. Beecham.   We have much satisfaction in recording a well-authenticated incident, highly honourable to an illustrious warrior and statesman recently deceased.   The duke of Wellington, being unable, from deafness, to hear the examination of the witnesses, had their evidence submitted to his perusal at the close of each day's proceedings. When the labours of the committee were drawing to a close, His Grace delivered his opinion to the effect that, in his judgment, no plan of colonization should be sanctioned by the legislature that would interfere with the beneficial labours of the missionaries.

This declaration was understood to have decided the fate of the Association, as the report of the committee was unfavourable to their claims.

2. A Bill, intended to secure the same object, was introduced into the House of Commons, in 1837, by Mr. Baring. This Bill was based upon principles already recognised in the settlement of South Australia. After much discussion, it was rejected by a majority of the House, chiefly through the opposition of the Church and Wesleyan Missionary Societies.

The executive of those bodies were of opinion, that the proposed remedy was calculated to aggravate all the social evils already existing in New Zealand. But should the affairs of the colony itself be well conducted, still there lay, beyond its geographical limits, at least one hundred thousand savages, for whose improvement the Bill made no adequate provision. It appeared to them, that as the measure did not contemplate the introduction of religious teachers into the interior, the only persons capable, at that time, of promoting peace and keeping up a friendly correspondence between the settlers and natives, it was not likely to reach the objects proposed; and that a trading company, having their own secular interests to serve, were not unlikely to be in constant collision with the aborigines. This Bill being thrown out,—

3. It was then suggested to place the country under the *protection* of Great Britain. Great Britain was to assume the office of trustee for the natives. The chiefs who signed the declaration of independence in 1835, were not likely, it was supposed, to object to this arrangement, and the consent of the others might soon be obtained. It was thought that, by granting the chiefs in the interior a small salary, their co-operation might be secured, in promoting the general interests of New Zealand. The public revenue was to be raised and applied by the protecting party. In carrying out this plan, the aid of the missionaries was to be solicited. Thus a native government was to be raised up under the protection of England. The reader will perceive that the success of such a scheme would entirely depend upon the agents employed in its administration; but, in any case, it was not desirable that the missionaries should be mixed up with the civil offices of the state.

4. An improved plan of residency was recommended by a select committee of the House of Commons. A war having broken out at the Bay of Islands, the resident complained of the want of power to deal with the contending parties. The governor of New South Wales sent the "Rattlesnake" ship of war, commanded by Captain Hobson, to protect British interests. This force was declared by the resident to be insufficient; as, in his opinion,

"some permanent authority was necessary, that should be supported by adequate military strength," to secure the efficiency of its measures, and prevent the tribes from destroying one another. "The representations of the missionaries," it was said, "induced the government to refuse this 'adequate military strength,' and rendered the proposed scheme abortive." It has been admitted, since then, that the true cause of failure, in this case, was a misunderstanding between the resident himself and the colonial authorities in New South Wales. "But for the missionaries, no European could live in this country. Let their greatest enemies say what they may, all such are equally indebted with myself to the general respect felt for the missionaries, for the safety of their lives and properties in time past." *

5. A system of factories was next recommended. It was maintained, that these centres of industry and sources of wealth were well calculated to repress the crimes of British settlers and improve the natives. The missionaries inquired, how? and declared that, in their judgment, these establishments were more likely to give accelerated force to the elements of evil that threatened the foundations of the social fabric. The missionaries had a more comprehensive knowledge of the country than any of the civilians then directing public affairs; and their experience and observation, extending over a series of years, convinced them that, just in proportion as Europeans increased in any given locality, did the natives acquire new forms of vice, and descend even below their own standard of morality.

In these circumstances the New-Zealand Land Company was formed, to effect the original object of the Association, without the sanction of an Act of Parliament at all, and entirely on the principle of a joint-stock company. But, according to their own showing, it seemed improbable that they should be able to manage their own affairs, which were sufficiently perplexing, and at the same time pay due attention to the civil and religious condition of a savage population. But while Christian gentlemen, such as constituted the directory of the Church and Wesleyan Missionary Societies, having the history of the past before them, looked upon these schemes with jealousy, and urged upon the government the probable evils arising from their hasty adoption, there were statesmen at home, and divines abroad, who maintained, with great pertinacity, that colonization alone could apply a remedy to the evils existing in New Zealand.

No writer, on either side of the controversy, evinced a more intemperate zeal than Dr. John Dunmore Lang, of New South Wales. This gentleman descended from the general principles involved in the question, and indulged a morbid mawkishness

* Marshall.

in a personal attack upon the missionaries. "The ground," he
observes, "on which the Bill for the colonization of New Zealand was successfully opposed in Parliament was, that the
establishment of a British colony in that island was likely to be
effected on infidel, and not on Christian, principles." "But
the case of the New-Zealanders cannot be trusted, with any
degree of safety, to the missionaries." "The Church-mission
settlement was for a long time a complete lumber-yard or factory, in which all sorts of labour were going on." "Whether
the individuals employed were originally bad men, or whether
the system was calculated to make them so, I cannot determine."
"There is still an abuse tolerated and practised, of sufficient
magnitude to neutralize the efforts of a whole college of apostles."
"The Church missionaries have actually been the principals in
the grand conspiracy of the Europeans to rob and plunder the
natives of their land." "My lord, I was unfortunately unable
to ascertain exactly the real extent of the land they possess."
"The case of these missionaries is the most monstrous that has
occurred in the history of missions since the Reformation."
"Your lordship will perceive how peculiarly out of place were
the declamations of the friends of the Church missions, in opposition to the Bill for the colonization of the island during the
last session of Parliament. The greater success of the Wesleyan
mission in New Zealand must, I conceive, be ascribed in no
small degree to the fact, that the Wesleyan missionaries are
strictly prohibited, by the fundamental laws and constitution of
their Society, from acquiring property of any kind, whether in
land or agricultural stock, at their mission-stations."*

On these severe reflections we remark :—

1. That, notwithstanding the slight compliment paid to the
"fundamental laws of the Wesleyan Missionary Society," the
doctor formed but a low estimate of the integrity and ability of
missionaries generally. "My lord," he observes, "in the course
of five voyages round the globe, and a residence of many years
in the uttermost parts of the earth, it has been my lot to come
in contact with many missionaries, who ought never to have been
honoured with so sacred a character. Instead of sending forth
to those important stations beyond the seas men of superior
talents and education, and piety and zeal, we have been sending
forth, with only a *few exceptions*, the lame, the halt, and the
blind of our national establishments."

2. We are not unacquainted with the personal history of Dr.
Lang: we have long respected him as an industrious student,
and an able writer; but we cannot pay homage to a judgment
that deduces such rash and momentous conclusions from such

* Letters to the Right Hon. the Earl of Durham.

superficial *data*. "I have only myself," he remarks, "*been once* at New Zealand, having touched at that island *for a few days*, in the months of January and February last," 1839. These *few days* were sufficient, it appears, to "confirm the information he had previously received respecting the island." That might be; and yet we cannot but think, that, notwithstanding the industry with which information was sought and obtained during these "few days," it was taking an unwarrantable liberty with those missionaries, some of whom were not inferior to Dr. Lang himself in moral worth or literary attainments, to represent them, to the government and their friends in England, as a set of convicted mercenaries, and to the newly-formed churches abroad as men destitute of every personal virtue. Dr. Lang was quite aware that there was no diversity of sentiment between the Wesleyan and Church missionaries, respecting his favourite theory of colonization.

3. We must now inform Dr. Lang, that persons as competent as himself to form an impartial opinion of the missionaries referred to, and who, from their official situation, must have known their character and proceedings for a longer period than a "few days," have expressed a much more favourable opinion of them. On appointing a gentleman to the office of resident in New Zealand, His Excellency the governor of New South Wales addressed him in the following terms: "You will find it convenient to manage the conference, to which I have called your attention, by means of the missionaries, to whom you will be furnished with credentials, and with whom *you are recommended* to communicate freely upon the subject of your appointment, and the means you should adopt in treating with the chiefs." "If, in addition to the benefits which the British missionaries are conferring on those islanders, by imparting the inestimable blessings of Christian knowledge, and a *pure system of morals*, the New-Zealanders should have the institution of courts of justice established upon a simple and comprehensive basis, some sufficient compensation would seem to be rendered for the injuries heretofore inflicted by our countrymen." "Having already mentioned the assistance which I anticipate you will receive from the missionaries, I have now only to impress on you the duty of a cordial co-operation with them in the great objects of their solicitude, the extension of Christian knowledge throughout the islands, and the consequent improvement in the habits and morals of the people."

Dr. Lang has inadvertently misrepresented circumstances and exaggerated facts. Suspected concealment has awakened jealousy and provoked retaliation; and the faults of a few have been indiscriminately imputed, by Dr. Lang and others, to all the agents employed in those missions. Even within a few years a writer, who may be regarded as an authority on all merely civil and commercial questions, has thrown a doubt upon the utility of their labours, and insinuated that they have placed the government and the country under a small amount of obligation; while another author, of some eminence in the literary world, has advised the subscribers to the Church Missionary Society to withhold their support from the New-Zealand mission. Having carefully and impartially analysed the books that have been written for and against those missions, examined the verbal and written testimony of Mr. Leigh, and other competent witnesses, and cautiously formed our judgment as to their character and progress, we aver, without fear of successful contradiction, that the directors of the Church and Wesleyan missions in New Zealand *have nothing to conceal.* That there have been cases of great unfaithfulness, on the part of some of their agents, is freely admitted; but they have been comparatively few, they occurred under peculiar circumstances, and were visited with a heavy measure of ecclesiastical censure. A clerical journalist observes, with the utmost candour, "The enemies of this mission most to be dreaded, were some of their own household. So far, indeed, did some of them dishonour the self-denying doctrines of the Cross, which they had been sent here to teach, that no less painful a plan could be adopted than an ignominious erasure of their names from the list of the Society's labourers." Yet these few cases, about which so much has been said and written, were not more aggravated than several that occurred under apostolic supervision, and stand recorded in the New Testament. Not that we would extenuate the offence of a missionary: on the contrary, we regard the character of the Christian missionary as being the common *property of Christendom.* Acting, as he does, under the *perpetual inspection* of immense multitudes of the children of God, including in their number many of the *wisest and best of mankind,* any defection in his character brings reproach on the general cause, clothing in sackcloth the friends of missions throughout the globe; and as the pages of the missionary annals are perused by thousands, in climes remote from their sphere of action, of various nations and languages, the conduct of a fallen member fills with sorrow the heart of the poor peasant, as he sits down, after his daily toil, to solace his friends and himself by the evening fireside, and reads the disastrous story. Even the converted savage stands confounded when he hears the intelligence; and devoted missionaries in various distant regions feel the loss of a brother, and are paralysed, exclaiming mournfully, "Tell it not in Gath!"

Having made these admissions, we write advisedly when we

say, that the modern history of the church does not supply an account of a more exemplary, laborious, or successful body of Christian missionaries, than those who have represented the Church and Wesleyan Societies in New Zealand. Dr. Lang supposes that either the " system or the men must have been bad ! " Not necessarily so ; but, as it regards the Church mission, a mistake was committed at the commencement of their labours. It was believed that civilization, morality, and the mechanical arts might be taught simultaneously, by the silent but powerful influence of living example. But God has never yet sanctioned with His blessing the inculcation of any system of ethics, that has taken the initiative in reforming mankind, although it may have been proposed to supplement it with the gospel of Christ. The moral principles of the scheme may have been good ; but, viewing them abstractedly, we may ask, By what process could they be rendered practically beneficial ? My crops may be languishing under the intense heat of a vertical sun ; the clouds that are slowly moving over the fields may be laden with refreshing moisture ; but by what mechanical contrivance am I to extract it ? God Himself, who has wrapped it up in these clouds, must put the laws of gravitation in motion, bring it down from the heavens, and spread it over my lands with His own hand. So in the regeneration of the world, the gospel must do every thing : the process is too lofty to be conducted to any satisfactory issue by human sagacity. Civilization, with all its train of blessings, is, after all, " of the earth, earthy."

To make a moral being of a savage is "the workmanship of God ; a new creation in Christ Jesus unto good works." Produce this change by the preaching of the gospel, and you at once raise a nation in the scale of intelligence, civilization, and morality ; for while there can be no sound morality without it, morality and every virtue will be coeval with the change itself. The mistake to which we have alluded consisted in not recognising this principle, and in introducing a merely mechanical agency. Satan had taken care, before the colonizing crisis came on, to strengthen all his natural defences by a fresh importation of auxiliaries from France. That country, at the instigation of the Baron de Thierry, sent over a Catholic bishop, and a body of subordinates, who established themselves on the Hokianga. It is due to the baron to say, that he denied having any connexion with the bishop and his party ; but it is equally due to truth, to inform the reader that there were strong grounds for believing that he first suggested it to France, and that the indifferent attitude he assumed when they arrived, was the consequence of his having discovered, in the mean time, that they could not now advance his political projects. The bishop called upon the country to submit to his episcopal authority!   He discredited the Protestant scriptures, and pretended to the exclusive possession of the truth.   The English and the Wesleyan churches he represented as being heretical, their teachers unauthorized, and the thousands they had instructed and baptized as being henceforth under his spiritual charge, and subject to his ecclesiastical jurisdiction.   He distributed crosses, and pictures of the blessed Virgin, which were eagerly received by the people, and worn in their ears and about their dress as ornaments.   He had the audacity to appeal to the Catholics of Europe, for pecuniary aid to sustain "so important a mission!"   This arrogance was rendered the more intolerable, since none of the members of this Popish hierarchy could either read or write the Maori language.   In learning the native tongue they employed as teachers some of the most depraved persons in the neighbourhood.   By their aid, they made a translation of the Ten Commandments; and, while the commandments themselves were mutilated, the translation was contemptible.   Their association with such scandalous tutors excited the suspicion of the natives, and greatly injured their character.   They were, however, very active, and succeeded in disturbing, for a season, the whole settlement.

To counteract their influence, the missionaries ordered one thousand copies of the New Testament in Maori, which had been printed by the brethren of the Church mission.   The Wesleyan press was worked with energy, and supplied many thousands of papers and tracts, illustrative of the errors of Popery, and confirmatory of the doctrines and worship of Protestantism.   The native mind was every where roused from apathy, and deeply agitated.   Twenty Wesleyan chapels had been built, in a comparatively short time, in the Waikato district, and many hundreds of souls were anxiously seeking instruction.   Towards the close of the year two of the brethren made a voyage round the southern extremity of the northern island ; and along the whole line of coast they met with one continuous appeal for teachers and books.

On the 10th of May, 1840, the ship "Triton" entered the Hokianga, having on board the Rev. John Waterhouse, a seasonable re-inforcement of missionaries, and a fresh supply of stores and provisions.   Mr. Waterhouse visited several stations, preached to the natives, inspected the schools, and expressed his gratification at witnessing such undeniable evidences of a vital and practical Christianity.   Having completed his arrangements on the Hokianga, he resumed his voyage to the Friendly Islands, leaving fifteen missionaries in New Zealand, with fifteen hundred communicants, and appointing Mr. Bumby to exercise a fraternal supervision over all the interests of the mission.   Mr.

Bumby accompanied Mr. Waterhouse to Kawia. On parting with his friends on board the "Triton," he resolved to pass through the Waikato country, to pay a visit to Mr. Fairbourn of the Church mission, on the river Thames. Mr. Fairbourn pressed him to remain all night; but, being anxious about his sister, whom he had left at home, and having confidence in the nautical skill of his natives, he attempted to reach Wangari by water, and perished, with thirteen others, by the upsetting of the canoe, on the 26th of June. He was a young man of an amiable disposition, deep piety, respectable abilities, and ardent zeal. Had he been spared to acquire a competent acquaintance with the native tongue, and maturity of judgment, he would have been a great acquisition to the mission.

Active preparations were commenced for translating and printing various portions of the Old Testament in the native language. Upwards of one hundred and eighty adults and twenty-nine children had been lately baptized; besides fifty adults and several children, who had been baptized by the brethren while on a visit to Oruru. The district-meeting, recently held, appointed one of its members to travel overland to Port Nicholson, in order to make preliminary arrangements for the formation of a new station there. The journey occupied three months, the distance being at least five hundred miles. The undertaking was at once laborious and dangerous. "Imagine," says the traveller, "one trembling on a precipice, climbing mountains, traversing wilds, plunging through bogs, wading rivers, penetrating dense, impervious forests, now drenched with rain, then burning in the sun, and travelling sometimes for days without meeting a single individual; and you will have some conception of this journey." On his way he visited the station at Kawia: here he "saw the grace of God and was glad, and exhorted them all to cleave unto the Lord with full purpose of heart." He observed the barrel of a gun hung up in one place, and used, as a substitute for a bell, to summon the people to public worship. "Blessed be God," he exclaimed, "the gospel of peace has triumphed over the demon of war here; for they have beaten their swords into ploughshares, and their spears into pruning-hooks." Some parts of the country were fertile and beautiful, while other parts were desolate and thinly populated. Their path led them to the magnificent lake called Taupa, which covers a surface of at least two hundred miles. The neighbourhood abounds with hot springs and boiling pools. The stupendous volcanic mountain, Tangariro, was in action, sending out dense volumes of smoke. At no remote distance stood the snowy mountain, called Ruapaka, whose crested summit penetrates the clouds, and is seen from the sea on either coast.

This district is frequently shaken by earthquakes, which the natives regard as being indicative of approaching calamity. For five days they travelled along the side of a snowy range of mountains, without meeting with a single inhabitant, or the vestige of a dwelling. They at last reached the river Wanganui, whence their road lay along the sea-coast to Port Nicholson. In travelling this distance, about sixty miles, they found above three thousand natives, who eagerly desired to have teachers. On entering Port Nicholson, the missionary and his attendants were surprised to witness the effects that had been produced by the genius and industry of a few Europeans in a comparatively short time. Up to a very recent period there was but one white man upon these shores.

The agent of the New-Zealand Company fixed upon Port Nicholson as the seat of their first colony, and landed twelve hundred English emigrants in 1840. The Honourable H. W. Petre calls this "a bold proceeding on the part of the Company, and still more so on that of the emigrants." But to remove those people and their families sixteen thousand miles from their native country, before the Company had provided even a landing-place for them, was a proceeding alike repugnant to justice and humanity, and might have been attended with consequences still more disastrous than any that ensued. On inquiry, the missionary ascertained that the Company had taken possession of the entire harbour, with the exception of *one tenth, which they generously reserved for the natives.*

The ship "Aurora" arrived, and landed an additional one hundred and eighty emigrants. This importation awakened the jealousy of the natives, and led them to inquire whether "the whole of the white tribe had not now arrived." Just at this time the Catholic bishop, and several co-adjutors, came to pay their first visit of inspection to the infant colony. As usual, his lordship magnified himself, his office, and his church: he informed the emigrants and others, that "nearly one half the entire population had become Catholics." All classes urged the Wesleyan minister to remain with them; but his duty had been defined by his brethren, and he could not prolong his stay. After accomplishing the object of his visit, he went on board the ship "Atlas," which carried him through a boisterous sea to the Bay of Islands in six days.

The fresh accession of missionaries, received by the "Triton," enabled the brethren to undertake a mission to Taranaki. The distance was about six days' sail from Mangungu. They learned that Taranaki formed an important centre, and that within a circumference of a hundred miles there lived several thousands of natives. The missionary and his family were cordially received, and commenced their laborious occupations of building and teaching, under the most encouraging circumstances. This district is remarkable for the beauty and diversity of its scenery. The most magnificent object within the range of the eye is Haupápá, or Mount Egmont. It rises upwards of nine thousand feet above the level of the ocean, and was formerly the site of a very active volcano. The base commences about three miles from the beach. This mountain answers all the purposes of a barometer to the natives: if any nebulous cloud rests on, or shadows, the lofty summit, bad weather is predicted; but if it be clear in zenith, the fishermen go to sea in their canoes without hesitation. "The whole of this day," says Dr. Selwyn, " we have enjoyed noble views of Egmont, the splendid monarch of Taranaki. It rises at once out of the plain, without other hills to break its apparent height. Its base is surrounded by almost impassable forests; the skirts of which are in flames, for the purpose of clearing the land for cultivation. On the following morning, the mountain came out gloriously from his veil of clouds, and gave me a sight of his snowy summit. On going out into the garden of Mr. Cooke, the view burst upon me of the whole mountain, running up in a white cone above the clouds, which were still clinging to it midway. At the extremity of the grounds ran one of those beautifully clear and rapid streams which abound throughout Taranaki; and all around the fresh foliage of a New-Zealand spring, tipping all the evergreens with a bright and sparkling verdure, formed a base upon which the white peak of the mountain seemed to repose. Taranaki is a lovely country, distinguished even among the many natural beauties which I have seen."

There was nothing, however, in the social condition of the people in keeping with the harmony of nature. In former years, the missionaries looked over the country with deep solicitude, gazed in pity upon the disorderly groups that attended their conversational meetings on the Lord's day, and met with but little encouragement from the young savages under instruction in the Sunday-schools. Writing under the pressure of discouragement, they said, "Where are the streaming eyes, the heaving breast, the uplifted hands, the faltering tongue, the contrite, broken heart? Seldom is the monotony of our usual duties interrupted with the cries of, 'God be merciful to me a sinner!' or, 'What must I do to be saved?' and seldom are we gladdened with the voice of praise and thanksgiving for the mercy and pardoning love of God. And yet, the more gloomy and overcast the prospect may be, the stronger reason is there for our continued labours and prayers, and that we should still go on sowing the precious seed, though it be with weeping; for 'they that sow in tears shall reap in joy.'"

It would have been difficult to have convinced those Christian men that they were on the eve of realizing, in their own experience, the fulfilment of the prophetic announcement just quoted. And yet, during the current year, 1842, they were privileged to witness such a baptism of evangelical truth as had not occurred since the first introduction of Christianity into the land.

The British and Foreign Bible Society, having completed a considerable edition of the New Testament in the Maori language, sent out 10,000 copies to the Wesleyan missions. These volumes were apportioned to the different stations, and received with acclamations of joy. Every marketable commodity was offered by the natives for those books. Many even learned to read, that they might be entitled to buy one. In one place ten pounds' worth of *kúmara* was presented as an expression of gratitude to the British and Foreign Bible Society for having sent the precious gift. The circulation of the word of God effectually checked the progress of Popery, and impressed a new character upon the religion of the natives.

The vast number of emigrants landed upon their shores by the New-Zealand Company, some of whom had been members of the Wesleyan church in Great Britain, led to the multiplication of stations and the erection of new premises; and added greatly to the perplexity, responsibility, and labour of the missionaries. Having new and extended spheres of usefulness thus suddenly thrown open to them, and a distressing paucity of appropriate means, they were under the necessity of pressing into their service all the available resources of both settlers and native converts. But the Lord had, for some time, been raising up a native agency to meet this crisis, so that several of their members were now so far advanced in knowledge and experience as to be able to fill, with some degree of respectability and efficiency, the situations of Sunday-school teachers, leaders, and local preachers. The arrival of another 5,000 copies of the New-Zealand Testament from England convinced the brethren that the church at home was in earnest, and led them to struggle with labours and local difficulties almost overwhelming.

The following works had been conducted through their own press; namely, 5,000 scripture lessons, 3,000 copies of an elementary school-book, 6,700 catechisms and prayers, and 6,700 prayers and hymns. At this period the missionaries occupied 13 stations; there were 3,259 persons in church-fellowship, and above 4,000 children in the schools.

But neither the liberality of the friends at home, nor the labours of the brethren and their press in the colony, could keep pace with the progress of the natives, and the increasing demand for teachers and books. Writing the civil history of the country, Brown observes, " Short as was the space of time from the formation of the colony in January, 1840, until Captain Fitzroy's arrival in December, 1843, the natives had, in the mean time, been making vast progress in the knowledge of *their own rights and interests, and also in intelligence;* and those tribes in the habit of frequenting the townships were fast adopting and conforming themselves to the manners of the Europeans. In the townships the system of barter has ceased, and money has become the medium of exchange. The natives can calculate the price as well as the Europeans. Many of the chiefs appear in town dressed like gentlemen, and behave as such. They have cultivated fields, sheep, cows, bullocks, horses, ploughs, and pigs. A native woman, *brought up with the missionaries,* is an excellent seamstress, and rears large quantities of poultry and other stock, which she brings to Auckland for sale, usually putting the proceeds in the bank. A chief, living at a point on the Waikato, keeps an hotel for the convenience of passengers, and a man-servant to wait at table, which is furnished with a cloth, plates, forks, and knives. Many of the chiefs are removing to the neighbourhood of Auckland, the capital; a proof of the progress of civilization, and of their desire to cultivate a friendly intercourse with the settlers."

The missionaries had been twenty years in bringing the natives to a knowledge of letters, and to the adoption of the mental and practical habits just described. Yet this general improvement in the state of society, and extension of knowledge, is not, say the brethren, wholly attributable to the "direct influence and labours of the European missionaries, but also to the quenchless ardour and zealous co-operation of those few natives who were originally converted to the Christian religion. Having imbibed its principles, and adopted its discipline and formalities themselves, they have gone about among their friends, from *pa* to *pa,* and from village to village, teaching, and exhorting, and reproving, and scattering the seed of Divine truth with both hands. Thus it is that the word has spread, and been so rapidly and extensively diffused amongst the people; and though many have doubtless espoused the form of Christianity from secondary motives, yet have they by this means placed themselves within the reach of the sound of the gospel, which we have a right to expect will issue in the saving application of its power."

This work of national regeneration was, however, suddenly checked by circumstances which we record with sorrow. The Rev. Samuel Marsden originated and superintended the New-Zealand mission until a bishop was appointed to New South Wales. New Zealand being a dependency of that colony, its ecclesiastical affairs were then placed under the jurisdiction of the bishop of Sydney. His lordship visited the islands in 1838, held an ordination and two confirmations, and consecrated burial-grounds at Paihia and Kororarika. New Zealand being separated from New South Wales, and the directors of the New-Zealand Company having voted considerable grants of money and land towards the establishment of an episcopal see, the government acceded to the arrangement; and on the 17th of October, 1841, the Rev. G. A. Selwyn, of St. John's College, Cambridge, was consecrated as the first bishop of New Zealand. He arrived in his diocese on the 30th of May. After calmly reflecting upon his new position, he wrote as follows: "I find myself placed in a position such as was never granted to any English bishop before, with power to *mould the institutions of the church from the beginning according to true principles.*" "I am fettered by no usages, subject to no fashions, influenced by no inspections of other men: I can take that course which seems to be best, and pursue it with unobtrusive perseverance. When we have been strengthened in our *intrenched camp, we will sally forth.*"* Having created archdeacons, filled up other ecclesiastical offices, and supplied himself with confidential advisers, his lordship then "sallied forth." But against whom was the first attack directed? against the cruel and inhuman atrocities of the aborigines? or the licentious orgies of his own country-men? or the aggressions of Popery? No; there was a more serious obstruction than either of these in his way to episcopal supremacy: that once removed, the others might be dealt with as minor evils. There had grown up, simultaneously with his own mission, another branch of the Protestant Church, very much like his own in doctrine, in its forms of worship, and in its administration of Christian ordinances, but not under episcopal jurisdiction. Up to this period the head-quarters of the Church brethren had been at the Bay of Islands, and those of the Wesleyans at Hokianga; one sphere of operation stretching along the eastern coast as far as the river Thames and Poverty Bay; and the other along the western coast and Middle Island, as far as Kawia, Taranaki, Port Nicholson, Nelson, Cloudy Bay, and Otago, with only a narrow strip of land between them. The missionaries of both Societies had lived in peace, and laboured in harmony; "the native converts of the one connexion being treated in all respects as if they were members of the other, and wisely kept in ignorance of the formalities of religion which distinguished the one set of missionaries from the other." "No sooner does the bishop arrive, however, than a line of distinction is immediately drawn between the Wesleyan and the Church-mission natives, the former not being allowed, as formerly, to

* Visitation Journal, part i.

partake of the sacrament with the latter. The Wesleyan missionaries were represented as not being of Divine authority, and their teachings decried as unwarranted and useless. The rite of baptism performed by them must be repeated by the bishop or his clergy, in order to be effectual. In his ardour for making converts to the Church, he has not rested satisfied with promulgating the doctrines of Christianity, but has waged war with his fellow-labourers, by denouncing their teachings as unsound. As this subject is of the deepest importance to the peace and welfare of the country, as well as to the spread of Christianity among the natives, every information on the point should be communicated to the British people."* Hitherto the missionaries of both Societies had laboured separately, each in his own communion, and in accordance with those distinctions of internal arrangement which are therein to be recognised; yet it had been a separation of *love*;—separate in form, but united in object, in affection, in sympathy. But his lordship, in his primary visitation of his clergy and the different stations of the Church mission, had created a considerable sensation by his bold and novel observations on the Wesleyan mission. That he might be better understood by the natives, he condescended to employ some of their figures of speech, describing the Wesleyan Church as a "*crooked branch*, and its people as *a fallen tribe*, who had no *scriptural ministers.*"

One of his lordship's clergymen had, in the exuberance of his zeal, crossed the line of demarcation, and obtruded himself into the Wesleyan fold. He had marked with the sign of the cross "several persons who had been baptized by the Wesleyan missionaries, and admitted them to partake of the Lord's supper, their baptism being now complete." The same clergyman, Mr. T., who knew but little of the Maori tongue, "travelled from Wanganui to New Plymouth, marking with the sign of the cross all who would submit to it, and admitting them, whether prepared or otherwise, as worthy members of the Church of England, to the Lord's supper."

The Wesleyan missionaries agreed, at their district-meeting, to address his lordship on the subject of these irregularities. He replied to their communication on the 31st of October, 1843. In his reply, he avowed sentiments he was only, till then, suspected of holding. "He declared them to be schismatics, their ordination to be invalid, and consequently their baptisms to be, at most, the acts of laymen." The brethren now felt it to be due to their own character, and to the relation in which they stood to their numerous churches, to address a public remonstrance to his lordship. In this document they inform

* Brown's "New Zealand and its Aborigines."

him, that their mission had been established above twenty years; that not less than £80,000 had been expended in its support; and that some of the most influential and important tribes in New Zealand, including many thousands of natives, were under their instruction. They complain that his lordship should have decided, "that in future the utmost distance is to be observed between the Wesleyans and Churchmen; that separate services are to be established in the same village; that the attendants of one native hut are no longer to enter the threshold, or resort to the services, of another native hut; that Wesleyan ministers are to be forbidden to preach in all consecrated places; that their ministrations are not to be attended by any but their own people; and that in some *pas*, (as at Wareatea, Mokotuna, and Warea,) they are not to be allowed to preach at all *within the boundaries of the village fence*." They urge upon his lordship the necessity of calmly reflecting upon the consequences of these exclusive and intolerant arrangements upon the principles and habits of such a people as the New-Zealanders. Having stated the case clearly and fully, they left the issue with God and the public.

The bishop soon found that he had evoked a spirit which he was not able to repress. "I was much pleased," he remarks, "with my stay at Ruapuke; though the advantage of it, in a religious point of view, was much impaired by the *dissensions among the natives*. Here, *as in other places*, there was too much discussion about *Weteri* and *Huhi* (Wesley and the Church). We do not wonder at the controversies which are raging at home, when, even in the distant part of this most remote of all countries, in places hitherto unvisited by English missionaries, the spirit of controversy, so congenial as it seems to the fallen nature of man, is every where found to prevail, in many cases to the entire exclusion of all simplicity of faith."[*] We appeal to the archdeacon of Waiapu and the senior clergy, whether *Weteri* and *Hahi* (Wesley and the Church) had not lived and laboured together as Christian brethren up to the very day on which Bishop Selwyn landed in New Zealand. While the Catholic clergy hailed the Protestant bishop and his Puseyism as valuable auxiliaries, they remained true to their own principles. They told the people that Bishop Selwyn and his missionaries were as great heretics as the Wesleyans; and that if they would be saved, they must renounce both, and join the only true Catholic and apostolic church.

For a season the half-instructed and half-enlightened portions of the natives were completely bewildered. They knew that for a number of years the agents of the Church mission had instructed their countrymen, without baptizing one of them; and

* Visitation Tour, part iii., p. 23.

z

were surprised to observe that, after the bishop came, his clergy baptized many without suitable instruction, and admitted them to the Lord's supper, the most sacred institution of Christianity. The Catholic bishop made the natives members of his church by baptism, and giving them crucifixes; the Protestant bishop, by baptism, with the sign of the cross, and the sacramental cup. This is the true key to Bishop Selwyn's success. "Auckland," says he, "contains a population of 1,900 persons, of whom more than 1,100 are registered as *members of the Church of England*."* But what a melancholy spectacle, to witness men clothed with literary honours, and acknowledging the Divine authority of the scriptures, allowing themselves to be so far influenced by superstition or self-interest, as to substitute externalism for the "weightier matters of the law," and thus to trifle with the realities of religion, and the solemnities of eternity!

How different from these cases was the apostolic method of induction into the church, as exemplified in the history of the eunuch, Cornelius, the jailer, and others! But this state of things is one of the peculiarities of the times. The claims of the Bible to be the only authentic revelation of the will of God to man, seem to be almost universally recognised. The confederates of Voltaire and Frederick of Prussia have died off; and it is a singular fact, that no individual amongst the nations of Europe, distinguished either as a statesman or a writer, stands forth as the avowed champion of their sentiments. The cause of the Bible is now injured by men who, while they admit its Divine inspiration, apply to it erroneous principles of interpretation, and thus weaken its claims upon the faith and practice of man. The condition of the church is equally anomalous. The sources of her weakness are not to be sought in the want of political power, wealth, or learning, nor in the hostile attitude of the nations, whether civilized or barbarous; but in her own social state,—her want of spirituality, producing party-spirit, the adulteration of the truth, and a fierce conflict about the mere symbols of Christianity. If the church possess any inherent power to remedy these enormous evils, she ought to put it forth to protect herself from the scandal of such a connexion, and, by a vigorous and decisive application of discipline, to insure the separation of the abettors of such inconsistencies from her communion.

Intending emigrants should read with extreme caution what has been written by parties deeply interested in the colonization of New Zealand. The statements of the bishop himself are not always to be depended upon. The accounts transmitted to the British government by its responsible functionaries are very dis-

* Journal, part i., pp. 8, 12.

similar to the pleasing pictures drawn by the soft and plastic hand of his lordship. The following is an official communication of recent date: "The number of Europeans now resident in New Zealand amounts to 26,000 souls: these persons are scattered over nine different settlements. One of these settlements contains a population of 9,000, while a population exceeding 17,000 is scattered over the other eight. There is no communication between these different settlements, except on horseback; and they are divided from each other by mountains, and hills, and rivers, over which there are no bridges."*

If the Wesleyans wish to spread evangelical truth over these beautiful islands, they must strengthen their mission by fortifying their position, and greatly increasing the number of labourers. While the party differences alluded to disturbed religious society, a variety of political causes conspired to change the entire aspect of public affairs. The vacillating policy of the government on the one hand, and the injudicious proceedings of the New Zealand Company on the other, led to the most disastrous consequences. The government had lost the confidence of all classes; while the native mind, roused by a sense of injustice, sought for opportunities to retaliate upon the colonists. As might have been foreseen, this state of things led to avowed hostilities, skirmishes, and massacres, between the natives and the civil power; and but for the prudent and conciliatory measures adopted by Governor Fitzroy, and the hearty co-operation of the missionaries, not only must the general peace of the country have been sacrificed, but, in all probability, the very existence of the colony itself.

At a meeting of the chiefs, held at Waitangi, in February, 1840, the political sovereignty over the islands was ceded to Her Majesty Queen Victoria. There are only two ways of getting possession of a country,—by physical force, or by a fair and equitable purchase. The latter seems to be the most likely means of securing the blessing of Almighty God upon a newly-acquired territory. The above treaty of Waitangi professed to be based upon this principle: for while the chiefs were required to yield to "Her Majesty the right of pre-emption over such lands as the proprietors thereof might be *disposed to alienate,* Her Majesty granted to those chiefs the *full, exclusive,* and undisturbed possession of their lands and estates, forests, fisheries, and other property which they may possess, *so long as it is their wish and desire to retain them in their possession.*" Had these stipulations been honestly carried out by Her Majesty's government, it would have saved much bloodshed, and some thousands of persons from pecuniary ruin. Unfortunately, the policy of the

* Earl Desart, June 23rd, 1852.

government was in conformity with the principles embodied in the " Land-Claims' Bill," which had passed the Legislative Council of New South Wales. That Bill assumed, that "the New-Zealanders, being wandering savages, *had no right to the soil of their own country !*" The chiefs, who had been parties to the above treaty, were indignant when they found that the right of pre-emption, as explained by the practice of the government surveyors, just meant the right of the queen to buy their lands when she pleased, where she pleased, and at her own price. They charged the government with the violation of the treaty; and, after warning the surveyors not to persist in their aggressions, proceeded to expel them from their territories. This brought them at once into collision with the regular troops.

In vindicating the part which he had taken in the massacre of Wairau, Rauparaha stated the whole case with perspicuity and eloquence, in the presence of His Excellency the governor, and an assembly of four hundred Europeans and natives. " Land," said he, " has been the foundation of all our troubles. The English say that it is theirs; but who says so besides themselves ?" He then entered into a detail of the grounds of their dissatisfaction, and concluded by justifying himself and his countrymen in defending their rights. After a silence of half an hour, His Excellency rose and addressed the assembly: " I have heard," he observed, "both sides, and now give my decision. The English were wrong in building houses upon land to which they had no claim; in trying to apprehend you, who had committed no crime; and in measuring your land, in opposition to your repeated refusal to allow them to do so. But you were wrong in resisting the authority of the magistrate; and very wrong in killing men who had surrendered and implored mercy. As you repent of your conduct, I will not avenge their death. I will punish the English if they do what is unjust; and your chiefs must help me to prevent the natives from doing wrong. In future, let us dwell peaceably." In this decision all acquiesced.

But notwithstanding the satisfactory adjustment of the misunderstandings occasioned by the tragedy of Wairau, the greatest excitement prevailed throughout the country relative to the rights of ownership of the land. The arrival, at a subsequent period, of a dispatch from Lord Grey, then colonial secretary, greatly increased this excitement; for while his lordship recognised the treaty of Waitangi, he applied a new and restrictive principle of interpretation to that treaty. The dispatch assumed, that while some parts of the soil were in *possession of the natives,* and could only be obtained by purchase, there were large portions of waste or uncultivated lands which the government might take without even asking the consent of the chiefs. " The savage inhabitants of New Zealand," said his lordship, " have no right of property in land which *they do not occupy.*" The missionaries, who, with six hundred chiefs, had been parties to the original contract, regarded this as sanctioning a practical departure from the obvious meaning and intention of the treaty, and protested against it. They maintained, 1. That the application of this new principle would enable the government, under one pretext or another, to take possession of nearly the whole soil of the country. 2. That there were no such lands as the dispatch described in New Zealand; for those lands not under the cultivation of the natives, were claimed as forests, as hunting-grounds, or as yielding the fern-root, on which they chiefly subsisted. The treaty of Waitangi stipulated, that "their estates, forests, fisheries, and other properties, should remain in the exclusive and undisturbed possession of the native chiefs." 3. That to carry the new interpretation of the treaty into effect, would inevitably involve the most disastrous consequences. The natives would regard the missionaries, at whose instance they had signed the treaty, as deceivers; they would abandon Christianity; they would again assume the ferocity of the savage; there would be a combination of all the tribes to resist an unjust encroachment; war and murder would, as formerly, spread over the land; the mission establishments, with every British settlement in the country, would be broken up; and the utter annihilation of British power, or of the Maori population, ensue.

These views were embodied in an elaborate memorial, and transmitted to Lord Grey, by Dr. Beecham. It is satisfactory to know, that such statesmen as Lord Stanley and Mr. Gladstone coincided in the same views. In replying to the Wesleyan memorial, Lord Grey assured the committee that he had not contemplated the violation of the above treaty, and that instructions should be sent out to the governor of New Zealand to preserve it in its integrity.

In the mean time, the natives felt an utter contempt for the government, and seized the slightest pretexts for showing the depth of their malignity. The British flag flying on the hill above Kororarika began to be regarded as a proof that the sovereignty of the native chiefs was at an end. It was supposed that signals were made from it to prevent the vessels of other nations from entering the port. In August, 1844, Heke the chief assembled a body of warriors, proceeded to Kororarika, ascended the hill, and cut down the flag-staff. The governor immediately dispatched a vessel to Sydney for troops, which returned to the Bay of Islands in three weeks, with two hundred men. The flag-staff was replaced, and protected by several guns. Block-houses were also erected, at convenient distances, from the beach to the summit of the hill, and defended by the military. Notwithstanding these formidable obstacles, Heke and his warriors attacked the Europeans at every point. He carried the heights, cut down the flag-staff, and compelled the military to take refuge on board their ships. The " Hazard " opeued a fire of shells upon the natives ; but they maintained their position, and only retired when they had laid the flourishing town of Kororarika in ashes. An eye-witness observed, " In the bosom of the dark hills the smoke of the town 'went up like the smoke of a furnace.'" The English buried their dead, and sent off above three hundred refugees and wounded, by sea, to Auckland.

This affair created the greatest consternation throughout the colony. The governor held meetings with the chiefs in the neighbourhood, and soon learned how deep-rooted were the sources of grievance, not only regarding the land questions, but also as to the customs' regulations, and the obstacles thereby interposed to the freedom of their commerce. This discovery induced the governor, in order to prevent a general rupture with the natives, and, at the same time, do them justice, to declare the Bay of Islands a *free port*. This bold measure acted like magic on both natives and Europeans ; and at a conference held immediately afterwards with Heke's tribe, and those in alliance with them, they acknowledged their satisfaction, and agreed that all disturbances for the future should cease. In the course of a few weeks the feelings of all parties were completely changed, the bustle and activity of business took the place of languor and despair, and the foundation of the prosperity of the colony was at last laid.

To the Church and Wesleyan missionaries this was a season of extreme trial. They retained the entire confidence of the natives, and were often obliged to step in as mediators between them and the New-Zealand Company on the one hand, and the government on the other. Considering the arduous circumstances in which they were placed, the bishop of New Zealand might justly complain of the conduct of those who " misrepresented the government and *slandered* the missionaries."

It would be a great dereliction of duty were we entirely to overlook " slanders," that are reiterated to this day by a certain portion of the colonial press. The case is clearly and forcibly stated against the missionaries by Hursthouse. " In contemplating the condition of those beautiful islands," he observes, " after the commencement of their colonization, *all men* must feel indignant that the former hostility of the colonial office to the New-Zealand Company, servilely copied by the early colonial governors ; and the settled hatred of the *missionary clique* to any interest but its own, virtually expressed by Mr. Protector Clarke, should have *caused the ruin* of so many of the early settlers, the *pioneers of civilization;* should have driven away *hundreds* of excellent men to other colonies, and so fearfully blasted the prosperity of the country. Nor is it to be forgotten that, under these rulers and their missionary promoters, the native interest, which they *professed specially to foster*, did in reality suffer more than any other." "In estimating the character and disposition of the natives, they have, however, been judged too favourably as to what they *are*, but not so as to what they may become, by proper treatment. It is said, that they have renounced cannibalism and Heathenism, in favour of potatoes and Christianity; whereupon 'Exeter-Hall' has declared them a regenerated and noble race. It is true, they are no longer cannibals; and equally true, that they have made such advances in Christianity as to be already divided into Catholics, Episcopalians, and Wesleyans. The abolition of cannibalism is a *great step in civilization*, and obedience to the forms of religion may tend to humanize the savage; but it is a great error to suppose, that, as a people, the New-Zealanders are yet converts to Christianity in aught save mere externals." The true ground of complaint is disclosed in the following passage: "In dealing with a Company opposed by the colonial office, Captain Fitzroy was *blinded by maudlin senti-mentality* for '*oppressed slaves*,' and spurred on by the *missionary clique*, so that he came to judgment in a spirit which soon stripped the unfortunate settlers of *their land*, and virtually dispossessed the Company of the *fairest territory they had ever acquired!*"

As regards the governor, we may just observe, that he was acting in a conspicuous theatre, with the eyes of Europe on his proceedings, and under a solemn conviction of his responsibility to the British people. As to the missionary *clique*, comprehending the Church and Wesleyan missionaries, it is sufficient to admit that they did successfully oppose the attempts of an English company of speculators to *deprive the natives of their acknowledged rights*, and to adduce the author himself to refute his other allegations. "The natives of this settlement," he says, "have already made such progress in education, chiefly through the philanthropic exertions of the Episcopal and Wesleyan ministers, that, of males between fifteen and thirty, it is estimated that three out of four can both read and write. The natives deserve great praise for their *honesty, sobriety*, and *peaceful habits*. They are becoming anxious to acquire stock, and already possess horses, and several head of cattle, of which they take great care. The tribe inhabiting the country south of the settlement, who are rich in native wealth, contracted with our millwright for the erection of three small grist mills; two of which, lately completed at a cost of £300, have been paid for entirely in pigs."

It was scarcely necessary for this author to have gone out of his way to censure the missionaries, in reference to the New-Zealand Company, since he himself sufficiently accounts for the failure of their enterprise, by the mal-administration of their affairs. "It is notorious in the colony," he remarks, "that if the New-Zealand Company had confined their attention to one or two places, their efforts and large expenditure would have been productive of more advantageous results. One of the greatest errors in the colonization of the country, has been the hasty planting of so many scattered settlements. The distance, by the west coast, from Auckland to the southern settlements is shown by the following table :—

From Auckland to New Plymouth is 126 miles.			Population, 1,800.	
From Ditto to Nelson	is 280 miles.		Ditto	2,100.
From Ditto to Whanganui	is 210 miles.		Ditto	100.
From Ditto to Wellington	is 300 miles.		Ditto	2,500.

"Several of these settlements have no commercial intercourse, while their distance from each other renders co-operation for mutual protection impossible. Auckland enjoys an excellent port, with a commanding position on two seas. Wellington possesses a fine harbour, with great facilities for trade. Nelson has considerable growing capabilities. Taranaki, (New Plymouth,) with a population of nine hundred souls, is, after all, the garden of New Zealand."

The conduct of those missionaries was viewed in a very different light by a gentleman better acquainted with all the circumstances of the case than Mr. Hursthouse. "The Wesleyan missionaries in New Zealand have acted the part of ambassadors of Christ: they have been enabled, by their influence, by their character, by their power among the people, to induce the natives of that country to accept a treaty which, I must say, is one of the justest treaties that was ever made between this country and any other; and I thank this Society for having come forward about a year ago, and assisted by their influence in maintaining the force of that treaty. I trust that the missionaries of this Society will continue, as they have hitherto done, to maintain those *just liberties which the natives of foreign countries have a right to demand at the hands of Britain.*"* "It is a strong expression," says Bishop Selwyn, "but I use it advisedly, that 'the land theory,' if it had been acted upon, would have made the New-Zealanders a nation of murderers!"

On the 17th of March, 1844, the Rev. Walter Lawry landed at Auckland, having been appointed to succeed the late Rev.

---

* Sir Edward N. Buxton, 1849.

PYRAMID FOR FOOD, ERECTED AT A NEW ZEALAND FEAST.

John Waterhouse. Governor Fitzroy received him with respectful attention, and assured him of his readiness to promote the objects of his mission. Mr. Lawry found the colony in a very depressed state: labour being scarce, and wages low, many were reduced to indigence. But, in regard to the mission, he observes, "All that I see and hear is satisfactory: every where the brethren are in good repute. On the stations the people are generally advanced in knowledge and morals, far above others, who, in some instances, I fear, have only copied the bad example of foreigners. The missionaries are publishing the gospel, and propagating those great principles on which, under God, the stability of political institutions and the welfare of society mainly depend."

The native tribes held a great festival on the 28th of April. The missionaries attended, with their respective tribes, from a distance of two hundred to three hundred miles. The provisions had been prepared and laid out for many days before their arrival. A wall of potatoes, in flax-baskets, five feet high, and three feet thick, extended above a quarter of a mile; and upon a rail over them hung twenty thousand sharks. There were twenty thousand baskets, containing more than one hundred tons of potatoes. The governor and his officers of state honoured the festival with a visit. All the ferocity of the savage was displayed in the war-dance; but, the missionaries being present, the Christian portion of the assembly stood aloof from their wild, raving, half-naked countrymen. On Sunday the chapel was filled three times; morning and evening, by a serious and respectable congregation; and in the afternoon, by native members of the church, who partook of the Lord's supper. They were of different tribes, who had come to the great feast, and had not met before on such an occasion. Mr. Whiteley delivered an appropriate address, and Mr. Hobbs read the service. They were then joined by the other missionaries present, and administered the bread and wine to their tattooed and other sable brethren. The scene was singularly affecting: "I never witnessed," said the general superintendent, "a missionary meeting half so telling as was this service, in favour of our missions. Such savages so tamed, such proud and haughty warriors so humble at the feet of Jesus, made its own appeal, without the magic touch of platform eloquence. They showed most clearly that they both knew and felt what they were about. And while the validity of the Wesleyan ministry is called in question by the Popish and Protestant bishops of the country, here were the seals of their ministry, 'epistles known and read of all men.' It was one of the most interesting demonstrations of the power of the gospel I had ever witnessed. Many besides myself saw the grace of God, and were glad."

Two days after, a public meeting was held, for the purpose of promoting the establishment of a seminary for the education of a select number of native youths in the English language; that they might have access to English literature, and thus become efficient teachers of their countrymen in matters of religion and civilization. The public meeting and the government heartily sanctioned the institution, and recommended its early establishment. The governor gave to the institution a suburban allotment of seven acres of land, close to Auckland: he also granted about two hundred acres, for agricultural purposes, five miles from the town. It was expected that suitable and extensive premises might be erected free of all expense to the parent society. The missionaries in the Friendly and Feejee Islands, regarding the proposed seminary as a substitute for Kingswood-school, heartily concurred in the proposal; and raised, among themselves and their friends, £1,000 towards the erection. By united exertion all difficulties were overcome, the premises were soon completed, and the contemplated benefits have since been fully realized. The general superintendent assembled the district committee; and, after a careful examination of the temporal and spiritual condition of the various stations, recorded his admiration of the judgment, zeal, and prudence with which the affairs of the mission had been conducted.

At a season like the present, when the grossest calumnies are propagated and believed respecting the "profligate expenditure" of missionary societies, it may not be deemed irrelevant to transcribe a memorandum, entered in his journal, by one of the brethren on retiring from this official meeting:—"The scale of expenditure has been reduced to the lowest possible amount. If it be reduced any lower, we shall begin to look with very sombre faces upon our poor children, as to what is to become of their education. Miserable enough in quality as New-Zealand education is, it costs much to obtain it: to educate them myself, is what my other duties will not allow."

The arrival of the refugees, consisting of out-settlers and missionaries from the Bay of Islands, created a great sensation in the public mind. "Unhappily," says a member of the legislative council, "the restrictions imposed upon commerce and the interminable land-question occasioned a rising of the natives. Three times was the staff, from which the emblem of British authority was displayed, cut down: the regular troops were faced in fair fight, and, though not beaten, the field was left in possession of the natives, who burned the township of Kororarika to the ground, and destroyed property to the amount of £60,000." The Popish converts were the most conspicuous in those atrocities. "The burning of Kororarika," say the brethren, "has spread terror throughout the colony, and placed the whole country in extraordinary circumstances. The refugees have sailed into port. All is bustle, the officers of government being engaged in making warlike preparations, fortifying the town, and training men to arms. Many are leaving for the neighbouring colonies; more would do so, had they the means, or were they at liberty. The regular troops have been beaten; a whole town has been plundered and burned; while the government is perfectly powerless, and obliged to intrench itself, without attempting to take the field against the natives. They plunder the colonists with impunity, shooting their cattle, and riding away with their horses; they cut down their fruit-trees, and set fire to their houses. Our lives will depend upon the measures taken by the governor. Nothing can now be done until two or three thousand troops arrive from England. How mysterious are the ways of Providence, that Popery and colonization should have been permitted to come in and lay waste this flourishing vineyard of the Lord!"

In a communication, dated "Wellington, May 2nd, 1846," they observe, "The prospect for this country is as gloomy as ever. Scarcely a day passes over without rumours, thick and fast, of war and its accompaniments. The natives who have been compelled to leave the river Hut, have strongly fortified themselves in one of the valleys of the Poniua harbour, where they are receiving large reinforcements from the interior. On the 15th they sallied forth from the bush, just before day-break, and attacked a company of fifty soldiers, stationed on the Hut: they killed eight and wounded three. They then retired into the woods, with the loss of only one man. All our people are loyal, and one of our chiefs has offered to join the troops with two hundred warriors. The government and the missionaries are blamed by some, and the Company by others; but the true cause of these calamities lies deeper than is generally supposed. In the midst of all, we labour on, through good report and evil report; and are cheered with several additions to the society. All the pews in the chapel here are let, and more are required. The native congregations are as good as we can expect; but until peace is restored, prosperity is out of the question. We see no deliverance, no way of escape, but in the living God. If the labour, life, and money employed in the work here, are to be turned to any beneficial account, the mission maintained in a state of efficiency, and the natives preserved from utter extinction, we must have more help."

The "state of society," they observe, "in this newly colonized and lately heathen country, is remarkable. Here are men of the world seeking their fortune; an array of military and naval men, 'like the English abroad,' and heathen natives and nominal Christians, sunk low indeed in the works of the flesh. Here is ' the Church,' whose bishop tells the natives that ours is no church, that we are not ministers, and that our people are deceived. Here is Popery direct from France: it serves the English bishop as he serves us; and declares that neither he nor his clergy are of the true church!"

Surrounded by such a state of things, the Christian natives were steady; and, while their religious fidelity was being severely tested, their progress in Christian experience was as obvious as it was satisfactory. In the following September, they were relieved in some degree from their deep solicitude, by numerous evidences of returning prosperity. "Of late," they remark, "a blessed influence has descended, most seasonably and graciously, on the Europeans and natives under our care: sound conversions are frequent; crowds attend the public worship of God; and, in the midst of war, our people are visited by the Prince of Peace, and testify, both by their lives and in the hour of death, the sufficiency of Divine grace."

At the love-feast held at Auckland, on October 5th, many of the natives were quite melted down to weeping and sobbing. Several powerful chiefs, fresh from the battle-field, were seen struggling in the pangs of godly sorrow, while the tears flowed down their tattooed, but manly, faces. Others were weeping tears of love, because Christ had revealed His mercy to their souls. We shall give the reader a sample of their experience. One said, "While Samuel," one of the young men, " preached, I fell from my seat, God showed me the greatness of my sins. Hell opened before me, and I prayed all day. For three days and nights my heart would not rest, or its trouble subside. While praying, on the following Friday, I heard the Spirit say my sins of theft, lying, adultery, and fighting, were all forgiven. The water of my eyes flowed abundantly. Great is the pain of my heart for the love I feel to the souls of my relations. Thus my experience continues." "I remember," said another, " my work in days gone by. I went to worship, heard preaching, met in class, was baptized, and received the sacrament of the Lord's supper. I thought this was religion. But when the word of God came home to my heart, I was afraid, and went to pray in secret. Whether I went to bed, or to work, my constant prayer was, that God would take away my sin. I, at last, obtained forgiveness." Hone said, "Under the preaching, God showed me hell: I saw the darkness, and my sins of many years. I had heard that man could not stretch out his arm to heaven, and blot out his sins with his own hand, and felt that I could not contend with God. I said, ' It is enough: I will make peace, and give up my heart to God.' Last month, on September 9th, I found the great peace of God: a voice called to my heart, 'Why tarriest thou?   Go and pray in secret for a new heart.'   I obeyed, and God manifested His love to me.   My joy now is the love of God in my heart, and I am for Him as long as I live."

And what is this but the primitive and apostolic faith working by love, and purifying the heart?   Truly we may address the subscribers to the New-Zealand mission in the sublime language of our Lord: "Blessed are your eyes, for they see: and your ears, for they hear.   For many prophets and righteous men have desired to see those things which ye see, and have not seen them; and to hear those things which ye hear, and have not heard them."

In many places the lay-helpers conducted the schools and public worship of God, in the absence of the missionaries, in the most solemn and edifying manner.   Angus describes, with much candour, a service of this kind, which he himself witnessed, in passing through the country, in October.   "It was Sunday morning," he remarks: "a small bell was struck outside one of the buildings, and it was an interesting sight to watch the effect it had upon the dwellers around the *pa:* one by one they came out of their houses, or crossed the little stiles dividing the one court-yard from another, and, wrapping their mats and blankets about them, slowly and silently wended their way to the place of worship.   On entering the building, each individual squatted upon the ground, which was strewn with reeds; and with faces buried in their blankets, they appeared to be engaged in prayer.   They then opened a Maori Testament, when a native teacher commenced the sacred service.   It would have been a lesson to some of our thoughtless and fashionable congregations in England, to have witnessed the devout and serious aspect and demeanour of these tattooed men, who, *without the assistance of a European,* were performing Christian worship with decorous simplicity and reverential feeling." *

Persons who had been absent from the country for a number of years were astonished to witness, on their return, the remarkable change that had taken place in the appearance and habits of the people.   One of the most intelligent and observant of this class remarked, "From the missionary villages, the ancient New-Zealander has almost disappeared: the present race is in a state of transition from the perfect savage life of their ancestors to the mild, orderly, and cleanly habits of civilized nations.   Formerly their persons and mats were covered with a casement of red ochre mixed with train-oil: now both the mat and blanket have been laid aside, and, in innumerable instances, the European costume has been adopted."   The period is not remote when they will take their stand amongst other civilized races, and exemplify the fruits

* "Savage Life and Scenes."

of Christianity in all the delightful enjoyments of personal, domestic, and social order, and comfort, and respectability. Instead of infanticide, the native woman now watches over her living child with maternal tenderness. The aged are no longer treated with neglect and cruelty by their own relations, but visited in their affliction, and relieved by Christian liberality. A collection has been introduced, as in Great Britain, in connexion with the sacramental service, which is exclusively appropriated to the relief of the sick ; and it is delightful to witness the cheerfulness and liberality with which the natives contribute to that object. The deepest malignity and most ferocious savageism have been compelled to yield to the power of the gospel. The barbarous chieftain has not only liberated his slave, but treats him as a Christian brother, and kneels by his side at the Lord's table. Old and young are emerging from their native darkness, and rising into a new state of intellectual enjoyment. " I am not aware," says one of the missionaries, "that there was one native in my circuit, two years since, who understood the multiplication table : now they can work with ease the questions in long division and practice. We shall soon hear of the New-Zealander being able to work all the problems in Euclid. They are making rapid progress in the English language. Their inquiries into the meaning and import of Divine truths are incessant. Some of them can repeat from memory five chapters of the Gospel by St. Matthew : several can repeat eight chapters of Paul's Epistle to the Romans ; and others the first four chapters of the Epistle to the Hebrews. Within the above period two hundred acres of land have been cultivated, and are now covered with wheat, besides patches of oats and barley. Our stock in horses, horned cattle, sheep, and goats, increases rapidly. The people have erected a water-mill for grinding their corn ; and it is curious to hear their conversation as they watch the revolutions of the machinery. Infanticide and murder are of frequent occurrence in some parts of the country; but here we have not heard of a single instance of either for two years. They now settle all their disputes about women, pigs, and land, amongst themselves. They have liberated their slaves, many of whom have returned to their own tribes and homes."

Surely additional evidence is not necessary to convince the reader, that the prejudices of ages have been overcome ; the sanguinary habits of former generations entirely changed ; and the melancholy scenes, the incantations, *tapu*, witchcrafts, and suicides, concomitants of Heathenism, been succeeded by "joy and gladness," arising from Christian worship, a sense of God's favour, and a scriptural hope of eternal life.

In April, 1841, the ship "Triton," which had carried missionaries and stores through the coral reefs of the South-Sea Islands for nine years, was disposed of for £1,000, and the "John Wesley," a larger and better appointed vessel, substituted in her place. After landing missionaries, schoolmasters, and stores at Auckland, she sailed for the Friendly Islands, on the 29th of May. On the day before she left, the foundation-stone of a new chapel was laid, £500 having been previously collected towards the expense of the building. A delightful work had been going on for some time amongst the young people of the congregation and sabbath-school. Several of the teachers had been made partakers of the saving grace of God, and went to their duties in the school, full of love and zeal. They spread "the savour of Christ" amongst the children; the general routine of teaching was suspended, and made to give way to prayer, when "out of the mouths of babes and sucklings God perfected praise." The influence of this juvenile revival was felt by the church generally; the members were quickened, and their number increased. The Native Institution had been put into efficient operation, and the youths under instruction were giving great satisfaction. They maintained their Christian consistency, and steadily advanced in the love of God and the various branches of secular education. The governor kindly offered to fit up a building in the immediate vicinity for me-chanical purposes, where the students might be assisted in learning the useful arts.

At a meeting of all the missionaries in the Friendly and Feejee Islands, held in May, 1847, special attention was directed to this Institution. After the necessity, expense, and utility of such a seminary had been amply discussed, they recorded their deliberate judgment in a few appropriate Resolutions. "Feeling as we do," they remark, "the extreme difficulty of training our children in Feejee, we most gladly enter into an arrangement for the establishment of a school in New Zealand, for the following reasons :—

"1. Our children can be conveyed to New Zealand, without expense to the committee.

"2. They will receive an efficient education, have good society, and be removed from the corrupting influence of the spirit and example of the Heathen around us.

"3. The missionaries will be able to remain longer abroad, and be relieved from much parental anxiety.

"4. After residing for years in a torrid climate, it is desirable that children be removed, at least for a season, to such a place as New Zealand, where the air is peculiarly salubrious.

"5. We are aware of the difficulties and expense connected with such an undertaking,—the erection of additional buildings, and providing every thing requisite for such an establishment; but we are prepared to bear our part of the burden.

" 6. This plan will be, in our judgment, advantageous to all interests: our children will be educated, the funds of the Society ultimately benefited, and the brethren enabled to prosecute their labours with greater devotedness and satisfaction."

CHAPTER XVI.

DESTRUCTIVE EARTHQUAKES—ACADEMY FOR NATIVE YOUTH AT THREE KINGS—GENERAL STATE AND RESULTS OF THE MISSION.

ON the 14th of October, 1848, God spoke to the southern portion of the colony of New Zealand, with a voice that made the barbarian and European alike quail under such developements of His power and supremacy as they had never before witnessed. On that day they were visited with rather a severe shock of an earthquake. Many of the buildings in Wellington were thrown down, but no lives were lost. On the 15th, the earth was in motion all day; but in the afternoon a shock much more violent than the former one was experienced. Nearly every brick chimney in the town was thrown down; and the buildings which had survived the former shock were shattered and rendered untenantable. "I was never so impressed," said an eye-witness, "with the almighty power of God, as when standing in the streets, and beholding the large massive brick buildings toppling over in every direction." A class was being met in the mission-house at the time; and while the people assembled thought themselves secure, the east gable of the large chapel was vibrating over their heads in the most frightful manner. Through God's mercy it did not fall, or they must have been all crushed to death under the ponderous mass. One of the local preachers, and two of his children, who were passing a store-house at the time it fell, were buried in the falling materials. They were devoted to Christ, and fully prepared by Divine grace to meet the Bridegroom. A still more alarming shock took place on the 19th, which laid the whole town in ruins. If the houses had been brick or stone, two or three stories high, the loss of life would have been immense. The mission families, being driven from their houses, erected a large tent, which afforded some shelter from the wind and rain that descended upon them with great violence. One thousand pounds' worth of mission property was destroyed by these successive shocks.

The governor issued a proclamation, appointing the 20th to be observed as a day of fasting, humiliation, and prayer to

NEW ZEALAND CHILDREN, NEAR BOILING SPRINGS.

Almighty God, that He would avert the recurrence of any similar visitation. The day was observed with profound reverence by all classes; and hundreds were led to reflection and prayer, who, previously to these earthquakes, had "cared for none of these things." Nor were these transient emotions: they ripened, in many instances, into religious principles, and issued in practical amendment. The native mind, just awoke from the slumber of centuries, discovered its ignorance and cupidity; and applied with earnestness to every source for information relative to the duties of life and the obligations of religion.

An ardent thirst for knowledge had been awakened in the minds of the young of both sexes throughout the country; and neither the efforts of the missionary, nor the liberality of the colonial government, could multiply means and agencies commensurate with the demand. It had long been observed with regret, that the senior boys in the day and Sunday schools suffered much from a promiscuous intercourse with their heathen families and relatives; but the application of a remedy seemed encumbered with a multitude of difficulties. It was at last suggested, that if an educational institution could be set up, in such a situation as would isolate those youths from their early associations, there was reason to believe that a considerable body of teachers might be raised up, competent to conduct the educational department of the mission amongst the natives. After due consideration, Manawa Tawi, or The Three Kings' Islands, were fixed upon as likely to afford all the requisite advantages for such an establishment. These islands lie about forty miles from the main-land, to the north-west of the North Cape. The inhabitants fled from New Zealand in the time of war, and subsisted for years upon roots and fish, which are abundantly prolific upon their shores. The governor heartily approved of this academy for the natives, and offered the brethren every facility in his power for the accomplishment of their object. Suitable buildings and accommodations being provided for a considerable number of boys, Mr. and Mrs. Reid were placed over the establishment.

The depraved habits of many of the colonists exerted an injurious influence upon the natives, and secularized numbers who professed Christianity; but the great body of the Christian converts continued to advance both in knowledge and piety. This was much owing to their conscientious observance of family worship. We select a few passages, and but a few, from the journals of the brethren; not only because they are full of instructive sentiment, but because they present to the reader a correct specimen of the every-day exercises and occupations of the missionary.

A A

The first is dated "Taranaki South, May 31st." "On the 28th of February I preached three times, held a public prayer-meeting, conducted the school with one of the teachers, and administered the Lord's supper to about one hundred persons in the evening. I held service on the evening of the 30th with the Europeans and natives at Petre, in Wanganui, in a place of worship lately built by subscription. During my journey to and from the south, I had three falls, twice from my horse, and once out of a canoe into the Patea river, but escaped each time unhurt. I enjoyed much of the Divine presence in the solitariness of the way.

"March 12th.—This day I preached to my own and the Church natives at Waiheke. The people do not, as they should, feel their obligations to support the institutions of religion.

"17th.— I again held service with my own and the Church people at Ketemarae. I also catechized them in the school, and was much pleased with their answers to my questions. The questions were taken from the Conference Catechisms, on 'death and judgment, heaven and hell.' One of the teachers prayed most affectingly in Maori at the close of the service. I had told them, in my remarks, that as all the rivers were running into the sea, so we were all tending to eternity, where we must 'stand before the judgment-seat of Christ.' The teacher caught the idea, and took it up most touchingly in prayer. Several wept, and breathed out their desires to the Friend of sinners. I met the classes in the afternoon. The people have been favoured with a prosperous harvest, and food of all kinds is abundant.

"27th.—I returned last evening from Turangarere, where I had held various services with the natives. They are building a large and commodious chapel in the settlement. I found several fine young men sinking under consumption. The road to this place is very dangerous, and the traveller must be very cautious, as a slip may cost him his life, in ascending and descending the precipices. Nature here, in time past, has been dreadfully convulsed. There are large rents, chasms, and pits, from earthquakes and other causes. I read to the people the dying experience of Mrs. Sherman, of Surrey Chapel, London, from the funeral sermon preached by the Rev. John A. James, of Birmingham. I related the dying saint's experience, and they begged me to write it out for their edification. O blessed religion! It has the same influence on the civilized and the savage. The infidel may laugh and scorn; but here are evidences of its saving power. The consolation it affords to God's people at home, it affords also to the dying New-Zealander abroad. The other day one of our people exclaimed in his last moments, 'My flesh and my heart faileth: but God is the strength of my heart, and my portion for ever.'

"March 6th.—One of our members died at Manawapou on the 4th. I visited him the day before. I found him in a small hut, resembling a dog-kennel, with a very small entrance. I could not get into it. The heat was oppressive, and the effluvia most offensive. He recognised me as I stood outside. I asked him if he knew me. He replied, in broken accents, 'Yes, you are my minister.' I asked the state of his mind. He said, 'It is dark, on account of my great pain.' I directed him to the good Physician. Next morning he died. His class-leader told me that when he was dying, he seemed to feel himself near to the invisible world, saying, over and over again, *Tangohia ahau, tangohia ahau,* 'Take away me, take away me,' and then expired.

"12th.—I went yesterday to Katotauru, and opened a new chapel, which the people have lately put up at their own expense, with the exception of my supplying a door and a bell. I was much pleased to witness their love to the public worship of God. The natives assembled from different places, and I dedicated the house to the Lord of hosts. The garments of some were poor and ragged ; but they were all clean in their persons.

"19th.—I returned last night from Keeteeonetea, where I had met the people of the surrounding settlements. I preached to them, and catechized in the school. It was interesting and encouraging to see men, women, and children, seated on the ground, reading the scriptures, and repeating the catechism. I also met the class: the experience of some was sound and hopeful; of others very superficial. On my way, I called at the Orakowai, where a flour-mill has been going for several weeks, under the superintendence of a European. It has ground between five and six hundred bushels of flour, which belonged to different parties. The wheat is very fine and abundant. They bake their bread in the native ovens. Some boil the flour, and make a dish they call ' white pot.' This preparation they enjoy with great relish, scooping it out to eat with their fingers.

" 22nd.—I went to Katotauru again, and preached to the people, who are busily employed in getting-in the last of their crops. Providence has dealt bountifully with them in sending them a plentiful supply of food. O that they more fully appreciated the loving-kindness of the Lord !

" On the 27th instant I preached to the Europeans at Petre. The weather was severe. The rain fell in torrents ; the wind blew the sand into my face like shot, and I was stiff with cold. I found the natives much excited by the trade and commerce going on in Petre and Wellington : they are in great danger of ' neglecting the one thing needful.' The young people, in particular, are most exposed : indeed, some have been already carried away by the seductions of the world. I ran some risk in crossing one of the rivers, which was flooded; but the Lord preserved me. The children are very troublesome; the young savages despise restraint. I am at a loss to know what plan to adopt, to awaken attention to education. Many are employed in making public roads near New Plymouth and Wellington: and, as they are paid in money, they are exposed to great temptations.

"On the 6th of April, Good Friday, I preached on the crucifixion, and described the events of Calvary. In the after parts of the day I continued the subject, and administered the Lord's supper to the people collected from different parts of the settlement. It was a solemn and profitable time. They were generally respectably clad, and clean in their persons. No one here rushes carelessly to this ordinance. While it is in hand, every thing is still as death. One woman appeared in a rich gown, a red silk bonnet, and white veil, which gave her a singular appearance. She removed the bonnet and veil on approaching the ordinance. Her appearance formed a perfect contrast to the mats with which the greater part were clad, with their dark tattooed faces. All had agreed to fast, and no food was eaten till the close of the day. This practice is observed throughout this circuit. The people have clear and correct views of the atonement.

"On the 7th, I preached at Ohangi and Wareroa, on the resurrection. They seemed much interested while I proved that the resurrection of Christ is a pledge that the bodies of His people shall rise again,

> 'And every shape, and every face,
> Be heavenly and Divine.'

"I went to Ketemarae on the 23rd, and preached to the Wesleyans and Church people. I started early in the morning, but was mistaken in the time of the tide. I was hemmed in, with my horse, among some rocks, and the sea dashed over us; but we got out without any accident. There is much sickness at present among the natives. Many have died, and others are in dying circumstances. They have so few comforts, that when sickness seizes them they seldom recover.

"On the 26th, I went to Patea, where I remained; preached five times, met the classes, and examined the children. I was gratified to find that two rebellious sons, who had run away to Kapiti, had returned to their parents and expressed contrition. The natives cannot bear to think of their former deeds of blood, nor to hear them mentioned. They have frequently declared, that they would all have been cut off, but for the saving influence of the gospel. They have often asked me, 'Why did you not come before? Had you come sooner, our parents, brothers, and sisters would have been alive. But they were cut off in their ignorance; and we weep for their souls.'"

The resident missionary of Kaipara wrote on the 2nd of August : " It has been my privilege to admit many into the visible church by baptism, within the last few months. I wish I could say that I believed those individuals generally to have experienced the great change implied in the term 'conversion ;' but, inasmuch as they appear to have been sincere in taking upon themselves a profession of Christianity, there is reason to rejoice on that account : and it is not too much to expect that, by a diligent use of the appointed means, many of them will receive grace to enable them to make their 'calling and election sure.' I preach at a place called Mareikura, about four miles distant overland ; but the narrow pathway through the deep wood is so muddy, and the rivulets by which it is intersected are so swollen at this season, that I am daubed with dirt and soaked in water by turns. The last Sunday and the two preceding days I spent at Kaihu ; but such was the state of the road, that I was afraid I should be seriously ill, from the utter impossibility of maintaining physical warmth in walking, and by having continually to wade through very cold water. Much of the road, for considerable distances, was under water from one to three feet in depth ; and one wood could be traversed only by paddling in a small canoe between the thick and lofty trees. Such is generally the character of this journey ; and, on one occasion, I was immersed to my chin in water, in wading through one of the inundated forests. I found the people, in general, attentive to their religious duties ; such as public worship, the daily reading of the scriptures, class-meetings, prayer-meetings, and Sunday-schools. I found it necessary to interpose, for the purpose of reconciling little differences which had arisen between them. This is generally the case ; and without pastoral oversight, the little disputes which so frequently take place, often from very trivial causes, would prove fatal to their Christian profession. The visit of their missionary is the time of general and public confession of the wrong-doings which may have occurred during his absence ; and this is done with much candour. After a fatiguing journey, I am often kept up to a late hour, in hearing mutual confessions, explanations, or recriminations, and in listening to a variety of matters that have been reserved for decision. Such matters must be regarded as coming within the duty of a missionary, who labours amongst a people of very limited knowledge and of superficial piety. I have given authority to the only son of Parore, the chief of the tribe, to read the scriptures and exhort in the public services. It is a great advantage, when we can thus employ the young Christian chiefs ; and I hope the educational means now in operation will, in a few years, raise up a much-improved class of young men for our assistance."

The information from Waima, under the same date, is equally

interesting. "Our congregations," says the missionary, "continue good, and the people generally hear the word with great attention ; and although of many it is evident, that 'the word preached does not profit them, not being mixed with faith in those who hear it,' yet many do receive it in the love thereof, and find it to be the power of God and the wisdom of God. It is truly refreshing to witness the influence of Christianity on the sick and dying. The New-Zealander has not many temporal comforts on a sick-bed, and in a dying hour. We often find him stretched on the ground, with little to cover him, no attention from his heathen relatives, and nothing within his reach that he can eat. In these circumstances he finds the blessed book of God a companion indeed, and is enabled joyfully to contemplate the hour which shall set him free from this world of suffering and woe, and admit him into the rest which remains for the people of God. The rising generation continue to give much satisfaction, by the general desire they manifest for knowledge, and the great attention with which they receive instruction. The government affords us every encouragement in our endeavours to educate the natives. His Excellency has just granted £120 to assist in building a school-house at Waima. The building, which is in progress, is sixty feet by twenty, and is very substantial. It will be capable of boarding and lodging. thirty children, and will be an ornament to the station. I have twelve lads living with me for the last four months, whom I have fed, clothed, and educated. I have spent at least three hours with them every day, when at home ; and have been highly gratified with their attention to all my rules and regulations, and with the very encouraging progress they have made. They can all now read the scriptures in their own language, and are well acquainted with the first part of the Conference Catechism ; in addition to which, they have made considerable progress in writing and figures, and are making great efforts to acquire the English language. Some of them are already reading in the English Testament, and are rapidly mastering the difficulties of the pronunciation. To all the means of grace they attend with great punctuality, and their behaviour during public worship is all that we can wish. Thank God, I have no other object in life than to please Him, and advance His cause."

·Writing from Waimate, September 24th, the missionary remarks, "This day, May 24th, I left home to open the new chapel, and administer the Lord's supper to our people at Turangarere. On my way I stopped at Warcroa, and preached to a large congregation out of doors ; but it was a noisy assembly : children yelling, dogs barking, and parties cooking food, all in the open air, made it difficult to engage the attention of the people with effect. After climbing precipices, and crossing rivers, I arrived at Turangarere on the following day, with my faithful guide and companion, a native local preacher. The rain fell heavily during the journey, and we were wet to the skin. I preached to a large congregation of Wesleyans and Churchmen in the evening. After the public service my attention was engaged till a late hour answering questions. It is impossible to describe the excitement which prevails on these occasions. On the following day we held a missionary meeting, which was a very crowded and peculiar one, on account of the singular addresses of the speakers. Some related their former degradation, their conversion, and present experience; but all urged the propriety of sending the gospel to the dark places of the earth. One chief from Patea was powerfully affected on the occasion. He was clad in a large dog-skin, and carried a native weapon in his hand. He jumped from the floor, flourished the weapon, shook his hair, and rolled his eyes, shouting in a screaming tone of voice, ' Send the gospel! send the gospel! O, it is good to send the gospel!' The collection amounted to £8. 0s. 6¼d.

" 27th.—To-day the congregations at the schools and public services were overwhelming. Being Whit-Sunday, I dwelt upon the operations of the Holy Spirit, and exhorted all to seek His saving and sanctifying influences. After the sermon ten children were baptized. In the evening I administered the Lord's supper to the members; it was a solemn and profitable time. On the 28th, a meeting of the chiefs took place respecting the sale of their lands. Nearly all present were opposed to sell. There was much innocent amusement in the speeches delivered. The chief of Whanganui said, ' I have sold my land, as I hungered for white men.' I preached again in the evening, and afterwards met the leaders and exhorters. I left the people on the following day, and commenced my journey homewards. The river was much swollen; but five of the natives stripped, and swam across, taking me with them. I had to ascend and descend deep ravines, extraordinary fissures from some convulsions of nature, and was liable to accident every moment; but I got out of danger, by the help of the natives and the blessing of God. I found my wife in deep distress, fearing lest something had befallen me.

" June 19th.—I left for Manawapou and Taumaha. I preached three times, and returned in dreadful weather,—wind, rain, and hail. The roads on the coast are broken and dangerous. I often wonder at my escapes. No one will repair the path without being paid for it. The greatest danger, however, is in crossing rivers near the sea. They are much swollen at this season by heavy rains. The solitariness of my journeys, too, is indescribable.

I travel sometimes twelve or fifteen miles, and do not see a human being; yet oftentimes, 'in the multitude of my thoughts within me, His comforts delight my soul;' and in the solitude of the bush, I feel it good to pour out my soul to God. How precious is a throne of grace in the desert!

> 'Here it is I find my heaven,
> While upon the Lamb I gaze;'

and to lead the New-Zealander to Him is my happiest employment. May I be faithful!

"July 2nd.—I returned last night from Katotauru, having spent a profitable and interesting sabbath with the people. The services of the day commenced with the usual prayer-meeting. After breakfast I visited the school. · It was superintended by Isaiah. The eighth section of the Conference Catechism, on prayer, was the part which engaged their attention. The remarks of Isaiah, in the course of catechizing, were both judicious and scriptural. At the close of these exercises I delivered an address. In the morning and evening I expounded 1 Thess. iii., and all listened with interested attention, excepting a few reckless young chiefs, whom I earnestly exhorted to 'flee from the wrath to come.'

"Hearing that the people of Manawapou and the neighbourhood were to assemble on the 6th, to make arrangements for the erection of a mill, I embraced the opportunity to spend a little time with them for religious purposes. I held several public services, conducted the school on the Sunday, met the teachers, and felt deeply impressed with the necessity of being 'instant in season and out of season,' in order to lead them in the way to heaven. Here the mortality has been great. What need to work while it is day! 'The night cometh, when no man can work!'

"On the 15th, I held services with the Wesleyan and Church people at Ketemarae. I expounded portions of the ninth and eleventh chapters of St. John's Gospel, and enforced the solemn doctrines of repentance, prayer, salvation by faith, and the resurrection of the dead, upon their attention. I found the minds of some, connected with the Church of England, imbued with the Popish notion, that the souls of the departed are confined somewhere after death. They had been told this by a Romanizing clergyman who occasionally visited them. One of our most sensible native teachers encountered this traditional error, and completely subverted it. On returning home in the dàrk, the waves of the rising tide dashed against myself and horse; but we got through without any serious accident.

"Last week the chief of Patea died in the Lord. The people of the surrounding settlements met at Katotauru on the 25th, to receive the Lord's supper. After a pensive journey on the mission-horse, I arrived, and found a large assembly collected under some trees, and the natives bringing food. This consisted of whole and cut-up pigs, potatoes, flour baked into large flat cakes, almost as hard as brickbats, with other food, which was distributed to the different parties who sat in groups, and all seemed to make a substantial meal. In the evening a meeting was held in the chapel, when I addressed them from the eighth Psalm, and afterwards met the leaders. On the Lord's day, as soon as the light appeared, they were all in motion. The first thing was to hold a prayer-meeting, then to breakfast, and afterwards attend the school. This was a most interesting service, especially the catechizing. The subject was the institution and design of the Lord's supper. After going through the usual questions, one of the teachers addressed them on their obligations to ' do this in remembrance of Christ,' in a feeling and eloquent style. After the school followed public worship. The chapel was crowded to excess. I preached from 1 Peter i. 16 : ' Be ye holy: for I am holy,' and baptized a child. In the after part of the day I administered the Lord's supper to the members. Several were kept back by the leaders, for uttering improper language ; others for family quarrels. This was a solemn and interesting season. They have clear views of the atonement, and of their obligations to observe this ordinance; and are most scrupulous in keeping back any who may have walked disorderly. Not a sound was heard during the administration of the elements, and all separated in the evening in peace. I was much interested between the services, by a discussion between two of our teachers, on the resurrection of the body and the immortality of the soul. Job and Paul were adduced, and 1 Cor. xv. expounded. The change from the worm to the butterfly was described in the most glowing terms. I was surprised and delighted with the manner in which the argument was conducted."

These extracts being sufficient for our purpose, we now direct the attention of the reader to an incident which occurred in March, 1850. But for the vigilance of Divine Providence, the Society would have sustained a severe loss, at this period, in the seizure of the missionary brig "John Wesley," off the North Cape, by a body of pirates. The particulars were published in the "Sydney Herald." The editor observes, "We have seen the legal depositions of the passengers landed from the ship ' Helen,' at the North Cape, New Zealand; and Captain Griffiths has furnished us with the following additional information : As soon as the pirates had obtained secure possession of the ship ' Helen,' they commenced disfiguring her as much as possible, by re-painting her and changing the colour from white to black. Her name on the stern was also obliterated, and the greatest care was taken to file it from the telescope, wheel, and other parts of the vessel where it appeared. After being confined in the forecastle for some time, the captain managed to creep through the hold to the cabin bulk-head, and overheard, from the conversation of the mutineers, that they had stood off the North Cape of New Zealand some time, with the intention of capturing the missionary brig 'John Wesley,' for which they were fully prepared, having swivels and muskets stowed away in their chests, with an ample supply of ammunition: but fortunately she passed them unobserved. On the 26th of December, the whaling barque 'Eliza,' and the brig 'Sabine,' from Sydney to California, anchored off the bay, where Captain Griffiths, and such of his crew as had refused to join the pirates, had been landed; and by the former they obtained a passage to Manganui, from whence they proceeded to Auckland. The plot must have been concocted before the 'Helen' left Sydney, as Wilson avowed his intention, that, in the event of his not being able to take the vessel with arms, he would have resorted to poisoning those who were averse to joining him, having provided himself with the necessary ingredients for that purpose. They had a well-organized band ready to join them on the coast of California. Their principal occupation on board was making cartridges, cast-ing bullets, and forming dirks, using the brass diamonds off the wheels as guards for the same. The head mutineer, Wilson, in-tended to capture, if possible, a larger vessel; but if he could not succeed in that, he would take the schooner on to Columbia river, to see if the coast was clear at San Francisco."

In 1850, His Excellency the governor made a short tour through several districts of the colony, and every where evinced a becoming interest in the welfare of the natives. His Excel-lency and suite spent the Lord's day with the mission family at Waipa, and attended the native services. The people assembled in great numbers to see the governor, and were delighted with his polite and affable manner, and condescending inquiries re-specting them. He spoke in strong terms of commendation of the Society's missions, seemed to be well acquainted with the labours of the brethren in Auckland, and considered the college for the education of the children of the missionaries as being a most important and valuable institution. That establishment was now in full operation, and enjoying a large measure of pub-lic patronage and support. The head master was conducting the educational department with zeal and ability. Several of the youthful students had been converted, and added to the church. The governor frequently visited the Institution, sup-plied funds for finishing the premises, and continued to take a lively interest in its prosperity.

The seminary for the training of native teachers at the Three Kings was also satisfactorily established. The prudent and efficient management of Mr. and Mrs. Reid commanded the respect and confidence of the public. They had under their care one hundred and fifty of the most intelligent and promising youths that could be selected from the different mission-stations. Though the school had not been long in existence, yet a public examination of the pupils had been conducted this year, 1851, to a very satisfactory result. The report is highly gratifying: "The academy for native youths, at the Three Kings, is one of the most interesting and encouraging institutions connected with the mission in this country. Mr. Reid is admirably qualified for his situation, and has been greatly blessed in the discharge of his duties; but he labours beyond his strength. Besides the scholastic exercises devolving upon him, he has a large farm to superintend, and keep the pupils at their industrial employments. During the year they have fenced in one hundred and six acres of land, and have now under crop, potatoes, thirty acres; wheat, twenty-five; maize, twelve; pasturage, fourteen. Several of the elder youths can plough and harrow, and ditch and fence; and others are learning carpentry under the instruction of an experienced carpenter: they have erected the necessary buildings. The girls make and mend and wash both for the boys and themselves, under Mrs. Reid's direction. She is devoted to the Institution: it is much to be regretted that her health is not equal to her zeal. The fame of the seminary spreads. Many respectable visitors have declared that, in their opinion, it is the most interesting object in New Zealand. Many civil and moral changes have taken place amongst the aborigines; but certainly this is one of the most delightful places in the land. To His Excellency the governor we are greatly indebted: he has ever manifested the most lively interest in this school, and largely helped us with funds. Having expressed a wish that some additional buildings might be erected, plans and specifications, of what was deemed necessary, were forwarded to him. His reply, addressed to the superintendent at Auckland, deserves to be permanently recorded. It was as follows:—

"'*Government-House, Wellington, August* 29*th*, 1851.

"'MY DEAR SIR,—I this morning received your letter of the 7th, enclosing the plans for the girls' and boys' school at the Three Kings. I have approved the plans, and written to the lieutenant-governor, authorizing the advance of the estimated amount, £600, in such sums as you may require for the purpose of erecting the buildings. I hope, therefore, that you will have the girls' school commenced without a day's delay. Both buildings might, I think, be completed before next winter fairly sets in. I hope, therefore, by the time I return, I shall find the school completed. Your account of the progress of the Institution is very satisfactory: pray give my thanks to its excellent master and his wife. I shall always feel grateful to them for what they have done. I often think of the school, and hope that God will grant me the pleasure of re-visiting it, and of finding it, as I expect, an institution of vast usefulness.'"

Wellington and other places have since applied for permission and assistance to enable them to form similar establishments to that at the Three Kings; and no doubt this will be adopted as the model school. Three additional places of worship had been opened in Auckland, and three additional clergymen of different denominations had been settled in these churches, during the preceding two years; yet the Wesleyan congregation was undiminished, and their church members increased. Six years since, they occupied a small weather-boarded house, that seated about two hundred hearers, and had twenty-eight persons meeting in class. Now, in 1851, they have a substantial brick building that will seat five hundred hearers, with exactly two hundred individuals in church fellowship. Nor were they indebted, as some have affirmed, to any extent, to emigration for this accession of numbers. "But few," they observe, "have come to us from a distance: the greater portion of our members have been raised up on the spot. God has blessed His own word, and caused it to bear fruit to His glory. As villages arise around us, we endeavour to spread His work. The Lord has raised up a few zealous young men as local preachers, so that we are able to get our entire system into operation. That system is, in our opinion, better adapted than any other to convert the world. It seems peculiarly adapted to meet the spiritual wants of a new country; for it supplies agencies that no other system adopts, makes available every modification of talent that a church may possess, and with the greatest facility strikes forth its roots in all soils."

It would be ungrateful were we not to pause, and shed a tear over a domestic calamity that occurred at Mangungu in June. Missionary Hobbs has furnished the narrative: "Mangungu," he says, "has lately been the scene of considerable excitement, in consequence of the death of Te Hira Tupanapana, son of the famous old peace-maker, Te Whare-rahi, of the Bay of Islands, who, in 1827, escorted, as a guard of safety, your then small mission-party from the scene of bloodshed and cannibalism, which ended in the demolition of our first station, and the death of the renowned 'Hongi. The worthy veteran Whare-rahi, since baptized Hori Kingi, 'George King,' had a family of sons, fine young men; most of whom lived on the banks of the Hokianga, and were members of the church of Christ. God saw fit to visit this family with consumption. Death first seized Te Runga, who had been named after that apostolic missionary, Nathaniel Turner; and next, Tarapata. He had been spared for years of usefulness, and his noble example had a happy effect on the less influential members of society. The third of these young men was baptized Wycliffe. Neither his faith nor his zeal faltered, from the commencement of his Christian profession, until his 'voice was lost in death.' What satisfaction would it not have afforded to the subscribers to the British and Foreign Bible Society, could they have seen the faithful wife of Wycliffe reading the words of consolation to her dying husband, from one of the Maori Testaments which their benevolence sent to this land! Te Hira, the first-born, was still spared, a chief about forty years of age, having two daughters grown up, and married to young chiefs on the Hokianga. After their marriage the hereditary disease developed itself; and, notwithstanding the medical attention of Dr. Day, they speedily declined and died. Such a series of deaths in the family caused the father, Te Hira, to sorrow as one without hope. Would that his had been a godly sorrow! but it was not. He said they were well and prosperous until they embraced Christianity; and, with one of his young widowed sons-in-law, he publicly renounced the profession of religion. A party of relatives came from a distance to visit them; and a new house, built on an imperfectly-drained swamp, very damp, and open at one side, was the place assigned them for the night. Te Hira, who had gone in haste to meet them, found, when he retired to rest, that he was rather lightly clad. During the night he was cold and restless as he lay in the open shed, in the month of June, the depth of winter, little thinking that within nine days the cold here caught would close his eyes in death.

"Four days afterwards, I heard that Te Hira was very ill. I immediately went to his place, and found him in a small rush-house, about three miles from our dwelling, with a little grass under him, not very dry, upon the earthen floor, with a pulse at one hundred and thirty, and complaining of thirst and of a hard lump within the right side of his chest. I addressed him, prayed with him, and hastened home to acquaint Dr. Day with his serious indisposition. Inflammation of the lungs, in winter, in a hut with an aperture to serve as a door-way and to admit light and air, into which frequent squalls of wind whirled the rain, with no bed, and no nurse, left little hope in the mind of Dr. Day of poor Te Hira's recovery. With such want of personal accommodation do the greatest chiefs in the country still content themselves. The doctor did not wish to send him any medicine, unless he particularly requested it, lest, in case of a fatal termination, his death should be attributed, by his heathen relatives, to the effects of the medicine. When he was informed of this, he said, 'Let me have the medicine immediately.' But all our efforts and prayers could not save him. The next time I visited him, his pulse was too quick to be counted: and in the middle of the following night the discharge of musketry gave public notice of his death. I am afraid he died without faith in Christ. How can these people become civilized while they are continually changing their residences, to keep up their title to the numerous pieces of land where they build temporary houses, to serve them while they take two or three crops out of each newly burnt-off patch? Such a system leaves them no home."

This picture, of "one of the greatest chiefs in the country," was drawn by one of the first and most experienced missionaries in New Zealand. Let it be contrasted with the soft and graceful touches given to the moral and social landscape by Bishop Selwyn, and the points of difference will be obvious.

Towards the close of this year, New Zealand was favoured with general peace, and Christianity was not only spreading, but taking a deeper hold of the public mind. But the inhabitants were passing from Heathenism to semi-civilization; and the great influx of Europeans to their various settlements rendered the stability of the professing portion of the community questionable. Many of these Europeans, claiming the sacred name of Christian, were deeply sunk in the most abominable wickedness. "These men," say the missionaries, "reproved by the superior conduct of the native Christians, strive, in every possible way, to induce them to give up their religion, and live as they themselves are living. And not unfrequently the seductive glass is given as an additional motive to join them in profligacy. Nor is this a solitary case; for men of this class are now found in almost every native village throughout the country. Under such circumstances, too much must not be expected from a people who are only beginning to 'see men as trees walking.' Christianity has, indeed, accomplished wonders among this people: it has succeeded in subverting a complicated and powerful system of heathen worship. The sanguinary laws and practices of the cannibal have given place to mild and peaceful Christian usages. The musket and tomahawk have been laid aside for the spade and reaping-hook. The obscene and horrifying war-songs and war-dances have been succeeded by the songs of Zion, and assemblies for the purpose of worshipping the true Jehovah. The question is not, whether the gospel has already been successful, but whether the precious seed sown, the springing plant of grace, shall be destroyed by the evil influences which now inundate almost every part of the land, particularly Otago. For many years, Waikowaiti was a centre from which whaling parties were supplied with the means of carrying on their business; and, at the close of the season, many Europeans would assemble for the purposes of drunkenness and revelling. It might with great propriety have been styled the place 'where Satan's seat was.' And since the whaling has been given up, the seeds of evil, so abundantly sown year after year, have not failed to spring up, to the great detriment of religion. Many of the young men have been, more or less, connected with the whalers, and have proved themselves to be apt imitators of the wicked practices of these degraded Europeans. Waikowaiti is now blessed with a resident missionary; but the circuit, which is above three hundred miles in length, runs along the whole eastern coast of the island, extending from the Kaikora mountains to Favoen's Straits, and is intersected by numerous rivers and harbours, which make it dangerous and difficult to supply the places with the means of grace. The difficulty is increased by the small amount of Maori assistance within the reach of the missionary. Many of the older men are unable to read; or, at least, read but imperfectly; consequently they cannot take charge of the public services. Many of the young men, who can read fluently, are unsteady; their moral character does not stand approved by the elder people. Under these circumstances, it is extremely difficult to carry out an efficient system of instruction. Had we labourers to enter the opening doors, and occupy the position already gained, Methodism would soon assume no mean standing in these districts. At present, it is rather like an advanced post of the army reconnoitring the country, or as a solitary herald, a precursor, 'a voice of one crying in the wilderness, Make straight the way of the Lord.' It is the seed-time here; and herein is that saying true, 'One soweth.' O when may the reapers be expected in this part of the Lord's vineyard?"

The general peace to which we have adverted, was interrupted in August, 1852, by the sudden incursion of a body of warriors into the neighbourhood of Kawia. They came from Waikato. For a number of years Kawia had enjoyed uninterrupted repose; the gospel had been producing its legitimate effects; and quietness, industry, and civilization had been the acknowledged characteristics of the rising population of the district. War was regarded as having gone out of fashion; and the people generally had sent their useless fire-arms to the government, who had cheerfully paid their full value in cash. The arrival of a war-party, consisting of some two hundred, or two hundred and fifty, men, all heavily armed and otherwise equipped for the field, threw the people into a state of great excitement. Some of the invaders called themselves soldiers, others policemen, and others contented themselves with their true designation of Maori warriors. One man had five cartridge-boxes buckled around him. Their professed object was to settle a land-dispute between two of the tribes of Kawia. They came to take the land from .the one, and give possession of it to the other. "I heard of their having encamped," says the missionary, "at a place a few miles distant, and rode over on Sunday to meet them and hold a religious service. They received me with civility, and listened with marked attention, while I addressed them from our Lord's invitation, 'Come unto me, all ye that labour, and are heavy laden, and I will give you rest.' I returned to our people in the night, and made arrangements for the reception of the Waikato warriors. It was agreed that a feast and welcome should be given them on their arrival; that afterwards they should be allowed to dig the boundary, break down the fences, burn the houses, or destroy property, or whatever else they pleased, without opposition or molestation, so long as they abstained from personal violence. They arrived early on Monday morning in formidable array, and halted in front of one of the *pas*. Here the chiefs gave them a formal meeting, and addressed them in respectful speeches. I also addressed them from 2 Cor. v. 10: 'For we must all appear before the judgment-seat of Christ: that every one may receive the things done in his body, according to that he hath done, whether it be good or bad.' A feast of pigs and potatoes was prepared for them; after which, they marched off to the place appointed by their friends for their encampment. Here they remained until Saturday; and I considered it my duty to remain in the neighbourhood nearly the whole of the time, in order to prevent mischief, if possible. Both Europeans and natives were unarmed; for all were unprepared for such an invasion. The tribe to be attacked yielded to my advice, and remained at home; so that the excitement which would have been occasioned by discussion and altercation was prevented; and, at their own homes, they continued praying without ceasing for the protection of Heaven, and the salvation of their enemies. I have visited the camp regularly for morning and evening service; and have not failed to urge, upon the leading men, the impropriety of such an hostile and uncalled-for interference with other men's quarrels. I have reasoned with my own people on both sides; and endeavoured to show them the importance of arranging our own disputes, on Christian principles, amongst ourselves. The chiefs for whom the warriors had come to fight protested against all forcible interference; and thus, by the Lord's blessing upon our endeavours, the question has been at last settled more satis-

factorily than I could have expected. Thursday was the great
day of excitement and demonstration of Maori and savage
wrath. The soldiers and policemen, as they called themselves,
threw aside the assumed restraints of their novel profession; all
merged in a regular exhibition of native savageism, and the
New-Zealand war-dance was performed in the style of olden
times. After the firing of muskets and the war-dance, followed
the speeches, some of them very violent, very decided, very
threatening, very alarming; but the tribe to be fought remained
at home. Attempts had been made to bring them out into the
field; but they utterly failed. After a long time spent in violent
speechification, the matter was concluded by two of the Ngati-
mahuta chiefs throwing their caps to a chief of another tribe,
favourable to the other party, thus signifying that the land in
dispute was given up to him for his friends, Ngatihikairo. This
was the signal for the instant departure of the warriors, and of
peaceful triumph to the Ngatihikairo. Truly, they have proved
the truth of the passage, 'Their strength is to sit still;' and
their hostile visitors, finding no foe to fight with, no opponent
to confront, and no orator to contradict, have gone back to
their homes in peace. 'Truly, God is good to Israel;' and 'if
it had not been the Lord who was on our side, when men rose
up against us, then they had swallowed us up quick, when their
wrath was kindled against us.'"

The subjoined communication is valuable, because it is of recent date, and throws considerable light upon the present condition of the Maori population. It is from the pen of missionary
Woon, and is dated "Waimate, October 4th, 1852:" "Yesterday,
Lord's day, I walked to Katotauru, an inland settlement, wading
through a river up to my middle, the old mission-horse being
now worn out, and unable to carry me any longer to my ap-
pointments; and visited a young man dying, I am afraid, of
inflammation of the chest. Of late the mortality has been great,
occasioned chiefly by their exposing themselves to cold, after
travelling or labour, and going out of hot-houses (for such I
may call their huts, from so many nestling together, and no
ventilation) into the open air. Yesterday, the young man
referred to was prompted, by the burning fever which raged
in his frame, to drink calabash after calabash of water, which so
increased his pain, that I was led to pray to the good Physician
to release him from his sufferings. Three chiefs have lately died
at a settlement on the Taranaki range; and three others, at a
settlement a little further off. From the nature of their illness,
I have rarely found the natives able to speak, so as to relate their
experience in prospect of dissolution; a circumstance I have
regretted exceedingly, so different to the records in the obituary

department of our Magazine, as furnished from month to month. I once heard an eminent Dissenting minister in London say, referring to the departure of Christians connected with our body, 'Your people generally die well.' There is a great disproportion of the sexes throughout this district : there are more men than women; and when a man loses his wife, he becomes unhappy and unsettled. One man who has lost both his wife and children during the last two years, has left the place, and gone to seek social comfort in another locality. A chief, speaking of the death of his wife the other day, told me that he had 'lost the prop of his house.' Another, referring to his partner, who was suddenly removed, said, 'My right hand is gone.' Another exclaimed, on the death of his wife, 'I am now an orphan!' When I arrived here in 1846, there were about eighteen hundred men, women, and children between Waimate and Patea. Now there are only twelve hundred, including Wesleyans and Episcopalians, as every one, great and small, is recognised as belonging to one or other of these denominations. The adults are familiar with the New-Testament scriptures, and quote them with great readiness. Popery has no footing in this district. Attempts have been made to prejudice the minds of the natives against the form of godliness taught by their missionaries, but without success. 'Thus it is written,' has repelled the attacks of the emissaries of the pope, who made a great mistake in expecting to bring the Protestant New-Zealander within their pale. To that noble institution, the Bible Society, we are greatly indebted for our success in this mission; and we earnestly pray that God's blessing may rest upon it. One of our tribes has been much agitated about their land; and for some time past meeting after meeting has been held to prevent its being sold to Europeans. This is uppermost in their minds, and forms the theme of their conversation. But thousands of acres lie waste, which they will never occupy. Their spiritual does not keep pace with their temporal prosperity. They have not yet learned the scriptural lesson, that 'it is more blessed to give than to receive.' They now eat the finest of the wheat; many are dressed with comfortable clothing, and ride on horses like gentlemen. While they ride, the missionary walks. A most objectionable custom has been lately introduced; which is, that if any one does wrong, payment in money or in property must be made by the transgressor! This is being carried to a most ridiculous extent, especially among the friends of the Church, whose minister originated the practice. A female of my own church told me yesterday, that she made a payment to her husband for a wrong expression she had addressed to him. A man called another *a slave:* payment was instantly demanded and readily paid. In many things they are but children in understanding; and a large share of patience is necessary to bear with their waywardness and self-will. But in the midst of trials, privations, and solicitude, I have many enjoyments: as the venerable Wesley, in nature's final hour, felt the presence of Him whose he was, and whom he served, so we prove, 'The best of all is, God is with us.'

> 'Alone, and not alone, am I,
>   Though in the solitude so drear;
> I feel my Saviour always nigh;
>   He comes the weary hour to cheer.'

When I read of the funds of the Church Missionary Society being in advance of our own, I said to myself, Why should not the directors of that noble institution hand over a portion of their receipts to meet our deficiency? I have often helped the sick and the dying members of the Church here, preached to them, schooled them, supplied their wants in various ways to improve their social condition; and does not one good turn deserve another? Help, men of Israel, help! Show your gratitude to Wesley, for kindling the flame of zeal in the Church, by assisting his children to carry on the conversion of the world! Is Christ divided? Let the Evangelical Alliance answer!

> 'O that the world might taste and see
>   The riches of His grace!'

The atmosphere here is remarkably clear, and heaven's hosts sparkle and twinkle with uncommon brightness,—

> 'Numerous as glittering gems of morning dew:
> ————————————— who can satiate sight
> On such a scene? in such an ocean wide
> Of deep astonishment? where depth, height, breadth,
> Are lost in their extremes; and where to count
> The thick-sown glories in this field of fire,
> Perhaps a seraph's computation fails!'"

In a dispatch of the governor, presented last session to both Houses of Parliament, His Excellency, after describing the general state of the colony, observes, "It only remains for me to add, that the exertions of our most excellent bishop and his clergy, together with those of the numerous, and I may say admirable, body of missionaries of different denominations, have secured to the colony a greater amount of religious instruction than any other young country has ever enjoyed: and this circumstance cannot fail ultimately to produce a very powerful effect upon the future population of the country; while at present it secures to New Zealand advantages which enter into all the ramifications of the society of the country, and the domestic life both of the natives and Europeans. There can be no doubt that the present state of tranquillity and prosperity of this country, and the rapid advances which the native population is making, are in a very great degree to be attributed to the exertions of the various religious bodies in New Zealand."

As Mr. Leigh commenced this remarkable mission, and continued, after his return to this country, to advocate its claims to the sympathy and benevolence of the Christian public up to the time of his decease, which took place in 1852, we have judged it proper to continue our narrative to the close of that year.

We cannot but hope, that it will be gratifying to the subscribers of the Wesleyan Missionary Society to be informed as to the state and prospects of the country and of the missions at the above date. This, however, must be done in a very few particulars, and with the utmost brevity.

1. When you opened your mission in New Zealand, little was known in Europe of either the country or its population. After a voyage of nearly sixteen thousand miles, your missionary landed amongst a nation of savages. With the exception of an occasional mat, they were naked, having their bodies besmeared with red ochre and oil; their habitations were inferior to the English dog-kennel, and equally filthy; while their food was the fern-root, the *kúmara*, and the flesh of men. The *customs* of their country were their only laws; and from the capricious decision of the chief there was no appeal. Polygamy embittered domestic society, and placed the life of the female in jeopardy "every hour:" while the casualties and wars to which the men were always exposed, were such that no man in the country expected to *die a natural death*. Now the laws of God and of Great Britain are recognised; the rights of property and of life are defined and held sacred; while many thousands have been brought to worship one God, marry one wife, and dedicate their offspring, in baptism, to one Mediator, "Christ Jesus."

2. When Mr. Leigh landed at Wangaroa, the natives were wholly unacquainted with the arts and habits of civilized life. It is true, they had seen with astonishment the European axe, and the ease and rapidity with which it brought the *kauri*-tree to the ground; but they knew nothing of the process by which the artizan worked it into shape and temper. They said, "Part of it belongs to Europe," referring to the head, "and part of it belongs to New Zealand," referring to the handle. Your missionary showed them how the axe, the chisel, and the saw might be successfully employed, not only in cutting timber, but also in manufacturing various articles of great domestic convenience. He made several agricultural instruments, a rude bedstead, sofa, and chairs, with his own hands. Now the natives can build houses, erect flax-, corn-, and saw-mills, and superintend the working of the steam-engine. Mrs. Leigh instructed the native females in the use of the needle and scissors; and now the blanket and

mat are giving place to the more convenient and ornamental costume of civilized nations.

3. When missionary Leigh commenced his labours, he had to deal with a language as barbarous as the natives of the country. It had, up to that time, been employed in promoting strife, licentiousness, and bloodshed.   It had neither felt the plastic hand of the schoolmaster, nor experienced the sanctifying influence of religion.   There was no book in the Maori tongue, and the first visible symbols of the civilized man were written in the sand.   The Grammar and Vocabulary of Professor Lee, of Cambridge, contained an outline, which has been successfully filled up by Archdeacon Williams, of 'Waiapu.   That venerable man, alike distinguished as a Christian missionary and Maori scholar, has placed his successors under great obligations by the publication of his "Dictionary and concise Grammar of the New Zealand Language."   Now, instead of there being but one schoolmaster and one elementary book in the country, there are innumerable Sunday and day schools, with several seminaries and colleges, in which the languages, the sciences, general literature, and Christian theology are being taught.   From these seminaries will come forth a body of enlightened statesmen, divines, and artizans; who will influence the deliberations of the senate, give dignity and efficiency to the pulpit, and carry intelligence, industry, and sobriety into all the occupations of private life and departments of public business.   They possess the word of God, and many thousands of volumes in the Maori language; have public reading-rooms, periodical publications, and political journals.   If their educational establishments and colonial press be conducted with the ability and vigour that now distinguish them, the literature of Europe will, in a few years, be within their reach.

4. When Mr. Leigh purchased his five acres of land from Tepui and his confederates, a pig from Te Tara, and a dog-skin with which to make himself a pair of shoes, there did not exist any regular commercial intercourse between New Zealand and any other nation.   It is true, that ships did occasionally arrive from New South Wales for timber and flax, while the French, American, and British whalers called to barter fire-arms and gunpowder for pigs and potatoes; but even these limited transactions were conducted with mutual jealousy, and frequently terminated in hostility and bloodshed.   The Europeans then in the country were either runaway sailors, who had fled from the rope's-end at sea, or runaway convicts, who had escaped the gibbets of Great Britain and the colonies.   At the above date, the European population alone amounted to 25,000 souls.   The improvement that has taken place in the internal commerce and foreign trade of the country cannot be described within our

limits.   We may, however, adduce the settlement of Nelson as an illustration.   From 1846 to December, 1848, the stock had increased,—horses, from 99 to 234; horned cattle, from 1,591 to 3,540; sheep, from 10,022 to 37,699; goats, from 1,029 to 5,353; pigs, from 2,866 to 8,739: 5,500 of these belonged to the natives.   The improvement in trade is equally striking. From 1843 to 1846, the imports fell from £28,867 to £3,082; while the exports rose from £629 to £9,819.   Advices have just been received in this country of the discovery of the precious metals at Coromandel Harbour, Auckland, and Canterbury settlement.   Coal has also been found, and copper dug up, within eight miles of Nelson.   The future can alone reveal the results of these discoveries.

5. When Mr. Leigh and the artizans of Marsden first revealed the true God to the natives of New Zealand,* explained the doctrine of man's responsibility, and brought that doctrine to bear upon the principles and habits of the people, they found them dishonest, turbulent, and cruel: in consequence of their feuds and wars, some portion of the soil was moistened daily with the blood of man.   The present governor has borne a distinct testimony to the deep and almost universal change that has taken place in these respects.   "The whole of these islands," he observes, "are now in a state of complete tranquillity; every settlement is in a prosperous condition: the *native race are loyal, contented, and rapidly increasing in wealth,* and the local government now possesses considerable influence over them." What, may we inquire, has tamed the ferocity of the "native race," produced on so extended a scale this feeling of "loyalty" to the crown of England, and "tranquillized" those roving masses. who, for centuries, had been going about, like the legions of Satan, "seeking whom they might devour?"

These, we are told, are the legitimate results of science and industry, emanating from colonization.   When it becomes necessary, we are prepared to show, that, but for the labours of Marsden's lay-settlers, and those of Leigh, Stack, Turner, Hobbs, and their successors, the country could not have been colonized when it was.   Unless the colonists had arrived in greater numbers than Britain at any time supplied, the natives would have baked them in their ovens, and eaten them at a meal.   Others, equally anxious to exclude Christianity from all claim to these lofty achievements, have ascribed them to the establishment of British authority, sustained by the British bayonet.   When these reasons have been assigned to the Christian chiefs for the general "tranquillity" referred to in His Excellency's communication, they have indignantly denied their relevancy.   They have said, in their own

* The first sermon was preached by Marsden himself.

simple yet forcible mode of expression, "Do not think that New Zealand is quiet and in peace because we feared the muskets and the soldiers. No; we did not fear them, only the word of God. It was this we feared.' It was this that chained New-Zealand hands, and bound them fast that they could not fight. By the word of God New Zealand is in peace." The truth of this must be obvious to any one at all acquainted with the relative strength and position of the two races. "The group of colonies," says Sir George Grey, "comprised in the New-Zealand islands, are composed at present of what may be termed nine principal European settlements, besides smaller dependencies of these. Their total European population may be stated at 26,000 souls. These settlements are scattered over a distance of nine hundred miles of latitude; they are separated from each other by wide intervals; and communication, even for persons on horseback, exists only between three of them. Their inhabitants have never been trained to the use of arms, and are so scattered that it would be found impossible to afford efficient protection. The wide intervals between these European colonies are occupied by a native race, estimated to consist of 120,000 souls, a very large proportion of whom are males capable of bearing arms. These natives are generally armed with rifles, or double-barrelled guns; they are addicted to war; have repeatedly, in encounters with our troops, been reported by our own officers to be equal to any European troops; are such good tacticians, that we have never yet succeeded in bringing them to a decisive battle. In fact, they are better equipped for warfare in this country than our own troops; and from the position they occupy between all the settlements, they can choose their own point of attack, and might even so mislead the most wary government as to their intended operations, as to render it extremely difficult to tell at what point they meant to strike a blow. They can move their forces with rapidity and secrecy; whilst, from the general absence of roads, the impassable nature of the country, and the utter want of supplies, it is *impossible* to move a European force more than *a few miles into the interior from any settlement*. In any thing like a national war, there can be little doubt that almost every village would pour forth its chiefs and its population. The centre of the northern island is occupied by a mountain range, the highest point of which is ten thousand feet above the level of the sea, and is covered with perpetual snow, having as one of its peaks a volcano of boiling water. The subsidiary mountain ridges or spurs, thrown off from the main range, are, for the most part, (where roads have not been constructed across them,) impassable even for horses: so that no overland communication, except for foot-passengers, can be considered as yet existing between several principal settlements. The European settlements are situated chiefly in the plains, whilst the Maori population inhabit the central mountain-range, or are scattered along the fertile banks of the rivers, or occupy the coast-line which intervenes between the several European settlements."

This is by far the most candid and important document ever published in this country on the relative strength and actual state of parties in New Zealand. Had the natives, at any period, broken out in one simultaneous insurrectionary movement, what would have been the consequences? And have there been no movements of embittered hostility? no conflicting interests? no national jealousies? no seasons of intense excitement? There have! What, then, gave cohesion to these heterogeneous materials, and afterwards consolidated the union? We say, frankly, The permeating influence of the word of God, and the missionary. Let the institutions of Christianity be vigorously sustained, and they will issue in the blending of the two races, the European and the Maori, until, in the feeling they entertain towards each other, they become as one people, strong for defensive purposes, if necessary; strong to repel unjust aggression, such as Tahiti has experienced; and strong for all benevolent and Christian enterprises. This state of society is fast setting in. Each European settlement has attracted to its vicinity, or contains mixed up with its white inhabitants, a considerable Maori population. In these cases both races already form one harmonious community, connected together by commercial and agricultural pursuits : they profess the same faith, resort to the same courts of justice, stand mutually and indifferently to each other in the relation of landlord and tenant, and are insensibly forming one people.

6. But "what is the chaff to the wheat? saith the Lord." What are these vast commercial and social advantages, compared with the spiritual and eternal benefits resulting from the labours of Leigh and his successors? We can only afford space for figures. Independently of those who have died in the Lord from year to year, the present number of communicants is 4,422; children in the day-schools, 3,500; in the sabbath-schools, above 7,000; 11,000 persons attend the public ministry on the Lord's day. This extended field is occupied by only twenty missionaries and their assistants. Alas! what a disparity between the number of agents and the momentous task assigned to them ! We ask the friends of the Wesleyan missions, Do you intend your agents to penetrate and influence the entire mass of society in New Zealand? to subvert the "customs" of ages? to create a national sense of responsibility? to excite feelings, anxieties, and conduct becoming the Christian, in the various relations of life, and to

promote habits of Christian zeal and liberality for the glory of
Christ? Then we tell you frankly, that you must double their
number!

CHAPTER XVII.

**MR. LEIGH RESUMES THE ITINERANCY IN ENGLAND—MARRIES—FAILURE
OF HIS HEALTH—DEATH AND FUNERAL—DISTINGUISHING EXCEL-
LENCIES OF HIS CHARACTER.**

HAVING established missions in New South Wales and New
Zealand, and remained eighteen years in connexion with those
missions, Mr. Leigh returned to England in 1831.   He had been
the subject of affliction for some time before he left the colony,
and suffered much from mental depression, occasioned by the
death of Mrs. Leigh.   Being incapacitated for public duty, he
spent the following year, as a supernumerary, in Liverpool.   This
season of relaxation proved so far beneficial, that, at the Conference of 1833, he felt able to resume the itinerancy, and received
an appointment to Gravesend.   The year was fully occupied with
the ordinary duties of the ministerial and pastoral offices, with
frequent excursions into other circuits, to awaken a more general
interest in behalf of the missions, and to increase the intensity of
their missionary zeal.

In November, 1834, he received the following interesting note,
from the Rev. G. Young, A.M., author of the " Life and Voyages
of Captain James Cook, F.R.S.:" " I received from a friend
some beautiful verses, composed by him on occasion of hearing
you relate an interesting anecdote of your having seen the name
' Cook,' inscribed on a rock in New Zealand, while you were there
as a missionary.   As I mean to notice this incident, and insert
the verses in my ' Life of Captain Cook,' which for some years I
have had in view, and now intend shortly to put to press, I shall
feel much obliged by your informing me, in what part of New
Zealand you met with the inscription, and at what time, and what
other letters or figures were inscribed on the rock, in addition to
the name ' Cook.'   Was there a date annexed, as the verses seem
to imply? and, if so, what was the date?   You probably took
a note of it at the time, and will be able to give me the particulars correctly.   I have been much encouraged, in preparing this
Life of the prince of navigators, by the Earls Mulgrave, Carlisle,
and Fitzwilliam, the Archbishop of York, and Archdeacon Wrang-
ham."   Mr. Leigh having satisfied the author on the above
topics, his work appeared in due time.

The following is a copy of the verses referred to, with the introductory observations of the author.   " On the main-land, two
small pyramids of stone were erected on two different hills, and

balls, beads, coins, and other European articles deposited in them. Yet these were not the only memorials left in New Zealand, to record the visit of our illustrious navigator : another was observed above seventeen years ago, by the Rev. Samuel Leigh, under circumstances particularly interesting.   This gentleman, connected with the Wesleyan Missionary Society, who commenced a mission in New Zealand in 1822, paid a previous visit to the Bay of Islands, and other places in the northern part of that country, in 1818 ; and in one of his walks near the shore he was delighted to meet the name COOK inscribed on a rock.   When Mr. Leigh, on his return to England, related the circumstance, the recital produced the following beautiful verses from the pen of a friend, which he has entitled—

"THE MISSIONARY AND THE MARINER.

" As once around the Hebrew sage,
    Sole monarch of their den,
The lions, crouching, still'd their rage,
    Till then unawed by men ;
So Leigh upon New Zealand's shore
    Calm and intrepid stood,
'Midst cannibals, untamed before,
    And hot from scenes of blood ;
For angels—answers to his prayer—
And God—even Daniel's God—were there.

" No Briton's foot to guide was found,
    No British voice to cheer ;
Each face was strange, as strange the sound
    That fell upon his ear :
But while he mused along the strand,
    Upon a rock sublime
He traced the carvings of some hand,
    Left legible by time :
When forth with quicken'd step he flew,—
A known inscription met his view.

" 'T was not the hand that once appear'd,
    Appalling Babel's king ;
'T was not the language to be fear'd
    When death is on the wing ;
But to the Briton, doomed to roam,
    A hand stretch'd o'er the seas,
Language that rapt his spirit home,
    Like music on the breeze :—
The name of COOK that mountain bore,
The date *when* first he trod the shore.

" The bold adventurer seem'd to rise
    In vision to his sight,
And with a voice, as from the skies,
    Inspired him with delight :—

'An ocean-ranger was *my* lot,
　With Britain's flag uufurl'd,
The guide to many a desert spot,
　While sailing round the world :
'T is *yours* to preach,—your Lord display,
And, Baptist-like, prepare His way.'

" No *written* words, from Nature's birth,
　In Zealand could be shown,
Till Britons, grasping sea and earth,
　Engraved them deep in stone :
And in that language, deeper still,
　And brighter far shall shine
Celestial truth,—Jehovah's will,—
　In characters Divine,
And letters, first on grauite spread,
Till nature's exit shall be read.

" These 'stones cry out' in Britain's praise,
　Far o'er the ocean's wave;
The mariners their voices raise,
　Though slumbering in the grave :
The name of COOK, and *but* the name,
　His culogy contains ;　　·
'T is like the hallow'd trump of Fame,
　O'er mountains, seas, and plains :　.
And rocks, uprear'd by Nature's haud,
His monumental piles shall stand.

" Aud, LEIGH, thy name like his shall live,—
　Survive the lightning's shock,
Though Time should his crasure give
　Those carvings of the rock :
The word of God shall be proclaim'd,
　And David's harp be strung,
The human savage sweetly tained,
　And converts, old and young,
As ' living stones,' shall build sublime
THY monument of praise through time."

Mr. Leigh was enabled to prosecute his public labours, with
very occasional interruptions, in several circuits during the following seven years.　In August, 1842, he married Mrs. Eliza-
beth Kaye, widow of the Rev. William Kaye, Wesleyan minister.
This lady he had known and respected for many years.　Possessing a sound judgment, deep piety, and an eminently meek and
amiable disposition, she was peculiarly qualified to sustain the
dignity of his ministerial character, and supply the elements of
social and domestic happiness.　In conducting female classes,
administering consolation to the afflicted, and removing little
obstructions to the peace and prosperity of the church of Christ,
the Wesleyan body possesses but few of her sex more successful
than Mrs. Leigh.

Towards the close of the second year after his marriage, his former ailments returned with increasing severity, and compelled him again to retire from the regular duties of the ministry. He selected Reading as the place of his future residence, and permanently settled there in 1845. Although freed from all ecclesiastical obligation to stated labours, he yet felt that the vows of God were upon him; and under this conviction was incessantly employed for the church. In meeting classes, conducting prayer-meetings, visiting and relieving the sick poor, and preaching the gospel, he found a congenial and extended sphere of usefulness. Having no family of his own, he adopted two of Mrs. Leigh's nieces, whom he brought up in " the nurture and admonition of the Lord." Anne, the eldest, now the wife of a Wesleyan minister, is an "example to the flock." On the birth of her firstborn, Mr. Leigh said, "Let his name be Sydney: who can tell but he may yet become an Australian missionary?" Young Sydney was put down in Mr. Leigh's class-book, and made a weekly and quarterly contributor to the cause of religion.

Being exempt from the constantly-recurring claims of the regular ministry, he was more at liberty to devote his intervals of health to the interests of the foreign missions. With a view to promote those interests, he travelled many thousands of miles, using all kinds of conveyances, at all seasons of the year, by day and by night. His public addresses were always characterized by perspicuity and earnestness. He gave vitality and action to every scene he described on the platform. His manly aspect and generous disposition inspired confidence and commanded respect. The reader may have been informed, that gentlemen travelling in a similar capacity, have, by adopting a respectable scale of charges, and a prudent economy in accomplishing their journeys, added considerably to their income by "gathering up the fragments." Without entering into matters of detail, we can assure him, that though Mr. Leigh's travelling expenses were supplemented by something additional from his own private resources, he generally returned from missionary deputations with an empty pocket. I find, from his correspondence, that, on one occasion, the accidental meeting with a friend, while passing through a provincial town, alone saved him from the necessity of selling his great coat. On another occasion, and under similar circumstances, he must have parted with his travelling cloak, had not an unforeseen hand relieved him in time to take his ticket for the next train. "A poorer than himself he could not see."

Those labours were continued with undiminished interest, on his part, till Monday, November 24th, 1851. On the evening of that day, Mr. Leigh, Mr. Puddicombe, and the writer left Reading, to attend a missionary meeting at Blackwater. While Mr. Leigh was addressing the meeting on the Australian mission, he had occasion to use a paper containing some figures which he had previously prepared.   On looking at the paper, he was surprised to find that the figures had entirely disappeared.   Turning round to the writer, who was standing by his side, he inquired, " Can *you* see any figures on this paper ?"   He replied, " Certainly I do ;" and, regarding this as an admonitory symptom, added, " Have the goodness to sit down, Mr. Leigh, and I will finish your speech."   With this request he complied, and resumed his seat.   At the close of the meeting, the writer took him by the hand, and said, " How do you feel now, Mr. Leigh ? "   He instantly replied, " I can complain of nothing but indistinctness of vision, and a little uneasiness about my head."   The carriage was immediately ordered, and he returned to Reading.   It was agreed to try the effects of a night's rest before calling in medical aid.   The next morning the opinion of Dr. Cowan was solicited.   After carefully examining all the symptoms, the doctor was of opinion, that, though severe, they might be mitigated, and further evil averted.   During the following night, however, paralysis ensued, and the use of the left side was entirely taken away.   He remained in this state, without much variation of symptom, until the beginning of March, 1852.   On the 3rd of that month, he had a succession of shivering fits, which shook his whole frame, and produced great debility.   In the evening he sent for the writer.   On entering his room, he observed, " Though my head is much disturbed, you must speak to me about the sufferings and triumph of Christ.   I wish to be wholly sanctified.   I have always admired those lines of Wesley,—

> ' Hide me, O my Saviour, hide,
>   Till the storm of life be past ;
> Safe into the haven guide,
>   O receive my soul at last !
>
> ' Plenteous grace with thee is found,
>   Grace to cover all my sin :
> Let the healing streams abound,
>   Make and keep me pure within.' "

Then, raising his hand towards heaven, he said, " Lord, I have often prayed unto thee since I have been confined to this bed, and thou hast as often answered me.   Glory be to God !

> ' Object of our glorious hope,
>   Jesus comes to lift us up !
>
> ' He hath our salvation wrought ;
>   He our captive souls hath bought ;
> He hath reconciled to God ;
>   He hath wash'd us in His blood.'

I want to be saved this very night.   Do, sir, pray that I may be fully saved, this very night."   The writer, having complied with his request, and spoken soothingly to him on the infinite willingness of God to fill his whole heart with holiness and love, and of the sufficiency of Divine grace to impart these blessings to him *now*, again commended him to God in prayer. Calm, firm, and decided, he looked like a man fully prepared for some new and great enterprise. He passed the night tranquilly; enjoying realizing views of future glory, and a guarantee, in the abiding witness of the Spirit, that he would soon be in possession of "an inheritance incorruptible, and undefiled, and that fadeth not away."

On Saturday, May 1st, his symptoms assumed a still more aggravated form, and it was now obvious that his end was near; but his mind was peaceful and happy. The following night was passed in restlessness and suffering; and at six o'clock on Sunday morning, May 2nd, he sent a request that the writer would lose no time in coming to see him. On entering Mr. Leigh's bedroom, he perceived that his breathing had become difficult, and his utterance indistinct; but his faculties were vigorous, and his mind buoyant with faith and hope. It had been agreed that he should receive the Lord's supper in the afternoon; but it was now apparent that he had not strength to endure the fatigue. Throwing his arm across his chest, he said, " I have much pain here." The writer replied, " No doubt you have; but God is making arrangements for effectually relieving you. If you have commenced this sabbath in pain, there is every probability of your spending the evening in heaven, in fellowship with a great body of missionaries, and all of them, like yourself, *returned* missionaries. The change will be wonderful." He replied, " The change will indeed be wonderful; but all will be well. And as it regards the returned missionaries, Dr. Coke will be at the head of us." His attention being directed to Hebrews vii. 25, " Wherefore He is able also to save them to the uttermost that come unto God by Him, seeing He ever liveth to make intercession for them," he was reminded of the importance and value of a confiding faith in the atonement and intercession of Christ, at such a crisis as had overtaken him. He said, with some emotion, " But for confidence in Christ I should, even now, be upset; but ' though He slay me, yet will I trust in Him.' "

He had the perfect command of his faculties, and continued to speak until within two or three minutes of his decease. At last the power of utterance failed, and, while heaving a sigh, the spirit retired from its " earthly house," to " a building of God, an house not made with hands, eternal in the heavens." He was attended during his last illness by Dr. Cowan, a gentleman as distinguished for the ability and eloquence with which he defends the Protestant institutions of his country, as for the successful application of medical science and experience to the relief of suffering humanity. By Mrs. Leigh the tenderest offices of conjugal affection were discharged, by night and by day, with a cheerfulness and promptitude that greatly mitigated the trial through which her husband was passing to "the valley and shadow of death." Mr. Leigh was interred in the Reading cemetery, in the presence of a large concourse of people, of all classes and denominations. On a monumental stone placed over his grave is the following inscription: " In memory of the Rev. Samuel Leigh, first Wesleyan missionary to Australia and New Zealand, who died May 2nd, 1852, aged sixty-six years. 'When it pleased God, who separated me from my mother's womb, and called me by His grace, to reveal His Son in me, that I might preach Him among the HEATHEN; immediately I conferred not with flesh and blood.' (Gal. i. 15, 16.)"

. The peculiar circumstances in which Mr. Leigh was placed, both in Australia and New Zealand, and the extraordinary interpositions of Divine Providence in his behalf, could not fail to impress upon him a remarkable character. With the exception of those of Dr. Coke, the results of Mr. Leigh's labours have been unparalleled in the history of the Wesleyan Missionary Society; and the time is not remote when the man to whom God assigned the honour of laying the foundation of the Wesleyan churches in the two sections of the globe so frequently referred to, will not be thought unworthy of having his name recorded on the same tablet with that "prince of missionaries," in the metropolitan church of Methodism. "In writing the life of Mr. Leigh," said Dr. Cowan to the author, "you have to define a character that combined all the elements of true greatness,—an original character."

We would place before the reader, in a few sentences, some of those excellences that more particularly distinguished Mr. Leigh, and were obvious to the most superficial observer of human life.

1. He was singularly qualified for the arduous duties assigned to him in the order of Divine Providence. He possessed a strong muscular frame, free from all hereditary disease; capable of enduring long-continued hunger, fatiguing journeys, exposure to cold and wet while sleeping in the woods at night, and the wasting labours devolving upon him during the day. His mind was of a sanguine temperament, eager and unswerving in the pursuit of its object, of indomitable courage, and imbued with the principles of true religion. These qualifications are indispensable in every one who would undertake a mission to uncivilized men. Indeed, all candidates for either the foreign or home departments of the Wesleyan ministry should be free from

constitutional infirmity and hereditary ailment; for a constitution originally impregnated with the seeds of disease will not be able long to sustain the pressure of the heavy duties unavoidably connected with the office.   In all cases mental fitness should be combined with physical competency.

2. Mr. Leigh was a man of earnest and unaffected piety.   It is a melancholy spectacle to witness a minister, and especially a missionary minister, laden with the responsibilities of the sacred office, and himself without religion, or possessing only so much as is necessary to carry him with gravity and seriousness through its duties.   Mr. Leigh was truly converted to God in early life; and "the love of God," then "shed abroad in his heart by the Holy Ghost," constituted the basis of his character, and the germ of all his excellences.   The religious principles co-eval with this event, were strengthened and matured by daily vigilance, reading of the scriptures, and prayer.   His profound concern for the salvation of men originated in love to Christ.   The price which He had paid for their redemption appeared to Mr. Leigh to enhance their value, and render it infinitely desirable that they should be made acquainted with the benefits which He died to purchase, and has gone to heaven to dispense.   While his zeal led him to seek in order to save the lost of every land, it moved him to select the outcasts of the human race as the objects of his preference.   To tell him that he had selected the *worst*, was just to awaken and kindle up within him all the sympathies of a generous nature.   To assure him that to attempt their conversion would be to put comfort, health, and even life itself, in jeopardy, was only to fire his ambition to place himself "between the dead and the living," as the next victim, should the "plague" not be "stayed."   Remind him of the loneliness of his situation, when "far hence amongst the Gentiles," the utter hopelessness of success, and the small amount of good which, under the most favourable circumstances, one individual would be likely to accomplish; that he might as well attempt to level the forests of either country with one axe, as to bring the barbarians of New South Wales or New Zealand to the knowledge of the truth by one voice; and he replies in the language of Paul, "None of these things move me, neither count I my life dear unto myself, so that I might finish my course with joy, and the ministry, which I have received of the Lord Jesus, to testify the gospel of the grace of God."   His heroism in danger, and patience in suffering, were nothing more than practical developements of the religious principle, "*Love* suffereth long, AND is kind.   *Love* envieth not.   *Love doth not vaunt*, is not puffed up: doth not behave itself *unbecomingly: doth not seek its own things* ONLY: is not *exasperated: doth not imagine* evil: *doth not*

rejoice in iniquity, but *jointly rejoiceth* in the truth: *covereth* all things, believeth all things, hopeth all things, endureth all things."*

To such foreign missionaries as may condescend to peruse these pages, we would say, with all humility, "Brethren, suffer the word of exhortation." We should be guilty of overlooking one important end of religious biography, were we not to call your special attention to this part of Mr. Leigh's character. We would therefore remind you, that your personal salvation, and the success of your enterprise, are mainly depending upon the cultivation of the principles we have just specified. A little reflection will convince you, that, without the daily accumulation of devotional power, it will be utterly impossible, in certain circumstances of temptation and opportunity, successfully to repel the seductions of the world, the appetite, and the devil. How can you expect the Spirit to "guide you into all truth," into the theory, experience, and practice of "all truth," if, by unfaithfulness to either God or His church, you are "grieving that Holy Spirit?" On what foundation can you rest your expectation of success, in your endeavours to negotiate peace between heaven and earth, if you forfeit your commission as Christian ambassadors? It is impossible that you should be able to look round upon the people of your charge, and say, "The seals of our apostleship are ye in the Lord," if you are aiming at other objects than the glory of Christ. If you suffer your devotional fervour to be cooled down to the temperature of the world's indifference, you become like the fig-tree upon which the anathema of the Saviour fell: "It soon withered away." O remember that the hopes of the Heathen, and the expectations of the churches, centre in you; that the eyes of Christendom are upon you; and that the labouring classes in Great Britain are contributing a portion of the produce of their industry to sustain your mission. We "beseech you, therefore, brethren, by the mercies of God, that ye present your bodies a living sacrifice, holy, acceptable unto God, which is your reasonable service. And be not conformed to this world; but be ye transformed by the renewing of your mind, that ye may prove what is that good, and acceptable, and perfect will of God."

3. Moral rectitude was another distinguishing peculiarity in Mr. Leigh. With him there was no affectation of qualities that did not belong to him, and no exhibition of equivocal colours calculated to mislead the inexperienced navigator: every part of his conduct was natural, transparent, and real. As figures in arithmetic are the representatives of definite quantities, so the words and actions of this good man were legitimate emanations

* Macknight's Translation.

from a heart permeated with candour, truth, and goodness. Of him it might be truly said, that, from honest conviction, as well as "out of the abundance of the heart, the mouth speaketh." It was a primary consideration with him, to keep his heart right with God; and his religious progress was marked by a continuous effort to bring his experience and practice to the strictest conformity to the requirement of "the first and great commandment," "Thou shalt love the Lord thy God with all thy heart, and with all thy soul, and with all thy mind." By this standard he tested the validity of his principles, and the rectitude of his actions. While integrity of motive characterized his intercourse with God, and fellowship with His church, it carried him cheerfully through all the social and relative duties of the Christian life. He was satisfied with an equality of power and privilege, and desired no pre-eminence amongst his brethren; but every approximation to distinction, by means of human patronage, gained by the suppleness of adulation, was abhorrent to his feelings.

We do not regard a desire to become eminent in the church as being in itself necessarily sinful; nor conclude, that the wish to avoid office must necessarily be religious. The apostle obviously intimates, that a man may innocently, and even religiously, " desire the office of a bishop;" but, in this case, the "work" and office must be combined. Where office and responsibility devolved upon Mr. Leigh, by the spontaneous suffrage of his brethren, he just looked upon it as enhancing his obligations to fidelity; and no circumstances, however arduous, could induce him to betray the trust. On relinquishing the general superintendency of the South-Sea missions, an office which was, even then, invested with considerable discretionary powers, he could say, with Samuel, " Whose ox have I taken? or whose ass have I taken? or whom have I defrauded? whom have I oppressed? or of whose hand have I received a bribe?" In the appropriation of the sums of money, or articles of barter, placed at his disposal, in the countries in which he laboured, he observed the most scrupulous regard to equity and economy. It is well known to the brethren who were then associated with him, that in all transactions involving the property of the Society, he evinced a more rigid frugality than when exchanging his own commodities. The savage would sometimes demand an inadequate, instead of an exorbitant, price; and when this was the case, Mr. Leigh would say to him, " The price you have named is not sufficient, and the true Jehovah requires me to give full value for your produce." In all his business dealings with men, he rigidly adhered to our Lord's injunction, " All things whatsoever ye would that men should do to you, do ye even so to them: for this is the law and the prophets." The law here laid down with such distinctness and authority, is of universal application; and just in proportion as the nations of the earth become impressed with a sense of their responsibility to God, will it govern the commerce of the world. It would be a remarkable thing indeed, (and, thank God, it has been of rare occurrence,) were a missionary so far to forget the peculiarity of his position, as to employ the smallest portion of the consecrated offerings of God's people, emphatically his "Lord's money," to any purpose not absolutely essential to his personal comfort, or the efficient working of his mission. Our Lord's admonition carries in it peculiar solemnity, when applied to the missionary: "Be thou faithful unto death, and I will give thee a crown of life."

Mr. Leigh possessed a noble and well-constituted mind, which claimed the right to exercise independent thought on the affairs of the state or policy of the church; and was, at the same time, ever ready to give a respectful attention to the opinions of others, and to pay a dutiful regard to competent authority, whether civil or ecclesiastical. "Whatsoever things are true, whatsoever things are honest, whatsoever things are just, whatsoever things are pure, whatsoever things are lovely, whatsoever things are of good report,"—these formed the substance of his "thoughts," and were interwoven with the whole texture of his life.

4. Mr. Leigh carried industry and punctuality into all the duties of life, and offices of religion. He considered the game of life too momentous in its consequences to be played heedlessly. His own observation had supplied conclusive evidence of the mischievous effects of indolence and irregularity on the reputation and success of the common tradesman. He had often marked how inconvenient those habits were to the man himself, the degree in which they obstructed his prosperity, and the amount of injury they inflicted upon others. In our judgment, such habits form a moral disqualification for the ministerial office; for whatever the intellectual character of the individual may be, they render it impossible for him to conciliate the respect, or command the confidence, of the public. Having no fixed system by which to regulate his studies at home, or his labours abroad, he is like a vessel at sea, without either compass, canvass, or rudder. The sailing qualities of the ship may be first-rate, and the nautical skill and experience of the commander unquestionable; but, in such circumstances, she must be entirely at the mercy of conflicting elements; and it must be owing to a rare concurrence of wind and tide if she escapes total destruction. The solemn words of Paul are as applicable to these habits as to voluptuousness: "She who liveth in pleasure is dead while she liveth:" her whole life is a fictitious one; it

wants all the substantial realities and enjoyments of life, while there is the positive death of virtue, honour, and happiness.

The Wesleyan ministry was intended to afford neither incitements nor opportunities for self-indulgence. Irregular habits are incompatible with its duties. The man who is charged with the instruction and supervision of a circuit, containing ten or twelve separate churches, with all their diversified and complex interests, and who is expected and required to promote the unity and prosperity of the whole, must either give himself wholly to those duties, or degenerate into a mere cumberer of the ground. No affectation of pulpit superiority should induce any minister either to neglect the less popular branches of his duty, or devolve them upon his less gifted brethren; for, unless every minister in a circuit takes an equal proportion of labour and responsibility, the work of God cannot be conducted to any successful issue.

It must be obvious, therefore, that the judicious division and diligent improvement of time are essential to personal respectability and ministerial success. It is an easy thing to waste, in superfluous sleep, agreeable recreation, or unprofitable visits, such portions of time as would, if sedulously improved, enable an ordinary man to realize, in a few years, an intellectual fortune. When Mr. Wesley instituted a service at five o'clock in the morning, he saw that while it would prepare his people for the duties, sufferings, or bereavements of the day, it would also operate as a grand auxiliary in forming the character of his preachers. He knew that, as, in medical practice, the administration of a strong narcotic in the morning will induce drowsiness all the day; so, in the science of religion, the vigorous exercise of the faculties at an early hour is like winding up the mainspring of the watch, and will keep the whole mechanism of the mind in activity throughout the day. The writer had it from the lips of Dr. Adam Clarke, that Mr. Wesley would invest no man with the office of the ministry who could not be moulded to a conformity to so reasonable and important a rule of duty. What but the reluctance of apathy prevents the Christian minister from enjoying the benefits of early rising? Let the beauties of Divine truth be laid fully open to the perceptions of the biblical student, and the practice now so irksome to him will become a perfect luxury. Long before the hammer of the artizan has announced the commencement of a new day of mechanical industry, will he be found prosecuting his inquiries into the revealed will of God, "with the Holy Ghost sent down from heaven."

Mr. Leigh could afford to be punctual in every thing, because he was methodical. No congregation calculated on waiting five minutes after the time, when he was to be the preacher.   What must the man of commerce, the systematic tradesman, and orderly mechanic think, who, having been accustomed to the utmost exactness in commencing and closing the business-transactions of the week, enter the house of God on Sunday, where every thing should "be done decently and in order," and find an assembly kept in suspense by the uncertain habits of the officiating minister?   They must surely conclude that, if he can swerve from the appointed time on so solemn and public an occasion, he is not to be trusted in reference to the more private, though not less important, duties of his profession. · Mr. Leigh was sure to be at the bed-side of the afflicted, so soon as he heard of their illness, to unveil the cross, and reveal the evangelical remedy in death. After he became a supernumerary, he would preach in the morning, and reprove the people for late attendance ; in the evening he would take his seat as a hearer five minutes before the time, and thus preserve his reputation for consistency.   In this country there are many circumstances to remind the irregular minister of the necessity of punctuality; but in some foreign stations, and in the absence of such circumstances, nothing but the force of religious principles, producing great tenderness of conscience, can sustain the habit.   Let the officers of the church conform to the apostolic order, which is, that they "wait on" their official duties, and not keep their official duties waiting "for them."   "Having, then, gifts differing according to the grace that is given to us, whether prophecy, let us prophesy according to the proportion of faith; or ministry, let us wait on our ministering; or he that teacheth, on teaching ; or he that exhorteth, on exhortation : he that giveth, let him do it with simplicity ; he that ruleth, with diligence ; he that showeth mercy, with cheerfulness."

5. The spirit of Mr. Leigh was truly catholic.   Many excellent men are so embarrassed by their doctrinal peculiarities or official restrictions, that they would consider it to be wrong, if not sinful, to diverge from the limits prescribed by their own ecclesiastical surveyors. Other branches of the universal church may be prosecuting some important enterprise, involving the honour of God and the salvation of men; but, unless they be allowed to act as the sole engineers of the undertaking, and to conduct its affairs within an enclosure which they themselves have selected and consecrated, they will not touch it "with one of their fingers."   We see no valid objection to their asserting the dignity, and vindicating the authority and sanctity, of the ministerial office ; but may not this be done, while they act like citizens of the world, and stand forth on the common platform of life, the avowed "friends of all, the enemies of none?"   Surely they should rise above sectarian bigotry and vulgar prejudices, and

breathe a spirit of benevolence, cheerful and expansive as the light and warmth of the sun, free and fertilizing as the drops of rain and dew that descend upon the fields of the husbandman. Free and independent in his principles and position, Mr. Leigh was always ready to advance " to the help of the Lord against the mighty," in co-operation with such as acknowledged the Christian atonement as the basis of the faith and hope of man. This liberality of sentiment and freedom of action he held in perfect consistency with a decided preference for his own system and people.   Whatever his opinions were in reference to the prudential regulations of Methodism, he considered its ecclesiastical polity to be as near an approximation to the apostolic platform as is necessary to enable the church fully and faithfully to fulfil her mission in the world.   Indeed, he considered it better adapted than any other to promote the knowledge and practice of Christianity amongst the nations of the earth.   Entertaining these views and sentiments, he regarded every occurrence that interfered with its unity or progress as a real affliction, alike perilous to the interests of religion and the souls of men.   Mr. Leigh was much exercised, during his last illness, by the audacity of Popery on the one hand, and the unsettled and divided state of the Protestant churches of this country on the other.   But schism, issuing in the disruption of churches, is not peculiar to the present age; for neither the authority nor the supervision of the apostles themselves could prevent the developement of this sin in the primitive times.   Nor did the apostle insinuate that the prospective schism in the Ephesian church would originate in either an undue exercise of authority or criminal remissness on the part of its " elders," but in other causes.   He said, " I know this, that after my departing shall grievous wolves enter in among you, not sparing the flock.   Also of your own selves shall men arise, speaking perverse things, to draw away disciples after them."   The men who originated schism in the Wesleyan church, combined with political dissenters, " of the baser sort," and made an attack upon the rectoral authority of the Conference.   They did not accuse that body of having corrupted doctrinal truth, but only of having been unfaithful in dealing with some of its own conventional laws.   They declared its assumption of power to be unscriptural, and then proceeded to clothe even *laymen* with the same prerogatives!   Methodism, they said, was " Christianity in earnest; " and yet they assured the people that to support its institutions would be sinful.   They denounced the enforcement of its fiscal regulations as being unjust and oppressive : afterwards they adopted those very regulations themselves, and applied the pecuniary proceeds to the purposes of faction.   If Methodism had really needed the organic changes which these schismatics recommended, and were anxious to enforce, their own acts had so completely subverted all confidence in their honest intentions, that they could not have been admitted as parties to an adjustment of differences. We allow that other evils may exist in a church, where there is neither schism, corruption of doctrine, nor perversion of discipline: the spirit of the world may paralyse the legitimate functions of a church, and render the enunciation of the truth powerless: but we cannot conceive how schism should supply a remedy for any form of ecclesiastical evil. Upon the whole, it may be laid down as a general rule, that whatever interrupts the aggressive movements of the church of Christ should be solemnly investigated and instantly removed. To the Wesleyan community we would say, " Whereto ye have already attained, walk by the same rule, mind the same thing." Look at the claims of the world, your obligations to Christ, your vast resources, and your multiplied agencies; and then, " forgetting those things which are behind, and reaching forth unto those things which are before, press toward the mark for the prize of the high calling of God in Christ Jesus." Unite with your ministers at home, and your missionaries abroad, in invoking a fresh baptism of the Holy Ghost and of fire: then let them go forth to " spread scriptural holiness over the earth." And neither the mammon of Great Britain, nor the idolatries of the East, will long be able to prevent the kingdoms of this world from becoming "the kingdoms of our Lord and of His Christ," and the Methodism of the future will supply materials for the brightest page in the history of the church militant.

CONCLUSION.

ALL who have written on the civil and intellectual condition of mankind, have admitted that the races among whom Mr. Leigh set up the institutions of Christianity were the most depraved on the face of the earth; that, in fact, they differed from the brute only in the shape of their persons and in the gift of speech. But if the gospel has effectually reached those extreme cases of human apostasy, who can question its adaptation to the diversified tribes of the entire family of man? Regenerated thousands stand forth, both in Australia and New Zealand, to attest its sufficiency to form their wandering hordes into worshipping assemblies, to endue the man-eater with the softest and tenderest feelings of humanity, to convert the ferocious cannibal into an industrious and peaceful citizen, and to transform even the devotees of *Te Tani 'Wa* into candidates for eternal glory. The mission of Mr. Leigh has demonstrated this. After witnessing this grand experiment, it now only remains for the church to proceed, at once, to extend the blessings of the new dispensation to the world. But in doing this she must follow scriptural precedents. At present, she is in danger of forgetting that "the law is the schoolmaster" that must bring nations, as well as individuals, "unto Christ," and that the introduction of the gospel was preceded by a general awakening. Where would have been the utility of the evangelical labours of either Paul or Apollos, if John the Baptist had not passed over the field with his legal plough, and "broken up the fallow ground?" The soil being thus prepared, Paul and Apollos planted and watered in faith and hope, and "God gave the increase." While we do not admit, that the church can have too much of the gospel, we yet maintain that she may have too little of the law. At the present moment she requires an agency analogous to that of John Baptist; a few able expositors of the law, to "convince the world of sin, and of righteousness, and of judgment." It is the first duty of the church to supply this agency; for "THE WHOLE WORLD LIETH IN WICKEDNESS!" This fact must be seized, as if it embodied a new revelation from God, and published in every part of the globe, where Christ has an official representative. Were this passage of scripture properly explained by the church, and effectually applied by the Spirit of God, it would produce a moral earthquake, that would rouse Christendom from her apathy, and stir her Protestant population to the depth of their sympathies. If it be not an exaggeration, but an ascertained fact, that the "whole world lieth in wickedness," the fact is so momentous that it ought to be carried, by Christian statesmen, into the British senate, and urged upon the legislature, until it is endorsed by the grant of a few millions from the national revenue to relieve so dreadful a calamity. This fact must be brought forward in every pulpit in Europe with a zeal proportionate to the magnitude of the subject, and enforced upon the people with a devotional earnestness and frequency that shall compel them to believe it. The Christian pastor must carry the intelligence into the families of his flock, and ask them plainly what they can do for a "world lying in wickedness." This text must form a distinct lesson, in all the educational institutions in the kingdom, and be reiterated until the youth of our land shall rise simultaneously, and "consecrate the first-fruits" of their industry to the mitigation of this enormous evil.

While the contributors to the Wesleyan Missionary Society look with astonishment upon the numerous and extended fields which their agents occupy, the churches they have formed, the religious and industrial schools that have been established, the languages that have been subdued, the translations that have been made, and the numerous converts that have been won to Christ, from the worst forms of barbarism; let them ask themselves, whether they cannot, by increasing diligence, economy, and liberality, greatly augment the income of this truly noble and godlike institution? Let the collectors, now spread not only over Great Britain but the world, take up the affecting theme of the above text of scripture, and carry it round their respective districts with renewed heroism, dwelling, with a deeper emphasis than ever, upon the mournful condition of the human race, and urging with vehemence the claims of a "world," a "whole world, lying in wickedness." Let this fact, so often referred to, be sent by the electric telegraph to the widest limits of human society, be struck upon every coin that passes under the dies of the British Mint, be printed on all the symbols of wealth issued by the national Bank, and float in the breeze from the mast-head of every ship employed in conducting the commerce of the world! Let the conviction be once worked into the national mind, that "the whole world lieth in wickedness," and the racing-stud of "his grace" will be disposed of, and the proceeds applied to ameliorate so vast a calamity; the hunting-establishment of "my lord" will be broken up, and the thousands *per annum*, now laid out upon hounds and horses, devoted to the elevation of mankind; the theatres will all be closed, the "laughable farce" being changed into a weeping reality, and the one million now spent in amusement and recreation consecrated to the conversion and salvation of men. A few, at least, of the millions now expended upon "strong drink" will be thrown into the same treasury, and appropriated to the relief of the deep and universal evil complained of. The vast masses of the precious metals that now contribute to gratify "the lust of the flesh, and the lust of the eyes, and the pride of life," in the banqueting-chambers and saloons of wealth and luxury, will be freely offered to recover a "world lying in wickedness."

When this shall have been accomplished in all lands, then Christ, as formerly, shall become "the Desire of all nations." God will then assist the church by extraordinary means to supply the universal want of mankind. The agency of man, being unable any longer to meet the demands of perishing millions, will be supplemented by a direct and summary interposition from heaven. "I saw another angel," says John, "fly in the midst of heaven, having the everlasting gospel to preach to them that dwell on the earth, and to every nation, and kindred, and tongue, and people." "And then followed another angel," who announced the effects of his ministry, "saying, Babylon is fallen, is fallen, that great city, because she made all nations drink of the wine of her fornication." Then shall the prophe-

cies and figures of scripture be fulfilled.   The " handful of corn
upon the top of the mountains" has germinated, "the fruit
thereof has shaken like Lebanon," and yielded seed for the
world: the "grain of mustard seed," "which indeed is the
least of all seeds," has "grown" up, "become a tree," and now
covers the earth with its "branches:" the tide of evangelical
truth which has been rising, swelling, and flowing through successive centuries, now "covers" the channel of "the great deep."
"The glory of the Lord is revealed, and all flesh see it together."   And "now is come salvation, and strength, and the
kingdom of our God, and the power of His Christ: for the
accuser of our brethren is cast down, which accused them before
our God day and night."   "The mystery of God is finished."
"Alleluia: for the Lord God omnipotent reigneth!"

THE END.

INDEX.

LONDON: PRINTED BY WILLIAM NICHOLS, 46, HOXTON SQUARE.